IN THE SHADOW
OF REBELLION

Gladys Smith

Llumina
Press

ISBN: 978-1-60594-070-0

Printed in the United States of America by Llumina Press

Library of Congress Control Number: 2008903605

This work of fiction is based on actual events. The characters are figments of the author's imagination, though she has included a few individuals prominent during those tumultuous times. Quotations from Theodore Roosevelt's speeches are included in dialogue as well as Clarence Darrow's brilliant defense of clients accused in the murder of Idaho's Governor Steunenberg. The date of Elizabeth Gurley Flynn's visit to Spokane has been shifted slightly to provide a smoother story line. The reader will find most place-names on a map of Idaho. However, there was no Bixbee, no Apex Mine, no Black Titan. These fictional names were used to allow the writer more freedom.

DEDICATION

To my son, Walt, whose interest in mining prompted me to write this novel. And to Walt for his unselfish dedication in caring for his sick father.

To my life-long friend, Barbara Cole, who continues to make me laugh.

And in memory of my late brother-in-law, Bruce Smith, who met life's challenges with courage and humor.

Heartfelt thanks to my sister, Andrea Smith, for copy-editing this novel during a period of great stress.

And belated thanks to my daughter-in-law, Sheila Berkeley, who copy-edited a previous novel, and due to my lapse of memory, was overlooked in the dedication.

Until when shall human beings honor the dead
And forget the living, who spend their lives
Encircled in misery, and who consume themselves
Like burning candles to illuminate the way
For the ignorant and lead them into the path of light?

Kahlil Gibran

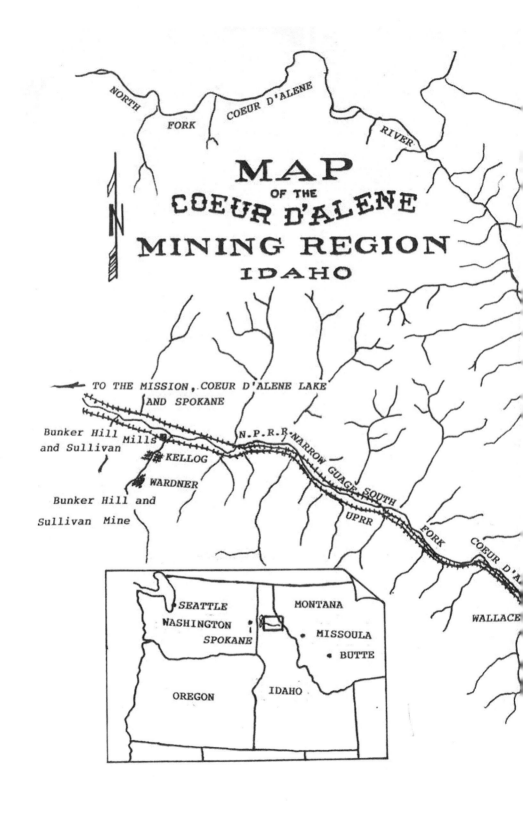

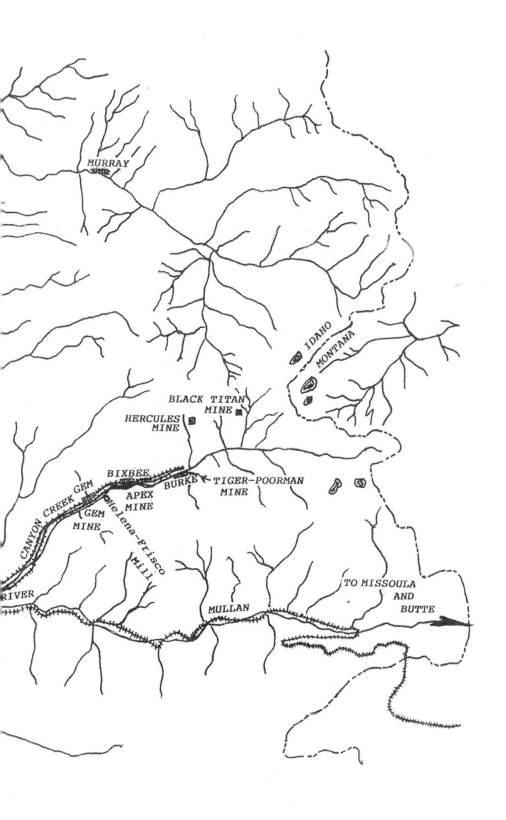

MURRAY

IDAHO
MONTANA

BLACK TITAN
MINE

HERCULES
MINE

BIXBEE
GEM
APEX
MINE
CANYON CREEK
BURKE ← TIGER-POORMAN
MINE
GEM
MINE
Helena-Frisco
Mill

RIVER

MULLAN

TO MISSOULA
AND
BUTTE

Part I

DISSENT
AND
DYNAMITE

CHAPTER 1

Wallace, Idaho
Providence Hospital, 1916

Dan lay in a coma, still and gray as death. My husband, my day, my night. He lived, barely, his breathing a slight filament of air, his pulse a mere trickle beneath my fingertips. The doctor had no way of knowing how long Dan would remain unconscious, much less how long he would remain in the hospital. Nor did he know the extent of the damage to his brain. He'd treated survivors of cave-ins before. Such accidents often happened to miners, but not to the owner of a mine, like Dan. The doctor had seen half the men regain their health after the effect of concussion had passed. The other half had remained in varying stages of dysfunction. A few had never wakened from their stupor, had simply lain in a sleep until death. The doctor hadn't said as much, but I gathered from his tone that he believed the latter would be true in Dan's case.

My heart sank at the thought of my husband never waking. From almost the day we'd met he'd become the fuel that fired my zest for life. Together we'd climbed the heights and descended into the valleys. We'd shared the bitter and the sweet, often walking the razor's edge between hope and despair. Now I might lose him. All because of the mine. I sometimes resented the way it had possessed our lives. Resented all the calamities it had visited upon us. But how could I blame the mine? It had no will. No power. It was man's ambition that drove him to bore into the mountains beyond the realm of safety.

Over the years, I'd dared to raise my woman's voice against the lack of safety in the mines, challenging a society of men that gave little thought to the workers who toiled and died underground to make men rich or to the welfare of their women and children. The rebellion of conscience had taken root early in my life, but I was twenty before it severed the bonds of propriety. It was one of perhaps a dozen moments during my forty-seven years on this planet that stood apart like signposts, pointing the direction I must take—places where the road forked, turned, or stopped. It happened in 1889, in the mining town of Williamsboro, Pennsylvania.

My family had always lived in the shadow of disaster, at first because of the potato famines in Ireland, then because of conditions in the Pennsylvania coal mines. Each morning at a quarter-to-seven, my mother would plead with my father and brothers to be careful as she handed them full dinner pails, then sent them down the hill to face twelve black hours working the coal seams of the Carbon Hills Mine. This particular morning had been no different. The men had left for work. With only the small fry at home to care for, Ma and I had sorted the wash and set tubs of water on the cook-stove to boil.

We were rubbing the men's work clothes over rippled boards when the mine whistle screamed through the thin walls of the shack.

"Lord! Not again," Ma cried. Within seconds, she'd plucked my baby sister from her cradle and hurried into the street.

It took longer for me to pull Carl and the three-year-old twins from their play at the back of the house, but I stepped into Maple Street in time to see my mother caught up in a swarm of townspeople hurrying down the hill to the mine. Men shouted and waved their arms to give directions, doubling their strides with each blast of the whistle. Tying on bonnets, women hurried from rows of grimy shacks and pushed their way into the scuttle of arms and legs. They sped along as fast as their skirts would allow, kicking up bits of loose slate from the street as they ran. Children dragged along by the hand sensed their mothers' alarm and added their cries to the shrilling of the crowd. Dogs added their howls to the siren's wail.

Everyone slowed to a stop at the foot of the hill, but the mine whistle continued to shriek through the wooded gap. In the hollow, the church bell tolled a warning. Dust explosions had no respect for season, and on that day heat rose in merciless waves from the red-earthed flat that fronted the mine. It intensified the smell and taste of coal dust. I hated the dust for the same reason I hated the colliery buildings that loomed stark and forbidding at the rear of the flat—they destroyed people's lives.

To the right of the buildings, the mine portal appeared as a murky gullet opening into the wooded hillside. It served as entry to miles of black, worm-like tunnels that riddled the mountain, tunnels with barely enough room for a man to crawl and work his pick. Williamsboro miners spent most of their waking hours in those cramped quarters, breathing coal dust and stale air, but union organizers hoped to improve conditions. I'd listened to hushed talk in the kitchen between my men-folk and fellow-miners who sympathized with the union cause. They believed it to be the only way to affect change in the mines. Until that happened, too many would lose their lives.

On this day, it seemed likely more had been killed, possibly my father or brothers. A dead-wagon standing beside horse-drawn fire wagons testified to that possibility. Beyond the wagons, men darted across the flat to pluck bandages and stretchers from carts sent by neighboring mines. On the fringe of the clearing, scores of townspeople waited for news. I stood on the edge of the crowd with the other women. A few clung to one another, weeping and moaning. Others were too paralyzed with fear to give voice to their feelings. To my damp eyes, women and men appeared as a blur of dark suits and blowing skirts.

Until my baby sister was born, I was the only girl in the family and it was my lot to help care for the younger children. At the moment, my attention was so fixed on the happenings at the portal I hardly felt the weight of my six-year-old brother Carl as he leaned his wiggly body against mine. I hardly felt the twins tugging at my hands. I barely sensed the sweltering sun that caused my threadbare calico to cling to my body like the skin of an over-ripe peach.

I was vaguely aware of tow-headed Sean, whimpering, "Maggie, pick me up. I'm tired." I'd slid him from my hip to the ground, and in his fright he'd torn a few strands of russet hair from my head. He clutched them in his tight little fist.

Poor little tots. If my father had his way, they'd grow up to face the same dangers as the older boys. He thought it manly, a tradition Irish families should keep alive. Despite that tradition, I hoped to steer the little ones in a different direction, and never would I allow children of my own to work in the mines and shorten their lives. In the meantime, Sean and the other two boys were my responsibility during the summer, when I was on leave from my full scholarship in English and journalism at Pennsylvania Women's College.

A woman squealed with joy when the first bedraggled group of miners shambled from the mine portal and stopped to look out over the throng with vacant, staring eyes. She broke through the restless stir of the crowd to hug kin, but angry guards kept the other women squirming behind locked arms.

Frantic for news, my mother worked her way to the front of the crowd, where she waited, hugging the newborn to her breast, her tired gray eyes filled with anguish. Strings of dark hair had straggled from the bun at the top of her head and stuck to her damp cheeks. I stood beside her, watching miners blackened with coal dust straggle from the mine portal onto the flat, straining to see if they were O'Sheas. I'd already lost one brother to an explosion. Four others, ages ten to twenty-two had scars and coughs from working the tunnels. If they continued to work in the mines, the coughs could develop into *The Dust*, a lung disease that resulted in a shortened life.

Three of my brothers held jobs as rock pickers in the higher levels of the mine. They dragged themselves from the head house and walked up to my thankful mother, their eyes dull and lifeless. I asked excitedly about their escape from the mine.

"We were lucky. Got just a few scratches," the fifteen-year-old said. "The explosion on our level didn't amount to much."

Thirteen-year-old Mike took a cap from his red head and slapped it against a blackened pantsleg to loosen the grit. "It was bad enough. Dust's been hanging heavy the past few days.

"I don't never want to go back in there," the ten-year-old said. His raspy words ended in a racking cough.

"What about Pa and Lennie?" I asked. Lennie was twenty-two.

Ned, the oldest boy, focused his eyes on the cap in his hand and twisted the brim. "It was pretty bad down on their level. Be a while before it's safe for the wrecking crew to go down."

●●●

The while seemed an age. I watched with a mix of hope and dread as miners who worked the upper levels stumbled from the tunnel and gave themselves into the arms of joyous wives and sweethearts. From the tunnel came the steady thud-ka-thump of a compressor blowing fresh air into the mine. From down the flat, a mill whined as it sawed lumber for coffins. Bees and flies droned in the heat. In the top of leafy hardwoods, ravens gave a reedy slunk, slunk. The church bell tolled.

"Can you tell me about Patrick or Lennie O'Shea?" my mother cried to each group of rescued miners. The weary men shook their heads.

An ominous groan rose from the crowd when a dozen men pushed coal cars filled with dead and injured down rails that led from the tunnel onto the flat. The rescuers piled the injured into horse-drawn wagons and hauled them to a drafty shed at the bottom of the gap, where they'd receive emergency care. Other men from the wrecking crew lay blanket-covered dead along the railroad tracks like windrows of hay. Now and then, one of the crew took a sock or shoe from the unrecognizable dead and held it up for someone to identify.

Forced to wait, my little brothers fretted and fought with one another. Carl punched each of the twins and called them stupid ninnies, then told me he was hungry and wanted to go home.

Savage with a hunger of her own, the baby tugged at my mother's nipples, but Ma was too tense to give milk. I thought I'd scream if we didn't receive news.

The flow of miners from the tunnel had slowed to nothing when the cavernous portal disgorged a handful of men. The mine superintendent pushed his way through the crowd and motioned us away from the path that led to the wagons. Behind the official hobbled a tall, gaunt miner, his pants blood-soaked. A long gash creased his forehead, and ooze from the wound trickled down his face. He held the front of a canvas stretcher, another bloodied miner the rear.

I pointed to the first man and shrieked, "It's Lennie!"

At the sound of my voice, the man lying on the stretcher moved, groaned, swore, and raised his orange head from the canvas.

"Patty," my mother cried. "Oh, Lord, he's hurt."

It took but a few seconds for the rest of the family to circle my father. Ma took one of his hands and held it up to her cheek. I held his other hand, not believing he lived. The little ones shoved one another for a closer look. Moved by some childish impulse, Carl pulled the blanket from my father's legs, revealing a mangle of scarlet flesh and bones. He let out a wail. My mother gave a terrible anguished scream.

I turned aside, a hand at my mouth to squelch a cry, and saw the mine official standing nearby. The sight of the man without a scratch on his hands or face, while my father was possibly maimed for life sent a wave of outrage sweeping over me, a blinding bolt of the hatred for mining and mining officials that had grown within me like a tumor over the years. Anger shook me like a leaf in the wind. I could have seized the man's neck and strangled him.

"You did this to my father," I shrieked. "You and your horrid mine. You don't give a jot about the men's safety. You deserve to go to jail."

I felt Lennie's gangly arms around me, pulling me away. "Leave him be. It's not just his fault. It's our fault, too—those of us who are poor enough and stupid enough to risk our lives for a loaf of bread. We're all to blame."

CHAPTER 2

In the dismal days that followed the explosion, my family tried to adjust to the reality of a father without legs or a job, one who'd lost his spirit, who hardly cared if he lived or died. We pretended that eventually all would be well, but none of us believed it.

A month had passed when my father called me onto the porch of our company shack, where he sat in a wheelchair, the legs of his pants pinned over the stumps that had caused such a change in his life. He motioned me to sit on the rickety step below him, disturbing a robin from her nest in a lilac bush. I couldn't imagine what was so important he'd call me from the after-supper chores. Before the explosion, we'd often sat on the porch of a summer evening, I with my mending, he with his pipe and newspaper, humming Irish ballads and telling stories. Since the accident, he'd drawn within himself and wanted no conversation, just sat nursing his hatred toward life. It made his request even more surprising.

He sat a few minutes without speaking, sucking on his pipe and drumming his fingers on the side of the chair in a preoccupied way. At last he said, "Maggie darling, I'm sorry the summer has turned out this way." His Irish brogue gave the apology the cadence of a musical lament. "I know how anxious you must be to return to school . . . know how much it means to you to become a writer or a teacher. But I must ask you to leave college for a while to help support the family." The lament had slid into a dirge.

I'd feared such a turn of events. Now that it might happen I was too stunned for speech. A long moment passed before I could say, "You know I want to help, and I will. I intend to spend more time at my job in the Dean's Office. But to leave school . . . I worked so hard for my scholarship . . . I'm getting top . . ." My stomach caved and my lips began to tremble. I could say no more.

My father studied his callused hands and rubbed them together in a distressed way. "It hurts me to ask, but you know how things are. We need your help until Ned is old enough to earn a man's wages." He paused several seconds, continuing to rub his work-scarred hands, then said, "Do you remember Bob Hanson?"

I nodded, recalling the anger I'd unleashed on mine superintendent Hanson the day of the explosion.

"He came here while you were in town this morning. Told me of a job you might want."

"Feels guilty, does he?" I said in a disheartened way.

"He knows the fix we're in, and I think he's truly sorry."

"That's hard to believe." I let bitterness gnaw at my thoughts for a moment, then asked, "What's the job?"

"Bob's brother, Harley, operates a mine in the panhandle of Idaho Territory. He's head of the school board in a town called Bixbee and needs a teacher. Not many women in that neck of the woods except for uneducated miners' wives."

My mouth slackened in disbelief. "So far from home?"

"'Tis that, all right. But the salary is twice what you'd get here in the East."

"And likely room and board is twice the cost. If I had a job near here, at least I could help Ma once in a while." I bit my lip to stop its trembling and said with a defiance I'd never unleashed on my father, "If I go west I'll be trapped. I'll never return to school."

Pa leaned forward and gripped my shoulder. "Now, now. You're a bright girl. When times are easier for us, you'll find a way to finish college."

I gave a little snort. "Easier? When will they ever be easier? And what about my scholarship? The Dean might cancel it. Why can't I work at something near the college, where I can take a course or two, maybe take a night job as a cleaning woman."

My father settled back in his chair and siphoned in a deep breath. "Don't be hasty," he said on an outward hiss of air. "Bob Hanson's known to hold a grudge. If we don't accept the offer, he might take it as an insult. He could make life hard for your brothers."

"He's just getting even for what I said to him the day of the explosion." Tears welled behind my eyelids as I considered the prospect of living in another mining town, the next one far from home. "You know I hate mining towns. If I have to work full-time, I'd rather find a job in some clean farm town."

My father's eyes narrowed until they sparked like burning coals. His face muscles hardened. "'Tis mining that puts food in our mouths."

"And men into wheelchairs." I couldn't keep the spite from my voice.

My father thumped the arm of the wheelchair. "I'll hear no more. The decision has been made. You leave in August."

I leaped to my feet, gasping tears of disappointment and outrage. "How could you agree to this without asking me?"

"This is how!" My father slapped one of the stumps, his expression as fierce as I'd ever seen it. "I expect you to make a success of this, Maggie. Hanson will give you three months to prove you can teach."

"And if I don't?"

"He'll find work for you in the company kitchen. But you can teach, Maggie. I know you can"

● ● ●

My father tried to be charitable the rest of the summer, but refused to speak of my departure and left the arrangements to my mother. Despite my dudgeonous mood, I knew it pained him that I must leave college and pained him to send me so far from home. He had his pride as well as his needs. Always the dutiful wife, my mother planned for my trip against her will and often looked at me with tears in her eyes. The strain of the last few weeks had stamped her face with weariness, but she stood tall, her head erect. I'd been told she'd inherited the stance of quiet determination from her father, the headmaster of a school in Norway, a man far different from Patrick O'Shea and his wild, stormy ways. I wondered, as I often had, how a woman of intellectual reserve, could have fallen in love with a man of such bluster as my father, a man so driven by the physical. But they had met and married while Patrick worked the Norwegian mines in Roros. Nine children had survived the union, two others lost at birth, one taken by the mine.

My features combined the Norwegian with the Irish. My face was oval like my mother's, my skin white, my nose seeded with freckles like my father's. My mother said my hazel eyes possessed an unusual translucence, "like a jar of honey lit by the sun." I doubted they held much glow on that day in late August, 1889 when I said tearful good-byes and boarded a train for Chicago. In that city, I transferred to an emigrant train, its engine belching smoke and cinders from a diamond-shaped stack. A forty-dollar loan from my mother's sister in Norway bought passage on a wooden boxcar crammed to the point of discomfort with restless travelers. Squalling children, quarreling husbands and wives, and eternal diapers strung across the car on sagging lines made it seem like a tenement house on wheels. The fare included space on a wooden bench that converted to a bed, which I shared hipbone to hipbone with a mail-order bride. It also included the use of a greasy cook-stove at one end of the car and use of the scant-curtained *convenience room*, where I often waited my turn while someone disgorged the miasma of motion sickness. My russet hair stiffened to a dark brown from the ever-present pall of smoke and from soot that showered in through open vents and windows. I became more grimy with each passing day.

The Homeseeker's Train was a third-class citizen and waited on sidetracks for hours at a time while passenger trains and freights rumbled past. Thus, two weeks crawled achingly by before the train groaned to a stop at Hauser Junction near the western border of Idaho Territory. There, I transferred to an ore train that had completed its run to the junction and would return to the Coeur d'Alene mining district—a bull engine, trailing two coaches and several ore cars, the kind of plug and peddler run that was common in the Pennsylvania mining country. After leaving Hauser, it creaked up the bottom of a canyon with steep mountains pressing in on both sides, the slopes heavily timbered with evergreens. Thickets of alder and mountain maple clogged the gullies, while other brush filled any space that remained. The Coeur d'Alene River flowed beside the track, deep and gray-brown with silt, likely the result of mining activity. Near the river, lonely draws and meadows held tiny homesteads, to which the engineer sent whistles of greeting.

This country differed from Pennsylvania, where hardwoods prevailed and where the mountains were molehills compared to these. Some ridges held the smoldering remains of fires that had raged in much of Idaho that August. When I mentioned this to a portly, well-dressed gentleman on the seat next to me, he spoke of scorching winds that had caused a single blaze in the town of Spokane Falls across the border in Washington Territory to spread into a conflagration that had destroyed half the business district.

"Burned thirty-two blocks," he said with a shake of his head. "As if the devil had sent up the fires of hell." He blew a plume of cigar smoke to emphasize the point. "That's the trouble with these boom towns. They put them up in a hurry. No care. They can burn down to nothing in a few minutes."

Farther up the canyon, the train passed three tiny settlements that lay along the South Fork of the Coeur d'Alene River, then steamed into the depot at Wallace, supply center for the Coeur d'Alene mining district. After a two-hour wait, I caught a ride on an ore-train, the only transportation into Burke Canyon, where the mining towns of Gem, Bixbee, and Burke were located. Sitting on a bench fastened to the bed of an open ore car, I watched the browning hillsides flow past, the canyon so narrow that at times I could reach out and touch the limbs of trees.

I shared the car with several other passengers huddled on benches. The car behind us had no benches, but a group of solemn-faced men sat or stood there, staring at the mine-scarred hillsides. They'd boarded the emigrant train in Michigan, and since the transfer at Hauser Junction, I'd decided they'd come to work in the mines. Like many of the men in Williamsboro, they couldn't speak enough English to ask for help or even make their most pressing needs known. Most of them were in their twenties, bundles slung over their backs. Some were quiet and wore the hollow looks of the displaced. Others poked fun at one another in Swedish, Italian, or in a cadenced Irish brogue. All were ashen-faced, as though they'd worked underground. Though they might laugh, their eyes were dull and unsmiling, like metal that had lost its sheen. A few of the men had watched me and made coarse jokes. I couldn't understand their comments, but their laughter and insinuating looks had warmed my cheeks.

Several of the men left the train at the tiny community of Gem, home of the Frisco Mine, then the train chugged up the canyon, snaking around curves that followed the canyon's twists and turns. When we reached the town of Bixbee dusk was closing in, but a dying sunset tinged the hilltops with the rosy hues of a September's eve.

Like Gem, Bixbee was squeezed between steep, mine-pocked slopes. With scarcely enough space for both railroad and town, the tracks passed within a few feet of slab and clapboard shanties, false-fronted stores, hotels and saloons, and within inches of telegraph poles set at a crazy tilt. Claiming first rights to the street, the ore train steamed up the tracks, rattling windows, forcing people on foot to back against the walls, and spewing soot on lines of clothes like black dragon's breath. The air reeked of the soot, engine oil, and rock dust from the mines, as well as a trace of smoke from the forest fires.

The engine came to a screeching, hissing stop in front of a small building of rough-sawed timbers, the Bixbee Station. As if on cue, a

man in a billed cap pushed open the batwings of a saloon next to the
station, releasing a rectangle of light along with the sound of rough
laughter. He took some portable stairs from the station-house, set them
on the ground at the side of the car, and motioned a handsome, stylishly
dressed couple of about my age down the stairs. They stepped onto the
railroad right-of-way and headed toward a bridge that crossed the creek
we'd been following. A sign hanging over the bridge said *APEX MINE
PROPERTY.* Next, a shabbily dressed woman herded a brood of
wriggling and bawling young children down the steps and walked
toward a flight of stairs opposite the bridge, one of several stairways
that clawed their way up the hillside to shanties clinging to the slope.

The stationmaster shoved my trunk against the front wall of the
stationhouse, then left to banter with the train crew, who stood
watching the engine suck water from a track pan. I'd set my satchel by
the trunk and was shaking the dust of two weeks travel from my skirts
when a silver-haired, rock-slab-of-a-man, six-feet-three if an inch,
walked from the bridge and strode up to the stationhouse in his baggy
tweed suit as if he owned the place. I had the feeling he'd squash
anyone who stood in his way. The well-dressed young man who'd
ridden the ore car from Wallace followed a step behind.

"Are these the men from Michigan?" the older man yelled at the
stationmaster.

"As far as I know. Nobody said."

Shoulders rigid, a determined thrust to his stride, the man in tweeds
walked up to the car that held the prospective miners and looked them
over as if he was buying cattle. "If you hear your name, step out of the
car," he blared at them. Holding a sheet of paper beneath a street lamp,
he read a list of names until a dozen men had left the car.

I'd had no inkling that the man in charge had noticed me, much less
knew who I was, but he looked my way and said to the younger man at
his side, "I think that's the new school teacher. I'd best introduce
myself, then I'll take these men to the Apex."

Both men walked the few feet to where I stood and tipped their
hats. "Miss O'Shea?" the older man asked. I said I was. "I'm Harley
Hanson, Clerk of the school board and manager of the Apex Mine. This
is my son Clyde."

I was surprised the younger man was his son, except that he
matched his father in height. The older Hanson had a craggy, florid

face, piercing gray eyes, and a trap of a mouth. Clyde Hanson had soft brown eyes and a smooth, gentle look to his face. The father had a brush mustache and a spade beard. Clyde's face was smooth-shaven except for a slick, dark-brown mustache.

We exchanged a few pleasantries, very few, then the elder Hanson said, "If you'll excuse me, I'm going to take these men to the bunk house. Clyde will escort you to Tuttle's boarding house. I've arranged for you to stay there."

The young man arched a dark brow. "At Della's?" he said in a theatrical baritone. "Do you think that's wise? You know what a trouble-maker she is."

"It can't be helped. There's no other place available."

A wry smile played on Clyde Hanson's lips. "Well, that will be an . . . an interesting experience for you, Miss O'Shea."

The older Hanson scowled at his son, gave me a condescending glance, and said in leaving, "I'll check with you after you're settled, Miss O'Shea. You can meet my daughter. She teaches at Wallace. Likely you saw her on the train with Clyde."

The younger Hanson took my satchel from the ground and turned to the stationmaster, who'd been observing our exchange with curiosity. "Bart, kindly have this trunk brought to Della Tuttle's place. There's a fiver in it for you." And to me, "Come, I'll take you to Della's den of rabble-rousers."

CHAPTER 3

Clyde Hanson and I walked up the narrow, dimly lit street, passing a general store that was shuttered for the night and two noisy saloons in addition to the one next to the stationhouse. A hound chased a cat from a garbage bucket that smelled of whiskey.

"Where are you from, Miss O'Shea?" Clyde said as we walked "Father has told me nothing about you."

"I'm from Williamsboro, Pennsylvania. A mining town like this."

"My, that's quite a distance. Almost across the whole continent. What made you come so far?"

I explained the circumstances, saying the move wasn't my idea, that I'd wanted to stay in college.

Clyde gave me an ingratiating smile. "Williamsboro's loss, our good fortune." His eyebrows changed their tilt with each nuance of speech. Even his cleft chin had a way of reflecting his tone. He stopped and turned toward me. "I know it's proper to call a teacher Miss, but would you mind if . . ."

"My name is Maggie—Margaretta, really—but I prefer Maggie."

"And you can call me Clyde." That decided, he continued up the dingy street, saying, "Tell me, how could a miner's daughter afford to attend college?"

"On a scholarship."

"Ah, a woman of intellect. Something new for the Coeur d'Alenes." Slowing his stride, he motioned toward several steep flights of stairs. They led to a rectangular building that looked like a boxcar stretched twice its normal length. "Tuttle's boarding house is at the top of those stairs."

The clapboard building stood on a bench cut into the hillside, where it could catch the first warm rays of sunlight in the morning, but at the moment, evening had spread a cool blanket of air along the creek bottom, intensifying the ripe breath of autumn. As if in answer to the chill, a stovepipe at the rear of the boarding house sent a filmy scarf of smoke twining across the lavender sky. On the ridge-top, a coyote yodeled a song of welcome to the emerging moon.

We dragged ourselves up the zigzag stairs to a landing where three men sat smoking their pipes. They were in their undershirts, suspenders looped over the hips of their trousers. Two said nothing. One muttered a greeting to Clyde, who gave a grudging response and set my satchel on the landing. A few feet away, a rain-barrel, bar of soap, and a towel on a nail invited some measure of cleanliness.

The wavering yellow light of a lantern glimmered through a doorway and through muslin window curtains at each side. When Clyde knocked on the door-frame, there was the sound of feet shuffling across a carpet, then a man wearing felt slippers, dark brown vest and trousers appeared in the doorway.

"Ah, Hank," Clyde said, "I've brought your new boarder." He made the introductions, identifying the man as Hank Tuttle, owner of the boarding house and of the town's general store. "I'll leave Miss O'Shea in your good care. Bart will bring her trunk." Then to me with a tip of his hat, "I hope to see you again, Maggie. Perhaps we can take a walk up the canyon."

I watched as he started down the stairs, then turned to face Hank Tuttle. He was of slight build, the cheeks above a bottle-brush mustache dimpled with pox scars, the sheaves of curly black hair parted in the middle and slicked with hair dressing. I judged him to be in his mid to late forties. He picked up my belongings and nodded me into the sitting room—whitewashed walls, a hodgepodge of furniture, and portraits of George Washington and Abraham Lincoln. A pump organ filled one corner, on it a kerosene lamp with beaded shade. Another lamp hung from a chain in the middle of the ceiling and cast a yellow light. A low table in front of a leather settee held stacks of magazines, papers, and several books. A pile of flyers announced a union meeting. Two men lounged on the settee, another man in a straight-backed chair, their bold, curious eyes upon me. They were using toothpicks, so I assumed they'd just eaten.

"Boys, this is the new teacher," Hank said. "I know I can count on you to show the proper respect. And you might wear shirts of an evening. Women don't like to see men in their undershirts." Ignoring their disgruntled replies, he said, "Come into the kitchen, Miss O'Shea. Della will want to meet you."

The door between the sitting room and kitchen stood open, allowing the heat of a cookstove and the lingering aroma of a recent supper to travel between the rooms. I hadn't eaten since breakfast, and the smell of food made my stomach gnaw at its linings.

Hank swung his arm toward a woman standing at a table that went the length of the room. Her hands were immersed in a pan of sudsy dishwater that reached the rolled-up sleeves of her blue gingham dress. "Della, here's the new teacher," he said to her. And to me, "This is my wife, queen of the roost. You can call her Della and call me Hank. That ought to give us the right to call you Maggie."

Whereas Hank was dapper, his wife was large and had folds of fat that shook beneath a white butcher's apron stained with the ingredients of supper. The hair pinned in a bun at the nape of her neck was ash-brown. She took a towel from the table, dried her hands, and held one out for me to shake. I took the warm, friendly hand. "Glad to meet you," she said in a hearty voice. "Too bad you're late for supper, but there's a plate of food on the warming shelf." She indicated a wood cook-stove on the outside wall, a huge blue enamelware coffeepot on one of the lids. While the pot wafted the aroma of strong coffee, the stove radiated a warmth that was uncomfortable for early September, though tempered by a breeze that drifted through a doorway at the far end of the room. The cackle of hens came from beyond the doorway.

"Harley told me you'd be coming in on the ore train," Della went on, "but a person never knows when it'll get here. We eat at six on the dot. The men have to keep to their shift schedule." She pulled a handkerchief from her apron and wiped it across a roll of fat beneath her chin. "Harley said you're from the Pennsylvania. Whereabouts?" She stared at me with inquisitive, light-brown eyes that spoke of a perpetual interest in life.

"Williamsboro," I answered.

"God in his nightgown! We're from right next door. We had a store in Muddy Creek before we moved here. Small world ain't it. How come you to move out here?" Once more, I explained the circumstances. "Sorry for your family's misfortune," she said when I'd finished, "but I'm glad you came. It'll be nice to have another woman in the house."

Hank smiled at his wife. "Della likes to jaw. She'll talk your leg off."

Della pretended affront. "You like to jaw just as much as I do, Hank Tuttle." Then to me, "Do you want to change your clothes before you eat, or eat first?"

"I'm about to starve. I'll change later. But I'd like to wash, if you don't mind."

Della pulled a hand towel from a cupboard next to the stove, set it on the table's white oilcloth, and took a small wash basin from a hook on the whitewashed wall. She poured two large dippers of water into the basin from a pail on the stove, set the basin on the table with a bar of soap, and resumed her dishwashing. I removed my bonnet and dipped my hands into the soothing hot water.

Hank had settled onto one of the wooden chairs that lined each side of the table and was cutting the tip of a cigar with his pocket-knife. "You picked a good time to come west," he said. "Montana's going to join the union this November. Washington State, too. Since we're in betwixt the two we'll be raising whoopee." Obviously pleased at that thought, he took a match from a jar that sat on the table and lit the cigar.

"Bad time for Spokane Falls to have a fire," Della said to me as I washed. "They'd planned a big whoop-ti-do come November."

Hank blew a curl of smoke and grinned. "Nothing's going to stop them celebrating statehood. They'll put up plenty of rag houses to party and gin-up in, you can bet on that."

"Idaho's hollering to get admitted before July of next year so we can have a big hoorah on the fourth." The glint of excitement in Della's eyes slid into a look of curiosity. "You going to be around?"

"That remains to be seen. I have to prove I can teach."

"Hope you have more luck with the kids than the first teacher," Hank said with a snort. "They ran her off."

"It's no wonder. She weren't much more'n a kid herself." Della fixed a skeptical look on me as if comparing me to that unfortunate girl. I was conscious of how I must appear—spare as a twig, freckles seeding my nose like a farm boy's, an unworldly expression, dressed plain as a wren in my brown lady's cloth. Her reaction reflected in the tone of her voice. "You old enough to handle them little monsters?"

"I've taken care of six younger brothers."

"The kids in Bixbee ain't like any brothers you likely had," said Hank. "They're a tough bunch. Especially them Tatro kids. Father's a mean bastard. I feel sorry for their mother. She just had another one. She'll die from over-work one of these days. Wait 'till you meet the older boys. They'll make your life miserable."

Della had taken the last plate from the graying dishwater and set it in a pan of clean water to rinse with the rest of the dishes. She dried her hands, took my supper from the warming shelf and set it on the table across from the dishpans. "It's a shame folks have more kids than they want or can take care of," she said as I sat down to a plate of chicken-fried steak and potatoes smothered with gravy. "Hank and me never could have kids. We feel kinda cheated." The thought obviously saddened Della. Caught up in her private reflections, she loosened the bun that had begun to slide from its fastenings at the nape of her neck and gave the long strands a twist. She wound them in place and anchored them with hairpins, then swirled a finger through flat ringlets that framed her face.

Prompted by her preening, I checked the fastenings on my own hair, something I hadn't done since early morning. I'd worn my hair in braids all my life, lately in a coil at the nape of my neck. When I left home, my brother Lennie had said, "You need to do something with your hair. Make yourself more comely. You'll be wanting to meet a nice man one of these days." I'd thought the remark silly. Meeting a man was the last thing on my mind.

Evidently my thoughts had found their way into Hank's musings. "There's lots of men in town, but not many to interest a fine lady like you. I'll introduce you to one or two. You've already met Clyde. He clerks in the mine office. His father has big plans for him with the company."

Della pulled a dish from the rinse water and started to dry it with a towel made from a flower sack. "Clyde's nice enough, I suppose. Talks kinda fancy." Then with an air of confidentiality, "Harley has two families, really. Clyde and his sister Nora are grown and earning their own way. A little girl came as a surprise. You'll have her in school."

Hank blew a puff of smoke and said in a calculated way, "Clyde'll make a good catch for some pretty gal if he can learn to leave the cards alone."

"I'm not really . . ."

Della shook a wet finger at Hank. "Shame on you for putting the blush on the girl." And to me, "Don't mind the way we rattle on, Maggie. We have a bad habit o' saying whatever comes to mind. We don't mean no offense."

"It doesn't hurt for her to know the possibilities," Hank countered. "Not that there are many. Some of the young miners are gentlemen, others are a tough lot. You'll find that out before long."

CHAPTER 4

Della and Hank rented me a room in exchange for helping with the kitchen chores. The room was small, with only a bed, chair, dresser, and commode, but it was all mine, something I'd never had before. When I wasn't busy in the kitchen, I wandered about town and up and down the canyon, becoming familiar with my new home. I wanted to look at the schoolroom, but the man who owned the building was out of town. When he finally returned and gave me the key, I left my chores to see the interior of the school for the first time. As much as I dreaded the teaching assignment, I felt a little thrill of elation, of excitement—of adventure. I was about to attempt a daring thing among strangers. To meet the challenge, I had my youth, my curiosity, an innate love for children, and a mule's determination, though they might lead me into a quagmire.

It was a hazy afternoon in mid-September and the town was quiet, half the men ending their shift in the mine, the other half sleeping or preparing for the night shift. The few wives in town were at home fixing supper in shacks along the railroad right-of-way and shanties that clung to the hillside back of town. Storekeepers stood in front of their shops, folding awnings to make room for the afternoon ore train. The narrow gauge tracks ended in the town of Burke a mile up-canyon from Bixbee, and the train began its run there.

As usual, the air was rife with the smell of engine oil, rock dust, creosote from ties stacked along the tracks, and sawdust from the Apex sawmill. As if that wasn't enough to foul the air, the odor of human waste rose from outhouses perched on platforms over Canyon Creek. The locals called it Shit Creek because of the corruption that spilled into the roily waters.

I'd already discovered that Bixbee was not just another mining town. It was worse. Drunken brawls, family squabbles, religious and ethnic feuds spilled into its one narrow street at all hours, every day of the week. According to Hank and Della, the town had been notorious for its muscle and quick temper since 1884, when it was nothing but a gold camp of tent houses. Evidently the gold hadn't amounted to much, but prospectors had discovered veins of silver, lead, and zinc in a belt about twenty-five miles long by eight miles wide along the South Fork of the Coeur d'Alene River. Burke Canyon was one of the main silver-bearing canyons that drained into the Coeur d'Alene.

By the time I'd arrived, large companies had merged most of the canyon's mining claims into a half-dozen working mines. They'd dug, drilled, and blasted their way into the hillsides, slashed greenery to fuel and timber the mines, and lined Canyon Creek with mine rigs and brown-board buildings capped with steep-pitched roofs. Harley Hanson's Apex Mine was one of those companies. It kept one-hundred-fifty men working in the stopes, ten hours each shift, seven days a week. Like Williamsboro, the town survived on rock.

Saloon-keepers were among those who kept their fingers in the miners' pockets. From Jack's Place came the sound of bawdy laughter and the sawing of a fiddle. A half-dozen men leaned against the saloon's false-front, lazing away the day, ignoring flies that clung to the building like a rash of measles. Drifters. I'd heard that the fire in Spokane had sent them straggling into the canyons. They watched me listlessly as I passed by.

"Ma'am, you got a dime for a beer?" One man asked around a wad of tobacco.

"Sorry, I spent my last dime to get here." It was true. I'd have to charge at Hank's store until I received my first paycheck.

The mine whistle ended the conversation. Its sustained blast signaled five o'clock, end of the shift. At the sound, two hard-faced women left the saloon by a rear door and rushed down the boardwalk ahead of me. Obviously, they wanted to reach their places of business before the constable caught them in town—five o'clock was curfew for Bixbee harlots. They took a few steps down the walk, then flounced up a crude earthen stairway to a row of cribs that stood high above the town on foundations of loose slate. I felt like a mudhen in my plain skirt and shirtwaist compared to the whores in their gaudy dresses.

As I neared the bridge leading to the Apex property a flux of miners began to stream across the bridge into the street, empty dinner pails and rubber boots dangling at their sides. They looked so tired their hip-pockets seemed to drag in their tracks. Their diggers—coveralls and boots they wore in the mine—were plastered with mud, their faces powdered with rock dust. The sight reminded me of Williamsboro, except the rock dust here was gray instead of black. I backed against the wall of a smithy to make room for them to pass.

I knew much about the men from talking to Della and Hank. Two-thirds were refugees from the misery of their homelands and had found a different kind of misery here—Irish, English, Swedes, Southern Europeans, Finns, men of all sizes with strong pulses throbbing in their throats. Most of them were full-time miners who'd taken on the look of the rock they worked. Men with more color in their cheeks were *ten-day stiffs, boomers, floaters*, men who worked a camp long enough to earn a grubstake before they set out for the next camp, possibly for a several days' binge.

Man after man stomped the mud and dust from his feet before stepping into a clapboard shanty or one of the businesses that crowded cheek-to-jowl for a quarter-mile up the creek. Many of them shuffled into saloons boisterous with comings and goings.

East of the bridge, men trudged up the slope to the company boardinghouse, a long, rectagular building notched into the hillside. I'd been told that most of the bachelors rented rooms there, but a few rented shacks in town or stayed at Della's. Down-creek from the boarding house, men dressed in suits rather than diggers walked toward a row of houses—the homes of geologists, engineers, and superintendents. Harley Hanson's house stood at the end of the row, the only two-story dwelling, the only one with a flower garden and picket fence.

The flow of men had dwindled and I was about to walk on down the street when one of the younger miners left the bridge, turned halfway to look behind him, and accidentally stepped into my path.

He removed his hat from a thatch of golden hair. "Excuse me. I should've watched where I was going."

"That's all right," I said. "No harm done."

I expected him to step aside. Instead, his blue eyes stared at me with speculation, at least one eye did, the other was swollen shut and bruised. A bandaged temple detracted from an otherwise pleasant face. "You're new in town," he said. The words were as much question as statement.

"I'm the teacher."

"Oh, that's good to hear. I thought maybe you were . . . though you don't look like . . ." He let the rest trail off, but his quirky expression said he'd thought I might be a new whore. "I wish you luck. Those kids—"

Before he could finish, an older miner bore down upon us, his red-bearded face like a storm about to break. He dropped his pail and boots, spun the blond around by the shoulder, and grabbed the front of his shirt. "Better watch your step, Rigby. If you don't stop bucking me on this union thing, I'll bloody you good."

The man called Rigby pulled his shirt from the redhead's grip and gave him a shove. "This is hardly the place for an argument, Rafe."

From Hank and Della's gossip, I recognized the name Rafe as the given name of Rafe Tatro, one of the more radical miners backing the formation of a union. He brought up a guttural laugh. "What's wrong, Rigby? Scared I'll embarrass you in front of your lady friend?"

Rigby flushed to the roots of his hair. "I repeat, this is not the place."

Tatro turned to me. "I'd say this man is a sissy. Wouldn't you, Ma'am?"

Before I could think of an appropriate reply, Tatro pulled back his fist and slammed Rigby in the jaw. Rigby lurched backward, caught himself, and charged Tatro, fists working like pistons.

There followed a brutal exchange of blows until Tatro belted Rigby in the stomach. Rigby gave a burst of air and doubled, holding his stomach.

By then, a dozen miners had come on the run and made a boisterous knot around the fighters. Dogs circled them, barking. One of the men took hold of Rigby's arm as he straightened and pulled back his fist. "Don't be a clod, Dan," the miner said. "There are better places for a game of fisticuffs."

The crowd disagreed.

"Go after him, young fella," one man said.

"If you want to get at Tatro's brains, kick him in the ass," said another.

"Yeze ain't going to let the bully show yeze up in front o' this comely lass are ye?" said a third.

The latter's words seemed to strike home. Rigby tore free of the miner's grasp and launched himself at Tatro. At that moment, a man wearing the badge of a constable pushed his way through the pack and up to the fighters. "All right, boys. 'Tis enough. Settle your grudges out of town or I'll have to put you in the clink." And to the disgruntled crowd, "Get on with you. Go buy a cool one or get home to your suppers."

Tatro and the other men were dragging themselves up the street when Della lumbered toward me with a rolling gait. I'd left her at Hank's store gathering the ingredients for supper, but it seemed the brawl had drawn her down the street. "I see you got to see some of Bixbee's hotbloods at work," she said, puffing.

"I couldn't avoid it. That man you told me about—Rafe Tatro—started the fight right in front of me. He even used my being there to goad the other man into a fight."

"Dan Rigby's not one to back down. But he can be a gentleman. I doubt he wanted to fight in front of you."

"I guess he couldn't take Rafe's taunts." I looked over to where Dan Rigby was dusting off his clothes and wiping blood from his nose and mouth. Dirt streaked the bandage on his forehead. "It looks like he's had an accident."

"Rafe caught him with the business end of a drill."

"Why on earth would he do a thing like that?'

"He got mad because Dan reported him to the super. Rafe left an unexploded charge of dynamite on the rock face and didn't warn the shift boss. Next men on shift coulda gotten killed. Any son-of-a-sea-cook who'd leave a sleeper without telling the boss outghta be snitched on. If I was the super I'd . . ." She went on and on while I watched Rafe and the other miners shamble up the street. "For the life of me I don't know why Dan wants to work as a hammer and drill man," she said. "He's had two years o' business college. I guess it's because he wants to learn the mining business from the bottom up. He'd like to own a mine of his own. Spends as much time as he can out prospecting."

"Are you telling tales again, Della?" Rigby said. He'd walked over to where we stood, hat in hand, apology showing through the cuts on his face. "I'm sorry this happened, ma'am," he said to me. "I'm afraid I let Rafe get me riled."

"No need to apologize. You didn't pick the fight."

Della pointed to Rigby's face. "Looks like the swelling's gone down on your forehead, but you better put a leech on that eye. And you better steer clear of Rafe. I've been told he can hold a grudge longer'n a kicked mule. When a man's been mining as long as he has, he takes to drink to forget how wore out he is. Whiskey makes a man like him real mean."

"He was born mean. Right now he's trying to strong-arm our new union. I'm for a strong union, but one that acts through arbitration not

violence." Rigby's crisp manner of speaking matched his appearance—
a man of action, one who wouldn't let himself be pushed around. It
showed in his wedged jaw, and in the dense, unbroken line of the brows
that overhung his eyes like bushy cutbanks sheltering a mountain
stream. Still, I noted a kindness there. He sent me a sheepish look and
said, "Like I said, I'm sorry this happened, Miss . . ."

Della raised an arm in apology. "I'm sorry. I plumb forgot my
manners. Dan this is Maggie O'Shea, the new schoolteacher. Maggie,
this is Dan Rigby."

"I'm mighty pleased to meet you," Rigby said with a broad smile.
He put his hat on his head at a jaunty angle and said in leaving, "Now if
you'll excuse me, I need to clean up."

I watched as he strode up the street, the swing of confidence in his
stride belying any misgivings he might have about union matters. I
hoped they wouldn't involve battles between the miners. My father had
suffered a bloodied head more than once during the struggle to form a
coal miners' union. I'd expected Bixbee to be more civilized, but from
Della's and Hank's tales, I had the feeling it would be as bad or worse
than other mining towns—forever in an uproar.

CHAPTER 5

Della and I parted company, she to return to the boarding house to start supper, I to continue down the tracks toward the school. The sun was about to slip behind the ridge that shouldered abruptly at my right and would soon leave the bottom of the canyon in shadow. The narrow canyon shortened the hours of sunlight, a blessing in summer, not in fall and winter.

Across the creek, the mills and out-buildings of Apex Mining and Milling hulked from the hillside amid the stumpage of pines. Near the crest of the ridge, a tramway connected the mine portal with a concentrating mill at the base of the hill. After a two-hour shutdown to clear the tunnels of rock dust and smoke from blasting powder, the night shift would scoop rock from the day's blasts into ore cars and the tramway would squeal with heavy cars riding down to the mill.

I'd walked a short distance when I heard a tittering behind my back. A glance over my shoulder revealed three boys ranging in age from about six to eight. They were dressed only in ragged knee breeches and shone a walnut brown from weeks of summer sun and ground-in dirt. One I recognized as belonging to the peevish brood I'd seen on the train. It was obvious the boys knew who I was—they were thumbing their noses. When school started, I'd see that they learned better manners. But for now . . .

"I'm going to the school," I said calmly. "Would you like to come along?" The boys ran behind an ice-wagon parked at the edge of the walk and peeked at me from between the spokes of a wheel. I smiled. "Just thought I'd ask." I stepped out at a brisk pace, looking to the rear to see if the boys followed. They did, giggling and making faces, a skinny hound at their heels.

At the edge of town, I heard shouts coming from the shadows of a railroad barn. Barely visible behind stacks of railroad ties, gangs of teenage boys were hurling rocks at one another. The oldest were members of Rafe Tatro's clan. The tallest was the first to notice me. He stepped from the shadows with a rude, arrogant stride, kicking at pebbles. The last slanted rays of the sun shone on his pimply face and a mop of hair the yellowish-gray of overripe hay.

 Eyes as yellow as a cat's squinted against the sun. "What you dumb little farts doing with the knuckle-thumper?" The boy asked the youngsters who'd followed me down the street. "Ain't you going to see enough of her ugly face when school's in?"

The blood rushed to my cheeks as I thought of things I'd like to say in reply to the boy's insolence. I'd known such hoodlums in Williamsboro, born into poverty and loveless homes, raised in an atmosphere of disrespect for others. In Williamsboro this boy would be at work in the mines. In Idaho he'd have to wait until he turned sixteen. In the meantime, I'd suffer his presence in school.

It took all my will power to resist speaking my thoughts. Instead, I said as politely as possible, "I'm going to the school, and the boys seem to want to come along."

The older boy turned to the gang peering from behind the ties and guffawed. "You pukes hear that? She's going to the school. Ain't that nice." He flourished his hands with mock femininity. "She's going to love what she finds." Churlish laughter erupted from the forts.

The other Tatro, an impish-looking redhead, stepped from behind the ties and stared at me, one hand stuck in the back pocket of his jeans, a hip slung out in a brazen stance. "You better not be mean to us, Teach. We run the last hickory-bender out of town. You'll be—"

He broke off as a man's voice blared from up the tracks. I turned to see Rafe Tatro bearing down upon us. "You rascals get home and help with the chores before I give you a good thumping," he said to the boys. Then to me, "Sorry if they was bothering you, Ma'am." I was surprised he'd bothered to apologize. Saying nothing more, he turned on his heel and headed up the tracks, the boys shuffling behind, the dog cowering at one side.

I arrived at the Bixbee School just as the little catchpenny train rounded the flattened hump of mine tailings that served as playground. It sent me a toot of greeting, then rattled down the canyon trailing cars of silver-lead ore. Twice a day the narrow-gauge made the trip down Canyon Creek collecting sacks of ore from a string of mines, each with its own small settlement. At the point where Canyon Creek flowed into the South Fork of the Coeur d'Alene River, the tracks turned west into Wallace, hub of the mining district.

I paused at the gate to the schoolyard, feeling a reluctance to enter the building and give myself up to the school for better or worse. Now that I'd met the Tatro boys, part of me wanted to leave town. The other part was determined not to let the insolent toughs get the best of me. Certainly the building did nothing to excite my fancy—brown rawboard about two years old. No windows cut the front wall, but the side walls each held three windows, tall and spectral, like those of a supposed haunted house in Williamsboro where Lennie and I had ventured once or twice.

Stairs led to the schoolhouse door. Beside them a locomotive bell dangled from a post. I climbed the stairs, unlocked the ill-fitting door and stepped into an entryway that held coat hooks and benches as well as three buckets and a scummy washbasin that lay upside-down on the floor. I set the containers on a bench and opened the door into the classroom, sneezing at dust and the smell of mice. The stench was the least of my shock. Someone had spattered the walls with ink and strewn ashes from a pot-bellied stove across the floor. Pages from books cluttered the room like fallen leaves. I recalled the Tatro boys' mocking voices and knew who'd caused the ruin.

I felt slapped across the face. "Why me? The boys don't even know me," I said to the walls. "Lord, how I wish I were back at the Women's College. Even Williamsboro would be better than this."

As I looked around at the clutter, my resentment grew. The more I thought of the mischievous devils who'd caused the mess, the more the school became mine and the violations against it became trespasses against me. "No one's going to put me down," I vowed. "I'll clean up the mess. Then I'll let those rascals know they can't tamper with what's mine."

My jaw set in anger, I put hat, gloves, and shawl on a desk and tore into the clutter, picking up broken slates here, torn books there. At the front of the room, a rickety table and a broken chair lay on their sides. Behind the table, a chalkboard's black oilcloth hung in shreds. To the left of the board, the door to a wood closet stood ajar, the latch broken. A section of the doorframe had been chipped away where it met the latch, the boys' point of entry.

I'd been working about a half-hour when boot heels clacked on the floor of the entry and Dan Rigby sauntered into the classroom. "What in the hell?" he said under his breath. Then louder, "I see the last teacher left the school in good condition."

The remark had come at the wrong moment. I turned my head aside as tears welled in my eyes.

Dan stumbled after his blunder. "I'm sorry. Somehow this mess struck me as funny."

What right did he have to laugh at my predicament? I swallowed at a tightness in my throat and said crisply, "What brings you this way, Mr. Rigby? I thought you'd gone home."

"I did." Then with a laugh, "Can't you tell?" Clearly he had. He was dressed in street clothes, a gray bowler, and had washed his face. He held a hand-rolled cigarette in one hand. "Della said you were here and I thought I'd stop by." He steered himself between the rows of desks and tossed the cigarette into the stove in the middle of the room. "It had to be Jim and Mike Tatro who did this. They were caught doing the same thing to the new church a while back. Only it wasn't near this bad. You ought to get them to clean it up."

I wagged my head adamantly. "No thank you. I've already had one encounter with them."

"They're a raunchy pair. Just like their dad."

While we talked, I picked up undamaged books and stacked them on the desks, noting that Dan was taking stock of me from my high-topped shoes to my hair. At the same time, I took inventory of *him*. Despite the bandaged forehead and cuts on his cheeks, the golden curls that framed his face and the handlebar mustache that turned upward gave him the look of a smiling sun. I felt reassured. Still, I wondered why he'd come.

He seemed to have read my mind. "I stopped by to see if you'd like to picnic at a pond down the Coeur d'Alene a ways. I have this Sunday off."

My mouth dropped open slightly. As much from shyness as surprise. "I-I hardly know you."

He smiled with a flashing white arch of teeth. "And I hardly know *you*."

"But what will people think?"

"There'll be a dozen boats on the pond," he said casually. "Lots of chaperones."

I ran nervous fingers along a desktop, fighting skepticism. "People watch every move I make. They'll think it's too soon for me to go out with a man."

Dan shrugged. "I wouldn't worry about the Bixbee folks. The men aren't going to care. And except for maybe Harley Hanson's wife, the women were sneaking into the woods before they were thirteen."

The comment caused a new rush of blood to my cheeks. My pulse quickened. "People have different standards for teachers."

"You can't let that keep you from having a good time." He set his hat on a desk and started to sit.

"Here, let me dust that first." I took a slate rag from the floor, shook it, and flicked it across the desk's checked surface.

Dan sat, studying me with wide-spaced blue eyes. "Would you feel better if I asked Clyde Hanson along? He could bring his sister, Nora. She teaches in Wallace."

"Mmm . . . I might consider that," I said hesitantly. "It would be nice to talk to another teacher. Della says she's a lovely person. She says you and the Hanson kids grew up together."

"Yeah, my father and Harley owned a placer mine in California. Clyde and I are sort of like brothers. At least we argue as much. Clyde was kind of a sissy. But I tried to see how far I could go without killing myself."

I relaxed a little at his candor. "Why did you move here?" I said as I wiped a rag across a broken slate.

"When our fathers split up, my dad moved to Spokane Falls and opened a furniture store. Harley moved here to manage the Apex. Clyde and I stayed in Sacramento for a couple of years and went to business college. Clyde lived at the race tracks, and I had a hell-roaring—" He broke off, seeming to regret his choice of words, and began again in a milder vein. "I came here because Harley offered to teach me about mining silver and lead. My dad didn't want me to go into mining, but I didn't want to work at his furniture store . . . anyway, my brother Aaron was there to help, so . . ." He seemed to have said all he wanted on the subject, simply sat picking at a fingernail, whistling *Oh Susanna* through his teeth.

I paused to rest, saying, "It must be hard to push for a union when Harley is your friend."

"Yeah, I have a boot in each camp. It makes for mixed feelings." Dan looked up from the fingernail. "What about Sunday. Will you go?"

"I-I can't say. I'll have to ask Della. I hate to leave her alone on Sunday when all the sundowners show." To hide my fluster, I scooped a stack of books from the table.

Dan slid from the desk and took the books from my arms. "Where do you want these?" I pointed to a shelf. "You'd better take time to enjoy yourself, Maggie. Come November, old man winter'll blow in here like he took a wrong turn out of Siberia. Last year it got down to forty below." He shelved the books with a grunt and added, "The mines froze up. Most of the men pulled out by January." He took his hat from the desk and stuffed it on his head. "I'd better get some rest. They'll be taking the cage down early in the morning. They're pushing to get out as much rock as they can before things freeze up."

I followed as he walked to the door, skirting what was left of the mess. He stopped at the entry and turned to face me, his eyes intense. "You find out from Della, and I'll check back with you tomorrow. Try hard, you hear."

I watched as he crossed the schoolyard, noting that although he was middle-height, he was so well proportioned he seemed taller. Despite ten hours working in the stopes, he carried his back and shoulders in a vigorous way and had a bounce in his step. It spoke of the same confidence I'd noted before as well as an elusive quality—something strong and sweet.

He was different from men who'd shown an interest in me in the past—clerks, storekeepers, and students at the men's college, polite young men devoted to serious pursuits. Dan thrived on mining, everything I deplored. How could I possibly have anything in common with him? Yet, I could hardly wait to see him again.

CHAPTER 6

Della gladly released me from my Sunday chores. Hank winked and said, "It didn't take you long to find a beau. Have a good time."

The train trip down the Coeur d'Alene River amid the sparkling hues of autumn almost blinded me with its brilliance. The day seemed timeless, one that warmed my heart and eased my longing for home. The picnic near the millpond was a delight, its setting a meadow tinged wheat-yellow from the frosts and fringed with cottonwoods in a trembling arc of gold. Magpies and bluejays argued over the biscuit crumbs we tossed their way and filled the woods with their ratchety calls.

I discovered a friend in Clyde's sister, Nora, a first-year teacher at the Wallace School—a petite brunette, with springy fly-away curls, whose manner was warm and honest. She'd graduated from a fashionable women's college and had traveled the country, yet she showed as much dread of that first day of school as I. We laughed at our anxieties, spoke of anticipated joys, and promised to keep in touch. It helped to have someone my own age as a confidant, one facing challenges like my own. If she'd been a different sort, I might have felt self-conscious in my drab brown dress as opposed to her stylish emerald-green suit, but she didn't put on airs, and I soon forgot that she came from a family that could afford such clothes. She hadn't trained to be a teacher from need, but to give her life purpose.

On the other hand, Clyde had taken advantage of his father's position in the mining world to indulge himself. He spoke with fervor of trips to San Francisco and Chicago, of visits to theaters, museums, and opera houses, and sang his favorite arias in a resonant baritone. Using a caustic wit and flair for the dramatic, he mimicked the players in a production of *Bohemian Girl* he'd seen in Spokane Falls. He proved so entertaining, I found it hard to tell when he was acting and when he was not. His eyes seemed always to be testing me, as if my words had hidden meaning. And I wasn't sure I could trust his. I was amazed that a brother and sister could be so different in that respect.

Where it was difficult to relate to Clyde, Dan's conversation and manner made only those demands I could satisfy with ease. At first, I'd thought that the exhilaration I'd experienced during his visit to the school had been an illusion springing from my loneliness and anxiety. But I found him all that I'd remembered—lively, funny, as comfortable to be around as a long-time friend. He poked fun at Bixbee, told of rollicking things to do in Spokane Falls, and spoke of animals, birds, and the sky. I glowed inside when I looked at his broad, fair-skinned face with its readiness for humor.

Clyde and Nora became involved in an animated discussion of family affairs, so Dan and I left the blanket where the four of us had been sitting and walked toward the pond, where a flock of mallards dabbled for insects. A clump of long-stemmed purple asters growing near the water's edge caught my eye, and I borrowed Dan's pocket knife to cut the tough-stemmed flowers. "These are for Della," I said as I inhaled the asters' sharp scent. "She likes to put flowers on the dinner table."

"Along with a stack of union propaganda and the best chow in the canyon," Dan said with an affectionate laugh. "If you ever need help, you can count on Della. She has a way of charging at trouble as if it was one of her hated roosters and she was wringing the life from its neck."

"I've already found that to be true. When I told her about the mess in my classroom, she grabbed soap, scrub brushes, and brooms, and led the attack."

I was tucking an aster into a buttonhole on my dress when I felt Dan's intense eyes staring at me from the shadow of his slouch hat. "You're very pretty," he murmured.

I lowered my eyes. My cheeks flushed. I knew I was nice-looking. But pretty? As far as I was concerned it took effort to be pretty, and I'd never had the time to stand before a mirror and primp, nor did I own clothes that would make me attractive. I rejected the compliment with a smile and a shake of my head. "Not really."

"Yes, you *are*, especially your eyes. They make me feel like you're seeing straight through me. My mom's eyes were like that. She knew when my brother Aaron and I had been into mischief just by looking at us." He paused to toss a pebble at a water snake that was wriggling through the weeds, then asked. "Is your mother living?"

I nodded and went on gathering asters, thistledown clinging to my skirts. "She's having a hard time since my father lost his legs."

"How did that happen?"

I explained, though I was heart-weary from telling the tale so often.

"Are you like your ma or pa?"

I considered the question while I wet my handkerchief at water's edge and wrapped it around the flower stems. "I suppose I'm like Ma . . . except she's put up with more than I would have. You'll never catch me marrying a miner." I realized the comment held implications I hadn't intended and sent Dan a look of apology. "I'm sorry. I didn't mean . . ."

He shrugged and smiled. "Being married to a miner is difficult at best. Not enough pay . . . too dangerous. I'll never marry while I'm working underground. I'll wait until I can make my wife a decent home." He took up a handful of round, flat stones and started skipping them across the pond. "It's a good thing I don't have to go to work until tomorrow evening. I can use another day like today. Maybe go prospecting."

"I don't understand why you work in the mine when you could get an easier job with better wages. You're not paid enough to face the danger."

He looked at me sharply, seemed to search my eyes for intent, then slowly slid his expression into one of agreement. "You're right. Us poor stiffs dig and blast for barely enough pay to keep us in diggers, groceries, and tobacco. And the operators don't give a hoot whether or not we get hurt. They just keep bellowing for more rock. The operator pushes the super—the super pushes the foreman—the foreman pushes the shift boss—and the shift boss rants up and down the stopes yelling for rock, more rock, more rock!"

We continued to stroll side by side, listening to the shore birds pipe as they scurried along on legs that looked like stilts. "Is Harley Hanson as bad as the other operators?" I asked after a bit.

"No different. He's beholden to the absentee owners and stockholders in the east. In his eyes, miners are expendable as loose change in his pockets." Dan indicated a downed cottonwood as a place to rest. After we'd settled on the trunk's shredded bark, he pulled a bag of Bull Durham and cigarette papers from his vest and let tobacco spill from the bag into one of the papers. Bag and packet of papers back in his vest, he rolled the cigarette and sealed it with his tongue.

His thoughts were still latched on mining. "I tell you, Maggie, men who earn a living by the sweat of their backs are in a struggle for their lives. The mining and smelting combines use their profits to gobble up railroads, oilfields, mines, land, and timber as fast as they can. All the while, they squabble among themselves for control. Soon we'll have to put up with a bunch of damned industrial lords. Robber barons, that's what." He seemed to be talking to himself as much as to me, clarifying his thoughts, his gaze wandering.

I made a nondescript noise of agreement and was going to add what I knew about men of wealth, but Dan seemed to have caught something of the thought and said, "Men like Carnegie—Harriman—and Rockefeller think God gave them the right to control all money for the workers well-being. We have to fight back or the steamroller will squash us all." He took a match from a supply in his vest pocket, struck the match with a thumbnail, and lit the cigarette.

"What about the union you've organized? Won't that help?"

Smoke strung through his lips as he said, "We've arbitrated a few small concessions, nothing big. Harley's promised to put in a change room with hooks and a shelf for each man, so we can put on dry clothes before we leave the mine in winter. The way it is now, a miner's sweaty clothes freeze to his back before he can get home." He paused to draw on his cigarette, laughed at some jays scrapping among themselves in a treetop, and went on. "Just about every mine in the district has a union now. The locals hope to form a central committee. That'll give us more clout. Our first objective is to have the mine owners build a miners' hospital in Wallace. Not that we need one," he said sarcastically. "A rock fall killed four men at the Apex. An accident in a shaft killed five at one of the other mines."

"What about demanding safety measures?"

"No luck there yet."

"You're taking a lot on yourself."

"I'm not alone. Lots of good men are interested."

Dan paused to smoke, while I watched squirrels scratch for nuts in the duff at the base of a pine tree. After a bit, he turned toward me in a manner of confidentiality. "Maggie, can you keep a secret?"

"I-I guess. Sure. What is it?"

"Before long, I'll own one of the richest mines in the district. When I do, I'll help the miner and I'll use my wealth to fight the goddamned leeches that are bleeding the country."

I sucked in a breath of disbelief. "You sound sure of yourself. How do you propose to own such a mine?"

Dan leaned close, as if he was afraid the jays might hear. I smelled the tobacco on his breath, along with the faint scent of cologne, and had an acute sense of his nearness. "I think I might already have that mine," he said in a near-whisper. "Last week I filed papers on an outcrop of galena that could turn into something big."

I stared at him in a skeptical way. "If it's that good, why hasn't someone else claimed it?"

He wagged a finger in front of my nose. "Because, dear lady, it'd been covered with brush. This summer's fire took care of that. Oh, Maggie," He lifted his arms as if in heavenly praise. "The gleam of it was enough to set me dancing."

I drew back, wary of the peculiar light that had come to his eyes. Since I'd arrived in Bixbee I'd heard tales of prospectors who'd spent their lives chasing a will o' the wisp. I hoped Dan wasn't as foolish. "It's a long way from outcrop to paying mine," I said as reasonably as I could. "It'll take more money than you can imagine to develop it."

His mouth slackened into a self-righteous expression. "I sure as hell am going to try. I've picked the brains of the supers, geologists, and engineers at the Apex. Harley doesn't have anything in that block of his that I don't know. I'm ready to make a go of a mine. All I need is the money." He took off his hat and rumpled his wiry curls in a manner of intense concentration of will, then went on talking more rapidly, every word filled with passionate conviction. "I'm not going to use any corrupt foreign or eastern money to get started like most of the operators around here. It may take years to get the backing. But just you wait. If the mineral's commercial, I'll make a producing mine." He stared past my shoulder into the amber afternoon, his eyes diffused with dreams of the future.

I didn't want to spoil those dreams, but I had to say, "I wouldn't want to own a business that keeps men in constant fear of life and limb, that pays them so little they can't strive for something better. I've lived with that kind of fear and in that kind of poverty. It shrivels the mind and spirit."

Dan drew his brows together in a look of affront. "I won't run that kind of mine. I'll make it safe and pay decent wages."

I studied his determined features as he stared across the pond, noting the many qualities I'd seen in him that day, from the comic to the zealous, each characteristic displayed openly, with a surety of self. I liked his spirit, but the near irrational zeal I saw in him now made me wonder. "Why are you telling me all this? How do you know I'll keep your secret?"

He turned toward me, grinning. "I'm a good judge of character. Besides, I don't want you to think I have no ambition. I'd—"

Clyde had come gliding up from behind us, his arm entwined in Nora's, and interrupted Dan's thoughts. "Whatever he's telling you, don't believe a word of it," he said with a laugh.

Dan waved the comment aside. "C'mon, pal. Don't put me down."

"Dan's been telling me what it's like to be a miner," I said, hoping to distract from the latest topic of conversation. I noted Clyde's smooth, uncallused hands, his fingernails free of ground-in dirt. "Do you spend much time in the mine?" I thought I knew the answer.

He gave a snort that smacked of disgust. "Not if I can help it."

"If you're going to fill your father's shoes, I'd think you'd want to find out about conditions first hand." I couldn't keep a sharp edge from my voice.

Clyde gave a careless shrug. "I'll cross that bridge when I come to it."

"Clyde's not one to put himself in danger," Nora said with a disparaging laugh. "I was always the one to take chances—rode bareback, jumped horses, played polo."

Clyde's eyebrows rose in a mix of affront and challenge. "I'd like to see you go underground."

Nora put her hands on her hips in an air of defiance. "I'm not afraid to go."

"Father would never let you!"

"He would if I begged enough."

Clyde's lack of responsibility had sparked a sudden resentment in my Irish soul. Without considering the consequences, I said, "I'll go into the mine, if *Clyde* will take us down."

"Dad won't allow women in the mine," Clyde said hurriedly. "It's too dangerous."

Dan brought up a chesty laugh. "Too dangerous for the women, or for you?" Then to me in a serious tone, "Are you sure you want to go? The first time is scary, even for us miners."

"I'm sure," I replied with more confidence than I felt.

"Then, I suppose Harley could arrange a time when there'd be less chance for harm, wouldn't you say, Clyde?"

Clyde mumbled something incoherent, while Nora clapped her hands.

"Sounds exciting," she said, bubbling over with anticipation. "I'll talk to Dad and let you know, Maggie."

I felt an abrupt caving of my stomach. I had no doubt Nora would get her way and one of these days I'd find myself in the dark of the underground, wishing I'd never offered to go.

CHAPTER 7

D ue to the opening of school, two weeks passed before Nora and I could go down into the mine. She'd sent word that she'd spend Friday night with her parents in Bixbee and suggested I arrive there a little before seven the next morning "I have a bicycling suit with knickers you can wear," she'd said in her note. "It will be more suitable than a dress. Dad said the draft going down the shaft would blow our skirts up to our ears."

After I'd borrowed Della's galoshes so I wouldn't ruin my shoes, I left her shaking her head at my lack of good sense and walked through town. It was too early for the stores to open, and men on day shift hurried past on their way to the mine.

I was approaching the bridge that led to the Apex property when Dan Rigby slammed the door on a hillside shack and hurried down a flight of rickety stairs, two steps at a time. He was dressed in his diggers and carried a dinner pail and rubber boots.

"Maggie? What are you doing out so early on a Saturday?" he said when he reached the street.

The explanation stammered from my lips. "I-I-Nora and I are going down into the mine."

"So, she talked her dad into it. That doesn't surprise me. She knows how to get her way."

I pointed to his dinner pail. "I thought you worked the night shift this week."

"I did, for half the night. The shift boss wants me and my partner back this morning to blast a tough ledge of rock. There's a new drill team and he wants us to see they do the job right."

He no longer wore a bandage, but there were gray puffs under his eyes. "You look tired. Will you have to work the full day?"

"Whatever the shifter wants. I'm his slave." He gave a cynical laugh. "At least I won't have to work with Rafe Tatro."

As if the devil had heard, Rafe Tatro and a slight man with a dark, lean, hungry look swaggered up to us. Like Dan, they were dressed for work. Rafe took a slouch hat from his mat of red hair and tipped it in an exaggerated manner. "Good morning, Miss O'Shea. Let me introduce my partner, Smutt Corrigan."

Smutt's thin face with its jug-handle ears seemed nothing more than an extension of his neck. It made his hard-shelled bowler look like it was about to slip down over his face. "I'm glad to be meeting you, ma'am," he said, mimicking Tatro's play on courtesy.

I could see the flush of annoyance rise into Dan's face, but he held his tongue, likely for my sake.

"I see you've got a new dinner pail, Rigby. Something happen to the other?" Rafe's taunting laugh made me suspect he was the reason Dan needed a new pail. "Don'tcha know it's bad luck to fetch a new pail into the mine? Hand it here, and I'll break it in for you so it won't look so new."

Dan tightened his grip on the pail and seemed about to swing it at Rafe, but thought better of it. "Mind your own business, Rafe."

Rafe sneered. "Your business is my business." Then to me, "If you want goldylocks here to keep his good looks, you should tell him to let go the reins of the union."

"Better yet, tell him to be leaving the district," Smutt said with an Irish slant to his words.

The scarlet in Dan's face deepened. He clenched his fist. Before he could follow through, a man with the build of Paul Bunyan called from a diner across the street and hurried to Dan's side. "Smutt, you and Rafe move on," he said with a jerk of his arm. The men sent him hateful looks and left, muttering oaths. "Better hurry," the Paul Bunyan type said to Dan. "We're going to miss the cage."

"First I want you to meet Maggie." Dan extended his hand. "Maggie, this is Bert Lacey, my drilling partner."

Bert tipped his hat. "Pleasure. Dan's told me about you." There'd been a Sioux in Bert's past. His walnut-brown skin, long humped nose, and almond-shaped eyes attested to the fact. His hair was dark-brown, almost black.

"I'm glad you're here," I said to both of them. "You can help me across the bridge so I won't get trampled in the rush."

On the far side of the bridge we met a stream of miners who'd left the company boarding house and were headed for the mine portal. Those on the upper end of the mining hierarchy—shift bosses, geologists, and the like—were leaving their homes on shifter's row. I said goodbye to Dan and Bert and walked down the row of small cottages to the Hanson's larger home. Harley and Clyde had left for work, Nora's mother in Spokane with her young daughter Lucinda, and Nora and I were able to dress without unwanted comments.

Nora's new black and white checked cycling outfit fit her trim figure to perfection, but she was shorter than I and we had to adjust the knickers of her old tweed cycling suit to fit me. When we emerged from the house I felt like a wart on a nose.

Nora sensed my discomfort. "Relax," she said. "These are the latest in sporting fashion. You'll be thankful you didn't wear a dress."

Clyde met us at eight o'clock in front of the mill that held the Apex office. I thought his business suit appropriate for the office, not for the trip into the mountain. The glint of humor in his eyes made it obvious he thought the same about Nora's and my suits. "I say, but you two look fetching," he said with a snicker. "If I was a cock I'd crow. You'll cause more than one pair of eyes to glance your way."

Nora gave a snort of a laugh. "It's your job to keep them from staring." She might laugh, but Clyde's remark made me want to crawl into a hole.

Avoiding further comment, the three of us began the steep climb up the path to the headhouse, a stark frame building that fronted the portal to the Apex mine. A tramway that paralleled the path creaked and clanged with ore cars riding the tram to the mill at the base of the hill. The farther we climbed, the more Clyde dragged his feet, clearly from a reluctance to enter the mine. "Do you really want to go through with this?" he asked me. I assured him that I did, though I had to work to hide my own anxiety. I felt like I was about to take a trip into purgatory.

The day foreman met us when we stepped into the headhouse. Clyde introduced him as Ted Busby—a middle-aged man with a pot belly, graying black hair, and laugh lines at the corners of his large, steely-gray eyes. He stuck his thumbs beneath his suspenders, as if it gave him a feeling of importance. "By Jesus, I've never seen outfits like that in the mine," he said with a grin. "You ladies might set a new style for diggers." Then to Clyde with a hint of sarcasm, "I see Harley's finally talked you into visiting the stopes."

Clyde looked as if he'd sucked a lemon. "Only because of Nora."

Busby took that as a cue to call Clyde over to a far corner of the room, where they spoke in low voices, looking now and then at us women. I caught snatches of Busby's conversation. "Can't . . . women . . . faint . . . won't be responsible . . . the men . . . ."

And from Clyde, " . . . can't talk them out of it . . . have to be careful."

When they returned, Busby pulled a watch from his trouser's pocket and glanced at the face. "We have to get moving. The shift boss is waiting to take you down." He motioned toward a man standing beside a window that opened into another room. Someone behind the window had just given him candles and a candlestick. He tucked the stick under his belt, the candles in a pocket of his trousers, then took a pipe from his mouth and stood in the glare of a lantern scraping the bowl with a carpenter's nail.

We scuffed across the gritty, match-littered floor and up to the man, a wiry redhead with little to distinguish him except a cauliflower ear. "Clyde and ladies, this is Red Mahoney, the shift boss," Busby said. "He'll show you around. And this man gawking at you from behind the window is Sarge. He'll give you candles and sticks."

Sarge stared at Nora and me as if we'd left our brains behind. "I've never known women to go down. Can't believe Harley would allow it." Shaking his head, he handed each of us two candles and a stick. "Better put these where you won't have to hold onto them. You'll be needing your hands to grab the cage."

Nora and I turned aside and discreetly tucked the candlesticks inside the waistbands of our knickers, the candles in the pockets of our jackets, then pulled on our galoshes. Clyde hadn't brought any rubbers, testimony of his ignorance of the wet conditions in the mine, or of his apathy.

"How much you got done on that new widow-maker?" Busby said to Mahoney."

"Stope five-o-nine? About half-way, first cut. The book miner wants to look it over. He's in your office checking maps and diagrams." Mahoney aimed a thumb several feet to the right of the window, where the door to a small, grimy office stood open.

While he and Busby spoke in miners' terms about progress in the stopes, I scanned a notice tacked to the wall beside the tally window. It was headed *Ten Commandments*. Two in particular caught my attention.

> Thou shalt not eat onions when going on shift,
> Even though they be as cheap as real estate in Bixbee,

Unless thy partner participateth likewise,
For that bulbous root exciteth hard feelings in the
Heart of the total abstainer, and causeth the interior
Of the mine to be an unpleasant place.

Thou shalt not go on strike lest thou
Be turned adrift on a cold and cheerless world;
Neither shalt thou demand thy pay, for the
Company's directors in the East know not that thou
Liveth, neither care they a tinker's dam.

A man had stepped from Busby's office, a rolled-up paper in his hand. He was a sturdy blond with a bearded face and high color in his cheeks, someone who didn't spend all his time underground. He had a candlestick tucked in his belt. He slipped the paper in beside it and walked up to us. "This is Rob Kessler," Mahoney said by way of introduction. "He's a book miner. Known more correctly as a geologist." He laughed as if he'd made a joke.

Kessler tipped his hat, his eyes kindling with interest as they met Nora's. "You ladies are brave. For your sakes, I hope we have a safe trip."

"Better be on your way before—" Busby broke off as two men in diggers hurried into the room. They hung their coats on pegs that lined one wall, then sat on a bench to remove their street shoes. "Late again!" Busby blared at them. "Two times in as many weeks. What's your excuse this time?"

"We went down to Gem," one of the men said as he pulled on his rubber boots. "Got into a fight," he added sheepishly. "The constable put us in the clink."

"You dumb hardrocks! You might be a good drill team, but you're not worth the trouble. Get here on time so you can take the chippy down with the rest of the men, or next time I'll pull your pins." Then to Mahoney, grumbling, "Guess they'll ride down with you. I'll talk to you when you come on top."

Mahoney muttered something disagreeable, then led the way to the rear of the headhouse. There, a doorway opened into a tunnel lit by lanterns that breathed a black smoke. Thirty feet farther on, the tunnel opened into a cavernous room that reeked of kerosene and engine grease.

"This is the shaft station," Mahoney hollered above the throbbing of motors. "The Apex is one of the few mines in the district that uses a shaft system." He pointed to a large, complex-looking machine against the right face of the cavern. Puffs of steam rose from its tank. "That's the hoist. The machine next to it is the compressor that sends fresh air into the tunnels." A miserly amount, I recalled Dan saying.

The engineer had begun to rev the steam hoist that would take us into the mine, and the combined pulsing of hoist and compressor struck the arched ceiling and rebounded three-fold. I thought my eardrums would burst.

Mahoney took a tin of Peerless chewing tobacco from his coat pocket and yelled above the throbbing, "I'll be right back. I want to give this to the motorman—insurance that the trip down will be a safe one." The hoist operator saw him coming and throttled the engine down to a comparatively mild rattle-clank and a hiss of steam that smelled of rust.

While Mahoney talked to the engineer, Rob Kessler led us over to a shaft he called the chippy shaft—*chippy or man-killer* were slang terms for the cage that carried men down into the mine. A platform about four or five feet square hung in the dark shaft. It was completely open except for vertical steel braces at each corner. The braces were attached to an identical platform above it that had a bonnet made of sheet iron, likely to protect miners from falling rock. The chippies looked like two animal cages, one above the other. The cable that held them aloft was wound around two wheel drums driven by the hoist.

At the collar of an adjacent shaft, a team of three men had brought the legs of a mule up under its belly and trussed it with eight-inch webbing. It looked like pictures I'd seen of Egyptian mummies. Two large metal rings were fastened to the webbing that encased the animal's neck and head. Hoisting the mule with ropes attached to the webbing, the men fastened the rings to a double hook on the underside of a cage.

I sickened at the sight of the abused animal hanging in the shaft, undoubtedly terrified, and felt shame at man's disregard for his fellow creatures. "That poor mule," I said to the geologist. "How can it stand such brutal treatment?"

"It was given a slight dose of chloroform to daze it and keep it from moving. It's been gaunted for three days so there's no liquid or food in its system to rupture its bladder or cause suffocation. Now, to add further insult, it'll be lowered to the five-hundred-foot level and rewarded for its ordeal with years of pulling one-ton ore cars, six at a time. How long he stays depends on how his heart and lungs take the strain." For a moment he watched the process, shaking his head in sympathy, then brought our attention back to the cage in front of us. "I need to warn you about the dangers of riding the chippy. You need to stay in the center. If you leave a hand or foot sticking out beyond the edge of the platform you're going to lose it."

Clyde had been standing mute. Now he took a few steps back from the shaft, his face like candle wax. Perspiration beaded his upper lip. "If it's that dangerous, we shouldn't take the women down."

"Are you just thinking of the women?" Mahoney said as he joined us. It was clear he had no love for Clyde.

Clyde made no reply, but his scowl spoke for him.

I'd been considering Kessler's warning. "Why aren't the cages larger so there's no chance of men getting too close to the edge?"

"Matter of money," Mahoney said in a matter-of-fact way. "We'd need a heavier hoist, bigger cable. We'd just put more men on them. Same problem."

"Then there ought to be rules that limit the number of men," Nora said adamantly.

I agreed with mild outrage. "There seems to be a lax attitude about safety."

Mahoney shot us a hard, closed look. "Miners know what they're getting into when they take the job. Lord knows, I have my scars." He pulled on the lobe of his cauliflower ear. "See this. Got it when one of the stiffs hogged my space on the chippy. My ear scraped the wall."

With a gesture of impatience, he showed us bodily where to stand, Nora and I in the middle of the platform, the geologist between us holding tight to our arms. The tardy miners had already boarded the cage and stood at one end. Mahoney pulled Clyde on last and stood with him at the other end. The hoist had resumed its pile-driving sounds.

I looked across my shoulder at Kessler as all sorts of dire imaginings flashed through my mind. "How does the motorman know when to stop the chippy?"

"There are strings tied to the returning cable. He counts them."

"Doesn't sound very accurate to me," Nora said. Apprehension was plain in her voice.

"A good man at the hoist knows almost by instinct when to stop," Mahoney put in. "Hal's been on the job for two years." Then to Clyde as he pointed to one of the braces, "Grab that bar and hold on tight." Mahoney already had a grip on a brace, as did the miners. The geologist let go of my arm and grabbed an overhead brace.

The motor churned. The cables vibrated in the shaft. The throbbing of the engine hammered at my breast-bone, joining the thud of my heart. I clutched the geologist's coat and took a deep breath to steel myself.

"OK ladies, hang on tight," Mahoney yelled. He drew a finger across his throat and shouted to the motorman, "Let 'er drop!"

CHAPTER 8

The trip down the shaft was the plunge into hell I'd expected. My stomach leaped into my throat. The blood pounded in my ears. I could hardly breathe with the walls rushing past my cheek. I closed my eyes, but I couldn't shut my ears to the weird clanging, groaning, creaking, and trickling that swirled around my head and transported me to a world beyond reality. All of it in musty blackness. Comments Dan had made about the dangers of riding the cage leaped to the front of my mind—defective machinery, flimsy cables, incompetent engineers, insufficient timbers, bad air, poor fire protection.

I opened my eyes for a brief second and saw a dimly lit hole that opened into the shaft. A man stood in the hollow alongside a mule. They were gone as quickly as they'd appeared, followed by a return to utter blackness.

"That was the two-hundred foot level," Mahoney said. His words sounded strange, as if spoken in a drum, then drifted upward out of hearing.

Water rained on the bonnet and the edge of the platform. The air turned warm and damp, oppressive, with a smell of creosote. The shaft seemed to narrow and I winced at the sense of being squeezed.

"Are you all right?" Kessler asked. I couldn't see him, but his words carried both anxiety and sympathy.

I tried to answer, but had no breath.

Meanwhile, the chippy sank deeper, deeper, down, down. We passed other obscure openings. More long seconds in darkness, then with a clank of chains, a trembling of timbers, and a howling gale of a draft, the hoist engineer brought the cage to a stop on mark. The chippy bounded and rebounded at the end of the cables like a ball on a rubber band. I clutched the geologist's coat for fear I'd fall.

"This is the lowest level in the mine," Kessler said with a bounce in his voice. "The cables get stretched pretty taut. I imagine you'd like to step onto solid ground." I gave a weak nod.

When the rebounding slowed, I could see into a large room lit by candlelight, much like the cavern at the head of the shaft, but without the yammering machines. Mahoney and Clyde led the way from the platform into the room. The geologist helped us women. The miners followed. My knees wobbled. Nora seemed just as unsteady. Clyde was making noises of discontent.

"Now I know why I've never ridden the cage," he said through a cough. I couldn't tell if the cough was from fright or rock dust.

"That's Clyde," Nora said with a wheeze of her own, "no sense of adventure."

The air in the cavernous room was foul despite a reassuring hum from an overhead ventilation pipe. Onion-eaters might be abhorred, but they could hardly compete with the smell of rock dust and blasting powder, the stench of warm bodies, human waste, and mule dung that couldn't escape to the outside. Add to that the smell of whiskey that followed miners around like eau de Cologne, and the result was a sickening atmosphere.

"It's nice to have light again," I said breathlessly. "Who keeps the candles burning?" The flames that were the subject of my question danced with the movement of our bodies, casting eerie shadows on the walls.

"A flunky goes ahead of the miners to light tallows extinguished after the last shift," Mahoney said.

He took my arm, Clyde at my other side. Kessler took Nora's arm with obvious pleasure. The two delinquent miners had gone ahead of us, pulling hammers and buckets of sharp drills from bins set along the walls of the station. Other bins held picks and shovels, axes, buckets of nails, and spikes for securing timbers that reinforced the tunnel walls.

A young man in his mid-teens walked from the darkness, a candle burning in the holder of his cap. He took a few drills from one of the bins, put them in a bucket, and left, staring over his shoulder at Nora and me as if he'd seen two apparitions. "That boy's a nipper," Mahoney said. "He carries tools and water to the men in the stopes. This hard rock dulls the drills and the men are always needing sharp ones."

A set of car rails cut through the center of the room. At the far end, they connected with three spurs that disappeared into shadowy tunnels to the left, right, and middle. The echoed braying of a mule came from the tunnel on the left. A man pushing an empty ore car faded into the tunnel in the middle. The tardy miners disappeared into that tunnel as well. Mahoney led the way down the right-hand tunnel.

Following the flaming candles, we skirted chest-high ore cars waiting empty on narrow-set tracks. I tripped over ties that held the tracks in place and slipped on loose rock. Mahoney's steady hand on my arm was all that kept me from falling. All the while, a steady trickle of water oozed from the rock faces onto the floor. Despite pumps churning to remove the seepage, my galoshes and the hem of my knickers were wet. I noted that Clyde's shoes looked as if he'd been wading in a pool.

Suddenly, the timbers creaked and groaned. I feared the walls were about to cave in. "Wh-what's that?" I stammered.

"It's the mountain settling," Mahoney said. "Superstitious miners say it's the spirits working. Some imagine pygmies coming out of the cracks."

Kessler had been listening and laughed. "Some miners say they're shriveled up little critters the size of two-year-olds, with big, ugly heads and faces like old men."

Clyde gave a snort. "If I worked in a mine for long, I'd see pygmies too."

We walked up the murky tunnel, barely able to see the walls, passing ladders that rose into utter darkness and ore chutes built from timbers as big-around as a man. Mahoney said the ladders led to small galleries called *stopes* located along a vein of ore. From the stopes came the ring of hammers on drills along with the scrape of shovels and the clang of rock hitting metal.

A man standing beside an ore chute opened a gate. Next instant, there was a rumble and clang of metal as rock was dumped down the chute into a waiting car. Farther on a man was hooking ore cars together. "He's one of our best muckers," Mahoney said with a tone of pride. "He mucks rock for a half-dozen drill teams and will load sixteen one-ton cars during a shift. The mule skinner will bring a mule in to pull cars to the shaft and load them onto a skip that lifts them to the tramway at the portal."

As if on cue, the squeal of metal on metal shattered the gloom. The car rails seemed to vibrate. Not far away, a mule complained and blew a loud breath. "Car's coming," Mahoney said. "Stand against the wall." Soon, a single candle appeared on the dim outline of a man's head, like a small moon glowing in the night. The tracks gleamed red in the faint light.

In an instant, the mule and car were upon us, squeal and rumble bouncing from the walls, the sound so loud I covered my ears. The smell of dander and sweaty animal hide were just as strong, the mule's labored breathing so close in the darkness I thought he'd step on me.

As soon as mule and car had passed, Mahoney led us up the tracks, away from the grinding wheels, steering us around a fresh pile of dung. "Where do they keep the mules when they're not working?" I asked.

"We've blocked off a drift that's pinched out. We call it the barn. The skinners bring oats, hay, and fresh water down on the skip."

"How long has that mule been down here?"

"A couple of years. Some have been in here three years. Not all on this level. They move them from level to level on cross-drifts."

A short distance up the tracks we passed an enclosed car with a half-moon on the door. No need to ask about that. We were about to reach the end of the tunnel when Mahoney pointed to the last of the ladders. "This leads to stope five-o-nine. I doubt you ladies want to climb the ladder, but the book miner and I have to see how work is progressing. You can wait here until we're finished, then we'll go back on top." Mahoney took a candle from his pocket and pushed it onto a wedge-shaped candlestick.

"How will we know the conditions unless we see for ourselves," I said as he lit the candle.

"I'm game to climb up there, if you are," Nora said.

Clyde's scowl penetrated the darkness. "Why all the sudden interest in conditions? Has Dan Rigby hooked you on the union cause?"

"Not at all," Nora said with a tilt of her nose. "I just want to be able to say that I saw it all." Clyde made a noise of frustration. "If you want to break your necks that's up to you, but count me out."

Mahoney thought about that briefly, then said with a groan, "All right, if you ladies must. The book miner will go ahead. I'll bring up the rear. That way you'll have light at each end without having to carry a candle." While Kessler lit his candle, Mahoney yelled up the ladder, "Nothing down." Then by way of explanation, "That's to warn the blokes up there not to throw any tools down the manway. They can't hear anybody climbing the ladder and might chuck something down the easy way."

I could barely see the rungs of the ladder as I climbed up the manway and had to feel my way along. I felt like a mole. I said as much to Kessler as he helped me onto the floor of the stope. He laughed. "If you look at the miners, you'll see the resemblance."

In this black dead-end room, the air was rank and hot, the smell of urine strong. Though three hours had passed since the end of the night shift, some smoke and rock dust remained to fill my lungs. Behind me, I heard Nora sucking air.

"The one hundred percent humidity makes it difficult to breath," Kessler said. "Sometimes the air carries lead dust that can poison a person. And vapors of unburned nitroglycerine from the blasts can cause headaches and vomiting. Muckers get sick from shoveling blasted rock into the chutes because it's saturated with gases. So you won't want to stay here long."

"The ventilating system doesn't help much."

"It does on the upper levels. But we keep punching farther into the mountain."

"What about the men who stay here for ten hours?" Nora said hoarsely.

"They take their chances," Mahoney said as he climbed onto the stope. "That's how they earn a living."

His words raised the hackles on my neck. "I'd say they have a right to demand better."

"Maybe so, but they won't if they want to keep their jobs."

Mahoney seemed to have depleted his store of patience. Clearly anxious to end the tour, he said tersely, "This is what we call a stope. Right now, it's six feet high and fifty feet long on each side of the manway. Dan Rigby and Bert Lacey are working the left face, breaking in a new team. Another team is working the right face. They share one mucker between them. Happens to be a young scissorbill on his first day in the mines." I'd heard my father use the term *scissorbill*. It meant someone new to the miners' trade.

Near the collar of the manway lay an assortment of blasting materials and tools, among them several long metal bars wedged at the ends. Mahoney picked up two of the bars and handed one to the geologist. "We'll need these to get a better look at that seam of ore." Then to us ladies, "There's always loose rock left in the walls from the night blasts. It has to be barred down. We'll check the left face first, see how that's coming along. You'll need your candle Miss O'Shea." Mahoney took the tallow I handed him, stuck it on my candlestick, and lit it. Kessler did the same for Nora.

Thirty feet to the left of the manway, miners were working to extend the stope farther into the mountain. The young scissorbill was filling a wheelbarrow with rock that had been blasted from the wall the night before.

"He's been sorting ore from the waste rock," Mahoney said. "Right now he's filling the barrow with the waste." Then to the young mucker, "Fill the heel of the scoop and let the toe fill on its own. Saves your back."

Mahoney explained once more that usually one team worked on the rock face at a time, but Dan's more experienced team was breaking in another team. We stood back for several seconds watching the men, the sweat on their shirtless backs glistening in the light of candles wedged into the walls. Dan was ramming a sledge-hammer onto a drill-head barely visible in the light of the tallows. While he was on the back-swing, Bert pulled the foot-long, one-inch steel out an inch, rotated it a tad, and reset it in the horizontal hole they were boring. With perfect timing, Dan slammed the hammer onto the drill, hissing to warn his partner and to give vent to his concentrated energy.

"It takes nerves of iron to hold a drill while the hammer whistles past your ear," Mahoney said above the ring of hammer on steel. "A slip could shatter your arm."

"How long can they keep that up?" I asked.

"All day, with a break for lunch. When the depth of the hole requires a longer drill, the partners switch jobs and the drill man takes over the hammer. That way they get a rest from the hammer."

The ring of steel was so loud Dan and Bert had no idea we stood behind him them. While they continued to drill, the other team picked up a hammer and drill and began to work on a second set of holes. "How many holes do they drill?" Nora asked.

"Eight or nine, each five feet deep, spaced in an appropriate pattern. Depends on the rock. This is a tough ledge, so it'll take more."

As I watched Dan bend his back beneath the hammer, I wondered more than ever why a man of intellect chose to work in a mine. I'd heard it said that mining flowed in some men's blood. That the swing of pick and hammer became a physical need. It might have been true in my father's case. He was driven by the physical. Even more, by tradition, a sense of manliness, and pride. Apart from that, he knew of no other way to put bread on the table. In a way, Lennie had succumbed to that way of thinking, my younger brothers not as much. They hoped to make better lives for themselves.

Dan was different in that he dreamed of owning a mine of his own, not to keep on drudging in the black dungeons. In my mind, the result would be the same. For him, men would breathe poisonous air and risk life and limb in the battle against the mountain.

CHAPTER 9

Providence Hospital, 1916

T wenty-six years later, I sat at Dan's bedside recalling that trip into the mountain, the bleach-white of the hospital room in stark contrast to the tunnels of darkness lingering on the edge of my remembrance. My visit to those tunnels had put a face on an enemy that had inflicted wounds on those I loved and would continue to do so. From that day on, I knew the reality of the danger that hung over miners' heads like a sword of Damocles. I'd felt the walls close in and breathed the stale, poisonous air. Yet, I still had no deeper understanding of what lured some men into the mines. Dan had achieved his dream of owning a mine. He'd basked in the glory and had suffered tragedy because of it. In spite of those misfortunes, mining had become as much a part of him as the air he breathed.

The door opened and Dr. Kendrick entered the room. He was a paunchy man in his mid-fifties, with iron-gray hair, a slight beard, and eyes that matched the hair. "It's disheartening to see him like this," he said after he'd checked Dan's pulse. "I remember him as a man in his early thirties, virile, radiating energy. I was the same age and had just opened my practice in Wallace. Dan had begun exploration work in his own mine and excitement gave him an added spark." The doctor paused to listen to Dan's heart and lungs through his stethoscope, then went on, "I didn't know him when he worked in the Apex tunnels. But it hadn't dampened his enthusiasm for life, like it does some men. Mines have a way of biting miners who spend many years in the stopes. Like this accident. I hear it wasn't much of a cave-in, but it doesn't take much to wreck a man."

"The foreman said a seam ripped open in a room they were blasting for a new compressor. One of the miners fell on top of Dan to save him."

"It saved him, but just about smothered him. That's why he's in this condition. Lack of oxygen. If he survives, he'll have to find a way to face each new day."

A nun walked into the room, a worried expression on her round, puffy face, and urged the doctor down the hall to help with another patient. I remained, listening to the sheets whisper with each shallow rise and fall of Dan's chest, smelling the carbolic acid that rose in strong vapors from bandages on his head.

When night fell, friends who'd come to pay their respects returned to their homes and left me with a creeping loneliness that drew me from the room to search for companionship. The hallway offered no comfort. Instead, the smell of urine and ether, the clang of bedpans, and the frantic rummaging of a nurse in a medicine closet reminded me of the nearness of death. A priest's dismal exit from one of the wards put an exclamation mark on the sense of mortality.

As I walked the hall, rubbing the stiffness from the small of my back, heels rapped the highly polished floor behind me. I turned as a tall, raw-boned woman with a red, angular face came toward me carrying a bunch of yellow chrysanthemums. She wore a heavy gray sweater over her dress, a frayed woolen scarf over her dark-brown hair.

"Is *Frau* Rigby?" she said in a deep, tired voice. I nodded. "My name is Helga Braun. I do not vish to bother at such a time, but I hear about Dan Rigby and I vorry. Is all right?"

"He's alive, but unconscious. The doctor doesn't know how things will turn out."

"Thank *Gott* he lives." She seemed truly relieved.

I thought about that in light of my own feelings. "I find it hard to give thanks right now."

"But you should. You should be thankful you haf a good man beside you all dese years. I do not know a man finer dan *Herr* Rigby." She hesitated, then added, "My Pietre vas killed in de mine."

"I'm sorry."

Helga shook her head. "No need. Is six years now. Ven it happen, Dan Rigby buy me and my little vuns a house on east side of Wallace."

Dan had always been charitable with his miners, but I had no idea he'd gone to that extent. I couldn't contain my surprise. "Why-why how nice."

"Is not many rich bosses who care about vidows. Not many know vat it is to feel de empty stomach."

My mind flashed back to the early days of my marriage, recalling the way Dan and I had struggled to keep a few pennies in our pockets. The memory made me suddenly weary and I motioned toward a bench set against the whitewashed wall. "Here, come sit with me." When we'd worked our bones into a small degree of comfort on the hard bench, I said, "My father was a miner. I was hungry half the time. I remember how my stomach hurt and how I shivered from drafts coming through the cracks in the walls. Dan and I were never that poor, but when we were first married we lived through hard times like every miner's family."

"*Ja*, I am thinking he know such things ven he gif me house and money to start bake shop."

"A bake shop? I didn't know there was a bakery at that end of town." I'd noticed Helga's clothes carried the aroma of yeast dough.

She waited for a nun to pass by, sweeping her long black robes across the floor, then whispered in an embarrassed way. "Not bake shop for everybody to buy. I bake for brothels on de hill. Dey pay good money for bread and cakes."

My cheeks warmed as I considered that. My sense of propriety kept me from replying directly to the comment. Instead, I said, "Perhaps you could open a shop at my end of town. I'm always in the market for a good loaf of rye."

The woman's face brightened. "It happen I bring loaf vith me. I tink I might see Dan Rigby's *frau*." She turned toward a boy peering around the corner of a cross-corridor. "Wilhelm, come here. Bring de bread." The boy started toward us slowly, his eyes downcast. "Come, no one vill bite you." And to me, "He is shy. My other little vuns show him dey is boss."

I stopped breathing for an instant as I noted the boy's round face, chestnut hair, and large gray, owlish eyes. Surely he was the reincarnation of a boy I'd loved as if he were my own.

"Vy you stare at my boy?" Helga asked.

Memories paralyzed speech. I was slow to answer. "He-he reminds me of someone," I said haltingly. "A boy I cherished. The resemblance is remarkable."

Helga studied my face. "It makes you sad?"

"A little."

"I am sorry." She pulled the boy down on the bench beside her and put a reassuring arm around his shoulder. "If he vas like *mein* Wilhelm, he vas good boy." She took a cloth bag from the boy and handed it to me. "Dis vill make you feel better."

I opened the bag, releasing the tantalizing fragrance of rye flour, chocolate, molasses, and caraway, and I smiled for the first time that day. "I thank you for this and for your kind words about my husband."

"*Und* I tank you for your kindness *Frau* Rigby." She laid the chrysanthemums in my lap. "Dese are for the good man's room. Ven he vakes, please tell *Herr* Rigby I pray for him." She hauled herself from the bench with a groan. "I must get back to *de liebchens*."

I took Helga's hand, a hard-working hand that felt like a rough board, and thanked her for coming. As I watched her disappear into the cross-corridor with Wilhelm, my memory compared the boy to the one I'd known and loved.

He'd entered my life in 1889, during my first trying weeks at the Bixbee School. I'd known teaching wouldn't be easy, especially with the Tatro boys in class, but the nightmares I'd had before the opening of school hadn't lived up to reality. The first few weeks, I'd cried into my pillow each night, wondering if I'd survive the next day. Jim and Mike Tatro were live matchsticks in a room of powder. They cared nothing about learning, just spent the time bedeviling the half-dozen children who wanted to learn. They had no more business attending school than the muskrats that lived in the creek. The few gentle souls in class who showed an interest in learning were all that kept me returning to school each day. I loved them for it, and they seemed to love me. Poor little mining waifs.

Then one afternoon in late October, something happened that would make discipline more difficult. The sun had slipped behind the mountains and I'd lit a kerosene lantern that hung above the rickety table that served as my desk. My hands resting on a copy of *McGuffy's Guide to the Teaching of Reading*, I sat, watching dust motes swirl through the path of light, imagining the vengeful things I'd do to the Tatros if I dared. Four o'clock always left me at the mercy of the empty room, the walls echoing my mistakes, reminding me I had until the end of December to prove myself. It was all I could do to face another day with seventeen children ages five to fifteen, a half-dozen of them Tatros.

The catchpenny's whistle shattered my thoughts. Engine smoke drifted past the ill-fitting door to join the smell of warm bodies, chalk, and lunch remains that lingered in the room. The train was on schedule, reminding me it was time to help Della fix dinner. First I'd wash the chalkboard and empty the trash—I'd forgotten to have the children do those chores before they'd left for home. Compared to its garbage-dump appearance in early September, the room was tidy, even cheerful. Children's charcoal drawings decorated the walls. Della's geraniums bloomed on the windowsills, and the chalkboard gleamed with new oilcloth. I pushed a damp towel up and down, releasing the black cloth's distinctive odor.

Behind me, the door to the entry rubbed against its frame and jerked open. I turned as a comely brunette stepped into the room, nudging a barefoot boy in ahead of her. He appeared to be at least nine years old and dragged a clubfoot across the floor. My heart wrenched.

The fact the boy wore no shoes was nothing new. Many Bixbee children went barefoot. My brothers and I had done the same when we were young. When we were older, our second-hand shoes wore through on the bottoms and we shaped cardboard to fit on the insides. Of course, it kept out neither snow nor slush. If the Bixbee children wore shoes this winter, likely they'd have the same problem. I don't know where this boy would find a shoe to fit his deformed foot.

He hung back while the woman walked timidly up the aisle between desks, her brown, child-like eyes focused on mine. I noted a hint of lavender perfume. "I hope I'm not bothering," she said. Her voice was husky, as if the breath vibrated behind it. "I came to see if you'd take my boy into your school."

I asked, "Does he live in Bixbee?" She nodded. "Has he attended another school this year?"

"No, Ma'am. I been teaching him to home."

"Why? Has he been sick?"

The woman glanced at the floor, then looked up blinking. "No, Ma'am, he ain't been sick. I-I entered him last year. But the teacher sent him to home. I thought you might do the same."

Surely this gentle-looking child hadn't caused trouble for the teacher. His expression was too open, too honest. My gaze wandered down his brown flannel shirt and patched coveralls to his gnarled stump-of-a-foot. Perhaps the foot had caused the problem. He noted my stare and tucked the crippled foot behind the other. Regretting my thoughtlessness, I pulled my attention from the child and turned it to his mother. "Your name is . . ."

"Nelly. Nelly Mearns." She called the boy to her side and pushed chestnut curls from his forehead. "This is Jeff." He leaned against his mother's shoulder and glanced at me with shy, deer-like gray eyes.

"Would you mind telling me why Jeff was sent home?"

Nelly hesitated, digging her fingernails into a leather pocketbook until her knuckles turned white. "It weren't no fault of Jeff's, the teacher's neither. It were Harley's . . ." She paused and gave the boy a squeeze. "Wait outside please, darlin'."

The boy walked a few steps, looked back over his shoulder at us, took a few more snail-like steps, and looked back again.

When he'd gone out the door, Nelly turned her wary eyes on me. Clearly, she was reluctant to speak. "Please, come sit," I said. I pulled my chair from the table for Nelly and perched on the edge of the table. "You were saying something about Harley."

Nelly pulled her lips into a near-pout. "His wife made the teacher send Jeff to home. She said Jeff weren't one of God's children and weren't fit to be with the other kids."

"Whatever possessed her to say that?"

Nelly said nothing at first, simply sucked her cheeks in and out and worked her mouth. After a bit, she confided, "I-I guess Mrs. Hanson meant 'cause Jeff don't have no father."

Thinking the father had died, I raised a hand in a gesture of sympathy. "I'm sorry about that. But what difference should that make to Mrs. Hanson?"

Nelly bit her lip and twisted the straps of her pocketbook. "Jeff never had no father. He . . . " She let the rest trail off.

Nelly's meaning dawned on me slowly, silence weighing heavily as I searched for an apt reply. "That-that happens sometimes," I said awkwardly. "But the circumstances of a child's birth shouldn't keep him from school."

"It's more'n that." I thought she'd say more. She didn't, just stared at the floor and continued to twist the straps of her purse. When she spoke again, she didn't look up, her voice so soft it was as if she was talking to herself. "I think maybe Mrs. Hanson don't like me 'cause of what I do. You see, I live at the top of town. You know . . . where the men go to visit." A blush brought life to her pale cheeks. "But I ain't like the others up there. One man keeps me in money . . . and I got two or three other regulars is all. I ain't never had no disease, 'spite of what Mrs. Hanson says."

She was a whore. My thoughts flew to a night in Williamsboro when my father's voice had pierced the paper-thin wall of the bedroom

I shared with my younger brothers. He'd raised his voice in anger at Lennie, two years older than I. "Stay away from them painted women! They ain't clean. Give you disease. They be making you sick the rest o' your life. Could even put you in a coffin. Stay away from them, you hear."

I'd found that in the West, sporting women were considered in the same matter-of-fact way as saloons. Evidently, that openness didn't extend to their children. Men could tear up a town on a Saturday night, visit whores, and gamble away money that should have fed their families, but a woman couldn't have a child without being married.

I'd never thought whores capable of motherhood. Funny how those childhood fancies had stayed with me. But this woman seemed different from other whores I'd seen around town. Nelly was demure, more sedately dressed.

She must have noted the question in my eyes. "I know what you're thinking, but I ain't a bad woman." Hurt lined her voice. "I don't steal from nobody, and I'm a good mother to my boy."

"I didn't mean to stare. It's just that I couldn't help . . ."

"Help wondering why I'm what I am?" She appeared to search for an answer. "Umm . . . no real reason," she said with a shrug. "Just seems the easiest way for a girl raised poor to earn a living. But my boy shouldn't be put down because of my work." She thrust out her chin in a sudden expression of defiance. "I ain't as bad as some of the wives around here, pretending to be goody-goodies while they do each other dirt." With that, she clamped her mouth shut and started for the door. "Sorry I bothered you. I'll teach Jeff my—"

"Wait!"

I pondered the situation while I closed the distance between us. What if Clara did object? Didn't the boy have a right? Was there really a chance for disease? I'd heard lots of old wives' tales, but that's probably all they were, tales. Besides that, I felt sorry for Nelly. Her manner showed concern for Jeff. And he seemed a nice boy. I needed more children like him in the classroom.

I said, "I'd like very much to have Jeff in class. And I promise, he'll finish the year."

The pout left Nelly's lips and her face wreathed into a smile. "Bless you, Ma'am. I'm real grateful. I hope you won't be sorry."

CHAPTER 10

Enrolling Jeff Mearns in the Bixbee School was like putting a fly in a hornet's nest. When I wasn't looking, the children taunted him because of his deformed foot and bared him from their play. It was humiliating for Jeff, especially when Jim and Mike were involved, and they always seemed to be at the center of the problem.

One morning, I started down the tracks toward school, passing storefronts with their awnings rolled up for the season. A rainstorm had blown into the district during the night. It had changed to snow in the chill of early morning, and had hurled itself into Montana, leaving a dusting of snow. A crisp breeze smelled of tannin, must, and damp earth. In the startling blue sky, a few tattered clouds trailed after the storm. I tightened the scarf around my neck.

Every now and then a child called to me from a crude wooden or earthen stairway that led to their shanties, reminding me of the problems I faced at school. Of course, I worried about Jeff, but I also thought of the beginners—three six-year-olds, willing to please and eager to learn. Two of them spoke little English, but all of them were beyond their years in experiencing the harshness of life. My heart went out to them. And there were the older ones, teenagers, some who'd attended school for only a year or two and couldn't read. If only I knew how to teach.

Lost in thought, I didn't hear Dan Rigby come from behind me. Rock dust coated his face, except for a circle where he'd wiped his mouth.

"Can I walk you to school?" he said.

"Yes, I'd like that."

"I was thinking of enrolling," he said with a sly grin. "You said you could teach me a thing or two."

I smiled to acknowledge the jest. "I wish you would. I could use some help."

"That bad, huh?"

"Worse than I thought it would be."

"Tell you what. Any time you want to take my place in the stopes, I'll trade you jobs." Laugh lines crinkled at the corners of his blue eyes.

I brushed that off and went on to bring him up-to-date on the happenings at school. He told me the latest news about the union. By then we were a hundred yards from the school. Suddenly, screams came from behind a tailings mound that fronted a patch of brush and cottonwoods.

"Get off me! Let me be." I was certain it was Jeff crying. He'd told me in confidence about a secret path that led from the cribs on the hillside to the tailings mound.

"Better stop bawling, you little baby." I recognized Mike Tatro's taunting voice. "Cain't let you go 'till we're done with our funning."

I shot Dan a look of outrage. "I've heard enough."

We skirted the pile of waste rock and shoved our way through clumps of brush to where Jeff lay squirming on his back. Mike Tatro sat astride his chest. "We wanna know 'bout all the whoring that goes on at your house," Mike said in a brazen tone. "Mus' be sumpin' to have all that hot love making going on right under your nose." He gave a coarse, cruel laugh.

"I don't watch." The words came gasping, almost unintelligibly from Jeff's lips.

"You're a goddamn liar!" Jim yelled in his phlegmy voice. He sat cross-legged and sunken-chested on a slab of shale, like a tribal chieftain savoring a ritual of torture. A ray of sunlight broke through the fringe of brush and lit his pimply face, making the tight, orange skin shine like a dimpled ball of cheese. He'd crammed his mouth full with a biscuit sandwich. When he saw us, a hideous grin spread across his face. "Hi, Teach, wanna biscuit?" He took one from the crust of snow and tossed it my way. Two other biscuits lay on the ground, spilled from an open lard pail I knew was Jeff's.

Dan sprang into action. He pulled Jim from the rock by the collar and gave him a shove that threw the boy off-balance. "Smart-aleck! Get your ugly face out of here."

Mike hauled himself from Jeff's chest and stood defiantly, hands on his hips. "You better not touch us. My dad'll knock your block off."

"Yeah," Jim added with a sneer.

Dan grimaced. "It'd be worth it to tan your hides." He took a menacing step toward Jim.

The bully stepped to one side, then the other, dodging Dan's outstretched hands, then took a boot from the snow, one the cobbler had made for Jeff's crippled foot. I assumed the boys had pulled it off. "We oughta heave this thing in the creek, don't you think, Mike? Wouldn't want to cover up that purty foot o' Jeff's." He tossed the boot to Mike as Dan closed in.

Mike dodged this way and that, holding the boot above his head. "The creek's the best place."

Jeff gave a savage scream and threw himself at Mike, kicking and clawing, trying to grab the boot.

The Tatros circled him, teasing. They'd hold the boot within reach, snatch it away, and lob the heavy leather back and forth over his head. They tossed it so that it brushed his fingertips, but not so he could take hold. Each time Dan closed in, they eluded his grasp.

With a bellow of grim frustration, Dan snatched a tree bough from the ground and advanced on the Tatros, swinging it. "You bloody bastards, give the boy back his boot."

It took Jim and Mike but a second to turn into a streak of plaid and denim, slipping and sliding from behind the tailings pile onto the tracks. Dan watched the shameless retreat. "Disappeared faster'n a duck chasing a June bug, didn't they, kid." He tossed the branch to the ground.

Jeff stood gasping, the boot clasped against his chest. The first time he'd worn the custom-made boot to school, he'd told me he hated it, even said he'd like to toss both his boots into the brush so he could go barefoot like the other boys. But to buy the boot, his mother had emptied the cigar box that held her savings and he knew she'd be angry. The Tatros taunts had transformed the boot into a treasure to be saved.

I stood sputtering with an anger that drove the chill from my cheeks, but Dan was panting from the chase. He put his arm around Jeff's shoulders and said, "C'mon, let's sit on this rock and rest a spell. Then I'll help you put on your shoe."

Jeff sat, wincing, and pulled up his pantsleg to lick some scratches. His knee was scraped and bleeding, his hands, too. I bent down to inspect the knee and covered the scrape with my handkerchief. "I'm sorry they kicked you."

Jeff shook his head. "They didn't do it. My foot caught on a vine and I skidded down the trail."

"I notice your pail's broken."

"It hit a rock. That's how the Tatros knew I was here. They heard it."

Still captured in Jeff's swollen eyes were the fear, the humility, and the anger of the encounter. He leaned against Dan and looked with adoration into his smiling face.

"You must be Jeff," Dan said. "Maggie's told me about you. Said you were a good student." He pulled a red bandana handkerchief from the back pocket of his pants and wiped the tears from Jeff's cheeks. "How about a tune?" He stretched his leg, slipped a mouth organ from the front pocket of his trousers, and wiped his hand across the mouthpiece. After he'd wheezed a few chords, he launched into a breezy rendition of *Oh, Susanna*. When he'd finished, he banged the harmonica against his knee to dislodge the spit. "What'll I play next?"

Jeff thought a minute, pressing a finger against his lips. "Do you know *She'll be Comin' 'Round the Mountain*?" The question rode a string of air that seemed to signal the end of Jeff's fright.

I interrupted, saying, "We'd best go to school. Maybe Dan can play for the whole class."

Jeff went rigid at the mention of school. "I'm not going to school. Please don't make me."

"You don't want those bullies to think they got the best of you," Dan said in a fatherly way.

"I don't care what they think." Jeff shook, either from the cold or from fear of the Tatros, likely both.

I pulled the loose sock up around his skinny leg. "Dan's right. Don't give them the satisfaction of thinking they won."

Dan stowed the instrument in his pocket and took the boot from the ground. "Give me your foot and we'll put this on. Then I'll walk you and Maggie the rest of the way to school." He grinned. "You don't want to make your teacher late."

Jeff gave a wan smile. "Will you play the harmonica for us?"

Dan shrugged as he fastened a buckle on the shoe. "Don't know if I should take school time."

"Please," I said. "It would be a wonderful way to start the day."

Dan thought about that and finally said with a grunt, "All right, but you sure know how to put a man on the spot."

●●●

I was amazed at Dan's talent. He captivated even the wiggliest five-year-old for an hour. At times he teased the organ to perform miraculously. At other times he breathed warmth into its reeds. And all the time, the children clapped and stomped their feet in rhythm, or sang along, whichever fit the tune. At ten o'clock, he left to rest for the night shift, but the thrill of his visit lingered on. Even the Tatros committed little more than mild mischief that day—likely because of the scare Dan had given them, not the result of a lecture I'd delivered on bullying.

Still glowing from the day's success and from a deepened sense of Dan's kind nature, I kneeled before the black mass of the wood stove, scooping cinders and ash into a bucket almost heaped to overflowing. Jeff had stayed after school—I'm sure to avoid meeting the Tatros on the way home—and he danced a broom across the floor, humming some of Dan's tunes.

It seemed I spent half my time shoveling ashes and stuffing lengths of pine and fir into the stove's rusted belly. It never heated the room evenly. Those who sat close to it sweltered, while those in the far corners shivered. First thing every morning I lit the fire, adjusted drafts and dampers, set a pail of water and teakettle on top, and put potatoes inside the jacket to bake in time for a mid-morning snack. The room still held the aroma of the roasted potatoes we'd had that day—fluffy white things dripping with butter, gifts from a farmer from eastern Washington who worked the mines after harvest. I'd discovered that a baked potato delivered a bundle of energy and kept the children's minds alert. It especially helped the youngest of the Tatros. They always arrived at school hungry.

I'd dumped the contents of the pail on the ash heap back of the school and was scooping more ashes from the stove, when shoe heels punched into the wooden stairs and through the entry. The door to the classroom opened, and two sour-faced matrons filed inside. A third set of footsteps clomped on the stairs.

I recognized the two women as mothers of children in the school. Hester Reap, a large woman with fat pink cheeks and pendulous breasts that swayed beneath her sweater, was known around town as a busybody and troublemaker. She entered the room with the expression of a bull primed to do battle.

The other was Clara Hanson, Harley's wife, a tiny, fashionably dressed brunette with heavy, well-matched eyebrows and hair piled high. The driven look in her dark eyes suggested nothing could be done fast enough to suit her. She was the mother of Lucinda, Clyde and Nora's eight-year-old sister.

Maude Tatro was the last to enter the room. I hadn't seen her since the day on the train. She took a skulking stand behind the other women, as if she was there on their orders.

Clara and Hester whispered to each other at the back of the room while they skewered Jeff with looks of contempt. I guessed at their purpose in coming. I'd been steeling myself for a confrontation since Jeff's first day at school, but I was astonished that Maude Tatro had come.

I clapped the ashes from my hands and wiped them on my sooty dustapron. "Ladies. You wanted to see me?"

Clara and Hester shot each other the kind of looks a pair of dogs send each other before they commit mayhem, then Clara gave Hester a nod, delegating her as spokeswoman. Hester flicked a hand in Jeff's direction as she marched toward me. "We come to talk about the boy," she said with a pronounced Swedish accent.

Jeff stopped sweeping and stared at the floor, his shoulders slumping beneath the straps of his coveralls. I should have asked him to leave as soon as the women arrived. How mindless of me. How tactless of Mrs. Reap.

"Jeff, I think it would be best if you went home," I said gently. "Thank you for your help. You can do it again tomorrow, if you'd like." I said the last pointedly to make it clear to the women that I planned to keep Jeff in school.

I invited the trio to sit in the larger desks and settled in my chair facing them, my back straight as a rod, my head held high, pretending confidence.

Hester Reap pounced immediately. "We don't want that boy with our leetle ones. His mama's a-a-bad woman."

"He's bound to have disease," Clara added in a high, metallic voice. "I don't want Lucinda getting it."

"You think his mama would stop putting him in school," Hester went on. "She knows we won't stand for it."

"Women like that are insensitive to others."

"Ja," Hester agreed. They think only of themselves."

The women's comments made it clear they were the insensitive ones. I studied them with a fixity that should have caused them to stir uneasily. It didn't, so I turned to Maude, who'd been listening like a frightened kitten. Her face seemed more pinched than it had that day on the train, her eyes more ghost-like, the bun at the top of her head about to slip from its pins. Her dress hung from her shoulders like a gray shroud, making her look the story of her life. "How do you feel about this, Mrs. Tatro?" I asked.

It was easy to see Maude would have preferred not to speak. She hesitated, then said in a voice that whined tiredly from her lips, "I don't have nothing 'gainst the boy. His mother neither, for that matter. I jess don't want my kids getting sick with biles."

"Or worse!" Hester bellowed.

Clara's nostrils flared in a ferment of self-righteous anger. "To say nothing of his affect on their morals."

I shot a spark of extreme dislike from beneath my eyelids. "Mrs. Hanson, what would you do if you were Jeff's mother? Wouldn't you want him to have the same schooling as the other children? Doesn't the boy have that right?"

Clara's chin took on added sharpness, and she pointed accusingly. "You certainly have your gall, asking me to consider the feelings of a-a-woman like that. Don't you think so, Maude?" Maude said nothing, just scratched the top of the desk with a broken fingernail.

Silence took over while I shaped the argument I'd pondered for a week. I pulled on it here, shoved on it there, trying to keep the acid of my feelings from affecting my judgement. "I understand why you feel as you do, ladies," I said, suppressing the fury that knotted my stomach. "There was a time when I might have felt the same. But I've learned a great deal from having Jeff in class. Children like him are innocent of their birth. They have the same right to attend school as any child. Here in the West, where a man's conduct is so . . . so free, I would imagine many sire a child like Jeff during their lifetime. Some of them good men . . . like your husbands."

I wished I could have reeled in those last few words. They'd left my lips with a meaning I hadn't intended. I bit back words of apology and braced myself for the attack.

CHAPTER 11

Hester Reap's breath exploded as if she'd been struck. "My husband never—"

"You don't have to reply to that insult, Hester," Clara hissed. Her face had turned brick red.

I hurried to say, "I didn't intend it as an insult. I just meant that perhaps we shouldn't be so quick to condemn."

Speech had no part of the battle of the eyes that followed. There was no sound except for the women's rapid breathing and the rustle of skirts upon discomfited bodies. Maude ran her fingers along a scar on the back of her hand. Clara dabbed at her nose with the corner of a handkerchief.

"As far as I'm concerned, ladies, there's no proof a child can infect others with the disease in question. And until someone proves otherwise, Jeff will remain in school." I rose, riding the crest of my courage. "Unless you had some other matter you wanted to bring up, I see no point in further discussion."

Clara's thin lips became a tight line across her chin. "I'll see that my husband has you dismissed, young lady."

That comment jolted me. I'd expected it, but now that it was a reality I had to swallow to clear my throat before I could reply. "Do as you see fit. Now if you'll excuse me, I have a stove to clean."

Hester and Clara arched their brows at one another and strode from the room with a show of ruffled pride. When Maude failed to do the same, Hester returned to the doorway and motioned for her to follow.

Maude waved her on and shuffled quietly to where I vented my feelings on the black maw of the stove. A pair of battered shoes with laces knotted in several places poked from beneath her dress. "You wanted something, Mrs. Tatro?" I asked.

Maude reached into a tote-bag she carried over one arm and took out something wrapped in a flour sack. It wafted the aroma of freshly baked cookies. "These be for you . . . for making my boys mind . . . and for teaching 'em to read and write." She held out the bundle shyly, as if it might not be worthy.

I noted the hesitation in her eyes and felt shame for the impatience I'd shown earlier. I opened the sack and sniffed the ingredients of sugar cookies that likely had taken a big chunk out of Maude's grocery money. "They smell delicious. But I'm not sure I deserve them. The boys don't mind as well as I'd like."

"You do better'n me. I cain't do nary a thing with 'em. The only way their pa can get 'em to mind is to beat 'em. Little ones ain't so bad, but them oldest . . ." She let the rest trail off as if words couldn't express her feelings of inadequacy. "The little ones tell me you're a real good teacher . . . fair, and don't make pets o' none o' the kids." She glanced around the room, studying the charcoal drawings, then let out a deep sigh, as though loathe to leave. "I won't be taking no more o' your time. Gotta get to home. One o' the girls is watching the baby." I followed her to the door, where she turned to add, "Don't take what we said about the boy as being agin you. It really don't make no never mind to me if Jeff stays. It's jess one o' those things that some women get lathered about."

I watched Maude's grayness shamble out the door, amazed at the woman's wealth of human understanding. To think she led such a harsh life, every other year a baby taken from the cradle to make room for another. She was like my own mother in many ways—a patient, enduring soul, existing so that her children might live, hoping fervently her children's lives would be easier than her own.

● ● ●

After the encounter with Hester and Clara, I'd fully expected to scrub floors full time at Della's boarding house. At first, I welcomed the possibility. Dismissal would free me to leave that horrid mining town, the Tatros, and conditions that turned children into monsters. But where would I go? Not back to Williamsboro as a failure. I'd have to wait until the end of the year to find another teaching position. Where would I earn the money to send home?

As my resentment faded, I realized that I was trapped. My family depended on the money I sent them. And there was Jeff. How would he fare if I left? Another teacher might have less sympathy.

After a week of worrying myself sick, Harley Hanson came to see me. To my surprise, he appeared to have come as one bound by duty rather than driven by anger. He first told me how much Lucinda enjoyed having me as a teacher, then asked me to account for my behavior during Clara's visit to the school. I reported in full with much blushing and trembling, certain I'd receive a tongue-lashing and a verdict of dismissal.

The most troubling moment came when he asked me what I'd said to Clara that had caused her such upset. When I repeated the remark that good men sometimes fathered children like Jeff, Harley seemed struck through, as if the lance of truth had stabbed a hole in his armor. His lips quivered and he flushed from his neck to his silver hairline. With a harrumph, he stammered, "That-that was rather crude. From now on watch how you phrase your comments." That said, he turned on his heel and strode from the room, his head and shoulders stiff as a plank.

Dismissal wasn't mentioned again, and during the next few months the children slowly accepted Jeff and treated him with less cruelty. Jim and Mike still tormented him, but a new fourteen-year-old student with long blond curls provided distraction. Ironically, Lucinda Hanson, a pretty little sprite who always championed the underdog, assumed Jeff as her special project. She played with him at recess and insisted on sharing her double-desk with him in spite of the other children's teasing. In light of Clara's intolerance, I wondered how Lucinda came by such strong feelings of compassion. Like her sister Nora, she seemed to have a mind of her own and a stiffness in her spine. The fact they'd developed such free spirits said much about their character. Perhaps Clara had shown more understanding in raising them than one might think.

Despite the difficult times at school, the time passed quickly, the seasons with it. Just before Christmas, arctic air shrieked down from the Yukon and brought a storm that piled four feet of snow on the level. Bixbee looked more cramped than ever, black and flattened in the snow. The town's bustle fled inside to escape temperatures that contracted the mercury in the bulb like a snail in its shell. Luckily the children had presented their Christmas program just before the storm, and I closed the school with a feeling of relief.

Lake Coeur d'Alene froze its entire length, stalling shipments of ore concentrates by steamer. A few weeks later, zigzags in temperature from a frigid thirty below to balmy Chinook levels sent snow avalanches hurtling down the hillsides onto the tracks, preventing ore shipment by rail. The Apex shut down, its ore bins heaped full and no way to empty them. Twenty feet of snow blocked the canyon. Food supplies dwindled. Men who could break through the drifts left the canyon to find work.

When flames licked the town of Wardner to ashes, Dan said goodbye and took a job helping to rebuild the town located twenty-five miles to the west. I was glad for the chance to fortify myself against his charms. I was falling in love with him, and the last thing I wanted was to let a miner snare my heart. Even worse was to marry one—to worry if there'd be enough food for the children—to say goodbye to my husband each morning, wondering if I'd see him alive at the end of the shift.

While Dan was in Wardner I fought the stirrings of my heart. I thought I'd prepared myself to keep our friendship just that, but when he returned in March we grew steadily closer. I seemed always to be holding my heart up for inspection, gauging the extent of my feelings for fear I was headed for the deeper relationship I feared. By the time the Fourth of July rolled into sight, along with the big celebration to welcome statehood, it seemed natural to stand at his side at the Bixbee station, waiting for the narrow-gauge to take us to the events in Wallace. Jeff stood at my other side. He'd formed a habit of staying after school and my fondness had deepened to love for the child. I'd watched over him when Nelly went to Wallace or Spokane Falls to shop. On this day, she'd asked me to keep him with me as she and the girls from the cribs were going to ply their trade among the celebrants.

Dan's brother Aaron had arrived from Spokane Falls and waited with us at the station. Della and Hank were there, as well as everyone else in Bixbee, picnic baskets in tow. Della had made both of us frilly white dimities, the yokes laced with red, white, and blue ribbons. The men's hatbands carried the same three colors. Despite the promise of a sweltering afternoon, the men wore vests, coats, and celluloid collars. Men who owned no suits wore work clothes they'd laundered for the occasion and shoes they'd polished with lard until they gleamed. Everyone was laughing, smiling, singing snatches of *America the Beautiful* and the few phrases of the national anthem their vocal chords could manage. Della led in her trumpeting voice.

While we waited, four men pushed through the boisterous crowd and walked up to Dan. The man at head of the group was tall, dark-haired, with bony features and fire in his cavernous eyes, the sort of man whose force of character showed in his face and reached out to hit you. He drew Dan aside, where he and the other three men spoke in hushed tones.

Della nudged me, "That's Hub Malone, a union organizer from Butte, Montana. They've got a strong union going at the copper mine and are trying to get other mining districts to form unions. He's here to help strengthen our union. I met him through one of the boarders."

I studied him carefully. "I don't like his looks."

"Can't tell a man by his looks. You'll get to meet him. I've invited him to dinner next week. He has strong opinions about the direction the union brotherhood should take."

Brotherhood, secret passwords, secret handshakes. I'd been through all that with my father and Lennie and was distrustful. The unions claimed to want equal rights for the common man, yet they set up their own system of coffer-dams.I'd hoped Dan could steer the new Bixbee union in a different direction, but it seemed he'd have to deal with leaders of other Rocky Mountain unions, some of them already committing violence against the mine owners.

The crowd broke into a wild cheer as the train clanged into the station trailing flat cars fitted with benches, sunshades of fir boughs, and bristling with flags of red, white, and blue. It looked like a gaudy caterpillar crawling along the tracks. The men from Butte took seats in one of the cars, my group of friends in another. Dan and Aaron sat at my left, Jeff at my right. Della and Hank sat on the seat behind us with the picnic baskets. I looked across my shoulder at Dan, so much the man, acutely aware of the scent of his shaving soap and the bulge of his shoulder touching mine. He turned an appealing smile on me, made all the more charming by creamy white teeth, irregular but interesting in shape. His startling, deep-set blue eyes were filled with excitement, also a hint of anxiety. While we'd waited for the train, he'd told Aaron about the drilling contest he'd entered with Bert, his drilling partner. That afternoon, the pressure would be on them to win for the Apex mine and it seemed to worry him.

Now he said to Aaron in his clipped manner of speaking, "It'd be a damned shame if Bert and I didn't get the hundred dollar first prize. We've practiced like sweat hogs."

"Why practice. You do it every day in the mine. I'd think swinging a hammer is the same whether you're aiming at a drill in the rock face or trying to drive a square peg into a round hole." Aaron's boredom showed in his sarcasm. Attending the celebration was an anti-climax, since Washington Territory had celebrated its acceptance into the union in November. He'd come along mainly to escape his father's demands at the furniture store.

Dan made a wry face and went on as if used to his brother's cynicism. "There's rules we have to follow. We have to change positions every thirty seconds without missing a stroke, the hammer man takes over the drill and vice versa. No time out to switch drills. It tests a team's ability to work under tough conditions."

"Is it supposed to prove you're some kind of a he-man?"

Dan shot Aaron a scathing look, and stared straight ahead without answering.

I'd met Aaron on one of his excursions to check on Dan's mining claim and had noted that he lacked Dan's sense of humor and spark, that he seemed angry at the world. Likely it was because he'd lost a wife and child to diphtheria. Physically, he bore a strong resemblance to Dan but was older and shorter, his eyes of such a light blue they approached white. His features were the same as Dan's but more refined, appearing to have been carved less from granite than from marble.

Aaron pointed to the car ahead, where Rafe Tatro sat with his tribe. "Bet Rafe was sore when you knocked him out of the preliminaries."

"It was his own fault. He and Smutt were too lazy to practice."

"Where's the contest going to be held?" I asked.

"Right in the middle of town. On a six-foot high platform with everybody gawking up at us like we're a couple of sideshow freaks. They've made such a big deal of it they've brought in Colorado granite and hoisted it up there." Dan took tobacco and a packet of cigarette papers from his vest pocket, his fingers so shaky he dropped the packet of papers on the floor. I understood his worry over the contest. All the Apex miners would hazard their paychecks on him, and Harley would expect his team to uphold the reputation of the mine.

When Dan went into the statistics of past contests, I lost interest in the dialogue and turned my attention to the mine-scarred hillsides, vivid in their greenery. Lupine, yellow balsam root, and Indian paint brush clung to the rocky slopes wherever they could sink roots. Even the tailings mounds along the creek wore garlands of blue bells and other tiny blue nothings that grew in silt at their base. I was reminded of the times my mother had sent me into the woods to gather wild violets and daisies. Sometimes I'd meet my brother Lennie on his way home from picking coal at the mine, and we'd stroll through the hardwoods, cutting asters for the kitchen table.

Jim Tatro's voice twanged from the car behind mine, destroying the memory. While waiting for the train, I'd noticed Jim and Mike slouched against a wall of the railroad barn with boys of similar ilk from the towns of Burke and Gem. Their caps were pulled down over their foreheads at an insolent angle and cigarettes hung from their lips. They were taunting girls in the crowd with words and gestures meant to shock.

I chuckled grimly within myself in private celebration. Jim and Mike had announced they wouldn't return to school in the fall. Jim had turned sixteen and was going to work in the mine. Rafe had given Mike permission to quit school provided he stayed out of trouble. I'd actually survived the year in spite of the boys, and the school board had asked me to return in the fall. I'd accepted, but not until I'd lost sleep over the decision. I disliked Bixbee and all that it stood for. I dreaded the fact there were other Tatros in school, one or two of them following in their brothers' shoes as town bullies. On the other hand, children like Jeff and Lucinda Hanson made teaching a joy. Perhaps they would inspire me for one or two more years. After that, I hoped to return to college—two of my younger brothers would be old enough to work the coal mines, something my father demanded of them. I'd sunk shallow roots in Bixbee's rocky soil. Time would tell how long they'd keep me anchored.

● ● ●

When the train pulled into Wallace, hordes of people swarmed through town, part of the three thousand predicted to take over the streets that day. Every slapboard building in town—each hotel, billiard parlor, store, bank, newspaper, and saloon sported flags and buntings of red, white, and blue. Streamers flowed between lampposts and buildings. The town looked like a huge flower circled by slopes that had once been furry with evergreens, but now were nothing but a jumble of rock, stumps, and brush, the trees having fueled the district's mines and the town's hearths.

The catchpenny paused long enough to spill us into the human flood, then coughed its way up the canyon of the Coeur d'Alene to collect celebrants waiting at Mullan. People from canyons too remote to travel by rail jolted into town in buggies, wagons, by stage, and on horseback. The squeal and groan of trappings rose above the babble of voices.

In a vacant lot provided for the purpose, horses stood head-hung and hip-shot, some with saddles or within harness. They switched their tails at a hatch of insects that speckled the hot July air. Gangs of dogs were not as thick as the insects, but they made their presence felt by scrapping among themselves and sniffing picnic baskets. At the west end of town, band instruments sharpened their voices for a parade that would feature local veterans of the Civil War. Everywhere rang the cry, "Forty-third! Forty-third! Forty-third!"

We jostled along with the hordes, elbow to elbow, bustle to bustle, through miniature dust storms raised by petticoats and boots. At the edge of town we parked our picnic baskets on a table that smelled of freshly planked fir, then adjourned to Bank Street for the parade—a procession of buggies and wagons polished to a high gloss and decorated with flowers and streamers. From there we walked to a pavilion that rang with band music and stentorian voices proclaiming the magnitude of the day.

Dan ate like a bird at the picnic and had little to add to the conversation. He coaxed Aaron from the table and left for the drilling platform, promising to meet me immediately after the contest. I wondered why he hurried. He'd have a long wait for his turn at the hammer and drill. Each of the six competing teams were allowed fifteen minutes to bore into the granite, and Dan and Bert were last. I wasn't going to spend all that time watching something so tedious. There were foot races on tap, horse races, and river races with men paddling the current in wash tubs.

After watching the river races, the Tuttles spied friends from down-river and became engaged in an animated reunion. Jeff went to see if he could take part in the sack races for children of all ages—a major step in confidence. Left to my own devices, I squirmed my way through a mob that jammed the boardwalk on Fifth Street, hoping to watch the horse races. In the background, Marshal Short and his crew of temporary deputies were visiting some of Wallace's twenty-eight saloons, whisking away gin-bibbers who'd swallowed too much liquid jubilation.

I noticed Clyde Hanson at the front of the walk, elegant in a white linen suit, his top hat looming several inches above the other hats and parasols. He was waving his arms in a frenzy. Beyond him, a brace of horses tore down the middle of the street, necks extended, nostrils flaring, hooves sending up explosions of dust. I slipped up beside Clyde to watch the end of the race.

He didn't notice me until he turned, shredding his race ticket. He took my hands, disappointment at his loss still on his face. "Maggie, it's good to see you. I like your new hairdo."

"I hope it's not too frivolous. The Fireside Companion says it's the latest style." Wanting to look my best for Dan, I'd swept my hair upward into a nest of curls at the crown of my head. I pushed at a froth of curls on my forehead and found it damp from perspiration.

"It's very becoming. Women in Chicago are wearing their hair that way."

"You've been there lately?"

He nodded. "Dad sent me there on business, but I managed to take in the sights. The Art Institute, the opera, theater, fine restaurants." He sighed at the memory.

"What business did you have there?"

"Investigating shipping rates. I spent enough time in Omaha and Minneapolis to discover the railroads are scandalously crooked. They fix rates among themselves, give rebates to volume customers, and charge the small shipper exorbitant fees. Because of their shenanigans the rates are on a perpetual seesaw. It's like a magic show using sleight of hand and disappearing hares."

"How do you deal with that?"

"Dad's hoping Sherman's new bill will help. But the railroad barons like to flaunt their power. Likely the government will lick the dust they walk on." He snapped his fingers. "So much for the law."

Having no further desire to discuss the mining business, I asked, "How long have you been home?"

"Two days. Time enough to take in the celebration going on in town. I tell you, Maggie, it's been a gambler's dream—dice, poker, faro. Played all over town, all night long, for incredibly high stakes."

"You should be more careful with your money. You won't always have your father to fill your pockets when you lose a wager."

"Aha, the Bixbee gossips have been tickling your ear. But they are mongers of false information. I gamble only money that is mine."

"It's still a bad habit. It could get you into trouble."

He shrugged that off and said, "Nora promised to meet me here for the last race. Will you be watching?"

"That depends on when Dan finishes his contest."

Clyde took note of a clock in a barbershop window. "Then it's time we went to the scaffolding. I have twenty dollars riding on his bulging muscles."

Knowing they wouldn't want to miss the drilling contest, I separated the Tuttles from their conversation with friends, and we let Clyde's tall rod of a figure wedge a path for us through the crowd at the drilling platform. A team from the Sullivan Mine in Wardner was whanging away at the rock, while of an audience of men wagered, heckled, or cheered for the team between swills of beer. Some spectators crowded one another for space behind a roped-off area that circled the platform. Others peered down from the rooftops of false-fronted stores like rows of roosting pigeons. The odor of hops and cigar smoke hung heavy in the windless day.

By the time Clyde had found us a place near the platform, time had been called on the Sullivan team. The judge recorded the depth of the drilled hole and told Dan and Bert to mount the stand. Like the previous team, they'd stripped to the waist, and the muscles rippled beneath their white-skinned arms and shoulders. Dan looked out over the crowd as he mounted the stairs, seemed to note Harley Hanson standing at a corner of the platform, and nodded in recognition.

I wanted to wave, but Dan had turned his attention to the double set of drills he and Bert had begun to arrange on the platform according to size, the sun glinting off the steels. Dan had explained the routine—fifteen pieces of steel in each set, enough to last the fifteen minute contest, three inches difference in length for succeeding steels, an extra set for emergencies.

Della poked me in the ribs with her elbow. "That boyfriend o' yours is some hunk. Is this the first time you've seen him without a shirt?"

I felt myself blush and glanced at Clyde to see if he'd heard, but looking like the tall and short of it, he and Hank were placing last-minute bets with others in the crowd. "You shouldn't talk like that," I told Della in reproof. "There's nothing between Dan and me but-but friendship."

Della gave a little cry of disbelief. "Don't pull that on me. I've seen that sick-calf look in your eyes when you're together. Dan's too. It's a marrying look if ever I saw one."

"I don't want to marry a man who works the stopes."

Della plumped a hand on her hip and sniffed with scorn. "What's wrong with a stoper?"

"It's not the stoper, it's the life he—" I broke off as Hank and Clyde turned toward me.

"Dan had better win," Hank said. "I have a tenner riding on him."

"You shouldn't fritter away your money," Della said.

"We've waited a long time for this day. Might as well live it up."

Dan and Bert had taken their positions at the slab of Gunnison granite, their hips slender and lithe, their faces as immobile as the stone. At the referee's signal, Dan swung the eight-pound, thirty-three-inch hammer in tight, rhythmic arcs while Bert crouched at the rock, turning the steel with precision, anticipating any variation in Dan's swing. Sweat streamed from their foreheads and glistened beneath the hot sun.

From the crowd rose mutterings, now and then a shout of encouragement. From nearby came the cry of a peanut vendor, in the distance a wild cheering at the sack races, all punctuated by Dan's explosive grunts and the ring of hammer on steel.

The crowd had begun to count the strokes per minute, starting each time Dan took the hammer and finishing with Bert's last swing. Dan had passed the fifty strokes per minute he achieved each day in the stope.

"Sixty-five strokes per minute, boys," Harley Hanson yelled. "You're doing great."

I shouted, "come on Dan, you can win."

Della blared, "Four dozen chocolate cookies if you do."

"Give it your best, old buddy." This from Clyde.

"A Havana if you win," Hank cried around a cigar.

The counting became louder, faster. Dan gritted his teeth as he swung the hammer in shorter, faster arcs. It was evident he was in pain from the effort.

Three more rotations. Seventy strokes per minutes for the third. Bert swung the hammer. Faster. Faster. The clamor of the crowd drowned the ring of steel.

Two more changes in position. Bert had the steel, churning, churning, churning. I could see that Dan was pushing himself to the limit, hammering harder, harder.

A resounding crack brought a collective groan from the crowd. The granite had split in two.

In less than a half-second, Bert snatched the short drill in the remaining set of steels and rammed it onto a different spot in the granite. Dan struck without loss of pace.

A sigh of relief swelled from the Apex supporters.

From a nearby rooftop Rafe yelled in slurred speech, "Some stupid team you got there, Harley."

"It could happen to anyone," Harley blared.

Dan's lips drew away from his teeth in a hiss. Stroke. Stroke. Stroke

My pulse pounded in my ears with each ring of the hammer.

Seventy-five. Seventy-six.

Dan's nose started to bleed from the sun and effort.

Eighty. Eighty-one. Eighty-two!

The referee flung up his arms. "Time! Eighty-two strokes per minute! A new record for the district."

The crowd yelled and whistled.

Dan dropped onto the granite, chest heaving. He took out a handkerchief and wiped the blood from his face. Bert folded his arms on the rock and rested his head on hands bloodied from the steel. Both men had given more than they should to the effort.

A judge measured the two holes and combined the depths for a total. "Another record for the district, boys. Thirty-six inches in fifteen minutes. Apex is the winnah!"

Hats flew into the air, teeth clamped on lips in shrill whistles, men slapped each other on the back. I swelled with pride.

I felt Clyde's arm at my waist drawing me from harm as men stormed the platform and doused Dan and Bert with beer. As I watched the mob heave Dan and Bert to their shoulders and promenade them up the street to the Short Stake Saloon, pride faded to disappointment. The presence of Hub Malone and the other men from Butte in the crowd entering the saloon made it likely I wouldn't see Dan for a while. I wished he wouldn't become involved with Socialists like Hub. Not that I had any quarrel with Socialism. My quarrel was with some of its leaders, men who might push the union cause to an extreme. Men like Malone. There was something in his face that made me fear his plans for the district.

CHAPTER 12

The following Sunday, I learned there was more to Hub Malone than his appearance might indicate. For one thing, he displayed a mind that was out of the ordinary. It become evident when Della invited him for dinner at the boardinghouse. She'd invited Dan as well, since it was his afternoon off work.

Dinner over, I stood at the table, taking dishes from a pan of rinse water and drying them with a towel. Della bent over the sinkstand, attacking pots and pans with a scrubber. She'd left all the doors and windows open, but it provided little relief from heat generated by the cook-stove. Sweat trickled down my forehead.

The boarders had retired to smoke on the landing, but Dan and Hub had settled in the sitting room. The open doorway allowed a view of Hub sitting in a rocker, his long legs stretched out before him, his cavernous eyes staring at Dan. His bony features, long coal-black hair and scraggly beard gave him the appearance of the grim reaper about to claim a soul.

Dan sat opposite Hub on a leather settee, a coffee-mug in his hand. He returned Hub's stare and said, "What's bothering you, Hub? You look mighty glum."

"Oh, I been thinking hard on union matters." The brogue of County Monaghan burred Hub's tongue. "The head o' the union in Butte wants me to take a job here and run for president of the local. If I do, I'd like you to be running for secretary."

"Hell, I don't want to have to take minutes. I never did like to write." The expression on Dan's face said there was more than dislike for writing behind his protest. He'd hoped to take charge of the local union himself. Mainly, to keep Rafe Tatro and his gang of dissidents in check.

Hub leaned back in the rocker and stuck his thumbs in his vest pockets. "It's not for taking the minutes that I'd want you to run. You and me, we've done a bit o' talking this past week. You seem to have a good feel for the union cause. You understand the tenets of Gronlund, Bellamy, and George. You have no trouble grasping the philosophy behind George's proposal for a single tax as a way to counter monopoly's control of nature's resources. I admire your intellect."

Dan frowned and pulled on the lobe of his ear. "Some intellect. If I were smart, I wouldn't be killing myself in the stopes."

"Now don't be giving me that. We both know why you're there. You've got brains me boy. We need brains. We need men with schooling. Half the stiffs in the mine can't read, write, nor even speak the language. All they're good for is the push and shove. Not the thinking. Not the planning. We can't let this fellow Tatro and his gang take control with their talk o' hate and violence. They're thinking o' torching the company beanery because Hanson's threatening to make all single men stay there. You'll have to leave your shack if he does."

"Harley wouldn't do that. It's just a bluff."

"Likely he'll be smart about it. I've seen it happen at other mines. The operators slip in the ruling when nobody's looking. They want to put the young ones in debt for board and room so they can't leave the job." Hub took a pocketknife from his pocket and began to work on a fingernail. "'Tis where the management has it over us," he said as he pared the nail. "They have the brains and the cunning. On top o' that, they have the money. They can buy their power. Like they did with Judge Pomeroy. I heard they put a nice wad in his pocket."

Dan sipped from the mug, his expression dark with some deep-felt thought. "If Pomeroy is on the take, that shoots the hell out of any justice we can expect if arbitration fails and we go on strike."

Hub leaned forward in the rocker, his dark eyes reflecting sunlight that shafted through the window. "Pessimism accomplishes narry a thing. You need to be putting your anger to work, me boy. Sound the clarion for the union cause. Help us rout the corrupt rascals from public office. Help us put our own boys in their place. You'd cut a fine figure in the legislature. As secretary of the local you'd be in a position to run for—"

Dan raised a hand to stop Hub's argument. "Oh, no you don't. I'm too busy with my own affairs to run for county office." He wagged his head back and forth adamantly. "I need to work my claim when I have time. Besides that, I'm too close a friend with the management to suit the boys. On the other hand, if I were take office, Clyde and Harley would toss me out on my ear." His eyes flicked nervously. "Why don't *you* run for the legislature?"

"I'd have to take up residence. I'm not sure what Butte has planned for me. I might not be here long enough." Hub seemed to think further about that. He put the knife away and rubbed a nose that was almost as sharp, like a blade between hollow cheeks. "I've too much of a history in the Emerald Isle," he went on. "Soon as the powers in the district learned of my union activities back home they'd be driving me out o' the state." He pointed a bony finger at Dan. "Getting back to the local union, there's something further for you to be considering. There's going to be trouble ahead for us miners—machine drills coming in and stealing jobs, powder and drill men trashed to muckers, their wages lowered. When we air our grievances with the company, we'll be needing a secretary who can deal with all the paper work. I'd like for you to think it over." Hub pushed back on his coattails as if to rise. "I won't be taking any more of your free time. I did want to mention, though, that my relatives in the East say it was the citizens raising a holy stink about the trusts that finally moved the Republicans to do something. Guess that millionaires' club decided they'd better be getting America off their greedy backs."

"Do you think Sherman's bill will help?"

"I doubt it has enough teeth in it. No, the best answer is for the working man to collectively own the railroads, mines, and steamship lines and operate them for the benefit of all. Not for the benefit of a few individuals who traffic in human life and misery. They suck the marrow from our bones." Hub pushed off from the chair and stabbed a finger in the air. "It's up to you and me to work for the Cooperative Commonwealth. If we don't, the working man'll remain in chains. Always haunted by the fear of poverty."

As I watched Dan follow Hub outside, I couldn't help marveling at the power of Hub's oratory. It was clear he'd spent time after a hard day's work fathoming the principles of socialism and unionism while other miners spent their poke of brainpower on cards. But something about his arguments disturbed me. Despite his comments about Rafe Tatro's radical leanings, I feared Hub's zeal and total commitment. When put to the test, he might lead the local miners down a dangerous path.

●●●

Through the fall, the local unions grew in membership and formed a central union to deal with the mine operators. The operators formed their own union, the Mine Owners' Protective Association, to take joint action against the unions when necessary. It wasn't long before the unions began to insist that all miners join their locals. At Burke, two miles up-canyon from Bixbee, the union asked the foreman at one of the mines to fire a man who wouldn't join the union. The foreman refused and the union ordered him to take the next train out of town. As a result, the owner closed the mine and pulled the pumps. When he sued the union, the district attorney ordered the foreman be reinstated and sent the union officers from the district. All the while, unsafe conditions took miner's lives and families bore the brunt.

I dumped my worries about the situation on Della one afternoon shortly after school had opened for the year. I'd changed into my calico housedress and stood at the kitchen table washing the supper dishes. Della was in the midst of baking tomorrow's pies from apples grown on a farm down the Coeur d'Alene River. The fragrance of apples and cinnamon spiced the air.

"So, what are you going to do about it?" she said in a challenging tone.

I raised my shoulders in a quandary. "I don't know. But I feel I should do something. If I could let the public outside the district know what caused the labor disputes and tell them about conditions in the mines, it might push the legislators to do something about it."

Della thumped a rolling pin onto a mound of pie-dough and said, "Why don't you write letters to the editor. Start with the *Wallace Free Press*. It has a circulation all over northern Idaho and in Spokane Falls. I've written a couple o' times. They weren't printed 'cause I can't write very good. And I think the editor was afraid of the wealthy mining interests who run the town."

I looked up from the dishpan and across the table at Della. "Then what chance do I have?""In the first place, you can write a darned sight better'n I can. In the second place, there's a new editor. Just bought the paper. Name's Adam Aulbach." She paused to fold the flattened dough in half and slip it into a pie-pan, then went on, "Aulbach's seen enough o' the real frontier to know what miners are up against. He started a paper in the gold camp of Virginia City, Montana during the time of the Plummer Gang. Might even have been a vigilante. For a while he worked for the *San Francisco Chronicle*, but he loved the frontier. Before he bought the *Free Press* he owned a newspaper in the gold fields of Murray, just north o' here. He's lived elbow to elbow with hard-working men. I bet he'll listen to somebody who writes in their behalf."

I gave a "huh" of a laugh that expressed anxiety more than humor. "Harley Hanson would fire me if I wrote about conditions in the mine."

"You don't need to sign your name to the letters. Just your initials. Maybe say the conditions are true in all the mines. Which they are."

I went on washing the dishes without knowing it, my mind fixed on Della's idea with a mix of trepidation and soft resolve. Finally I said, "All right, I'll try it. See if he'll print a letter."

Aulbach did print the letter and many more, enough that it rekindled the love for writing that had led me to major in English at the women's college. But my efforts to stir public opinion were soon to receive the ax.

It all started in late February, in a way that had no bearing on the unions. Winter had frozen the district to its marrow and forced me to close the school in December. The mines had shut down, and Dan had left for Spokane Falls to help at the furniture store. To satisfy a need for companions my own age, I made frequent trips down the snow-bound canyon on a scheduled sleigh-run and entered the whimsical world of Wallace Society with Nora and Clyde Hanson. We whirled our way through a social calendar that thumbed its nose at the cold and ignored outlaws and ne'er-do-wells who'd taken refuge along a new section of the Northern Pacific Railroad that connected Wallace with Missoula, Montana.

Then one evening in late February, when Nora lay in bed with a cold, Clyde and I watched a road production of *A Double Wrong* held at the Theater Comique, a theater so filthy the actresses insisted the stage be swept before the first act. A boisterous audience filled the theater—Wallace patrons sitting on rows of hard wooden chairs at the front, transients dressed in rough-spun coats perched on wooden benches at the back. Teenage boys climbed the rafters for a better view, and when the players appeared on stage, they whistled shrilly and threw a barrage of rotten eggs and vegetables. Some of the missiles hit the audience below.

Later, Clyde and I sat in Nora's warm kitchen, the room lit by electricity provided by the town from four in the afternoon to seven in the morning. Tea and cookies on a round table in front of us, we were reminiscing on the shameful event. Clyde's expressive eyes crinkled with laughter. "I'll never forget the look on your face when that rotten potato hit your head."

I snickered and countered, "You still have some stuck to yours."

Clyde touched his sheath of walnut-colored hair and looked with disgust at the gooey mess left on his fingers. "I doubt if slimy potatoes will ever become a popular hair dressing. Not unless the chemists concoct something deliciously fragrant to cover the stench." He shot me a grin of reprisal. "Speaking of looks. You should have had a mirror in hand when that egg dribbled down your nose."

I laughed at the image. "If I'd had some bacon I could have cooked breakfast. Can't you see me holding a fry pan in the air to catch the eggs and potatoes as they flew by."

We laughed until our cheeks were damp. Then, as the spasms of hilarity subsided, Clyde reached across the table for my hand. "I love to hear you laugh. Why does it come so easily to the Irish?"

I smiled uncomfortably. "I-I suppose I inherited a quick laugh from my father . . . at least, he used to laugh a lot . . . before . . ." Ill at ease with the show of affection, I tried to withdraw my hand, but Clyde held fast.

He was still focused on the last comment. "Does your mother laugh easily?"

"Umm . . . not so much. Her laughter is catching, but she holds it in reserve, as though she has only so much of it to spend."

"She's not happy?"

I stared past Clyde at the shadow of my own misgivings. "A miner's wife is never truly happy. My mother is no exception. Maybe she was at first. She and Pa had to marry when Lennie came along. My grandfather forced them to leave Norway." I wondered at my ability to speak to Clyde with such candor. Usually, I squirmed beneath his intense gaze.

"What was an Irishman doing in Norway?"

"He worked the mines near Roros, where my mother lived. I guess he was quite charming then, and my mother . . ."

"Succumbed. With repercussions."

"My grandfather was headmaster of the local school and didn't want the scandal. I think my mother half-way expected to find happiness in America."

"Ah, happiness. What an untenable bit of pettifoggery." Clyde curved my fingers over the palm of his hand and stroked them, his eyes on mine as if searching for some elusive sign. "Maggie . . . dear Maggie . . . in spite of my cynicism, you've made me divinely happy, and I love you for it." His voice was soft, fibrous. "There, now I've said it. I've wanted to lay that piece of romanticism at your feet for weeks. I hope I haven't offended you."

An unpleasant warmth spread upward from my high lace collar to my forehead. I wanted to run, but all I could do was slowly pull my hand free. Why hadn't I seen this coming? But of course, I had. I'd chosen to ignore it. I'd been wearing blinders so I could have Clyde's and Nora's company. Now Clyde had torn off the blinders and made me face the fact that he'd fallen foolishly, embarrassingly in love with me. How in the world, without hurting him, could I make him see that romance had no part in our relationship?

I gulped back my fluster and stammered, "I-I'm not offended. I-I'm flattered. You're one of the nicest men I've ever known."

Clyde raised a quizzical brow. "You're not very convincing."

"I mean it. But that-that's as far as it goes. I like you very much. But I don't love you."

Clyde drew back in his chair with a disheartened expression that slid into a hardening of his jaw. "It's Dan?"

I acknowledged the question with a deepened blush and a nod.

"Oh."

From experience, I'd learned that single syllable coming from Clyde's lips could have any number of meanings. This time it smacked of extreme indignation. He picked up a cookie and bit into it decisively as if snapping off my head. "You're promised?"

"No-no, not promised. Dan and I just have a silent understanding."

For a long moment Clyde was silent, drumming his fingers on the tabletop, scowling at his teacup. Every muscle was on the defensive, no ease anywhere. When finally he spoke, his tone was filled with resentment. "An understanding? That's a pretty broad statement. Just what do you understand?"

The question jolted me. It was not what I'd expected, but I refused to let the barbs in his voice draw blood. "Dan and I understand that we like to be together," I said as calmly as possible. "We understand that he's my beau, and I'm . . . I guess you'd say I'm his lady friend. I didn't mean to make you angry. I thought you knew."

Clyde pushed off from his chair and began to pace the floor, flicking a bitter glance my way each time he changed direction. I could see that I'd stomped on his ego. "So, it's been Dan all winter, has it? I thought he no longer had a claim on you. Why didn't you say something, instead of letting me think I had a chance. It was . . . it was cruel of you."

I felt pummeled, also a bit angry. Clyde was not taking this in the way I would have liked. But I had to admit he was right. I should have said something. Now his monstrous ego was bleeding. I studied his profile, wondering how this could be the same man who'd display such chivalry earlier that evening.

Heat throbbed in my temples as I said, "I had no idea it was necessary or fitting to speak of such things. I've gone places with you and Nora because I was lonely and enjoyed your friendship. You made the winter bearable. I thank you for that. I'm sorry if you thought my motives more complicated."

At a loss for anything more to say, I left my chair and began to clear away the dishes, my nervous fingers clattering saucers and dropping a spoon on the floor. My head hit a naked electric light bulb that dangled from the ceiling by a cord. Clyde said nothing, just sulked at the far end of the kitchen. He lit a cheroot and took quick puffs on it while he watched me work. How complicated life could be. My brother Lennie had feared I would attract no man, now I had two men wanting my hand. As much as I'd come to admit the need for romance in my life, love could certainly muddle one's existence.

Clyde broke the silence by saying in a threatening tone. "What will you do if I tell my father about that poison pen of yours?"

The insinuation startled me. I thought I knew what he meant by it, but I didn't want to give the accusation credence. "Wh-what do you mean, poison pen?"

"Don't play innocent. I know you've been writing those letters to the editor about conditions in the mines. I've expected something of the sort ever since you went into the tunnels."

"I-I what letters?"

"Look me in the eye and deny it."

I looked him in the eye, but could say nothing.

"See. I'm right."

I fished for a plausible explanation, but all I could say was, "How did you find out?"

"I put two and two together and the answer was 'Maggie.' The prose is that of a woman. The initials fit."

I thought about that as I squirmed beneath his glare. "Are you going to tell your father?"

He smiled wickedly. "Likely I'll let you wiggle in the wind for a while."

CHAPTER 13

I soon learned that love and a rejected suitor could do more than muddle my life—they could jeopardize my job and put an end to my journalistic efforts. The first indication was a request from Harley Hanson to come to his office at the Apex mill. He gave no reason for the command appearance, but I feared it didn't bode well. As I trudged down the tracks to the Apex bridge, I looked to neither right nor left, seeing nothing but my own fearful thoughts. I was nearly deaf to the dogs yapping at my feet, to children throwing snowballs in the street, and to the wind that buffeted me this way and that. My anxiety held me in its grip, all thoughts feeding it, none diminishing.

The mine was closed, but evidently Harley was preparing for the opening in mid-March, thus the meeting at the five-story mill. The snow lay in clinging folds on brittle weeds that had set roots in front of the building, and it outlined every branch of a pine that had survived the slaughter of timber. The mill blotted out the hillside behind it, each of the five levels smaller than the one below, somewhat like a pyramid. At the rear of the building, the bearing wall from each level met the steep slope. Harley's office was at the front of the mill near a railroad spur where empty cars waited on the snow-covered tracks.

As I approached the mill, a notice on a bulletin board caught my attention.

AS OF MARCH 15TH ALL SHIFTS WILL RUN FOR
TEN HOURS. WAGES STAY AT $3.50 PER SHIFT.
SHIFTS START AS USUAL—7:AM AND 7:PM

I read the notice again. Three times. Then once again in disbelief. Anger grew within me as doubt translated to understanding. Harley had agreed to the union's demand for an eight-hour day along with a uniform wage for all miners. It was clear he intended to return to ten-hour shifts to make up for the wage. Dan had helped negotiate the agreement. He'd be mad as a hornet when he learned about the deception. I stewed as I climbed the steps to Harley's office, framing words that could speak of my anger. I could hardly wait to confront him.

The Apex office was of sturdy pine—gray-walled, bare-floored, the only breath of color a huge graph that detailed shipments of ore for the past three years. Four desks stood against opposite walls. A huge double-desk was piled with books, charts, graphs—obviously the geologist's domain. A smaller desk held manila folders. Another desk was clear. A roll-top desk held wire baskets, ledgers, and spindles stacked high with receipts. The only other furnishings were a Regulator wall clock and a bench along the front wall flanked by brass spittoons. An incandescent light with reflector shade hung over each desk and at the entry, a luxury paid for dearly with the purchase of power from the Poorman Mine's hydro plant, power too expensive for use in the Apex mine. In the center of the room, a stove made from a boiler tank belched waves of heat. A two-gallon coffeepot steamed a thick aroma from its perch on top of the stove.

A blond, round-faced man with a balding head was seated at the roll-top desk. A pipe tucked in the corner of his mouth breathed a twirl of smoke. When he heard my heels click on the bare floor, he turned and took the pipe from his mouth. "Ma'am can I help you?" he asked.

I was about to tell him why I was there when Clyde Hanson sauntered from a small storeroom at the rear of the office, his dark hair combed to perfection. His eyes widened. "Maggie? What are you doing here?"

"Your father wants to see me."

The corners of his mouth twitched. He flushed. "What about?"

"I don't know. He didn't say."

"He-he's talking to someone," Clyde said in a discomfited tone. "If you'd like, you can wait at my desk." He motioned toward the desk piled high with manila folders. "I can pull up another chair."

Nettles of chagrin prickled my spine. I had no desire to make awkward conversation with the suitor I'd rejected. "I don't want to bother you," I blurted. "I'll wait here on the bench."

"In that case, I'll be off for town." Hurriedly, he took a hat and overcoat from pegs on the wall and turned to the man at the roll-top. "Adam, tell Father I'll be back in an hour."

I settled on the bench, feeling as much relief to see Clyde walk away as he seemed to find in leaving, but Harley Hanson's stentorian voice tempered the sense of release. It came from a room to the right of the storeroom, the door ajar. He was saying, "I believe that's all we can accomplish right now, Simon. When am I due in court?"

A small, curt voice, "A week from today, ten in the morning."

Another suit, I thought. Operators were always suing the competition for one transgression or another. They not only reigned over their mines, the towns, the people, but they dominated the natural order of things. They'd slashed acre upon acre of timber for use in the mines and had spewed rock down the slopes into streams until nature had lost her fragile control. If they saw a piece of ground they liked, they grabbed it—from strangers, from each other, it didn't matter, just so they seized the advantage. Before the unions appeared on the scene, a few operators had treated their workmen with a hearty friendship. Others were ruthless. Harley's manner with his men had been mid-stream. He'd always considered miners simply a necessity, part of the business, to placate only to the extent it kept the business running smoothly.

I heard a briefcase snap shut, and soon a slight, dark-haired man with a thin face and spectacles appeared in Harley's doorway. He turned back as Harley asked, "Will I see you before the hearing?"

"I'll check back in a few days." That said, the man brushed past me, his nervous, puttering walk aimed for the coat pegs.

When the man had donned his hat and coat and left, the blond left his desk to tell Harley I was waiting. Soon, he motioned me into Harley's office, where I was met with a haze of smoke. Most of it came from a cigar that lay in a silver ashtray on Harley's massive desk. A few wisps escaped the creaking belly of a stove that strained against the chill of a blustering wind that plucked bits of ice from the brush at the side of the building and chinked them against the window panes.

Harley sat like a granite monolith behind his acreage of desk, much like a slab of rock used to mark a property line. His eyes were heavy-lidded, his silver hair tousled from a rumpling he'd given it, likely from concern over the legal matter. He shot me a chill look over the bridge of his nose, then jerked his head toward the door. "Shut the door. Then sit down." He flicked a hand toward a chair at the front of the desk.

I did as asked and sat with my eyes fixed on Harley's six-feet-two frame, noting the precision-cut of his silver imperial, the storm-gray eyes, watching him tap his fingers on the desk in a manner of impatience or anger, I couldn't tell which. I soon found out it was both.

"Young lady, you certainly have your gall, writing those letters to the editor complaining about conditions in the mine."

Just as I'd feared, Clyde had decided on revenge. I lowered my gaze to the desktop, wondering whether to play innocent or admit to the charge. I decided on the latter and looked up into Harley's glaring eyes. "How did you know?"

Harley didn't reply immediately, as if deciding whether it was any of my business. At last, he said grudgingly, "If you must know, Clyde told me. I suspect because he's nursing a grudge. Something about you taking advantage of his affections." Harley gave a twist to the corner of his mouth, implying more than he'd said.

The comment stirred some primeval reaction in my glands. I felt a terrible pressure rise within me, like I was filling with air and would explode if I didn't release it. "I didn't take advantage! Nora invited me to Wallace to attend the balls and theatricals. Clyde was the logical escort. I had no idea he was falling in love with me. I had to resist his advances."

Harley's expression of displeasure bled into one of annoyance. "Mmm . . . I see. Clyde is like that. But that's beside the point. The point is, by writing those letters, you've been biting the hand that feeds you. I'd call it a stupid betrayal."

I stammered a reply. "I-I wrote about mines in general, not specifically the Apex. Surely you'll admit there are problems."

"Of course there are problems. Mining is dangerous. Besides that it's expensive. We have to get out the rock or shut down from lack of profit. You're twisting the blame to obscure the fact you've committed a blunder." He paused, breathing heavily, nostrils flaring. "If you weren't such a good teacher and such a good friend of Nora's, I'd fire you here and now." He continued to wheeze angrily through his long nose and to glare at me. After a bit, the breathing slowed and the fire in his eyes dimmed to embers. "You're just like Nora. Speaks her mind without considering the consequences. What is it with young women these days? You can't seem to accept your place in the world."

Instant resentment burned on my cheeks. I straightened in the chair, back rigid. "What is that place? To wait on our lords and masters and serve as brood mares. We have minds, you know. As much intelligence as you males. All we need is a chance to show it."

"Now, now. Simmer down. I've heard all this from Nora. I grant you have a right to assert yourselves. But not when it affects my business. If you write any more letters you'll lose your job." The fire and brimstone had come and gone in his eyes, but I had no doubt I'd received a serious warning off.

I sat fuming for several seconds before I said, "I was through with the letters, anyway. Aulbach has asked me to report the news in Burke Canyon. No more opinion pieces. Strictly news."

Harley leaned back in his chair and looked skeptical. "Better not slant the reports to reflect your sentiments. And don't let it interfere with your teaching."

"I majored in English and journalism when I was in college. I know the rules of good reporting. And I won't take time from my job."

Harley drew in a deep breath and gave me an emotionless stare. "Well, now that's settled, you can go. Adam will see you to the door."

"First, I want to speak to you about the ten-hour shifts," I said as evenly as possible under the circumstances. "Dan and the grievance committee bargained with you in good faith. Did you know when you signed the agreement you were going to lengthen the shifts?"

Harley's scowl returned. "And if I did?"

"Then you bargained in bad faith."

He threw his weight forward, chin jutting in defiance. "You have a short memory. You seem to have forgotten you work for me." The words hissed over his teeth.

"I'm not talking to you as an employee of the school district. I'm asking as a citizen of the mining community."

We sat for a while, waiting to see whose glare would weaken first. There was no sound except Harley's harsh breathing and the monotonous movement of the pendulum wall clock. At last, he slumped back into his chair, swallowed some coffee from a mug that had been sitting on his desk, and rattled his throat to make way for words. "Are you asking as a representative of the press?" I said not and that his words would go no farther than his office. "Very well, since you're so damned stubborn, I'll give you a lesson in practicality. First off, there's the economics involved. The price of silver is down, freight rates are up. They're always on a see-saw. But the miner expects a constant wage. The only way us operators can even the odds is to lengthen the shifts."

"And give the miner the short end of the stick."

His face darkened and grew forbidding. "So! We're a wicked race of devils straight from hell, are we? Starving the poor forsaken miner."

He shook his finger in an accusatory way. "Then how do you account for the fact we lowered the boarding house rate from seven to six dollars a week?" Without waiting for an answer, he went on, "The country's headed for a depression. If the miners want to eat, they'll be happy to work on the new terms."

"And what about conditions in the mine?"

"Look, Maggie, there's only so much I can afford. The investors back east are always hollering for more dividends."

"I feel for them," I said with cynicism.

Harley threw back his shoulders in an imperious manner and lifted his chin. "If it weren't for investors there'd be no mine. If you spent some time in this office it would open your eyes. That's why us operators banded together to form the MOA—for protection against unreasonable union demands, against the unfair practices of the smelting trusts, and against the railroads' outlandish freight rates."

"I'd say the main reason was to keep the unions out of the Coeur d'Alenes."

He gave a laugh with no humor in it. "We saw trouble ahead. We don't like having a bunch of miners tell us how to run our business. I wasn't all that anxious to lengthen the shifts, but the rest of the operators were. If I don't go along with them on this, they won't help me when I need their support. Business is business. A man does what he must do to keep his whistle." He nodded toward the door and said curtly. "If there's nothing more you want to discuss, I see no point in your taking more of my time."

I pushed back my chair and was headed for the door when Harley said, "If I were you, I'd give Dan a bit of advice. Tell him the union is headed for a cliff, and if he keeps filing grievances he'll take the plunge with the rest of them."

CHAPTER 14

I passed Harley Hanson's warning on to Dan, hoping he'd take heed, but he continued his active role in union affairs. He had such faith in the union and gave so much of himself to keep it alive that I said little to him of my concerns about his welfare. I kept hoping tempers in the canyon would improve. They didn't. For the next year, the mine operators and the central union engaged in a tug-of-war over a uniform wage and payroll deductions to be paid into a fund for a union hospital. Strike—compromise. Strike—compromise. Whenever the union announced a new strike, the mine owners threatened to bring in miners from the East. In rebuttal, the union growled a warning to non-union miners from other districts to stay out of the Coeur d'Alenes or face the consequences. Meanwhile, death continued to haunt the stopes. At the Apex, the hoist operator was caught in a flywheel and killed. Four men died in a blast at a neighboring mine, two men in a blast at another mine. I reported it all for the *Wallace Free Press*, stifling my impulse to editorialize.

Union problems didn't seem to stunt business growth in the district. More than four thousand five hundred people lived in the seven mining towns strung along the Coeur d'Alene river from Wardner to Mullan and up Canyon Creek. Mines gouged over four-and-a-half million dollars worth of ore from the hills each year, making the Coeur d'Alenes the most vigorous lead and silver producing region in the nation. When a tide of goods flowed into the district on the recently completed Northern Pacific Railroad line that connected East with West through Wallace, the greenbacks of progress fell to earth like autumn leaves. Yet, the Mine Operators Association waged a constant battle with the railroads. In January, the railroads said they'd submit to a shutdown of the mines rather that cut freight rates. As a result, the mine operators discharged fifteen hundred men from the stopes, leaving about four hundred to work on development and to keep the tunnels from flooding. In mid-March the MOA announced that a looming depression had caused the railroads to lower freight rates and that the mines would reopen in April, but with ten-hour shifts for the three-fifty wage.

As if nature conspired with the miners, the soft air of spring 1892 drifted from camp to camp swelling buds on trees and awakening men's souls to possibilities the long winter had repressed. A restlessness seized the district, a quickening of passion and fury. Hank spoke of men hunched in saloons, heads together in excited murmurs. Outside the mine portals, they bunched as wasps around a bit of flesh, their voices rough, angry as they complained about the wage scale, the lack of safety precautions in the mines, the lack of company-funded hospital care for the maimed, and the continuing threat of being forced to live in company boarding houses and shacks.

To add to the problems, the machine drill had bared its hammering fist. Powered by compressed air, the drill punched into rock at a rate of three hundred strokes per minute as opposed to a miner's fifty. Tunneling with the new drills cost the operators $2.30 per foot as opposed to the $17.50 per foot cost of hand drilling. The men were frightened. Machines meant less need for hammer and drill men. Many were scrubbed to muckers or carmen, their wages lowered to three dollars a day.

Dan was given a *buzzy* that drilled three inches into the rock in one minute at six hundred strokes per minute, sending rock dust showering onto his face and chest. He felt as if the machine would shake his shoulders apart. Bert had left the district to care for his ailing mother, and when Sil Crego, Dan's new drilling and batching partner, was trashed to mucker, Dan saw red. He'd already lost respect for Harley Hanson because of Harley's dogged stand on union matters. As secretary of the Bixbee union, Dan reported to the *Wallace Free Press*, "We aren't about to let our fellow workers lose their former wage. We demand three-fifty a day for all candle holders, regardless of their job. We damned well better get it or we'll strike!"

Harley Hanson said in reply. "With the price of silver down, there's no way I can raise the wage. If miners don't like the conditions here, they can take their asses somewhere else. I'll bring in workers from the East."

Knowing there'd be trouble if he imported non-union labor, Harley bribed Judge Pomeroy to free prisoners from the county jail, then he gave them Winchester rifles and put them to work guarding the Apex. To increase security, he hired carpenters to build a fence across the front of the property as a barrier to union members. In protest, the union set up a picket line.

One day as I walked home from school, I saw clouds of dust rising from the rhythmic punch of the pickets' boots as they tramped up and down in front of the bridge that led to the Apex. Rafe Tatro, Smutt Corrigan, and Jim Tatro were among the pickets carrying wooden rifles to mimic the Apex guards. Jim had mined for two years, Mike Tatro was in prison for stabbing a drifter during a brawl in one of the saloons.

Rafe led the column of men, shouting, "Hup, two, three, four. Hup, two three, four. About face, march!"

Bored with their duty, the mine guards looked out from beneath the brims of their hats with a blend of humor and disgust. Now and then, they shouted obscenities from across the creek.

I looked for Dan among the pickets, only half-way expecting to see him. When he wasn't picketing, he took advantage of the strike to trudge up-canyon to his claim, the Black Titan, named for the charred ground in which it had been found. He'd traced the vein of ore and had begun to put hammer and nail to a cabin, but today he was in town. I saw him in front of a false-fronted diner that had a replica of a sandwich and beer bottle hanging from the eaves. He was leaning on a signboard that said *APEX UNFAIR TO UNION LABOR*. Hub Malone was with him.

I walked up to them, pulling a shawl around my shoulders to ward off a chill breeze that whisked down from the ridge-top. The crest loomed stark against a silver sky that darkened and lightened with constantly shifting layers of clouds. "It looks like it might rain," I said to make conversation.

Both men tipped their hats. Dan gave me a warm smile. "Hope not," he said. "I'm on picket duty in a few minutes."

"Will picketing really accomplish anything?"

"Nothing else seems to work"

Hub looked glum. "Arbitration has accomplished nary a thing. Picketing is all we have left, short of violence. We must—"

He broke off as a volley of hoots and hisses erupted at the bridge. Five carpenters who'd been building the fence had left the Apex property, tools in hand, and were trying to cross the picket line. Four of the carpenters, likely drifters pressed into service, fought their way through the picket line and hurried up the street. But Rafe's gang of radicals circled the oldest man, a local carpenter well-known for his skill. Rafe took him by the collar, scattering his tools, and held him fast.

"We better look into this," Malone said to Dan in an urgent tone. He started for the bridge, Dan and I alongside.

We arrived in time to hear Rafe blare at the old man, "You sucking up to the kingpin, Lew?"

"I've got to earn a living," Lew said as he struggled to free himself. "If I don't do what Harley says, he'll blackball me in this town."

Rafe took a strangling grip on Lew's collar and said through gnashed teeth, "We'll do a lot worse if you set foot over there again."

Hub closed on Rafe. "Let him go. We have no quarrel with him. 'Tis no time to be showing your muscle. You're here to picket, nothing more."

For a long, tense moment a hard look held between the two men. Finally, Rafe loosened his grip and flattened his lips in a smile of derision. "What's with you, Malone?" He aimed a thumb at the Apex mill hulking behind him on the far side of the bridge. "Are you too chicken-livered to do anything about that horse's ass? Harley charges twice what he should for my shack. And me out o' work."

Hub narrowed his eyes with an unfathomable expression. "We tried to negotiate that before the mines closed."

Jim bawled, "Three men've been killed in the cage since you took office, Malone. Others in blasts. You say, 'We'll talk to Harley about it.' Ha! What Harley needs is a stick o' dynamite up his rear end."

I saw the fury rise so suddenly in Dan's face I was afraid he was going to attack Jim. He did lunge at him, but stopped when they stood chin to chin. "Don't use that kind of language in front of a lady."

Jim sneered. "Is it the woman? Or what I said about Harley? You're nothing but a turncoat."

Dan pulled back his fist ready to strike a blow, but Hub caught his arm, checking the forward motion. "Fisticuffs will accomplish nary a thing. We have to work together."

Rafe manufactured a false tobacco-stained smile. "That's why I was going to invite Lew in for a beer." He took hold of Lew's arm.

"I don't want a beer," Lew wheezed as he struggled to pull free. "I need to get home."

"'Course you want a beer. You been working hard all day," Rafe said through the deceptive smile. "Might even buy you two beers." He started Lew up the walk, the gang of radicals with him, passing beneath symbols and one-word signs that advertised a variety of wares and services.

"Stay with them, Dan. They're up to something," Hub said ominously. "I have to go to Burke to meet with the union brass."

●●●

Later that evening, I was in my room at Della's boarding house, undressing for bed, when Della pounded on the door. "Maggie, I need your help. Dan's been bloodied good."

A blue wrapper over my nightgown, I rushed into the kitchen, orange hair flowing loose over my shoulders. Dan sat at the table, gripping his side, while Della dabbed at his cheek with a wet cloth. His face was bruised and swollen. Blood flowed from his nose and mouth. His brown corduroy coat was torn and hung from one shoulder like a peddler's sack. The flannel shirt hung in two long shreds, the four-in-hand tie ripped and slung over his back. It had been raining and the clothes were wet. Dan's batching partner, Sil Crego, stood to one side holding a hat, an expression of worry and anger on his face.

"Good Lord," I cried. "What happened?"

Dan raised his head, pried one eye open, and tried to speak through swollen lips and jaw. His words had the sound of mush bubbling in a pot.

Della had concerns other than the reason for Dan's condition. "Maggie, bring some clean sheets and a pillow case. Sil, help me get Dan into an empty room. He needs to lie down."

When I returned with the sheets, I spread one on a bunk in the vacant room while Della removed Dan's coat and shirt. "Help him lie down," she told Sil. "Maggie, make some tea and stir a little laudanum in it."

Dan was barely able to swallow the tea containing the pain-killer and winced when I put a tea compress on his swollen eye. Della treated the cuts with witchhazel and carbolated Vaseline, then covered them with strips cut from a flour sack. Next, we bound two broken ribs with lengths of sheeting. In between moans, Dan moved his tongue around in his mouth and tried to tell us in a thick voice what had happened.

"You know how Rafe was giving Lew Barnes a bad time . . . because Lew's building the fence," he said with extreme effort. "Well, I followed them to Jack's Place to make sure Rafe didn't hurt him." Dan paused to hold a handkerchief at his mouth. He cleared bloody phlegm from his throat, then continued in a labored way, "Rafe forced Lew to drink beer until he got him stinking drunk . . . I tried to stop him . . . but the bartender was on Rafe's side . . . he threw me out." Spent from the telling, Dan rolled his head to one side, breathing heavily.

A few pain-filled minutes passed before he went on to say that Rafe had planted his money pouch on Lew, pretended Lew had stolen it, and had the constable put Lew in jail. "When I heard about it, I bailed Lew out of the clink and helped him stagger home . . . I was heading up the steps to my shack when five men came up from behind." Dan broke off, coughing, holding his side in pain.

"Who were they?" Della said with a huff of anger.

"They had bandanas over their faces, but I recognized Rafe's voice . . . Smutt's . . . and Jim's . . . not sure about the rest."

Outrage constricted my voice to a squeak as I asked, "Just because you bailed Lew out?"

Dan nodded and closed his eye. I put a fresh tea-soaked pad on the swollen eye while Della held his head steady.

Sil had been listening in silence. Now he put in, "I was late getting home and found Dan lying at the bottom of the stairs. Managed to drag him here. Damned miners have a case of Shit Creek fever."

It was hard to tell from Sil's tone where his allegiance lay—with the union, the battered carpenter, or a mix of both. I'd first met him in December when he moved to the district and I'd observed him on several occasions—a man of middle height, olive complexion, slimmer than Dan and several years older, likely in his mid-thirties. He wore his black hair slicked with pomade until it looked like a wet otter's. A scar streaked one cheek above a lightly waxed mustache. He claimed to have worked the mines in Colorado, but I'd noted that his hands were smooth, unscarred, without the telltale calluses and leathery appearance that resulted from working in mud and rock dust. I'd noted as well that his cheeks lacked the death pallor of the underground miner. Something wasn't genuine about Sil Crego.

At the moment he was leaning against the wall, listening to Della grumble, "The boys are getting out of control. They aren't going to change a thing by beating each other to a pulp." No one was more aware of the miners' mood than Della. Her kitchen was always open to union men, and small groups gathered there, nourishing their bellies with her pies and nourishing their rebellion with her impassioned words. "They claim it's mainly short-stakers who start the trouble" she went on. "Men who loaf around in the saloons and talk about shooting scabs, dynamiting the Apex, and showing Harley who's boss."

"There's some truth in what they say," Sil replied. "But Rafe and his gang aren't short-stakers. Malone had better put some salve on their discontent before it festers into outright war."

Shooting scabs. Dynamiting. Outright war. As I listened to the comments, an image seized my mind of our drafty kitchen in Williamsboro, where my mother was nursing my father's battered body after the Molly Maguires had attacked him for opposing their acts of violence. The Molly Maguires belonged to the coal miners' union, but operated secretly on their own against the mine owners and scabs. They even dressed in women's clothes to hide their identity, hence the feminine name.

Like Dan, Pa had abhorred violence, and my mother had suffered the consequences as much as he had. Now here I was, nursing another miner, my mother's ghost hovering over my shoulder. I couldn't believe I'd let myself exchange the worries of Williamsboro for a set of anxieties just as troubling. Why would I want to perpetuate the pattern? Yet, no matter how I'd tried to reason with myself and loosen my ties to Dan, love was always there, holding me fast.

CHAPTER 15

In the evenings that followed, I went to the room where Dan lay and tended his injuries. I thought about him often when I was at school, fearing that when he left the safety of Della's boardinghouse he'd meet with foul play. After a week, he returned to his shack and took a limited part in the picketing. Now and then he stopped at the school to let me know he was well. Still, I fretted. If Bixbee followed the same pattern as Wiliamsboro, this was only the beginning. The fighting would have no end.

The crossing of the swords between Harley Hanson and the union was hard-felt in town, especially with a depression creeping into every corner of the nation. Many families had left Canyon Creek, and the children who remained seemed always to be on edge and distraught. Men who remained in the district wandered idly about town. Neighbor women who used to stand in their doorways and gossip across the narrow span between houses now ignored one another. Even those women whose husbands worked for the same faction plied their gossip with an air of despondency. Only the smallest children still laughed their laugh of innocence, the men in the bars their laugh of escape.

Houses stood vacant, and shopkeepers boarded up windows. Business at Hank Tuttle's mercantile neared a standstill. A few customers entered the store to soak up the warmth of the pot-bellied stove, fewer yet to buy from the neat displays of household goods and miners' paraphernalia. Those who could afford to patronize the store were non-union employees kept at the Apex to keep the mine from flooding. Union customers stopped in when they couldn't find items at a commissary the union had organized at the union hall. And then they had to scratch deep in their pockets to pay.

When the wives of men in opposing camps met, the sparks flew, such as the one-sided catfight I observed one day when I was shopping at Hank's store—a self-contained, dimly lit world that contained everything from whiskey to Bibles, calico to kerosene. It held a variety of smells—tobacco, leather, fresh-ground coffee, cheese, dried and pickled fish, and the distinctive aroma of bacon. Three wooden chairs and an open cracker barrel clustered around a pot-bellied stove in the center of the store—an island of warmth in the winter as well as a year-round place to visit.

On this day, I was bent over a shelf near the front of the store judging a remnant of calico for an apron. Hank stood at a glass-covered cheese-case near the cash register. A pencil tucked behind his ear, his dark hair parted in the middle and combed to each side as always, he was running a knife over a sharpening steel. Behind him, a goggle-eyed parrot in a cage squawked, "Polly wants cheese. Polly wants cheese."

Hester Reap, wife of a staunch union man, the shrew who'd protested Jeff's enrollment in school, had been shambling among boxes of tools at the front of the store. She came to a stop in front of a bucket that held a few axes. "What? Six dollar for the axe?" she said loud enough for Hank to hear. "We will do without before I pay that price."

"They're getting hard to find," Hank said as he sliced into a wheel of cheese. "The price is just a few cents above my cost." He tore a sheet of paper from a roll on the counter, wrapped a wedge of cheese in it, and tied the package with string.

Mira Appleby, wife of one of the non-union men who'd been kept on at the Apex, walked from the back of the store, toting a pair of men's high-topped rubber boots. A coil of ash-blond hair framed a thin, care-lined face. She dropped the boots to the floor, dug into a ragged purse, and put a few coins on the counter. "I can't pay but a little on these boots, Hank. My man's been dropped down to three dollars a day. And him working a level where they cut water. We'll be eating beans for the rest of the month. And that only if we're lucky."

Hester gave a warning intake of air and advanced on the counter, her heels pounding the plank floor, her eyes glaring to set up the attack. "How dare you complain, Mira Appleby. Your man works while the rest of us go hungry. Anybody who will not join the union so he can keep his job deserves to be hung."

Mira's wan face blanched further. For a moment she seemed at a loss for words, then she said in a tired, defensive way. "Jeb's just trying to keep us in food and clothes. Besides, he thinks a man should have the right to join or n—"

Hester broke in, snapping Mira into silence. "And let the rest of the men strike to get him better wages. That is what he is doing. Some right!"

Hank opened and closed his mouth, managing a syllable here and there as Hester continued her tirade. Finally, he jumped in with, "Will that be all, Hester?" he held out the brown package. "Want it on your tab?"

Hester ignored him and pointed an accusing finger at Mira. "Believe you me, Mira Appleby, if our men get cut off by the mine owners, your children will go hungry chust like mine. The union will see your man gets his lumps." She yanked a shawl tight around her chest, jerked the cheese from Hank's hand, and stormed into the street.

In the awkward silence that followed, Hank busied himself by whisking bits of cheese from the counter into a crumb pan and sorting change in the till. I picked up another remnant of calico.

Mira just stood there, head hung. "I hear you favor the union, Mr. Tuttle," she said in a tremulous voice. "At least they say you and the other store owners gave your support at the town meeting."

Hank's puffy cheeks slackened. He looked up from sorting change and said hesitantly, "Well . . . as a matter of fact I do support the union."

"Then you probably don't approve of my man working." Mira's face assumed a bruised look. "We came here from Ohio to get away from all the strikes and the beatings my man took. Now we have the same thing here. Nobody gives a man a choice any more. Where are we going to go?" Before Hank could reply, she caught up the boots and fled the store, her eyes on the brink of tears.

With a constricting of my heart, I walked to the door to watch Mira's small figure hurry down the walk. Men standing outside the batwings of Jack's Place sent ugly gestures her way. Too bad a woman like Mira had to suffer because of her husband's decision. For a moment I felt complete sympathy for the Applebys. Then, as several idle men trudged by the store, gloom on their stony faces, I felt as sorry for them as I had for Mira.

What was the answer? Why couldn't men respect the decisions of their peers? Why must there be this constant warring? I hated it for making enemies of friends. Hated it for ruining people's lives.

I saw the hostility reflected in the behavior of the children. At a time when they should skip down the tracks to school bearing armfuls of pussywillows, they arrived tired, resisted study, and fought constantly among themselves. Then one afternoon, the Appleby problem brought tensions to a frightening head.

The children had left for home, and I stood at the chalkboard writing a penmanship lesson on the black oilcloth when Lucinda

Hanson tore into the classroom, screaming, "Miss O'Shea! Miss O'Shea!" She ran to the front of the room, her long black curls bouncing up and down like springs.

"What's wrong?" I said with a start. Lucinda wasn't prone to yelling unless there was a good reason for it.

"They're kicking Susan. Hurry! Tom's hurting her bad."

I rushed from the room and followed Lucinda across the yard and through the gate. Fifty yards up the road, seven-year-old Susan Appleby writhed on the ground crying, her arms folded over her head to protect herself from fourteen-year-old Tom Tatro's hammering feet. Blood pumped from a gash on her forehead and splattered over her hair and dress.

Jeff Mearns had picked up a stick and was beating Tom's shins. Einar Reap and another shy child named Robby stood to one side, their eyes stretched wide. The air reeked of steamy bodies and asafetida worn around necks to ease coughs.

Tom's blond head bobbed up and down with each thrust of his foot. "Dirty scab! Dirty scab." he yapped. Two of his brothers threw rocks at Susan while his sister chimed in on the taunts. Their eyes glittered from the savage play.

The terror and anguish in Susan's cries stabbed at my heart, causing me to bear down on the children with such outrage that the taste of it rose in my mouth. "Stop it! Stop it this minute," I shrieked.

I must have looked like a banshee with murder in mind, because Tom shot one glance my way and raced up the railroad tracks, his brothers and sister with him.

"I'll see you pay for this!" I screamed at their backs. And to the other children, "Lucinda, you and Jeff stay with Susan. Einar, get a pail of water from the pump at the school. Robby, you run up to Susan's house and tell her mother to come."

I flew back to the classroom, grabbed clean towels, a bottle of witchhazel, carbolated Vaseline, and muslin pads from a cupboard, then ran back to Susan. As I fell on my knees at her side, a passion of tenderness swept over me, a deep sorrow for the humiliation the child had endured. Damnable strike. Hurting the innocent. It seemed women and children always received the brunt of men's squabbling.

Soon Einar arrived, slopping water over the sides of a pail, and set it on the rocky ground. I washed the cut on Susan's forehead and treated it with witchhazel. Then, while Lucinda held a muslin compress on the dripping wound, I cleaned the scratches on Susan's face and arms. When I pulled up her dress, I discovered several hard welts on her knees.

It wasn't long before Susan's father appeared and bent over her, his worried face white, startled. He'd left home in a hurry and wore no shirt, just longjohns under his suspenders, a lean man who looked too old to be Susan's father. He took her hand as she burst into a fresh wave of tears. "My God, what happened?" When I told him what I knew, he shot me an accusing look and said with reproach, "Don't tell me you let those bullies go without punishing them." The words were a question as much as a statement.

His censuring tone hurt. After all, I'd done what I could to help his daughter. Still, I understood his anger. It rose as much from worry as from outrage. "The boys ran off as soon as they saw me coming," I said wearily. "It was more important that I stay with Susan than chase after them."

Jeb Appleby blinked a couple of times, blew air, and ran a hand across his chin in a contrite way. "I'm sorry. I didn't mean to snap at you. But to see my daughter like this . . . the strike's gotten to my nerves." He looked up the street, then back at me. "I sent Robby for my wife. I was having trouble sleeping . . . I'm on night shift . . . so she took the little ones for a walk up the road. I don't think we should wait until she comes. We need to get Susan to the doctor." He lifted the child in his arms and started up the tracks that led through Bixbee and on to the mining town of Burke, two miles up the canyon. Dr. Pettit had an office there. A long way to carry a child.

I took a clean muslin cloth from the grass and hurried to catch up with Mr. Appleby. Jeff and Lucinda tagged along behind. "Why don't you take Susan to your house?" I said to her father. "I'll stay with her until your wife comes. You can get the doctor."

Jeb looked across his shoulder at me with an anxious smile. "I'm beholden to you, Miss O'Shea. You seem to care about the child. There are those in town who'd like to see me and my family in our graves."

I knew the truth of the remark. I could see it on the faces of men who stood along the walk and watched us with expressions of hate, contempt, and ridicule. Staying with Susan was the least I could do in the name of compassion and justice.

••••

The next morning, Hester Reap walked to school with Einar and raked me up one side and down the other with her verbal claws, claiming it was improper for me to ask Einar to help Susan, the daughter of a *scab*. She stood so close I could smell the odor of fried bacon on her sack-like dress. Her moon face was crimson. "Why you take the side of the scabs?"

Why did I what? The accusation heated my face. "Mrs. Reap, as far as I can recall, I said or did nothing to support any faction."

The spleen in my voice fueled Hester's animosity. "My Einar say you held Susan in your arms a long while. Now if that is not taking sides I don't know what is."

How could a sweet child like Einar have come from the womb of such an overbearing witch? I held my breath, trying to find the patience to deal with Hester's idiotic reasoning. Finally I said, "Mrs. Reap, I'd give comfort to any child in Susan's condition. If Einar was hurt, I'd do the same for him."

She sneered down her nose. "I doubt you would."

I felt myself losing control and closed my eyes. I didn't open them until I'd calmed myself and could say as reasonably as possible, "These are difficult times in Bixbee. We both know that. But why should children bear the burden? Growing up is hard enough without having hate eat at their insides. It's up to us adults to help them control such ugly emotions."

Hester said no more, merely gave a huge grunt, and in the same belligerent way as she'd arrived, elbowed her way through the children entering the room.

My blood simmered all day from Hester's visit, then a half-hour after the children had left for home, other visitors returned it to a boil. I was sweeping the ashes from around the base of the stove, my green satin sleeves rustling with the movement, when Clara Hanson entered the room, Harley a few steps behind.

Clara started her harangue the moment she cleared the door. "Lucinda tells me you lectured the class today about bullying, but allowed Tom Tatro and those other urchins to remain in class. Why in heaven's name didn't you expel them? It's clear you're on the side of the union."

I stiffened at the metallic sound of Clara's voice and rolled my eyes in a feeling of frustration. Hester Reap had accused me of being too soft on the child of a strike-breaker. Now I was being told I was on the side of the union. It seemed my attempts at impartiality in the classroom had become lost in the madness of battle. I set the broom aside and indicated two newly acquired wooden chairs. "Won't you sit down?"

"We can't stay," Clara said brusquely. The pointed brim of her small Marlborough hat was pulled down over her forehead in a way that accentuated the sharpness of her nose. Her lips were a thin, tight line below the pinched nostrils. "I felt we must talk about what happened yesterday. Like I say, you should have expelled the Tatros."

I wondered if her reaction would have been as strong if the victim had been the child of a union man. "Mrs. Hanson, if the attack had happened on the school-grounds I would have. But it didn't. All I could do was to have a serious discussion about bullying and try to ease the children's anxiety about the strike. They're as emotionally involved in the town's problems as everyone else."

Harley towered like a granite pillar beside his wife, his critical gaze on me. I could hear the air labor up his humped nose. "What if the same thing happens during school hours?" He asked in his booming voice.

"I'd be forced to expel the guilty party. But even if it happens on the schoolgrounds, expelling one or two children will do nothing to ease the tension. Susan is new in town, the child of an outsider who's taken a union man's job. Tom is carrying on at school in the same way his father is with the non-union men you employ. It's up to the adults to resolve the problem."

Harley's jaw hardened. Affront glittered in his bulging eyes. "I'd say you have to deal with conditions the way they are, young lady. You can't sustain discipline if you let this sort of thing slide by. I've learned that in working with miners."

I put a leash on my resentment and replied, "Children are different, at least in some ways. They're in their formative years. There are times when it helps to talk things out and think things through. It gives them a chance to change their behavior of their own will. We did a lot of talking today."

Harley snorted and shook his head. "I can't see the Tatro kids ever changing."

"And I don't want them picking on Lucinda because of Harley's position," Clara said with a curt tilt of her nose.

"I doubt that will ever happen. The children respect Luci too much." I said simply. "She's everyone's friend. She has more compassion than any child I know."

Harley chose to reply to my comment. "That's my point. Her compassion deserves your support. Today she came home disappointed. She felt you'd left an opportunity for the Tatros to hurt Susan again."

I had to admit there was some truth in that and felt a surge of regret. "I'm sorry if I disappointed her. I truly am. It's clear you both love her dearly. But compassion amounts to nothing if it finds reward in the punishment of others."

● ● ●

Two days later, punishment took on a new meaning. I knew about Rafe Tatro's crew of *scab* beaters, but the full realization hit as I stood at the stove in Della's kitchen, stirring the morning's batch of eggs. The room swam with the smell of biscuits, strong coffee, fried steak and gravy. Beyond the window, a slight breeze sent serviceberry petals drifting to the ground like falling snow.

One of Della's boarders came to the table, yawning, an older man, heavy-set, with a face like a bull terrier. Big gray puffs lay beneath his eyes, and he showed other signs of having had little sleep. He took the only empty chair, which happened to be near the stove, and leaned over the heaped platters of food to speak to a man sitting opposite him. He clearly wanted the conversation to be confidential, but excitement carried his cockney speech to my ears.

"We had us a right bloody night, man. 'Ave we got them scabs on the run." He looked my way, pulled his chair closer to the table, and lowered his voice. I strained to hear. "Ye should've seen Jeb Appleby. By the time we was through with 'im he was spitting blood. 'Is face was a pulp. 'Is leg broke at the knee, facing opposite of what it should." The man snorted a laugh. "Should've heard 'im scream."

I imagined the beating and the screams as if they were there in the room and wanted to retch. I had to force myself to stir the eggs to keep them from burning.

The man speared a biscuit with his fork and went on while he spread butter. "We finally let 'im go. Told 'im to get the hell over the hill or we'd kill 'im. Should've seen 'im trying to crawl off." He gave a coarse laugh.

It was more than my nerves could stand. "You men are acting like a pack of wolves," I cried. "No! Worse than wolves. Wolves wouldn't torture for the fun of it." I dropped the stirring spoon onto the floor in shock and used the search for a clean spoon as an excuse to distance myself from the Englishman.

How utterly brutal. How insane. I recalled Len Appleby's face when he spoke of the strike, his eyes full of torment. That poor man!

CHAPTER 16

I slept little that night for worrying about Jeb Appleby and his family, but two days passed before I could speak to Dan about the beating. He'd made the rounds of the local dives and shacks to distribute food donated by other mining districts and had taken the rest of the day off from his responsibilities at the union hall. Lunch basket in hand, he led me up the wooded trail beyond Burke to picnic at the Black Titan. The air was crisp and the May sunshine glistened off the new leaves of willows and cottonwoods. Most springs, my heart filled with joy at the sight of buttercups, shooting stars, and bluebirds and at the sharp scent of evergreens. It seemed ironic that in this year of 1892 the season of rebirth and hope should come at a time when human expectations withered on the vine.

Dan did little to lift my spirits. Though he championed the union cause and thought its claims against the Mine Owners Association just and necessary, the trend toward violence tore at his conscience. He was disturbed most by the fact that Hub Malone was doing little to stop it. As we headed up the canyon he seemed preoccupied and to walk without perception. I tried to draw him from his gloom by pointing to cottonwoods growing in the creek-bottom, their tips swollen with bright, sticky leaves no bigger than the ears of a squirrel. We stopped to admire mourning cloak butterflies that had gathered around a puddle of rainwater, their velvety-brown wings rimmed with glowing hues of blue and yellow. We noted deer tracks that cut the meadows and a scattering of grouse feathers where a lynx had ambushed its evening meal.

When Dan's interest lagged, I asked questions about the mine, though I knew the answers to most. I knew that whenever he could break free of union problems, he'd worked at the Titan from the first gray slant of dawn across the crests of the Coeur d'Alenes until the sky caught the crimson twilight. Before he'd run out of powder, he'd cut the mineral vein at twenty-five feet from the surface, had found fair-looking mineral for one hundred feet beyond that, and had continued to bore for another hundred feet. The latest assay report showed the mine as a break-even prospect. Yet, Dan held fast to a hope that seemed to have little basis. He had no money for blasting powder or the heavy nails needed for timbering. His father was ill, which meant his brother, Aaron, had no money to sink into the mine nor the time to take up a pick, which he sometimes had done on a Sunday. Still, the Titan set Dan's imagination afire. He thought of that cold fortress of rock as a living thing, a child to be nurtured to its full potential. Like a father dreaming of his child's success, his plans for the mine far outstripped the reality of its infancy.

A mile above Burke, we left the damp woods that lined the creek-bottom and zigzagged up a steep, rocky hillside. There, the fires of '89 had burned most of the trees, leaving room for a jungle of brush to grow in the ashes. Several months had passed since I'd visited the mine. During that time, Dan had rented a horse with jump-scraper to add a number of switchbacks to the trail. A few piles of dirt still ridged the path where the scraper had bounced over boulders and dumped some of its load. Old tree roots needed to be cleared away and rocks needed to be tossed over the side, but the extra sections of trail made the climb more gradual. I was glad for that—neither my lungs nor my shoes were adapted to the thousand-foot climb.

The cabin Dan had raised with the help of a mule stood in a small tree-rimmed basin that had escaped the fire. I was amazed at the size of the cabin. Made of huge, unpeeled logs, the building shamed the flimsy shacks in town. Several cords of firewood lay stacked against one wall. A stovepipe poked its black neck from the roof.

Knees wobbly from the climb, I dropped onto a bench at the front of the cabin, leaned against the logs' rough bark, and listened to the sounds of that breathless noon. A pileated woodpecker hammered at a towering snag in the creek-bottom. A chipmunk scolded from a nearby slab of rock. A bee whined among the yellow blooms of a holly-grape. From my vantage-point near the crest of the ridge, I could see multi-fingered mountain ranges fan out into an eternity of wilderness. A few hillsides held the scars of past fires, but most shone with the livid green of early spring. Snowfields still crusted the sunless, north-facing slopes, revealing winter and spring beneath the same spotless sky. The one exception to the intense blue were clouds that wisped from a snow-capped peak like the spokes of a wheel. The pattern repeated itself on the hillside in long stringers of shadow.

The sky's brightness flashed behind my eyes as I turned to Dan. "What a beautiful view. No wonder you spend so much time up here."

He brushed aside a mound of pine husks left from a squirrel's feast and sat beside me on the bench. For a while he gazed out over the rumpled landscape, then he turned his eyes toward the mine portal fifty yards to the left. The gaping black hole looked like the den of a giant badger. On the far side of the portal, waste-rock had spilled down the slope. On the near side lay mounds of lead-gray ore. "I'm going to miss the Titan," Dan said with sadness.

The comment startled me. "What do you mean?"

Dan's silence lasted so long I wondered if my words had been lost in space. I repeated the question.

"I don't want to talk about it." He set the picnic basket on the bench and removed a tea towel that covered the contents. "Mmm . . . smells like chicken sandwiches."

Impatience twitched my mouth. "We're not going to eat until you tell me what you meant."

"Likely you won't eat if I do."

"Dan!"

There followed a moment of uneasy silence while his blue, sulky glance touched mine. Then he said with a sigh of reluctance, "All right. It-it's just that I don't know how much longer I can take these strikes. A lynch mob's taken over."

I thought of the beating they'd given Susan's father and shuddered. "They did some terrible things to Len Appleby. Don't you have any say in what they do?"

"I tell them beating scabs is hurting our cause—that it'll make it harder to settle our grievances. At the meetings, they just hiss me down." A slow resentment clouded Dan's face. He propped his elbows on his knees and stared at his feet.

"Maybe they'll come around to your way of thinking." Though I said it, I had little hope it would happen.

Dan seemed just as pessimistic. He gave a humorless laugh and muttered, "Not a Chinaman's chance. It's going to take the operators and the union a long time to come to terms. It'll boil down to the union demanding a closed shop and the operators refusing to let the union in the mines. I'll be trapped in the middle. If the union wins the right to work, I'll be on shift with men who hate my guts for talking peace and compromise. If the management bars the union from the mines, I'll be out of a job, unless I damn the union, and I won't do that. My quarrel isn't with the union, it's with the bastards who've taken over."

I put my hand on his thigh with a fervency that brought his head up. "Someone has to speak out against the cruelty."

"As long as Rafe heads the crew that goes after the scabs, it'll happen again. And he's laying for me for pushing arbitration. I'm always looking over my shoulder, expecting him to do me in."

"Surely, Malone doesn't approve."

"He's the one who appointed Rafe and his crew. He figured it was better to give them responsibility than try to keep them in line."

I wondered in disbelief at Malone's action. With all his talk of equal justice and social opportunity, he seemed to think only those who believed in the union cause deserved a place in workers' heaven.

For a while I sat mute, only slightly aware of ravens clacking overhead and of the creek gabbling in the bottom of the canyon. A sudden breeze stirred the branches of a pine at the side of the cabin. Smoke from trash-burners at the mines near Burke curled up the draw.

I glanced at the man beside me, surprised at the changes I saw in him, surprised at his willingness to accept defeat, yet hoping it would keep him from harm. "What do you intend to do?"

I was sure Dan had been expecting the question, perhaps dreading it, yet it seemed to come as a jolt. "I-I've considered leaving," he said with hesitation. "Have been for several weeks. There were things that held me here . . . men I didn't want to see hurt . . . the Titan, and . . ." Color flared beneath his fair skin. He looked into my eyes with such deep affection I thought I'd wilt. "I didn't want to leave you." Abruptly, he turned aside, his face darkening into partial eclipse. "I-I might go to Canada for a while. There's lots of jobs there in the mines." Then tongue-in-cheek, as if to hide his pain, "You wouldn't have me cluttering your doorstep."

"You haven't done much of that lately." I said it half-joking to cover the disappointment that knotted my stomach. Imagining life without Dan made my heart sink as if in a cold sea. For the first time, I admitted to myself that it was only because of him I'd stayed in Bixbee rather than look for a teaching position elsewhere. Not for the lame excuses I'd given, whatever they were. At the moment I couldn't remember. I put my hand on his. "Things will improve. This strike has hung on for five months. The men aren't themselves right now. Their actions say less about them as people than it does about their need for a job. It's being out of work that makes them act like fools."

Dan swung his head around and caught me with my mouth slack, my eyes filled with concern. "Listen to you! Making excuses for those sonofabitches. There's such a thing as ethics, you know. Ways men should act regardless of the dirty deals life hands them. I thought you hated the things they've done to the scabs." He left the bench and paced back and forth at the edge of the basin. Even at a distance, I could see his fingers shake when he took cigarette makings from the pocket of his coat.

I hadn't wanted to anger Dan. I'd only wanted to persuade him to stay. I waited until he'd lit the cigarette and went to his side. "I'm not trying to excuse anyone. It's just that I can't bear the thought of you leaving. Isn't there some way? Why don't you simply work at the mine?"

"Not when you have Rockefeller's disease as bad as I do. The mineral is looking real good, but I've hardly a cent to my name to develop it."

"What about working at your father's store?"

"The depression's hit. Aaron said he couldn't hire me. The papers say the depression could get a lot worse before it's over. The best thing for me to do is go where I can get a job and save my money until better times come along." Dan had been talking to the dark hole in the hillside. Now he swept his arm toward it in frustration. "God, Maggie, I want this mine to work. I want to prove I can make money and still give the miner a square deal." He glanced around at me as a trickle of tobacco smoke made it through his mustache like a wispy gray cloud. "You can't imagine how it makes me feel not to have the bucks to put it into production."

I thought of how I disliked mining—disliked what it did to the countryside, abhorred what it did to people's lives. Yet, I couldn't bear to see Dan in such a dismal mood. I curled my fingers around his arm. "I'd like to help. Maybe when Della can pay me again, I can work extra hours to—"

"I won't take your money." Dan glared at me, eyebrows raised in affront.

The tone of his words hung like a wall of nettles between us. Why did a man's pride always get in the way of practicality? A few moments earlier I'd have done anything to keep Dan in Bixbee. Now, his rancor made me wonder. My cheeks warmed with an anger of my own. "I was only trying to help. And don't think I can't understand your frustration. I've had all I can take of vulgar men who have nothing better to do with their lives than to get drunk, go on strike, and beat each other up, while their wives drudge away their lives trying to do with nothing. I'm tired of teaching children who have little to look forward to but more of the same. I want to work where people exist with pride. Where they talk of something besides mining and unions and poverty."

Dan hung his head, the scowl fading from his face. "I'm sorry. I didn't mean to be such a grouch."

An awkward silence held between us for a minute, two, three. Dan stood with his shoulders hunched, his gold brows ruffled with worry. I considered the consequences of his leaving while I watched a chipmunk eat from his winter store of seeds at the base of a boulder.

After a bit, Dan sighed, threw the cigarette to the ground, and took me gently by the arms. There was something different in his face, an added dimension to his feelings, a certain expectation and sense of trust. "Be patient with me, Maggie. When I bring in this mine, I'll make a wonderful life for us." The only time I'd seen Dan's eyes burn with such intensity had been when he'd spoken of the Black Titan. It seemed I'd been elevated to the same importance as that dream of his. He tilted my chin and pushed a stray lock of hair from my face. The caress of his fingers sent a chill sweeping over me, something as soft as the touch of a feather. It filled me with such a profound sadness that tears broke through my eyelashes and rolled down my cheek. I wished I could pluck my rantings from the air and bury them unspoken.

"Are . . . are you asking me to marry you?" I said in a near-whisper.

He wiped away my tears with a fingertip and pressed my head against his shoulder. I smelled tobacco and the sour-sweet scent of his flesh. "I hadn't intended to ask so soon. Not until I could give you the things you deserve." His thick, breathy voice resounded in his chest. "When I think of going away without you, I can't stand it. So, I'm asking you now—will you marry me?"

The thought of marrying Dan and going with him to Canada stunned, also frightened me to the core, sending a soft paralysis up my spine. One part of me wanted to throw my arms around him and say, "Take me with you, Dan. I can't bear to stay in Bixbee without you." I opened my mouth with the thought on my lips, but could utter no sound. Instead, I listened to the calm voice of reason. If Dan continued to work underground, I'd lead the same worrisome life as my mother. And there was Jeff. I couldn't abandon him. In spite of those doubts, I loved Dan more than I'd imagined and wanted to be part of his life. I felt torn asunder, pulled in a hundred directions.

I looked up slowly, Dan's face blurring through my tears. "I love you, Dan. I love you with all my being. But I just don't know . . . I need time to think." *Time?* Time was an aching anxiety with no certainty ahead.

Dan seemed to sense my distress. "Maggie darling, that's all I ask. That you think about it."

He drew me closer, so close I felt the drumming of his heart and felt his veins pulse when I threw my arms around his neck. He kissed my lips softly, gently, until the happiness of it filled my whole being and made me feel as if I had wings.

In that heartfelt moment, I knew what my answer would be. Not today. Not tomorrow. I'd take time to think. But as surely as the sun would set on this lovely spring day, someday I'd become Dan's wife.

CHAPTER 17

All that night I lay in my bed, wide-eyed, my mind latched on the day's events. In the soundless hours, I could hear Dan's voice as if he were in the room and tingled at his words of endearment. I recalled each syllable and held them up for scrutiny, feeling my heartbeat slow or quicken with the meaning of each new phrase. Before the first pink rays of dawn crossed my windowsill and the hillside robins greeted the day, I knew I wanted to be with Dan more than anything else. Still, the shadow of my childhood lingered on.

I'd written my mother just two days earlier, but I wrote her again for advice. It seemed to take forever for her letter to arrive. When it did, her words of wisdom reflected the skillful use of English she'd developed as the daughter of a headmaster in Norway.

Williamsboro, Pa.
May 16, 1892

My dearest Maggie,

I appreciate your letters. I read them again and again. Sometimes they are all that keep me going.

I don't envy you for the decision you must make. It seems that is what life is all about, one decision after the other. At least you have a choice. If there is blame for the life I lead, it rests upon my shoulders. One little indiscretion gave me a single path to follow. You have many choices.

Even if you should never finish college—and heaven forbid that happening—you have the education to make the most of your mind and talents. When you love, rather than allow it to rule your life, use the passion of your heart for the strength and nourishment it can provide, never forgetting to nourish your mind as well.

What you say about the lot of a miner's wife is true. When Dan bosses his own mine, he will continue to face danger in the tunnels.

Union violence can be just as deadly. Is your love strong enough to endure those problems. You might not know until they happen.

If Dan's love will allow you to grow into the woman you dream of becoming and to accomplish at least part of your goals, then follow your heart. Life without love is difficult at best. From what you say about Dan's prospects in Bixbee, the marriage will not be easy, but poverty will not chase true regard.

If you must choose between love and a career, promise me you will consider long and hard before you decide. Do not let yourself be pressured into marriage. If Dan must leave for a while, parting will not discourage true love. But once your decision is made, you must face it squarely. You can never run away from life.

Know, my dearest, that whatever you decide you have my blessing. Always look up to see the light. Never look down at the shadows.

With all my prayers,

Mama

My mother had put the burden of the decision where it belonged— on my shoulders. Still, I needed to explore my feelings with someone. Della was out of the question. For two years, she'd urged Dan to propose. The only other person who had my confidence was Nora Hanson. She was more worldly than I. Surely, she could offer some advice. I took the next Sunday off from my chores at the boarding house to visit her in Wallace.

"Dan loves you deeply," she said as we sat at her kitchen table sipping tea. "I see it in his eyes when you're together. He has a lot to offer. Smart. A hard worker. He'll do his best to make the Titan a success. That fact scares my brother. He's afraid of the competition. Don't tell Clyde, but I'm pulling for Dan."

"What if the mine isn't a success? I'm afraid he'll keep sinking his money into the mountain in spite of it."

"If he loves you as much as I think he does, he'll move on to better things." Nora leaned across the table and took my hand, her blue eyes intense. "Maggie, every woman takes a chance when she marries. At the time, she thinks everything will work out. The truth is, wedlock is a compromise. I'm not married, but I see it on all sides. Women have to rein in their expectations to make their marriages work. If they don't, there are problems. My own mother hasn't had an easy time of it. They had nothing when they were first married. I suppose their marriage has worked as well as any, but I think it's hardened my mother's attitude toward many things."

I thought about that, fearing the possibility I'd become another Clara Hanson. "I guess that's what I'm afraid of. Disillusionment."

"It's part of this crazy life. You can't tell me you haven't found disappointment in the classroom."

I gave a nervous laugh as I recalled the days I'd hated teaching, days I'd considered marriage a means of escape. I stared at Nora quizzically. "Why haven't you married? I'm sure you've been asked."

She shrugged her slender shoulders, leaned back in her chair, and spent a moment absently winding a finger around a long strand of curly black hair. Her eyes were fixed on her teacup as if it held the answer to my question. "At first I wanted my freedom," she began slowly. "I was having too much fun. Since I moved here, it's been a matter of not finding the right man. That's one problem with teaching in the district, choices are limited. You're lucky you found someone like Dan."

"Yes, but he's a miner. I'm afraid that the danger and tragedy inherent in mining will create a veil of thorns between us, to say nothing of sadness and regret."

"Then you do have a problem." A wry smile spread slowly over her lips. "You could marry Clyde. He'd give up mining in a minute if you asked. But I can't see you married to him, as much as I'd like that. He's not as stable as Dan. Too prone to fritter his money away. The only reason he's in mining is the chance for wealth—travel—the theater—concerts—rich food—and gambling. Of course, you might like that." She gave a little laugh that sounded like tinkling chimes.

I wanted to say I couldn't marry anyone like Clyde. Instead, I smiled and said, "Luxury might be nice for a while, but I think I'd tire of it. I want something that challenges my mind. That's another thing that makes the decision so difficult. I want to do more with my life than raise a family and keep house. My mother drummed that into me so long and so hard it's become a real need."

"That's part of the reason I haven't married. Most men wouldn't consider letting their wife work. Does Dan object?"

"I don't know. He seems proud of the fact I'm a teacher."

"I hope you continue. The district needs teachers who care. The strikes are hard on children. Always moving in, moving out. Their home life is stressful to say the least."

● ● ●

It seemed that fate had heard Nora's statement about the needs of children. Before I'd decided about marriage, I was forced to consider a proposal of an entirely different nature, one that complicated my decision further.

I was standing at the rear of the classroom one late afternoon, running my fingers along the bookshelves to determine which books I would need to order for the next school year, when the entry door opened and slammed shut beneath the force of a blustering wind. I walked the few steps to the doorway to see who'd braved the storm that had blown torrents of rain in from the northwest. I was surprised to find Nelly Mearns stomping mud from her feet on gunnysacks I'd placed at the entry. It had been months since Nelly had visited the school. Why now?

"You must be chilled through," I said. "I'll put more wood in the stove."

She pushed strings of damp brown hair from her face. "Don't bother. I won't be staying long."

"At least sit down." I led the way to the front of the room, dragged a chair from the wall for Nelly and sighed into my teacher's chair. The rain drummed on the roof and slid down the windowpanes. The wind roared in the trees. I'd kept the children inside all day, and I thought I must look as school-worn as I felt. My hair had begun to slip its fastenings and a couple of orange strands dangled over my shoulder onto my white shirt. The shirt had lost its starch, and chalk dust smudged my green plaid skirt.

Nelly looked even worse. She was dripping wet, her face swollen and red, as if she'd been crying, and without the usual powder and rouge whores liked to wear. She had an expression of urgency. For a moment she stared at the soggy gloves she'd set in her lap, then said haltingly, "I don't rightly know how to ask you this . . . it seems the only thing I can do. Jeff likes you so much . . . better'n anybody . . . so

I thought it might work out all right." She fell silent, picking at a thread that poked from a seam in her black glove.

"How can I help you?" I said to prod her to the point of her visit.

"Well, Ma'am . . . I'd . . ." She snatched a breath and blurted, "I'm going to be gone for a while, and I'd like you to take Jeff in."

The request didn't surprise me. I'd watched over Jeff several times when Nelly had gone to Spokane for the day. But the words 'take Jeff in' hinted of something more prolonged. "How long will you be gone?"

"A year or two. Maybe three."

My mouth dropped open with a gasp.

"I-I know it's asking a lot," Nelly stammered. "And kinda sudden. But you see, there's a man wants to marry me and take me prospecting up to Alaska. There won't be no schools up there. And it'd be hard taking care of Jeff in the wilds. I hear it's real cold there. We'd live in a tent most of the time. I thought if Jeff could stay with you . . . if you don't mind . . ."

If I didn't mind! Did Nelly know what a huge favor she was asking? And what about Jeff? He'd feel abandoned. "You must love this man a great deal to leave your son."

Nelly's lower lip quivered. "You don't know what it means to be my kind. It ain't often a woman like me has a good man ask her to marry him."

"If he really loved you, he'd keep you and Jeff together. Why doesn't he stay in Bixbee?"

"He can't. Not the way things are. And they're going to get worse."

"You mean the strike? It'll be over soon. Then he can—"

"It ain't just the strike. It's what goes along with it." Nelly hesitated, biting her lip, her eyes wide as an owls, as if she were afraid to speak her thoughts. "You see Blade . . . that's my man . . . he don't believe in unions. Rafe Tatro and his gang been roughing him up, telling him if he don't join they'll run him out of town on a rail. They done that to some of the others."

"I know," I said ruefully.

"Last night, Blade come to my place all bloodied and with a big slice out of his forehead. He just ain't gonna stay around here no more."

I touched Nelly's hand. "I know what your man faces, but can't he stay in the States so Jeff can be with you?"

"It'd be the same anyplace he went. Blade says the unions are trying to take over the country. They don't give a man no choice in the matter."

I fished for some other way to solve the matter and came up with, "Why doesn't he work at something where unions aren't involved?"

Nelly's expression said the idea hadn't occurred to her. "I-I guess he don't want to. He says the only way he can make us a good life is to put lots of money in the bank. The best way to do that is to find gold in Alaska. I know it's gonna be like finding a button in a ton of hay, but it's our only chance." Her gaze touched mine, wistful, questioning, pleading. "We'd come for Jeff as soon as we could."

Jeff was a dear and I loved his gentle ways. But to take him on as my own, in addition to teaching and helping Della, possibly marrying Dan? I didn't know what to say.

Nelly sensed my grave doubts. Disappointment crept over her face like a graying sky. She pulled on a glove. "I can see you don't want to take Jeff. I don't blame you. It's asking too much."

"I-I didn't say that. I-I just don't know what to do. I'd need help with the grocery bill . . . I might need a larger place to live . . . I . . . I need more time to consider it."

• • •

Now I had two decisions to keep me from sleep. I told Della and Hank about Nelly's proposal, but they were poor ones to ask for advice. Every stray down-and-outer in the district could find a handout and a bed at their house. I thought about asking Dan, but his vested interest in me would hardly allow for an unbiased opinion. My mother's voice sailed across the thousands of miles that separated us, reminding me of something she'd once said. "Don't open your heart too wide to the world, or you will open it to sorrow." True, but what would life be without an open heart? In the end, Jeff's eyes decided for me—soft, gray, beseeching eyes that stared at me from the darkness of my room seeking refuge in my heart.

When I told Dan I planned to take care of Jeff, his face sagged with disappointment. "Does that mean you won't marry me?"

"I . . . I . . ." I blushed, averted my gaze for a moment, then looked back at his hurt-filled eyes. "I want to be your wife. But not now. Later, after the strikes are over. When you can make a go of your mine and not have to work the stopes. Or until—"

Before I could say more, Dan took me in his arms and kissed me so soundly I had to gasp for air. Slowly, he released me, stroked my cheek and kissed it tenderly. His expression was one of profound love mixed with resignation, "Maggie, my dearest darling, I wish it could be tomorrow. But I agree. Times are too unsettled. And mind you, I'll do whatever it takes to make us a good life."

"Understand, my decision has nothing to do with Jeff."

"I know that. I like the boy as much as you. If Nellie hasn't come for him by the time we marry, I'll be the father he never had." He laughed. "Just don't let him get the idea he's the only man in your life."

CHAPTER 18

T he minute I decided to let Jeff stay with me, the Tuttles tucked him under their wing and lavished him with clothes and gifts. With hardly a second's thought, they said Jeff and I could use their two-room apartment, claiming they'd planned to build larger quarters onto the existing house anyway. Many of the boarders were gone, and it would be a good time to make the alterations.

Since men were out of work, it was easy to find help, and lumber was lying idle in Wallace, the price cheap. Before long Jeff and I had an apartment made from the old sitting room and Tuttle's adjoining bedroom. We should have been content and at ease, but tensions that plagued the town sifted through the walls like an insidious disease. Six saloons had closed in Bixbee, and Hank had boarded up his store with a satirical sign that read, *Closed by Order of the Mine Owners Association.* Della spent her free time attending rallies and making impassioned speeches for the union cause. Whenever an agitated crowd gathered, she found her way there, as if she scented ferment on the breeze.

Dan stayed in Bixbee for the time being, not entirely because of his love for me—he was certain our love would endure even if he left—but he needed to prepare the mine and cabin for his departure. Events made that seem more imminent each day. The Mine Owners Association threatened to bring in government troops, and strikers were deserting the picket lines to work the stopes of small mines that had opened their portals to both union and non-union workers. Rumor had it that two large mines in Burke, the Tiger and Poorman, were desperate to get back into production and would hire any miner, no questions asked about union membership. Yet, the war itself ground on, the battle cry no longer wages, rather the very life of the union.

The MOA, grown to seventeen members, pressured the government to squelch the strike. The central union courted other industrial unions, the farm block, and the railroads in an attempt to put the squeeze on Congress to remove the tariff on Mexican lead. If it did, the MOA would be forced into higher production and the need to employ union men.

The union had lost a million dollars in wages since the beginning of the strike and was shrunk from the previous two thousand members to a solid core of eight hundred veteran miners. The railroads had lost a million dollars in freight fees, to say nothing of the cost to the mine owners. Business was at such a standstill that bored merchants in Wallace tossed a football in the streets. Still, the MOA continued to bring non-union miners into the district, and union pickets doggedly met every train, sometimes hiding beneath the loading platforms to escape detection by MOA guards. Time and lack of progress in the strike had worn down both sides to a nubbin of their former selves. Any rash move by either side could precipitate the final decisive battle.

By the first hot days of July the banners of war had become frayed. No longer could they buffer the head-on collision of two great efforts—the MOA's desire to lock the union from the district and the Central Union's determination to close the mines to all but union miners.

One evening I was sitting on the landing with the Tuttles, enjoying a cool draft that flowed up the dusky canyon. Jeff sat at the top of the stairs whittling on a stick. Suddenly bells rang in the street below. Through the twilight, I saw union criers hustle along the railroad tracks ringing their bells and crying, "Citizens' meeting! Union hall. Citizens' meeting!"

"Did you know there was going to be a meeting?" Della asked Hank.

Hank took a cigar from his mouth and shook his head. "Likely Rafe's bringing some scabs in for justice." He took a bowler from his knee and stuffed it on his head, then pulled a jacket from the back of his wicker chair.

Della slipped an apron from around her waist and pushed off from her chair. "I'll get my bonnet."

Hank shot her a disapproving look. "Things could get rough. I told you last time you tagged along that women have no business at these meetings."

Della plumped a hand on her hip. "Then why do they call it a citizens' meeting? I'm a citizen."

I took a shawl from the arm of my chair. "I'm going to take notes for the newspaper."

"You gals would knock on the gates of hell if you had a mind to." Hank got to his feet. "Come along if you must, but I won't be responsible for your safety."

I threw the shawl over my housedress and retrieved a notepad, pencil, and bonnet from the apartment. When I returned to the landing, Jeff had set aside the willow stick and stood at the head of the stairs with the Tuttles. From the cap on his head, I gathered he intended to go. I said, "I'd rather you stay home, Jeff."

"Why can't I go?" he complained. Jeff had always tending toward shyness, but lately he'd become more social and spent time with Einar Reap and Robby Townsend, two of the nicer boys in town—evidently Hester Reap had decided Jeff was a more suitable companion for her son than the rest of the boys. Likely Jeff thought Einar and Robby would be at the meeting.

On the one hand, I didn't want to expose Jeff to the churlish dogfights that took place at some of the meetings. On the other hand, I'd tried to make him aware of the problems inherent in mining and unionism. "All right," I said reluctantly. "Wash your face and comb your hair." Then to Hank, "Go ahead, we'll catch up to you."

We found the Tuttles wedged inside a throng of Bixbee's male citizens who'd gathered in front of the union hall—a large raw-board building in the center of town, a flagpole jutting from the false front. The crowd was shouting expletives at five men dressed in muddy diggers. They were being held at rifle point by Rafe and Jim Tatro, Smutt Corrigan, and the rest of their henchmen.

"Strike-breakers," Hank said to me by way of explanation.

We waited until the jostling crowd had entered the building, then Hank helped me settle beside Della on a bench at the rear of the hall. He joined a few merchants and saloon-keepers who sat in the row ahead of us. Jeff huddled in a corner with his two friends. Like Jeff, their faces held the soft-clay look of early puberty, the features changing with each passing day. This evening, those features expressed curiosity mixed with excitement.

Miners of all shapes, sizes, and complexions lined the rows of benches in front of us, most of them without coats, their vests open in the stuffy room. Many faces were familiar. Those not so familiar belonged to miners from neighboring camps. Voices buzzed and eyes gleamed with excitement in the light of lanterns that hung from the ceiling. In the front row, Rafe Tatro's thatch of red hair was as conspicuous as a cock's comb alongside Smutt Corrigan's jug-shaped head. The five men they'd driven into the hall at gunpoint slouched in dread between Rafe and the rest of the scab-beating crew.

When the last of the benches filled, late-comers lined up along the bare walls, among them six men with rifles. I noted that Clyde and

Harley Hanson had slipped into the room and stood to the right of the doorway, as stolid as the room's center posts. Clyde had attended other mass meetings. Not Harley. The miners watched Harley, grumbling their displeasure, blood in their eyes and hate in their souls.

Della leaned toward me and whispered, "Harley being here is gonna cause trouble."

An immediate confrontation was avoided when Hub Malone and other union officials clumped through the rear door of the building and took their places at the officers' table facing the benches. Malone put a sheaf of papers and gavel on the table and slipped a pair of reading glasses over the end of his nose. His cadaverous face seemed leaner, his cheeks bluer than ever, his eyes darker and deeper in their sockets.

Dan's batching partner, Sil Crego, sat to the left of Malone. He flourished a cheroot that sent up a stringer of smoke. Dan had resigned his office as secretary of the Bixbee union to protest its actions against strike-breakers. Sil was filling in until someone could be appointed. The intensity in his black eyes, along with the way he held his shoulders and jerked his head, suggested intense anxiety.

I pointed to the table and asked Della, "Who are those men next to Malone?"

"The gray-haired fella is Tom O'Brien, President of the Central Union. The others are officials from there, too."

I'd heard Dan speak of O'Brien. He considered him a good man and a peace-lover. He said O'Brien was doing his best to keep the combined locals from getting out of hand.

I made some notes on my pad, then focused on Malone. His gaze darted this way and that, scanning the crowd, then settled on Harley Hanson with an expression of distrust. He picked up the gavel and rapped the table. "Quiet down, me boys. Let's be getting on with the meeting." The Irish burr resonated from his long thin nose. "We first need to be discussing Mr. Hanson's presence here. I'm not sure having him here is in our best interest. Or his, for that matter."

Harley's voice boomed from behind my shoulder, saying, "You announced this as a citizens' meeting. I'm here as an interested citizen, like Hank Tuttle and some of the others." Benches creaked as miners turned to get a better look at their adversary.

"Don't use my husband as an excuse," Della yelled at Harley.

"Yeah, don't give us that," a miner hollered.

"Ve know vy you are here," said another.

Malone rapped the table. "Show your manners, boys." Then to Harley, "Since you be the opposing party in our dispute, you have no right to be joining our meeting. I won't proceed with the business at hand 'til you state your purpose."

Harley pointed to the five men Rafe and his crew had dragged into the hall. "I'm here to see that the rights of my workers aren't jeopardized. You had no cause to pull them from their work."

"I say we did. They're taking the bread from our mouths."

"And your damned union is taking it from mine," Harley countered. "You're going to ruin me. I can't operate with a third of the miners I need. Most of the men I'm bringing in from the East have never seen a mine before. A lot of them hobo a ride on our trains, then desert to get a free meal ticket from you." He sucked in a breath and went on with his tirade, gesturing angrily. "Not only do I have to pay dumb hayseeds to guard my property, but I have to pay their fines when they get caught in town with their guns. I'm losing my shirt."

Resentment flared in the eyes of the union members. Their grumbling gathered momentum. "We feel for you, Harley," one man said with sarcasm. Another said, "Go home to your wife."

Malone's brows hung brooding over eyes filled with dislike. He pulled the glasses from his nose and raised a sharp voice above the noise in the hall. "Now that Mr. Hanson's had his say, union members will be voting to see if he can stay. Those who be in favor o' his—"

"Hold on!" Harley yelled. "That vote should include all the businessmen in the room."

"You be the only businessman here with an axe to grind," Malone said dryly. "I'll repeat the question. Those who be wanting Mr. Hanson to leave the hall signify by saying aye."

The crowd roared an aye.

"Those opposed."

A few bartenders who managed the company's saloons raised quiet, dissenting voices.

"You've heard the decision," Hub said. "I'd appreciate it if you'd leave peaceably."

Clyde edged toward the door, but Harley stood as adamant as an Indian staked for the attack. The thunder of his voice split the rumbling in the room. "You'll pay for this! And if you so much as lay a finger on my men, you'll land in jail. The Association has already sent for injunctions to keep you from bullying our workers. And let me tell you—" He let fly an oath as six men with rifles pushed him out the door.

Clyde was given the shove, too, but not before he sent a vengeful look my way. The union had taken its toll on his friendship with Dan. Now, he seemed to consider me the enemy as well.

Malone stuck the glasses back on his nose, rapped the table, and waited patiently for quiet. "It sickens me heart to know that after all these months we still have not won the battle. To know the rich still suck the marrow from our bones. But 'tis temporary, me fellow citizens. 'Tis temporary. We must hold together as brothers. As sailors upon the sea. If we stand as one, we shall rise against this tyranny." He got to his feet and leaned over the table, pumping his fist in the air with each subsequent appeal. "Rise against it citizens! Rise against it. We shall overcome." His voice had grown more intense, like a mounting fanfare of trumpets. "Rise against it, Brothers! Rise against it."

The miners burst out with measured shouts of "Rise! Rise! Rise!" clapping and stomping to the beat. Della hauled herself to her feet and added her brassy voice to the rest. Their bawling hammered at my brain. I felt sick. Never had I seen anyone as anxious as Malone to arouse others to violence. For a long moment, I couldn't bring myself to look at him. Instead, I scribbled from one side of the notepad to another. When I did look up, Hub was back in his chair, skimming a sheet of paper.

He waited for the yelling to abate and said, "Since this be a special gathering we'll dispense with the usual proceedings. But I do have a few announcements." Referring to the sheet of paper, he went on to report that Butte and other unions in Montana as well as the Spokane Labor Committee were sending food for the strikers.

The miners put fingers at their mouths and whistled, pulled stoppers from flasks of whiskey and passed the bottles from man to man. One man pounded his approval on the wood heater at the side of the room.

Malone waited for the noise to die, fingering the stringy black handlebar mustache that seemed about to slide from his upper lip. At length, the room turned so quiet I could hear the sputtering of a kerosene lamp in need of adjustment. "Here 'tis a dirty bit o' news, citizens." Malone's voice was subdued, grave. "I've just learned that the Association has sent Pinkerton detectives disguised as miners to spy amongst us. Some as long as a year ago. They're here to ferret out our secret plans—build a case against us—manufacture lies—put us behind bars. Be wary, me boys. Be wary."

A wave of outrage rippled along the rows of hunched backs and grew into the rumble of a breaking storm. The miners looked around for likely culprits, the heat of their anger warming the room. The smell of it filled the air.

Malone called for order. "Now, to the main purpose o' this meeting. There be those in camp who've worked amongst us but do nothing to help our cause." His voice cut like a sharpened steel. "They let us push for higher wages, let us push for hospital benefits, let us push for safety regulations while they do nothing. And keep their jobs to boot." His smoldering eyes indicate the five men sitting in the front row. "The time has come. They quit their jobs and join us—or else." His fist hammered the table. "The Association and their injunctions be damned!"

The crowd responded with the greatest din of the evening. Dozens of voices took up the beat, halooing their anger in support of the articulate spokesman who'd put his finger on the pulse of their resentment.

Rafe Tatro exploded to his feet. "Let's put the fear o' Christ in 'em!"

"The fear of the devil, I say," Smutt yelled.

Jim Tatro leaped from the bench, his pimply face as ugly as ever. "Let's castrate the devils!" He spit tobacco juice on the floor and wiped his mouth with the back of his coatsleeve. "These men are goddamned, lowlife sneak-thieves. If they don't have enough guts to take up for their own rights, they oughta hang."

Yammerings around the room grew in volume and became one voice in answer to the man who'd called their anger into being. Malone smiled as if he took delight in the din. His expression of triumph turned my stomach. This man of intelligence, this man of social and philosophical thought had become rabid. The crowd? Crazy.

The outrage I felt was almost more than I could stand. I lurched to my feet and shouted above the bedlam. "Look at you. You're a bunch of red-eyed monsters. You're no better than the operators who caused you to band together in the first place."

Della yanked at my skirt. "Sit down, Maggie, you're going to get into trouble."

I ignored her and wiped at sweat leaking onto my forehead. "The MOA brought men in from the East, knowing full well you'd mistreat them and it could put you in jail. Is that what you want?" My voice had a brittle, desperate sound.

Rafe Tatro blared in a slurred voice, "Si' down. We don't wanna listen to you. Go home to your dishes."

"Scab lover," Smutt croaked.

Others took up the cry.

Malone drummed on the table. "That's uncalled for. Miss O'Shea is a respected member of this community. She has a right to speak her mind."

More cat calls and hooting.

Malone waited for the noise to subside and went on. "I will ask you to hand over the notes you've been taking, Miss O'Shea. I wouldn't want you to write a report unfavorable to the union."

I clutched the notepad to my waist. "You have no right to interfere with the press."

"I'm just looking after the interests of the union." He nodded toward a rifle-bearing guard who stood near me. "Gus, get the writing pad." The man took a purposeful step toward me.

"I will not surrender my notes!"

Again, Della yanked at my skirts. "For God's sake, Maggie. Give it to them before you get hurt."

"Throw the snoop out," One miner yelled.

"Shouldn't be here in the first place," yauped another.

"Maybe she's one o' them Pinkerton spies." The comment ended in a guffaw.

Malone's sharp voice rose above the rest. "That's enough. Maggie is no Pinkerton. I just don't want her coloring the facts to suit herself."

"I don't color facts," I said as I struggled with the guard to keep my notepad. "The facts are colorful enough without any embellishment."

Despite my efforts, the guard tore the pad from my hands and was taking it to Malone when Tom O'Brien grabbed Hub's gavel and pounded the table. "Gus, return Miss O'Shea's notes to her and get back to your post. She's always been fair in her reporting. The union has no complaint against her." He waited for the guard to do as ordered and went on, "I'm ashamed to hear this kind o' talk in the brotherhood." His deep Irish voice shook with anger as he spoke.

"We're not here to insult people. Nor are we here to spill men's blood. We're here to find other means o' persuasion." He pointed a finger at Rafe. "You men who worked over Len Appleby went too far. From now on when you deal with non-union men, it must be done through the brotherhood. I'll have no more of this carnage."

Angry mutterings rose around the room.

"Go home and suck your thumb, O'Brien," Smutt yelled.

Malone drew the back of his hand across his mouth. His gaze was on the table as if he was caught in the dilemma of whether to support O'Brien or the miners of his local. He cleared his throat. "All respect to Tom, we need to be deciding for ourselves. What do you wish to be doing about these five men and any other non-union men that stay in camp? Do you want to pay some amongst yourselves to approach the scabs? Or do you want the services of the men the Central Union hired for such purposes?" He motioned toward the six men with rifles.

A shout came from the rear of the room. "I move we pay some of our own to send the scabs over the hill into Montana."

"I second it," Rafe bellowed.

"All in favor?" Malone said. A roar. "Opposed?" No dissenting voice. "So be it. I appoint Rafe Tatro, Smutt Corrigan, Phil Hanks, and George Smothers. Phil and George to see that Rafe and Smutt behave themselves."

I sat through the final moments of the meeting, fuming, wondering how I should word my report for the *Wallace Free Press.* Adam Aulbach was on the side of the union and always read my reports carefully. He often asked the source of my information, but seldom told me to change any aspect of my writing.

When the meeting was adjourned, the Tuttles stayed to speak with other merchants. I separated Jeff from his friends and pulled him through the noisy crowd. Behind us, the union hall thundered with the miners' heavy tread as they left for various destinations.

We hadn't gone far when we met Dan on his way home after a long day at the mine. He asked why all the miners were in town, and I explained. "You should've been at the meeting," Jeff said excitedly. "Maggie told them off."

Dan looked at me with raised eyebrows. "Told who off?"

I gave a brief account that ended in a "huh" of a laugh. "I might as well have been talking to the wind."

"Maybe, but you weren't afraid to say what you thought," Jeff said with pride in his voice. Then to Dan. "Maggie says sometimes it takes more grit to say what you think than to punch somebody in the jaw."

A quirky look crossed Dan's face as if he was considering the comment in light of his own impulsive nature. He smiled knowingly. "There's something in what she says."

From immediately behind came the sound of feet crunching cinders along the railroad tracks. We turned as Sil Crego caught up to us.

"How could you just sit there without saying anything?" I asked peevishly. "You could have given me a little support."

"There are times when a man can't account for his actions," Sil replied in a cold voice. "He shouldn't have to with a friend."

I thought calling me a friend was a stretch. I knew Sil only through occasional meetings when he was with Dan. I'd never felt comfortable with him. And most certainly would not have shared my home with him as Dan had, though I assumed Dan had done it as a matter of obligation to a drilling partner.

That thought was pushed aside as Rafe Tatro and a knot of lantern-bearing men lumbered past, shoving the five non-union men up the canyon. Smutt beat on a pan to announce their march.

"Makes me so damned mad," Dan muttered. "I've heard of this sort of thing happening in the East and in the Isles. I kept hoping we were above that."

"There's always some bad apples want to take over," Crego said. "And the madness of the pack lets them. Most of the miners wouldn't do anything seriously wrong on their own. But they're all steamed up. It takes only a few blood-thirsty howls for them to set their mouths for the kill." He paused to watch Rafe's crew stagger and bellow up the tracks, then looked back at Dan. "One thing's clear. Men like you and me had better look out. We might have to make a run for it."

CHAPTER 19

After that night at the citizens' meeting, I lived in constant dread that something terrible might happen to Dan. The Mine Owners Association served injunctions against the Central Union, claiming one-hundred-thirty members had interfered in the functions of the mines when they'd hazed non-union workers. Dan was spared an injunction. Evidently, the Pinkerton spies had reported his stand against violence.

Representing all the locals in the district, the Central Union quickly assembled in Wallace. Through Sil, Dan learned that union officials had hired Gabe "One-Eyed" Dallas from Butte, Montana to scent out the Pinkerton detectives who'd infiltrated the union and kill them. He also learned that guns and ammunition had arrived in the district and were waiting to be shouldered in the name of the union cause. Urgently aware he should leave Bixbee, Dan boarded up the Titan.

I walked around in a daze, hardly knowing what to do. I'd imagined the worst, and it had happened. What would I do if the battle continued? The uncertainty made me want to resign my teaching position and take my chances with Dan, wherever that might be. But as long as I remained in the canyon I'd chronicle events for the newspaper, hoping that an accurate account would lead the way to justice.

One evening, I sat at the kitchen table reviewing the notes I'd taken at the latest meeting. Beside my notepad lay a newspaper with headlines that told of a union riot in Homestead, Pennsylvania, where steel workers had trapped three hundred Pinkerton agents on a barge and killed several of them. Though I disapproved of the MOA's use of detectives, I didn't want the Pinkertons in the canyon to receive the same treatment. Our men had been on strike as long as the steelworkers. They might commit horrible crimes when they had nothing to do but take out their frustration. Especially when they felt betrayed.

It was past the usual suppertime, and I was waiting for the Tuttles to return before I added flour-paste to a pot of stew simmering on the stove. That afternoon, they'd left to attend a meeting in Gem, the tiny slapboard town located a mile down the tracks from Bixbee, the site of the Gem Mine and the Helena and Frisco mining properties owned by Esler, head of the Mine Owners Association.

"Something's brewing at Gem," Hank had said. "There's going to be a mass meeting there in a half-hour. Rumor has it that Gabe Dallas has tracked down the Pinkerton spies and is going to point them out. We don't want to miss that."

I'd felt obligated to attend the meeting and report to the *Wallace Free Press,* but an inexplicable premonition had compelled me to stay at the boarding house. I'd thought it based on a reluctance to expose Jeff to a meeting that promised to be worse than the last. I could have left him at home, but I knew his curiosity would lure him to the scene. Beyond that, I'd felt a strange need to be at home and had asked Della to take notes.

At the moment, Jeff was in the sitting room, playing a solo game of marbles. He'd started the game on the landing, but a cloudburst had drenched the canyon, the drops as loud as stones falling from the sky. They'd increased in intensity until it seemed the storm had dumped a sea of water onto the roof, wave after wave after wave. I'd closed the back door against the storm, but suddenly it opened and Dan rushed into the room, his face masked with fright. His clothes dripped from the storm and carried the herbal scent of wet shrubs he'd brushed against. He clasped my arms and pulled me from the chair. When he drew me close, I felt steam radiate from beneath his shirt and denims. His breath was warm in my hair. There was a tension in him, as if he was going to say something I might not want to hear, something that would change our lives forever.

He made a sound that was part moan, part sigh. "Maggie, darling, I don't want to leave without you."

Leave? Time seemed to stop in mid-second, the room a prison of rising heat and pounding anxiety. I pulled back to look into his eyes and saw a nervous mist on his brow. "What happened?"

He held a finger at his lips. "Shh, I don't want anyone to know I'm here."

"Nobody's here but Jeff."

"I don't want him to know, either." The rain had stopped, and Dan pulled me onto the stoop outside the kitchen, the eaves dripping water all around.

"Is Rafe after you?" I whispered.

"Not yet. But he will be soon." Dan's voice was hoarse, very distracted. "There was a mass meeting in Gem. They fingered Sil Crego as one of the Pinkerton spies."

"Oh, Lord, I always thought there was something suspect about that man. Didn't you?"

"Not until I caught him high-tailing it out of the shack a few minutes ago." Dan gave an exclamation of self-loathing. "I've been a stupe. When Sil sneaked out at night, I thought he was visiting some fast piece. Instead, he'd walk to Wallace and mail reports to the Pinkerton office in Minneapolis. They'd forward them to the MOA."

"He admitted all that?"

"After I threatened to knock his block off unless he told me what he'd been up to."

"You should've turned him in."

"I couldn't. Sil says the union thinks I conspired with him. They've hired professional gunmen to make sure he and the other Pinkertons don't give them the slip. They'll be gunning for me, too. They won't give me a chance to explain. They'll kill me on sight."

Fear paralyzed my spine as I pictured gunmen abroad in the night looking for Dan. "Did anyone follow you here?"

"Not that I know of."

From down the tracks came the sound of an avenging mob on the march. In the light shining through the kitchen window, Dan's face had the look of kiln-dried clay. "I can't stay any longer. They may search for me here."

I clutched Dan's arms to keep him from leaving. "Take me with you."

He shook his head in a despairing way. "Not now. It wouldn't be safe."

"Where are you going?" I uttered the words in tone of complete hopelessness.

"To Canada. I'll write when it's safe." For a brief second he clamped his jaw tight, as if to keep from blurting things that could change his mind. Then he said simply, "Just know that I love you. Nothing will change that."

"And I love you." My eyes gave no message of hope, but I squeezed his hand to let him know I'd be waiting for his return.

He darted a look down at the tracks, then took a slim leather pouch from his coat pocket and handed it to me. "Aaron and I are equal partners in the mine. I've signed my half over to you. Hide these papers where they won't be found. I figure if anything happens to me, you'll have something to help with Jeff's expenses. I've written instructions inside. "

My stomach cramped. I started to cry. "Don't say that. It sounds too ominous."

He lifted my chin and wiped away the tears. "I'll be all right. Remember, I love you." He kissed me gently on the lips, pulled his arms from my grip and disappeared into the silent, rain-soaked brush of the hillside.

In the street, the voices grew louder. Soon boots clumped on the long flight of stairs. I rushed into the sitting room, sat in the rocker, and stuffed Dan's pouch into my sewing basket. To appear as if nothing had happened, I took out a sock and darning ball and began to mend. I hoped I didn't look as frightened as I felt.

Evidently I did, because Jeff looked up from his marbles with a quirky expression. "What's wrong with you? Did you see a spook?"

Before I could fake an answer, someone pounded on the door. "Crego! Rigby! You sonofabitches in there?" The door shook beneath the pounding fist.

I steeled myself and went to open the door, my nerves as taught as mattress springs.

CHAPTER 20

I opened the door a crack and was met by the smell of kerosene from several lanterns that shone, hissing behind Rafe Tatro's bulky silhouette. A voice of rage growled from deep within his beard. "Is Rigby here?"

"No-no," I stammered. "Why would he be here?"

"You're his girl ain't you?"

I didn't answer, just fished for a lie. "He must be at the meeting in Gem. Della and Hank are there."

A look of suspicion shot from beneath Rafe's heavy brows. "He wasn't at the meeting. Why ain't you there? You're usually out snooping."

"I thought there might be violence. I wanted to make sure Jeff didn't—"

"I think you're lying! I think you stayed here to help Rigby escape."

I feigned innocence. "Escape? Why would he want to escape? Why are you after him?"

"We think he's been in cahoots with that Crego."

"What do you mean, 'in cahoots?'"

"We found out that Crego's a Pinkerton spy. We think Dan's been helping him."

"Dan wouldn't do that," I said with true outrage.

"Shuddup! I don't wanna hear your screechy voice." Rafe slammed the door back on its hinges and stood on my newly braided rug in his filthy boots, the barrel of his rifle at my chest. His watery, blue-gray eyes were red from too much whiskey and he smelled of it. He motioned his son Jim and several other rifle-bearing men inside and shouted orders. "You blokes check every room. I'll stay here and see that these two stay put."

"They can't go into the other rooms," I cried. "They're private."

"We'll go where we wanna go."

Rafe shoved me into the rocker with such force I groaned in pain, then he grunted into a chair by the door. Across from me on the settee, Jeff eyed Rafe with a look of spite that matched the hate in my soul. In the rest of the house, doors opened and boots rapped on the floors of each room. Doors to clothes cupboards creaked open. A shoe hit the floor. Rafe took a flask from his vest pocket and drank. After what seemed an eon, the motley crew scuffed into the sitting room.

I ventured a word of defiance. "I told you he wasn't here."

Rafe curled his lips into a sneer. "That don't mean he won't come. When he does, we'll string him up alongside Crego." Rafe hauled himself to his feet, belched, and said in a mocking tone, "Did you ever see a hanging? I have." He used the tip of his rifle to trace an arc across my neck. "I seen the poor slob's eyes bug out at the pull of the rope. Seen his face turn blue. Seen his blind eyes staring at the buzzards. All that'll be left o' your lover boy will be a raggy bunch o' bones."

I clutched my throat, the feel of the rifle translating to that of a rope. My mouth was dry, my palms damp. My heart pounded against my ribs, fearful, angry.

Rafe removed the rifle and blinked, as if trying to force his drunken senses to work. With a sudden resolve, he arched a brow at each man in the room and finally settled his wavering glare on his son. "Jim, you and Phil stay here in case Rigby shows up. The rest of us will go after Crego."

Jim's mouth dropped open slightly, revealing a wad of tobacco between lip and gum. "Hell, Pa, I wanna be there when you run onto Crego."

"You heard me!"

Jim slumped onto the chair Rafe had vacated, his face sullen. The burly, squinty-eyed miner named Phil nudged Jeff over and sat beside him on the settee. A pile of bedding lying on the floor beside the settee became a nest for his rifle.

I went rigid at the thought of being left alone with such renegades. Rafe seemed to notice and shot me a wicked smile. "Might as well relax, Miss O'Shea. It's going to be a long night."

●●●

To avoid watching the two louts across from me, I sat darning, my back and neck stiff as a board, my thoughts leaping from one dire imagining to the next like monkeys trying to outdistance each other. I blamed the district for bringing this to pass. Blamed Malone. Blamed Sil. Blamed myself for keeping Dan from going to Canada when he'd first mentioned the possibility. Now he might die at the end of a rope. My eyes leaked tears. My mouth trembled.

Jim and Phil had damped their lanterns and sat at the edge of the yellow light cast by the ceiling lamp, Jim's amber eyes staring at me from the shadows in a sinister, scornful way. Now and then he leaned sideways to use the cuspidor beside his chair, then continued to chew the wad in his mouth. I thought it ironic that the boy who'd caused so many hours of misery at school now held me prisoner. What a perversion of justice.

Phil was a big man who'd let indulgence purple his face and sink his reddened eyes into pockets of flesh. In the mix of light and shadow, his expression bordered on the depraved. He was the filthiest man in Rafe's crew, all hair, beard, and eyebrows as bristly as wire, Tufts of hair sprouted from his ears, giving him the appearance of a lynx, but at the moment, he seemed a toad with no good intentions.

Both men smelled like they'd bathed in whiskey. I wanted to close the window against the after-storm chill, but that would worsen the stench. Brazen from the flasks they held in their laps, they made lewd remarks about me and taunted Jeff. I pretended to ignore them and drove the needle in and out of holes in the sock with a vengeance. When Jeff reacted to their jibes, I told him to hush, explaining that they wanted him to do something untoward so they could harm him. I was certain they'd welcom any suspicious move on our part as a chance to get rough.

Through the men's odor of whiskey, I caught the spicy aroma of the stew I'd left on the stove and realized my stomach was gnawing at its linings. I wanted to stir the vegetables before they stuck to the pot, but that might prompt the men to ask for a portion. As far as I was concerned, they could go hungry. Likely the fire had dwindled to nothing, anyway. I could resurrect supper when the Tuttles returned. I couldn't imagine why they hadn't come.

The aroma of the stew had attracted a few blowflies. One had trapped itself behind the roller blind on the window and buzzed against the screen like a bumblebee. Another circled my head in an irritating way. When not swatting flies, the men would slump forward for brief seconds, eyes closed in drunken half-sleep. I'd tense and lean forward slightly, hoping I could steal into Hank's room for the Enfield rifle he kept hidden under the foot of his mattress. But each time, one of them would rouse with a start, blink, shift on his chair, and yawn.

When I needed a rest from the darning, I avoided the men's baleful stares by reading the insulating newspapers Della had used to paper the walls. Since I'd moved in, I'd hung wallpaper with a faint tan and gold design on two of the walls and was waiting for Hank to order another roll. Now, to pass the time and keep from worrying about Dan, I read advertisements I hadn't noticed before—ads for elixirs guaranteeing long life, for corsets, cough syrup, for cemetery plots, for schedules of trains leaving the district. A crack in a ceiling board had the outline of a child's toy gun, a reminder of Hank's rifle. It was of no help with Jim and Phil on guard.

Sometimes Jeff and I would stare at each other for long moments, our eyes speaking of a terrible dread. Afraid of what the night might bring, I studied him intently to etch his features in my mind. He still possessed the round babyish face, the large thoughtful gray eyes, and the straight chestnut hair of three years earlier. But now he was taller than my five-feet-three, long-legged and short of trunk, ridiculously out of proportion like most boys of twelve.

Thus, the minutes dragged by, the half-hours, the hours, until dawn washed the black of night from the window. Not until then did I close my eyes, my head full of nightmares. When the door banged against the wall, my eyelids shot open onto the sight of Rafe Tatro and his slubberdegullion escort of nine clumping unsteadily into the room. In addition to the Winchester that dangled from Rafe's hand, a revolver was tucked into the band of his trousers, and a knife protruded from the top of his boot. His chest worked in and out like a bellows beneath his greasy vest, as if he'd been running or climbing the hills.

As he stepped toward me, his breath hit me full in the face, carrying with it the imagined smell of sulfur and brimstone mixed with the real odor of sour whiskey. "Did you get your beauty sleep?" he asked with a hideous grin. He reached out to touch my cheek.

I lurched to my feet, my heartbeat pounding in my chest. I wanted to slap him. For Jeff's safety I didn't. Instead, I asked worriedly, "Did you find Dan?"

"No. Thanks to you. Crego neither. If 'twas up to me, I'd hang 'em both the minute we find 'em, but Malone said he'd snug *my* neck with a rope if I didn't bring 'em in to stand trial. Makes me wonder whose side Hub's on."

"If Hub doesn't hang you, the law will," I said between clenched teeth.

Rafe grimaced and pulled back his hand to strike me. To his credit, he let the hand drop slowly, but the menacing look remained. "Better not sass me, Miss O'Shea. After what's gonna happen today, your man don't stand no more chance than milking a he-goat into a sieve."

Phil Hanks gave a vulgar laugh. "Rigby's gonna miss this little redhead o' his. Now I can have her all to meself. I can see how she sleeps a man."

An image of that foul bear of a man between my sheets leaped alive in my mind and loomed in all its nakedness before my startled eyes. Jeff must have had a similar vision. He lunged across the settee and pounded on Phil's chest. "Don't talk like that about Maggie. Say you're sorry, or I'll punch you in the nose."

With a swipe of his arm, Phil shoved Jeff onto the floor, then hauled himself to his feet and stood over the boy wagging a knife at his throat. "Better behave or you won't be around when I come courting."

"I'll kill you first!" Jeff wrapped his fingers around Phil's knife hand and tried to push against it. Phil hovered over him, the tip of the knife nicking blood from Jeff's neck.

"Stop it!" I lunged at Phil, but Rafe caught me by the shoulder and threw me onto the rocker. "Pick on somebody your own size," Rafe said to Phil as he pulled him backward. "We ain't after kids." He belched, swayed a bit, and added, "Don't let me catch you touching Maggie. She's a good—"

"What's going on?" It was Hub Malone's piercing voice. He and another man had entered the house, letting in a draft that cooled the anger on my cheeks. He worked his way through the men slouched around the room, ducking his head to avoid the lamp. He must have been up all night—gray puffs hung like brooding storm clouds beneath his eyes. He glanced around at the other men, then settled his angry stare on Rafe. "You better not be harming this young lady!"

Rafe met Hub's glare with a sulky, wavering stare of his own. Two willful men. At the moment Hub had the advantage due to the fact he was sober. Rafe seemed to scour his sluggish brain for an argument, finally came out with, "Whyn't we hold 'er hostage? Maybe Dan'll come out o' hiding to save 'er hide."

I waited in terrified silence. If they took me hostage, Hub would send word by way of the invisible network that kept miners abreast of events in mining districts throughout the West, likely in Canada too. Dan would return as soon as he learned of my capture, whether in days or weeks. I hugged myself against a fearful chill that had settled in my bones.

Malone seemed to consider the proposal, rubbing the nose that cut the plane of his face like a spearhead. When he spoke next, his voice sliced like a sharpened steel. "Wipe your nose, Rafe, your brains be leaking. We're willing to stand and fight, but we aren't going to use women for bait." Static electricity seemed to snap the air between the two men, a friction common between men like Rafe Tatro, who twisted the ideals of others to suit his own ends, and men like Malone, whose intelligence and zeal made use of the Rafe Tatros of the world. Malone shot Rafe an annihilating glance and motioned toward the door. "Take the rest o' these blokes and get some coffee. We'll be needing you sober for what's ahead." He nodded at the man who'd come with him. "Joe, go with them and see that they do what I ask."

Malone went to the door to watch the grumbling men tramp down the stairs, then turned back into the room, the disapproval of what he'd seen reflected in his face. He fixed his embalmer's eyes on me. "I'm sorry if those men have done anything to offend you. It wasn't at my orders."

Despite the apology, outrage heated my blood. "You're as much to blame as those men for what's happening to me and everyone else on the creek. If anyone hangs, it should be you."

For an instant we glared as enemies, then Hub turned aside, his shoulders raised as if he was holding his breath. When he turned back, several reactions flickered across his face—anger, sadness, and something else that was not easy to read, a sense of tragedy or foreboding. He put his hand on my shoulder. I jerked it away as if I was shrugging off an insect. Hub smiled cryptically then said in a measured way, "I'll ignore what you've said because of who you are and what you mean to a man I've admired. What's happening may run against your current, but your life is on the line. Despair breeds rage and a hunger to retaliate against the lack of justice. If I were you, I'd hold my tongue from now on. Right now men are ready to kill at the slightest insult."

I tried to think of a suitable reply, but nothing could express my dread and disgust. Giving up on that I said, "I'm worried about the Tuttles. Have you seen them?"

"Della's at the union hall in Gem cooking for the men gathered there. Hank's been rounding up groceries. You need to stay here and keep the boy with you. As I said, I won't vouch for anybody's safety."

CHAPTER 21

The night had frazzled Jeff's nerves to the point of exhaustion, and after the men left, he slept so soundly that a thunderstorm didn't waken him. Wanting him to sleep, I straightened covers that had rumpled onto the floor below the settee and started down the long stairway that led to the railroad tracks.

Below me, the morning sun sulked down on scores of miners who'd begun to converge on the town like armies of ants, many of the men from Burke. They wore knives tucked in their belts, holstered handguns, and carried Winchester rifles sent by the union in Butte, Montana. A terrible droning rose into the hot, still air, the low-pitched growl of the wolf pack. Some of the miners stomped mud from their boots and entered the union hall. Others continued down the tracks toward the town of Gem.

Half-a-dozen miners stood at the entrance to the union hall, their heads together in agitated conversation. I heard them speak of a union man who'd been shot at Gem when he'd attempted to cross the Frisco Mine's scab line to visit friends. And they spoke of Pinkerton detectives who'd disappeared. There was speculation about Dan's part in one detective's escape. From the tone of their voices, I could tell that the brotherhood's rage had grown overnight. If caught, Dan would have a hard time convincing them of his innocence on the spying charge.

Most of the chatter centered around the proposed union attacks against the mine operators—one attack on the Apex, another on the mining properties at Gem, and a third on John Hammond's Bunker Hill at Wardner located several miles west of Wallace on the Coeur d'Alene River. The operators were to be given a choice of sending their non-union miners from the district or seeing their mills blown to bits.

I felt a strange lapse of reality, as if living a dream or of being transported back in time to the days of the American Revolution, privy to the militia's plan to attack the British garrison. Certainly, the expression on those soldiers would have been as full of anger and revenge as the grim faces of these miners.

A loud voice prodded me back to the present. "We don't want no snooping reporter in here," said one of the six men. "Go home."

The cautious part of my nature said I should heed the advice. The other part resented the insult. "I'm not snooping. I need to speak to Hub Malone."

"I told you to go home!" The man seized my arm and tried to turn me.

"Take your hands off her, Bud," said another miner. "We have no quarrel with her."

Grumbling, the first miner loosened his grip and allowed me to push my way into the hall, then past men standing in the aisle between benches. Other men sat, gabbling loud as a flock of turkeys, their rifles reflecting a strip of sunlight that filtered through a pall of cigar and cigarette smoke.

Hub Malone sat with other union officials at the officers' table, where flattened grocery bags served as platters for slices of bread, bologna, and pickles. Bottles of beer stood here and there. Malone looked up as I approached the table. His expression said I was intruding. "What do you want, Miss O'Shea?" His steely voice cut through the loud talk and laughter. "We haven't found Dan, if that's what you want to know. And I'm not giving a statement to the newspaper."

I ignored the lack of welcome and stepped toward the table. "I'm not here for either of those reasons. Della Tuttle and I are worried about the safety of the women and children. We'd like to offer the boarding house as a refuge. There'll be food and places to sleep. We'd appreciate it if you'd send someone around with that message."

Malone pondered the request a long while, pulling on the tip of his black handlebar mustache, breaking his deliberation with sighs that signified gravity of thought. I had no inkling what thoughts lurked behind the dark, appraising look he'd fixed on me, but I was certain they were critical.

"I don't like you barging in here like this," he said at last. "But I appreciate your concern. We men tend to forget our obligation to the families. I'll send a man around with the message." He pointed toward the door. "Now, you'd best be leaving. And don't come back." I started to leave, but he added, "If you hear from Dan, tell him he'd best show his face. We'll listen to what he has to say about the Crego thing. We'll be fair. If he doesn't come back, I'll have him barred from the district."

● ● ●

Hub Malone's warning hung in my mind as I stood on the stairs that led to the remodeled second floor of the boarding house. Below me, in the

Tuttle's new sitting room, women and children had gathered in a state of worried confusion. Hub had sent a messenger to the few wives left on the creek and they'd fled their homes with their young ones. A few women from Gem crowded in along with those from Bixbee. Others walked up-canyon to find safety with friends in the town of Burke.

Della greeted the women with a broad smile and bellowed instructions. "You gals take your things upstairs. There's plenty of room for the grownups. The kids can bed down on the floor. And, Maggie," she yelled up at me, "while I'm getting these folks settled, you can peel a couple o' dozen potatoes. There's a few carrots, too, and onions. We'll make a big pot o' potato soup and biscuits. I think there's plenty o' canned milk in the pantry."

The kitchen stifled from the July sun beating in through the south window. Ivy on the shelf above the window had begun to wilt, and sunlight that lay in a pool on the table's blue-checkered oilcloth made it smell of oil. The room would be even hotter when I built a fire in the stove. Despite the heat, I was thankful for something to keep my hands busy. Still, nothing could pry my thoughts from Dan. I was afraid to tell anyone where he'd gone for fear they'd think him a traitor, and I had to suffer the worry alone.

After supper, we gathered on the new porch that ran the length of the boarding house and watched the ominous movement of men and arms down the canyon. We pretended bravery as we spoke of the impending battle, but a subdued, tremulous quality invaded our voices. Even Hester Reap's tongue had lost its acid and Della's trumpeting its blare. As sure as we knew the ingredients of soup from its aroma, on this day we smelled death in the pot.

Hank went to Gem to check on happenings there and returned after night had fallen warm and still. He reported that the union had entrenched itself on the dark hillsides surrounding the Gem and Frisco mining properties. It would wait until morning to dynamite the Frisco mill, then move up to the Apex.

The women retired to their beds so the children would sleep, but I was too upset. Wrapped in a blanket, I sat on the landing outside my apartment and watched a full moon rise above the steep ridge behind the Apex mill. Along the crest, stars winked among the black silhouettes of trees like lanterns wandering the night. At the foot of the slope, the mill reflected the light of the moon. Except for the recurrent ta-hoo of an owl, not a sound could be heard, not a light seen. The rows of darkened shops and houses seemed as empty of life as graves in a cemetery. The only movement was that of cloud shadows rippling across the hillsides, but wind currents that sent clouds sailing across the face of the moon brought no breath of air to the canyon.

Around two in the morning, my sluggish mind awoke to the fact that the union had changed its plan—or perhaps the plan as reported to Hank was meant to deceive spies that remained on the creek. In any event, from my vantage point on the hill, I was able to see scores of shadowy warriors skulk along the railroad tracks, then hide behind stumps, small second growth timber, and outcroppings of rock on the hillsides back of town. Some hid on the Apex property across the creek. Because there was no wind, their movements were a tremor on the air rather than an audible sound. As I strained to hear, an eerie feeling vibrated along the cords of my senses.

When the first light washed across the eastern sky, shots erupted from the hillside above the whores' cribs. Dirt spit from the ground in front of a barricade where replacement guards were relieving the Apex night guards. The guards returned the fire. A scream told of a union man wounded or dead on the hillside.

A second burst of union rifle fire tore into the barricade. There were shouts and an anguished cry from one of the guards. At the same time, distant gunfire broke out at Gem. Before my eyes, men were killing one another over jobs. It seemed the whole lot of them had gone mad, and I was witness to the lunacy.

The gunfire brought startled women and children onto the porch, throwing coats and shawls over their nightclothes. Hank yawned onto the porch to watch the battle.

Jeff sat cross-legged on the floor beside my chair, sleepy-eyed. "What's going on?" he asked in a frightened, half-drowsy voice. I told him what I'd seen. "Is it safe up here?"

I put my arm across his shoulders and pulled him close. "If the fighting gets too near, we'll go inside."

Jeff seemed to think about that, his wide eyes intent on the battle at the edge of town. "Aren't you glad Dan's not here," he said after a bit. "He could've been out there getting shot at."

I'd been so rapt on the warfare I hadn't related it to Dan. Jeff's comment jarred me at the same time it offered relief. "I'm glad there's *something* to be thankful for."

Across the narrow canyon, a tram engine at the top of the mill began a loud rattle and clank. It revved several times, then wound down to a steady grinding hum that started ore cars on the tram crawling over the ridge to a mine portal beyond sight. Men who'd hidden themselves on the slope fired at cars riding the tram, as if they held persons making an escape. When the cars climbed out of view, the men hurried over the ridge in pursuit.

Meanwhile, men who'd seized the portal directly above the mill worked feverishly around an ore car sitting on a track that led down to the mill. Next instant, the car moved down the track, slowly at first, then gained momentum, wheels squealing. It rolled faster and faster until it rammed the mill in a blinding flash of light that shook the ground and sent a pulsating roar rolling up and down the canyon. The mill rose into the air as if launched into flight, stayed suspended a brief second, then collapsed in a heap of rubble. Debris rained onto the railroad siding and onto piles of cordwood used in the mine and mill. The smell of dynamite and potassium cyanide used in the milling process stenched the air.

The barrage of gunfire stopped and men rushed from concealment, yelling, whistling, and waving their rifles. Some slid down the hill back of town onto the tracks. Others ran down the slopes that flanked the mill. Several men prowled the row of houses on the far side of the creek, those belonging to Harley Hanson, the supervisors, and engineers. No one came from inside the houses. Apparently, Sil Crego had warned the occupants and they'd left the canyon.

The blast had hammered my bones and slammed into my eardrums. I was swallowing at my deafness when several guards walked from behind the barricade at the Apex bridge, the man in the lead carrying a white flag. Union men wove their way through the shredded lumber and twisted metal, took the guards prisoner and searched the barricade. They'd begun to carry out men on makeshift stretchers when a thundering blast in the vicinity of Gem caused them to stop and give a wild cheer.

The second crime against all that was rational made outrage surge from my toes to the roots of my hair, made the veins in my neck throb, and drove me into the house. My first stop was the kitchen cupboard where Della kept medicinal supplies. I gathered what I thought I'd need, then hurried to the storage closet for sheets we used as rags. They'd make good bandages.

When I walked onto the porch with an armload of supplies, Della piped suspiciously, "Where are you going?"

"To tend the wounded."

Suspicion faded to a grunt of support. "Good idea. Hold on, I'll go with you." Then to the other women, "Any of you gals want to come along?" Women stirred from their chairs and gave children instructions to go into the house, prompting one last order from Della. "Hank, you stay here, and watch the kids."

"Aww Della, come on. What do I know about taking care of kids?"

"It's time you learned. Jeff and the older kids can help. Just see that they stay here where they won't get hurt."

CHAPTER 22

I spent two hours at the union hall with Della and the other women, helping Dr. Pettit treat the wounded guards and union men. Most of them had been wounded by rifle fire, their arms, legs, and heads wrapped with blood-soaked bandages. When we returned to the boarding house, Hank went to Gem to check on happenings there. He reported back, saying the Frisco mill was in the same condition as the Apex, that the union had taken the guards prisoner, and that both union and non-union men had died in the battle preceding the blast. He'd learned that a host of miners planned to steal a railroad car in Wallace and coast seventeen miles down the tracks to Wardner, hoping to dynamite the Bunker Hill's concentrator before government troops arrived to squelch the uprising.

As Hank spoke, it dawned on me that I'd forgotten my duty as a reporter. "I should get this information to the *Free Press.*"

"No need," Hank said. "Aulbach sent a reporter up from Wallace. Guess he was afraid you wouldn't be able to leave the canyon. Anyway, the guy's going to check with you before he goes back to Wallace. I told him you'd be here at the boarding house."

With the mood of rebellion running wild, and unrestrained drinking going on up and down the canyon, Hank warned me and the other women to stay at the boarding house. Then he left for the local union hall to keep abreast of events. Heeding his advice, we pretended a deceptive calm while we baked huge batches of bread, cake, pies, and cookies for the return of hungry men. When the worry became more than we could bear, we'd descend the stairs as far as the boardwalk and beg news from men making their way back to Bixbee and Burke after taking part in the hostilities at Gem. The union volcano still rumbled beneath us, threatening further destruction, and the women were afraid to return to their homes until their men had dynamited the mill at Wardner and returned to their beds.

When lamplight flared along the walk and in the windows of the union hall, Della herded the guests inside for tea and cookies, but I sat on the porch, a shawl drawn around my shoulders against the evening damp, and waited for Hank to return. My eyes wandered in and out of focus from lack of sleep. My head throbbed. Thankfully, the reporter had come and gone before I'd reached that state of mental torpor.

Jeff brought me a cup of tea and sat beside me on a stool he favored when he wanted to whittle on a stick. I'd failed to convince him that he needed to wear a shirt, and in the light shining through the window, I saw that his nut-brown skin was covered with goose-bumps. He was even quieter than usual, likely sorting through recent events. Like my brother, Lennie, he retreated within himself when something caused him distress. He could wander through hours at a time completely absorbed in his thoughts, seeing nothing, knowing nothing of what was going on. Though on this night, he was acutely aware of the day's turmoil.

He sat a long while, squinting at the stick he was whittling, before he said without preamble, "What'll we do if they've found Dan and killed him?"

A chill crept over me as I dredged up a reply to his question. It must have pained him to ask. He'd grown to love Dan and craved the attention Dan offered so willingly. I put my hand on his head and traced the shape of his skull in a soothing way. "I'm sure he's alive. He'll send word to us soon." The words were meant to reassure, but my anxiety had crept into them and made them sound hollow.

Jeff pulled a harmonica from the pocket of his jeans and turned it over and over in his hands, possibly recalling it was a birthday gift from Dan. "I hate this fighting," he said glumly. "I wish my mom would come and take me away." Slowly, thoughtfully, he put the instrument to his lips, wheezed a chord or two, then eased into a melancholy tune. I knew the words to the song and they added to my heartbreak.

> Oh, my darling, oh my darling,
> Oh, my darling Clementine,
> You are lost and gone forever,
> Dreadful sorry, Clementine.

I wanted to ask Jeff to play a happier tune, but in my somber mood I could think of none appropriate for the evening.

From beyond the musical lament, rose the chuffing of Haggarty's engine. I wondered what the ore train was doing on the track. Surely, there'd be no run today. Below me, Hank panted up the stairs, having returned from his vigil at the union hall. He accepted my invitation to sit and told of the march on the Bunker Hill and of the wounded miners Haggarty would take from Canyon Creek to the hospital in Wallace. I wanted to ask if he'd learned anything about Dan, but feared the answer.

He paused to draw on a fresh cigar, then searched my face with speculation, as if he sensed the question on my mind. "Got good news for you—or bad, whichever way you want to look at it. Nobody seems to know anything about Dan. Guess he got away." He blew a ring of smoke into the night air, then said in a sad, reflective tone. "Likely we won't know until this trouble blows over and he comes back to town."

He comes back? What if he never returned? How would I know if he lived? A terrible foreboding clawed at my insides and left me a hollow shell.

Frantic shouts at the foot of the stairs dragged me from my brooding. I recognized Einar Reap's voice. I'd thought he was in the house with the rest of the youngsters. Evidently, he'd slipped away to spy on union activities, as he sometimes did with Jeff. Curiosity seemed to rule their behavior.

"Miss O'Shea! Miss O'Shea!" Einar yelled as he bounded up the stairs.

I rose to meet him. "Einar, whatever is the matter?"

The boy gasped for breath. "The school's on fire. I saw Tom Tatro run out the gate."

I gave a distracted cry. "Why tonight of all nights?"

"That bastard! He thought nobody'd be around to put it out." Hank snatched the cigar from his mouth and shouted orders. "Einar, you and Jeff come with me. We'll get some help with the fire cart. Jeff, you can ring the alarm bell. Not that it'll do much good with all the men gone." Then to me, "Maggie, tell the women to tote buckets and gunny sacks down to the school. The pump's far enough from the building you oughta be able to reach it without getting burned. If not, make a chain of women and pass buckets of water up from the creek."

When I arrived at the school, I stopped dead in my tracks from horror. The rear of the school was a sheet of flames and the mine tailings that formed the playground glowed orange from fire that danced against the night sky. Seized by a temporary panic, I dashed around the yard, my mind in too much of a whirl to settle on a course of action, but Della quickly sized-up the situation.

"You gals quit milling around like you been sent for and couldn't come," she blared above the snap and roar of the fire. "Bring them buckets and sacks to the pump." Operating the pump handle with one hand, directing the women with the other, she sent this woman here, that one there, wherever flames threatened to engulf a different section of the building. The older children worked in pairs using wet sacks to smother flaming grass and weeds at the base of the hill—the small children had been left at the boardinghouse with one of the mothers.

I worked like a mechanical toy, dousing water on the flames wherever I could without getting singed, ducking sparks that exploded like fireworks and floated upward on columns of heat. The smoke-filled air had the feel of a torch against my cheeks. I had to gasp for breath. My eyes smarted. My ears rang from the roar of the fire. My soggy dress steamed.

Worse than the physical discomfort was the sight of those insatiable flames gorging themselves at my expense, gobbling hundreds of hours of effort. All because of that damnable fiend! Hatred for Tom Tatro swelled within me until I wanted to scream. How dare he? How dare the Tatros bring so much misery into my life?

Hank, Jeff, Einar, two teenage boys, and a few shopkeepers had arrived and added their excited voices to the din. They set a portable pump near the creek, put their shoulders to the harness of a hose cart, and pulled it up a short incline into the schoolyard. By the time they'd put the hose to work, the back half of the building had become a furnace with no hope for containment. The only option was to concentrate the spray on the front of the building, which they did until heat seared their hands and faces, then they backed away, taking women and children with them. All they could do was drench the surrounding trees and brush to keep the flames from spreading onto the hillsides. Even then, the needles on fir trees at the rear of the school wilted and burst into flame.

Within minutes the entire building became a raging hell that generated its own gale-force winds. The walls crashed in upon themselves, spewing showers of white-hot embers into the ashen sky. Kindled by a splash of fire, the bell-post flamed like a torch and disintegrated into a heap of livid coals. The bell clanged to the ground, sounding the death knell for the Bixbee School.

CHAPTER 23

Rain had pounded the canyon during the night, and the black scar that had been the schoolhouse reeked of wet ash. The odor seemed as foul as the act of arson itself. Sickened by the sight and smell, I turned my back on the ruins and rocked myself in a rope swing at the edge of the schoolyard, the skirts of my blue gingham tucked beneath me to keep them from touching the ashes. The gnats were terrible that day. Tiny black things that bit into my scalp, neck, and ears. I slapped at them with the Spokane paper Hank had rustled from somewhere, then opened it to read the headlines blazoned across the front page—*UNION TAKES OVER BUNKER HILL WITHOUT VIOLENCE—MINERS LAY SEIGE TO SHOSHONE COUNTY— GOVERNOR DECLARES MARTIAL LAW—ONE THOUSAND GOVERNMENT TROOPS ON THE WAY.*

Old news. I'd already seen two companies of troops file through Bixbee on their way to Burke. Another company, unable to find space to cluster its barracks tents, was stringing them along the railroad right of way within sight of the school-grounds. Townspeople had gathered in the glaring sun to jeer their efforts and pelt them with questions.

No union miners were there to watch the tent-raising. I'd heard rumors that they'd all been arrested except miners who'd managed to slip over the border into Montana. What an ugly affair. Like a real war, even to the soldiers. So great had been the shock, my inner senses still listened for the report of rifles. Even without further exchange of bullets, the battle had changed the course of life in the canyon. Why had it come to this? Why couldn't I have gone on living in a predictable way? But no, the world had come tumbling down around my shoulders, and there was nothing I could do about it.

These were my thoughts when I saw Maude Tatro shamble down the tracks past the soldiers and onto the playground. She hadn't taken refuge at the boarding house with the other women, and until the night of the fire I'd thought she might have left the district. I'd put that idea to rest when Tom was seen running from the schoolyard. I wondered how Maude would deal with Tom and with the fact that Rafe, Jim, and others linked directly to the bombings and the abuse of non-union miners would be put in prison. I'd expected to feel a sense of relief at the news of Rafe's and Jim's capture. But the fear still lurked at my elbow—they'd be released someday. Just thinking about them made my skin crawl. One part of me argued that the Tatros had been thorns in my side too long to feel sorry for Maude. The other half considered the heartache she must have endured as Rafe's wife. In the end, sympathy for Maude won, and I smiled as she approached the swing.

She looked in poor health, as barefoot as the grimy toddlers she dragged at her sides. Her face seemed all eyes and there was little to her inside her shabby calico, much like a broom dressed to scare crows. She lowered herself onto a swing beside mine and pulled one of the runny-nosed toddlers onto her lap. The other child whined to be lifted onto the swing, and soon both were in Maude's gaunt lap. The hands she held on the little girls' bellies were red and swollen, with large black cracks at the corners of the fingernails.

"How are you Maude?" I asked with true compassion. "These last few weeks must have been hard on you." An understatement.

"Tolerable, I guess. Cain't do nothing 'bout it anyways." She seemed steeped to the hairline in misery.

"Have you had enough to eat?"

She shrugged in a doubtful way. "Enough to get by. The state soldiers is divvying up the goods at the union store, and we'll be getting our share. I'm not counting on much. Them militia generals ain't here to play Santy Claus. Their boys have nothing to eat but coffee and hardtack. Likely they'll help theirselves to most o' the supplies."

I twisted the ropes on the swing so I could face Maude squarely and said with suppressed doubts, "Have hope. We have to trust them to do the right thing."

"Don't have to trust 'em at all. Rafe says they ain't nothing but the mine owners' tin soldiers. They'll do anything them kingpins tell 'em to do." She set one squirmy child on the ground, then wiped the other's nose with a wadded handkerchief.

When she'd moved that child to the center of her lap, I said, "It sounds like you've seen Rafe."

"I visited him to Wallace this morning . . . took some poultice for where he got shot."

"Is it a bad wound?"

"Could be worse. It's his shoulder."

I thought of the brutal injuries Rafe had inflicted on the innocent and thought it just retribution. "Will he and Jim be free soon?" For my sake, I hoped the answer would be negative.

Maude dropped her gaze to her folded hands and rubbed a thumb over veins that stood above the reddened skin like rivers of ink. Her face showed no emotion. "The sheriff's taking the both of 'em to Boise to stand trial. Hub Malone and the other officials, too. Rafe says they could get two years in jail."

"How will you manage without them?"

Maude stared at the ground and ran her teeth over her lower lip in thought. When she spoke, her reply wandered, as if she were talking in the lapse of illness. "It don't make no never mind. Rafe don't help me none. Jim neither. More trouble'n they're worth. I'm glad to see 'em gone. As for making out, soon's the union gets in some money they'll gimme help, and I'll take my crew back to Kentuck."

"You have folks there?"

"Yep, and I'm real wanting to see them. Even if Rafe don't get sent to jail, it won't do him no good to try for work here. I hear tell the mine owners got a blacklist. If a man's name's on it he won't get hired." A sudden boldness brightened Maude's eyes, as if an ember of the real Maude had sprung into flame. "Iff'n he wants me and the kids he'll have to come begging on his knees and promise to do better by us."

I swelled with pride for Maude. She'd been batted around and used for a brood sow too long. It was time she spoke out against her husband. "If there's anything I can do to help, let me know. Food . . . packing . . . taking care of the children . . . whatever."

"'Tain't much to pack. But I sure thank you for the offer. I'm surprised you wanting to help after what Tom did to the school. I come to tell you how purely sorry I am." Remorse made Maude's voice sound like a rusty hinge.

"I don't—that is—we have no way of knowing he did it for certain," I stammered.

"You don't need to pretend. Not for my sake. I been 'shamed o' Tom for so long I couldn't hurt no more iff'n I tried. I know he burnt the schoolhouse 'cause I heard Jim tell him to do it. I was too scared o' Jim to say nothing." She set the toddler on the ground, took the handkerchief from inside her long sleeve, wiped her eyes, and blew her nose.

I patted her thigh. "Please don't take it to heart. It's not your fault. You can bring a child into this world, but you can't change what's inside him."

"I knows what you mean. You're gonna have to be on the watch for Jim. Iff'n he were to come back to Bixbee it wouldn't be . . ." Maude let the rest fade and rubbed her cheekbone in thought, as if she was unsure whether to finish the statement. I didn't prod her, just let her take her time. After a bit, she went on, "Iff'n Jim comes back it won't be safe for you. I heard him tell Tom he was gonna git both you and Dan Rigby some day. Knowing him, he ain't gonna forgive or forget."

Part II

HAPPINESS
AND
HEARTACHE

CHAPTER 24

Providence Hospital, 1916

Dan lay on his hospital bed, his head seeming twice its size in the white mummy's wrap. He'd been confined now for six days, and just as his coma held him prisoner, it kept me in chains. Dr. Kendrick had advised me to return to the apartment in Spokane, promising he'd phone if there was a change in Dan's condition. With great reluctance, I was considering his advice. The newspaper of which I was owner and publisher required daily guidance, and I'd been away too long.

Suddenly the walls seemed to close in. The shades at the two narrow windows had been drawn to within a foot of the sills, and the light shining through the bottom of the panes was growing dimmer as evening approached. It made two rectangular patches, one at the foot of Dan's bed, another on the floor near the doorway. Pinpricks of light shone through the blind where the olive-green canvas had been scratched. I went to the windows, drew up the blinds and opened the windows a crack.

When I turned back to the bed and saw my dear husband lying there, the prospect of leaving him in the hospital prompted the same feeling of desolation that had consumed me when he'd left for Canada in the summer of '92. Out of the long, cluttered years, the day he'd left camp loomed as one of prophecy, its meaning concealed at the time, but as glaring as the sun at mid-day when I looked back twenty-four years later. That day, more than any other, had bound me to Bixbee, to the Coeur d'Alenes, and to mining. Though every fiber of my being wanted to run from the madness, I waited in the gray dawns and purple evenings, in the thunder of heat storms, and in the bone-chilling winters, thinking of Dan, tucking my love deep in my heart for safe-keeping until his return.

I recalled that I'd tried to forget Maude Tatro's warning about Jim taking revenge, but it had found a niche in the back of my mind from which to haunt me. I felt some relief in the fact that the Tatro men had been kept in prison when most of the union men were released from the crude, unsanitary barns where they'd been left to swelter and turn their irritation upon each other. Once freed, they'd deserted the Coeur d'Alenes for lack of jobs—the mines had opened, but few operators were willing to hire union miners, especially those involved in the uprising. In Bixbee, a population of ten-day miners drifted in and out of camp, giving the town the stability of a ship on the open sea.

Suffering the void caused by Dan's absence, I tried to concentrate on overseeing the carpenters who were building a new school. Jeff was intrigued with the process and kept an eye on the builders when I was helping Della. In fact, he spent most of his time working with hammer and nails, watching the new school rise from the ashes. Often, I found Lucinda Hanson there, engaging Jeff in lively conversation. It was obvious their friendship had ripened into puppy love, and I wondered what the Hansons would do if they found out about Lucinda's visits to the construction site.

The government troops left Burke Canyon in November of '92, and the union reorganized. Hub Malone and other union officials were released from jail, but Rafe and Jim Tatro, Smutt Corrigan, and the rest of Rafe's scab-beating crew were to remain in the state prison for an additional two years for their brutal treatment of non-union miners. The release of the officials gave spark to the union's daring and it renewed its war with the Mine Owners Association, resulting in threats and acts of violence on both sides. The MOA had cleared Dan of conspiracy, but shootings and stabbings had returned to pre-militia level and I feared for him if he returned.

Two years crawled by in that unsettled way, a time when I focused my efforts on teaching and newspaper reporting. At first, Dan had sent letters from the nearest trading post, tender love letters that included news about his job as hoist operator at a mine in the hinterlands of British Columbia. The job paid well and he was saving money for exploratory work at the Black Titan when he returned. Then the letters arrived less frequently, scarcely enough to count on my fingers, until I heard nothing. I felt abandoned, drifting in a sea of doubt, wondering why I remained on the creek. In May of '94 I was offered teaching positions in Wallace and Spokane and was biding my time while I decided between the two. Holding those offers as security, I'd composed a letter of resignation to Harley Hanson, but kept it in reserve in the faint hope that something would happen to change my mind. My roots had grown deeper, nourished by the Tuttles' love. And Jeff had become part of my life. His mother had failed to return, and it seemed he'd always be mine to care for. I had to consider that possibility as I contemplated a move.

It was Sunday afternoon, the letter of resignation in my skirt pocket, when I headed down the tracks toward the school. Winds had battered the canyons for days, shattering trees burdened with late snows, and I wanted to check on damage to the schoolgrounds before I delivered the letter to Harley. I'd closed school early on Thursday, the last day of the school year, because it was too risky for the children to be out. Now, three days later, the winds had stopped howling, the snow squalls had blown themselves out, and spring had put on its warmest smile. The day was crisp around the edges, yet the sun was a soothing poultice on my back, the air a sweet balm filled with the scent of warm pine and fir resin that drifted down from the upper reaches of the canyon.

As I worked my way around mounds of debris, I sometimes paused to gaze at the striking green, blue, and white of May's earth and sky. The blue that ribboned overhead looked like pictures I'd seen of the ocean, whole swells of foaming clouds here, bubbly stringers there, wisps and swirls of froth. A red-tailed hawk wheeled upward into the imaginary brine.

I was about to enter the schoolyard when I noticed a recently erected bulletin board in a place where anyone entering town couldn't help but see it. In the center of the board, a large notice featured a caricature of a Chinaman being herded from the district at gunpoint. Bold lettering below it warned, *All Chinamen Must Leave this Mining District as of June 1, 1894, by Order of the Coeur d'Alene Unit of Western Federation of Miners.* A notice below that declared, *Non-union Men, Your Days in the District are Numbered. Get Out Now, in Peace.* This notice, too, was by the order of the WFM. It seemed the powerful union in Butte had united all the miners' unions of the West into one organization and was continuing to press its demands.

There was a photo of Hub Malone in the lower right-hand corner of the board. A caption beneath it read: *Put Your x by Hub Malone for County Commissioner—For Free Coinage of Silver—Against Corruption in Government—Burke's Outstanding Representative at the Populist Convention in Boise.* So, Hub was in Burke now and into politics despite his former protest against it. Memories of Hub's and Dan's conversation about local politics rushed out of the past, bringing pangs of regret, as well as an image of the vibrance Dan had shown in

those early union days. As I had each day, I wondered if he still lived
and if he still loved me. At night he invaded my dreams, only to lie
beyond grasp, his face forlorn, pleading. I'd wake fearful for his safety,
fearful our love had never been more than a figment of my imagination.
It had been so long since he'd taken me into his arms that I felt like a
tree with the sap long gone. I almost wished I'd never met the man. I'd
lived on memories for month after month and they'd turned bitter.

When I reached the school, I found the yard cluttered with
branches. Other limbs blocked the steps leading to the school's entry.
After I'd determined none had caused damage, I threw the limbs from
the steps and went inside to do the final cleaning for the year. I always
saddened when I closed the school for the summer. As much as I
yearned to give my frazzled mind and nerves a rest, I hated to say
goodbye. Many of the children would return in the fall, but some would
leave the district and I'd never see them again. Others would move on
to the high school in Wallace. Jeff was one of those. He'd ride the early
ore train to school each morning and would board with friends of
Della's when the weather was bad. Nora, Clyde Hanson's sister, had
married a young lawyer and was mother of a toddler. Likely, Lucinda
would stay with her during the school week.

Gripped by end-of-the-year melancholy, I was standing outside the
entry, shaking dust cloths, my skirt and blouse covered with a full-
length apron, when I saw a man walking down the tracks. He carried a
carpetbag in one hand, a box bound with twine in the other and dragged
his feet as if weary or burdened with care. At first, I thought him a
stranger, thin, but broad-shouldered, likely a transient searching for
work. The moment of recognition hit when he opened the gate to the
schoolyard and smiled faintly, sparking the memory of a day when that
same man had swaggered out the gate with two small boys at his side.
Now, five years later, I was struck dumb at the sight of him, void of
emotion. At one time I'd been so in love with him that everything he
said and did affected my life. That love had almost crippled me, had
left me frayed and vulnerable, and in the end I'd built a protective wall
around my feelings.

He set down his belongings, his eyes darting from me to the ground
in a self-conscious way. As I watched him, I suddenly felt queasy, as if
I'd faint. He must have noticed, because he came toward me in a
tentative, uncertain way, then stopped. That look of uncertainty did

more to revive me than anything else he could have done. What was wrong with him? Didn't he want to come near? After all this time, didn't he want to throw his arms around me? The feelings I'd kept in check for so many months came pouring out and swamped me—the mental and emotional pain, the confusion, the resentment, and yes, the love. I was so angry and confused that, as he mounted the steps and took my arms, I convulsed with tears and beat on his chest, babbling incoherently about the trespasses he'd committed against me, as if I'd waited a long time to speak my mind. Through it all, Dan said nothing, just held my arms and let me vent my feelings, until finally the hurt drained from my heart and I threw my arms around him, quaking, sobbing quietly.

Firming my lips against another wave of tears, I pulled back to let my damp gaze crawl over him. "I haven't heard from you for so long I thought you were . . . " I let the rest fade as a second numbing shock stunned me. I'd been so possessed by my rantings, I hadn't realized that Dan looked crumpled and sick, ten years older than his thirty years. "What's happened to you?" I asked with a new sense of worry.

"I-I've been ill," he said haltingly. "Been living on quinine and flaxseed syrup for half-a-year." He crinkled the corners of his eyes with forced amusement. "Gotten so my mouth's in a permanent pucker from taking the awful stuff."

I studied the pale, drawn face, the faint lines left by illness. The wheaten curls and the crystal blue of his eyes were the same as always, but he'd shaved his mustache, the skin around it sallow. "What was the problem?"

"Typhoid."

I gave a little gasp. "I wondered why there was so little to you. You might have died."

"Nothing to worry about. I'm on the mend." Dan smoothed a strand of hair from my face, and tucked it into the poof of curls at the crown of my head. The gesture brought a ripple of affection to my heart.

I took a deep breath and asked, "Why didn't you tell me you were sick?"

I didn't want to come back until the disease was past." He seemed restrained. Unsure of himself.

I, too, was unsure of myself. On the one hand, I wanted him to kiss me soundly and erase the endless months that had separated us. On the other hand, I feared that he might not want to kiss me. My heart dropped at the thought.

He pressed my head against his shoulder and said as hesitantly as before, "I started so many letters . . . tore them up. I didn't have the nerve to tell you what the typhoid had done to me. I was afraid . . ." His voice trailed off.

I drew back and looked up at him through wet eyelashes. "Afraid of what?"

"Afraid there wouldn't be enough of the old Dan left to interest you. You wouldn't want half a man, now would you?" He gave a spontaneous flicker of a smile.

I relaxed a little, wondering why men were so concerned about what they termed manliness. "I wouldn't care," I said, sniffling. "I've missed you so. I thought you'd never come back." I burrowed my head into his denim jacket, smelled tobacco and the sweet-sour odor of his flesh. "I've been so lonely without you, as if I was half alive."

"I'm sorry." He nuzzled my hair.

"It seemed . . . forever," I said in a near-whisper. "But now that you're here and I can touch you . . . it's as though you'd never been away."

He kissed the top of my head and my wet cheeks. "Oh, Maggie darling," he murmured, "I love you so. Forgive me for being gone so long . . . for not writing." He took my chin in his warm hand and tilted it upward. "I just couldn't put on paper what I felt in my heart. Forgive me?"

I replied with a kiss planted on his neck. One arm still around me, he pulled a handkerchief from his trousers pocket and watched while I wiped my eyes and blew my nose. I felt better now, felt the full force of the old love returning. All at once, the world was right-side-up again. Dan had returned and was holding me, saying he loved me. Suddenly I knew that, despite his absence, I loved him more than anyone else on earth. Somehow, I'd see that nothing ever separated us again.

He smiled a shade. "I have some good news. I landed a job as accountant at the Poorman Mine in Burke. I saw a notice at the railroad station in Wallace and rode up to Burke to see about it before they hired somebody else."

"They were willing to hire you in spite of your history with the union?"

"The manager knows I didn't take part in the blasts. Besides, he needs a man who knows the business as well as how to keep the books."

"That's wonderful! You won't have to work the stopes."

"And I'll make enough to support us." He drew a long breath and gazed lovingly into my eyes. I felt his muscles relax, as if he was reassured of his place in my life. "Maggie, there's no reason for us to wait any longer." His voice had changed in a subtle way, had become deep and filled with affection. "There's no reason for us not to marry . . . so will you?" His eyes seemed to cry out the great need of his heart.

I felt strangely limp. For a long breathless moment, I tingled all over. Then came a sudden, irrepressible glow of body and soul. My hand crept up Dan's shoulder until I felt the pulse throbbing in his neck. "I'd be happy to marry you, Dan. I want that with all my heart and soul."

He gave a huge sigh and kissed me softly, then long and hungrily, the way lovers do when they've been apart for years, as if we were the only two on earth.

Gradually, faint sounds made themselves evident—the clacking of crows, the ripple of childish laughter, the rattle of a horse-drawn wagon, and close at hand, the burbling of the creek. A breeze stirred the branches of a pine at the rear of the schoolhouse making me aware of time and place, of the rise and fall of Dan's chest, and of the sweetness of his breath. I felt as if I'd found a haven where no one could separate me from the man I loved.

CHAPTER 25

Dan and I exchanged marriage vows in early June in a meadow a mile above Burke, the air fragrant with awakened greenery and damp earth. The spring-scented evergreens were the walls of the chapel, the blossoming scrub our bridal bouquets. Soon the clearing would serve as a baseball diamond, but no games had been played as yet, and sunlight showered through the trees onto a carpet of glacier lilies, buttercups, violets, and meadow mushrooms. From the woods came the persistent drumming of grouse, from the meadow rose the burbling of a spring into its basin.

To reach the sylvan wedding, guests who lived along the creek merely trudged up the canyon. Aaron and Adam Rigby took the train from Spokane to Burke and went on foot from there. Adam looked like an older Dan but without Dan's open, friendly expression. From what Dan had told me, he considered his father a skinflint, devoid of any compassion.

Della was one of my matrons of honor, Nora the other. Nora rode up from Wallace with her husband, but Clyde and the elder Hansons chose not to attend. The reason was twofold—when Harley and Adam Rigby had dissolved their partnership in California the separation had been caustic, and besides that the Hansons were still angry at Dan for organizing the union.

Della had sewn my dress in three days—a creamy silk with wasp waist, over it a tight-fitting jacket with huge puffed sleeves and roses embroidered on the lapels and cuffs. "I'm sure gonna miss you," she said as she worked on the hem. "Nobody to listen to me rattle on. I'll miss Jeff, too. I love him like a son."

"We're just moving next door," I said with a little laugh. "You won't be rid of us that easy,"

Now, I stood in that lovely dress, the corset laced so tight I could hardly breathe. Dan was more comfortable in a black suit, his cap of golden curls glistening in the sunlight. If only my mother stood near me and I could look into her face for comfort. A woman shouldn't marry without her mother at hand to offer support. Loving, generous Della tried to fill the role, but it simply wasn't the same. Even if Ma had been at my side, I might still have felt a sudden fright while listening to the justice of the peace expound on the duties of marriage. I turned to Nora, standing at my left in wine-colored satin, and shot her a frantic glance. She seemed to sense my anxiety and gave me a reassuring smile that said, "It's all right, Maggie. I went through the same thing and survived."

Even so, I listened with panic as the aged justice of the peace mumbled his way through the vows. "Do you take this woman . . . sickness . . . health . . ." Then Dan's nervous voice saying, "I do." Perhaps he, too, was seized by wedding fright. When the justice turned to me and uttered the final, irrevocable question, "Do you take this man . . ." I knew I'd reached the point of no return. My heart throbbed in my ears. My nerves prickled as if I stood in a briar patch. I could hardly find the voice to say "I do." But I did, and Dan and I became man and wife. When he pulled me gently into his arms for the post-nuptials kiss, I trembled like the quaking aspens at the fringe of the meadow.

Self-conscious and ill at ease, we accepted the congratulations of the guests and joined them at linen-covered tables made by setting planks across sawhorses. By the time everyone had ravaged Della's fried chicken with all the trimmings and devoured a tower of a wedding cake, Dan and I had relaxed, and he and Jeff sat astride boulders, coaxing tunes from their mouth organs. One of Della's boarders used a thick spruce for a backrest and strummed on a banjo he'd brought to pleasure the noon, his frame so lank he looked like a daddy longlegs wrapped around the instrument. Thus, as the afternoon passed in song and jovial conversation, my earlier panic dissolved into a feeling of contentment.

●●●

We spent a three-day honeymoon at a modest hotel in Spokane and made love around the clock. I'd thought it would be distasteful, something done to please my husband, to consummate the marriage vows, and I was surprised at my total enjoyment of the act. When we returned to Bixbee, we had to restrain our moans and groans and the thumping of the bed for fear Jeff would hear through the flimsy wall that separated our rooms. He was raised in a whore's house and knew all about such things, but I didn't want him to compare what he'd heard in those days to Dan's and my connubial joy.

There were just two bedrooms in the clapboard house we rented near Della's—a gray, weather-beaten shack staring onto the tracks, a privy leaning into the hillside a few steps from the back door. Cramped parlor, tiny bedrooms, kitchen and pantry patched onto the side, a wood range used for cooking and heating, a holding tank at one end for heating water. But I tackled the moving process with the flush of excitement that comes to a woman when she flitters about arranging her own nest. Beside the precious books that fit on a shelf, I found the perfect spot to display our wedding photograph, one of the O'Shea family, and another of Dan's mother who'd died when he was in his teens. On a walnut dresser that was a gift from Nora, I arranged an ivory brush, comb, and mirror, a wedding present from Dan.

I refinished the used furniture Aaron Rigby liberated from the store in Spokane and managed to keep Della's taste within bounds when she sewed curtains, linens, and the like. Among the items from the store was a china cabinet I painted scarlet and gold to match a red lamp with yellow flowers, a present from the Tuttles. In the center of a tea table, I set my pride and joy, a large nutbowl Jeff had carved and polished until it felt like satin.

Despite my previous qualms, I was thrilled to be Mrs. Dan Rigby, to have a home of my own, and to have dreams fluttering in my chest that at one time had been only wisps of my imagining. I looked at everything with a new sharpness of vision and woke each morning with remarkable vitality, with the feeling I'd never been alive before.

●●●

Sadness dampened my bliss when I received word in August that my father had passed away—the official word was that he'd had a heart attack, but my mother wrote, "It was from the heartache he'd suffered because of his legs. I was surprised he lasted this long."

To my amazement and total gratitude, Harley allowed me to close school temporarily and paid my train fare east to attend the funeral—he called it a belated wedding present. While there, I said a tearful goodbye to my mother—her widowed sister had invited Ma and the younger O'Sheas to stay in her spacious home in Roros, Norway. The older O'Shea boys, young men now, had found work in the growing railroad industry and would remain in Pennsylvania. All but Lennie. To my utter delight, he chose to return with me to the Coeur d'Alenes to help Dan develop the Titan. I'd suggested the exchange of work for room and board to Dan before I'd left for the east, and he'd said, "We'll give it a try. The more help the better. Just so Lennie understands I'm boss."

Lennie's placid manner made it easy for him to fit into the household. Jeff took a liking to him immediately and didn't mind a bit when we put an extra cot in his cramped room. Dan worked days at the Poorman Mine's office and spent every hour after work until dark at the Titan teaching Lennie what he needed to know about mining silver/lead ore. I continued to teach, and despite Dan's reluctance, put most of my salary into the mine.

Not many weeks had passed when our household faced another life-altering change. In the early stages, I kept my pregnancy a secret, even from Dan. But it wasn't long before I overheard one of the town gossips say to another woman known for her loose tongue, "Have you noticed how that school teacher is filling out her dress?"

"Who does she think she's fooling?" the other woman said in a catty way. "She has no business in the classroom."

Despite the remarks, I remained in the classroom until winter put a lock on the district and I had to close the school. Then I stayed home to prepare for the baby. In the latter stages, when Dan and I retired to our bed for the night, I'd hold his hand on my stretched belly so he might feel the sudden ripplings and protuberances that meant an active baby.

"It's too bad a man has so little to do with bringing a child into the world," I said one night. "He misses so much, never to feel the stirring, the sense of giving new life."

Dan replied with a crinkle of humor in his eyes, "I believe I had quite a bit to do with it. If not, God help the man who did."

The lightness had left my steps long before the hoary fogs of January and February congealed the canyon, turning every leaf, twig, and stem, every rafter and lamppost into visions of crystalline wonder. Unable to mine because of the frigid conditions, Lennie left for the coast to work the docks until the spring thaw. The Poorman Mine closed for the winter and Dan found a temporary position as substitute for an ailing accountant at a store in Wallace. When the trains were stalled because of deep snows, he walked the five miles back and forth to Wallace, but sometimes he had to remain in that town because of a blizzard. I worried that he wouldn't be at home when the baby arrived.

I wanted the house to be presentable for visitors after the birth, so I scrubbed the floors with much awkwardness and discomfort, washed and ironed the muslin curtains, spread fresh paper on the shelves, and polished the furniture until its gleam hurt the eyes. Then, so I'd have a clean bed for the birthing, I boiled all the bedding and hung it out in the below-zero weather, where it froze fast to the line.

When I was certain no one could find fault with my housekeeping, I put the baby things in order—squares of muslin, soft baby flannels and woolens I'd embroidered around the edges. With a quivering heart, I arranged them neatly in a white chest of drawers trimmed with pink and blue roses. I'd already made a bassinet from a basket decorated with hand-sewn lace and ribbons.

In one dresser drawer, I assembled items necessary for the birthing—Vaseline, cornstarch, granulated carbolic acid, piles of clean rags, pieces of linen I'd boiled and browned in the oven, packages of safety pins, and bands made from flour sacks. Two washbasins waited on the dresser and two kettles of water simmered constantly on the kitchen stove. Each night I filled the lamps to brimming with oil.

When Dan and Jeff were at home, I kept them busy preparing for the cold. They gathered a small mountain of cordwood and chopped it to size for the stove. Since the pump was likely to remain frozen, they lined up buckets of snow for melting until they looked like tin handmaidens waiting in a row.

The fog continued to hang like a muffler in the creek bottom and fern-like crystals collected on the windows until I could hardly melt a circle to look outside. At night, my breath turned to frost and made the covers stiff around my face. Dan insisted I sleep between two featherbeds so I'd stay warm.

In the last weeks before the birth I became ill. My legs swelled, and I was delirious much of the time. Dr. Pettit ordered me to bed and urged me to go to the new union hospital in Wallace for the birth. Nora said I could stay at her home in Wallace until then, but I resisted. There was little money to pay the hospital, and I knew as surely as if I were a Cassandra that everything would be right.

The night of the birth, I lay in bed, warmed by a roaring fire Della had built in the cook-stove. I'd had difficult labor for twelve hours and I'd sent Jeff to the boarding house, where he'd stay with Hank until called back home. Hank stopped by now and then to see if he could help Della. The last time he'd come, she'd sent him to fetch Dr. Pettit from his home in Burke. My mother had given birth several times at our shack in Williamsboro, and wished I could be as strong and uncomplaining as she'd been. How I wished she sat at my bedside now.

Dan walked in late from Wallace, letting the fog's stagnant smell inside to mingle with the odor of woolen underwear steaming on a rack by the stove. He sat down on the bed beside me, took my hand and held it at his breast. His expression was one of deep concern and guilt. "Is there anything I can do?" he said gravely.

I held my breath, fighting pain, and wagged my head.

"I wish you'd gone to the hospital."

"Don't . . . worry . . . I'll be all . . ." I let the rest fade as I endured mounting pain. I wanted to be brave, but deep inside I felt a pang of resentment that a woman must suffer the torture of birthing while the man felt none. In a moment my muscles relaxed, but my lower lip stung where my teeth had clamped onto it.

Della stumped in from the kitchen with the air of a general and blared, "You'd better get out o' here, Dan. A man gets underfoot when it comes to birthing. You don't want us to end up with half a baby do you?"

Dan forced a laugh, but his face said he felt unwanted, an outsider in a female world, barely tolerated in his own house. After he'd kissed me and gone into the parlor to pace the floor, I could hear him rage at himself for being the cause of such suffering and felt shame for the resentment that had sneaked into my heart.

At bedside, Della said, "Bear down harder, Maggie. I'm holding you."

I tried, but by the time the doctor arrived, I was out of my head, moaning, crumpling the starched sheets with clenched fists. The doctor blurred before my eyes—a small man with a catfish face and beard. He made a quick check on my condition, then barked instructions to Della. She'd turned silent, except for the sound of her heels punching into the floor as she fetched cloths and instruments from the boiling water. She'd brought a small table to bedside and set two washbasins there. She filled one with boiling water and another with the carbolic solution the doctor ordered. When he threw the sheet back from my distended belly, I could smell the medication on his hands.

The pain had become so fierce I screamed and arched my back, twisting with one convulsion after the other. Through my agony, I felt the doctor's stethoscope explore my vast belly, "There's no heartbeat or movement," he told Della in a strained, subdued voice. He inserted his hand in the birth canal. "The baby's breech first. It's large and

Maggie's pelvis is all wrong for childbearing, more like a man's than a woman's. I'm going to have to use forceps. Better tie her ankles to the bed."

I heard Della tear a sheet into strips and felt her bind my feet to the bed. I heard the doctor rummage among the rattly instruments in his satchel and dip something metallic into one of the basins. "Della, hold her down so she can't rear up," he said crisply. Then his voice from the foot of the bed, "Maggie this'll hurt, but it can't be helped." I thought to myself how could it possibly hurt more than it does already?

Muttering directions to himself, the doctor inserted the forceps into the birth canal and I let out a scream. Never had I felt such agony. In the bulge of my eyes, I saw Della leaning over me, pushing down on my shoulder, her face contorted with imagined pain. The doctor tugged with the forceps—paused—tugged—paused. With each tug I screamed, wishing I was dead.

Then a sudden release from the torture. Somewhere in the haze of my mind I heard the doctor say, "Poor thing. He's dead. It was the eclampsia did it. Not enough oxygen going to the placenta."

CHAPTER 26

The first few days and nights following the baby's stillbirth seemed a vague nightmare. The doctor stayed on, refusing other calls, his face gray-green, with dark pouches under his eyes. I held onto a mere filament of life and often lay in a drugged sleep. When the crisis had passed, the doctor insisted I remain in bed, and Dan hired a young woman named Ginny to keep house and to attend to my physical needs. Della brought meals from her kitchen, and Dan and Jeff did what they could to help at night and on the weekends. Above all else, Dan gave me the strength to endure a belated funeral, then put me to bed with kisses and tears when it was over. I suffered for Dan. He'd wanted the baby terribly. "After all, I'm going on thirty-one," he'd said before the birth. And I'd disappointed him.

My greatest heartache was for the baby and myself. We'd been cheated. I felt as though everything had been carved from my insides but ribs and lining and I had nothing to show for it. All those months of anticipation. All the plans. All the affection felt for the unborn child. And that poor little dead thing. Nine months inside my dark womb struggling to survive. And for what?

Thus, the days stretched emptily ahead one after the other, until an afternoon in late March when I sat bundled in blankets at the parlor window. The hired girl had gone for groceries and my only company was the squeak of the rocker, the snap of a fire burning in the Home Comfort range in the kitchen, and the metallic tick of the wall clock. I held a recently published volume of Emily Dickinson's poems in my hands. Beneath the volume lay a jacket I'd been mending before I'd paused to read—work had resumed at the Titan, and the scrubby jacket was one that Dan wore to toil at the mine after putting in a full day's work in the office at the reopened Poorman Mine.

It was a bleak day with a hint of sunshine peeping through. Dickinson's poems warmed my heart, but the thin sunlight seeping through the parlor window did little to warm me physically. Outside, a hard wind blew in great gusts and swells, took hold of the shack and rocked it, rattled the windowpanes, and moaned through the crack around the door and down the stovepipe.

With the approach of evening, the sky faded to subtle grays and increased the dragging gloom. That ended when Della opened the door against the wind and swept into the room with a basket in her hand. "Brought you some custard and sourdough rolls. I know Ginny don't cook that sort of thing." Through the doorway, I watched her set the basket on the kitchen table and touch the kettle on the stove to see if the water was hot. Soon she returned with two cups of tea. "You remember me talking about Elsie Springer, my friend from Wallace?" she said as she set the cups on the pine teatable I'd refinished before I'd become pregnant.

I considered Della's question and dug up an image. "Umm . . . was she the woman who pushed so hard for equal suffrage?"

"Yep, she's the one. She went after them delegates at the constitutional convention like a fretful porcupine." Della settled into a wicker armchair across the table from me as if ready for a long dialogue. "Anyways, Elsie's in Boise now. She's still working on that suffrage thing. She wants us Idaho women to do some stumping before the legislature meets in January. If we can get a women's suffrage bill passed, we can vote in the '96 election."

I thought about the need for the women's vote while I sipped my tea, then answered measuredly, "It's going to be an important election, what with all the splintering of the parties . . . the Populists gaining voters . . . there's the silver question, too. It would be a good time for women to press for the vote."

Della wagged her head at some disagreeable thought and said sourly, "We don't wanna get caught short like the ladies in Washington state. The hee-haws in their legislature called for a vote on suffrage and gave the ladies only three months to organize, knowing they'd lose."

"Do you think the men in Idaho are ready for—"

"They dang well better be! We come close to getting suffrage put into the state constitution. Our own county was for it and a couple o' the others."

I'd lived in Pennsylvania at the time, but Della had told me about the scrap between those who favored suffrage and those who opposed. It seemed the tide had changed slightly. "I know the Populists are in favor of it. But a few of the leaders are rather strange in their approach."

Della gave a little snort. "Sure, but that's how they get people's attention. They raise less corn and more hell. The union's strong for the

Populists, too, because it's for free coinage o' silver and double standard—gold and silver."

"It's encouraging that they're for the women's vote."

"Hank's thinking o' registering Populist. He says they're the people's party. He says they're getting ready for a big pooferah between the people and the pluto . . . pluto . . . what do you call them big moneybags who run the country?"

"Plutocrats." I smiled inwardly as I reflected on the pleasure Della found in using such words.

"It's still going to take a lot o' pushing from us women folk." Della drank heartily from her teacup and went on with enthusiasm. "Elsie wants to start women's rights groups all over the state to work together and plan an attack. You know, sorta like getting ready for a big Injun war. Each group'll send delegates to a convention in Boise. They'll set up a battle plan there."

"I hope you're more successful than the W.C.T.U."

Della gave a whoop. "Now hold on, we ain't gonna get fussed up about no temperance issue. Temperance sure as hell wouldn't go over here. Anyways, when the legislature meets, a bunch of us will go there and give our argument. We'll hound the cats 'till they run up a tree and yowl for help."

I shook with the first belly laugh I'd had in weeks. When my stomach stopped bobbing up and down, I said with the remnants of a laugh, "Knowing you, you'll have the most persistent pack of hounds there."

Della wagged her finger at me. "You're going to be one of 'em, Maggie. I figure you need something to keep your mind off your problems."

"But I promised to teach school in the fall."

"You'll have all spring and summer. The legislature won't meet 'till January. You'll have the school closed down for the winter by then."

Della drank tea and eyed me expectantly while I pondered the idea, cautiously at first, then with growing interest. After a bit, I nodded in agreement. "I think I'd like that. I'm tired of sitting in this rocker. I can record our progress for the newspaper. That will please Aulbach. I don't want him to think I've given up reporting."

●●●

Dan gave his blessing to my involvement in the suffrage movement—as long as I fed him on time and helped him keep the books for the Titan. That settled, I plunged my mind and soul into the cause and worked with Della to organize the district. I spoke to literary societies in the handful of towns, to ladies' aid societies, and attended neighborhood teas. I walked the streets holding suffrage literature under the noses of passers-by and knocked on doors hoping to coax wives to give their support. I left the tougher nails to pound to Della's flaming oratory—such as the few men's clubs willing to hear pleas for equal rights.

In January, weather closed the mines and the school. Lennie left for the coast, Dan for Spokane to help at his father's store. That freed me to make the interminable train trip through Washington, Oregon, and down into southern Idaho, where Della and I, along with other Shoshone County feminists, added our voices to the clamor for suffrage. I returned home a month later to report on a legislature that had closed the session by throwing paper wads dipped in ink, and had stripped the capitol of wastebaskets, inkstands, paste, and books. But that same body of lawmakers sent me back to Bixbee with the sweet taste of victory on my lips. Idaho women would cast their votes in the '96 election.

Nationally, it was a period of fist pounding and shouting. The major parties squared-off over the issue of the gold standard, Democrats and Populists declaring for silver, Republicans for gold. When the campaign for the presidency turned into a boxing match between William Jennings Bryan and President McKinley, the nation itself jumped into the ring, the South and West aligned against the Northeast, farmers and laborers against business. Excited about their vote, women in the Coeur d'Alenes took time from their hum-drum lives to argue the issues while their husbands gathered behind the bat-wings of saloons and on cracker boxes in the local stores to trade verbal and physical punches.

Miners took up Bryan's cry for a monetary standard of sixteen ounces of silver to one of gold. "Sixteen to one!" was heard around the West. The splintering of the Democratic party in the mining district divided Bixbee down the middle. One merchant bribed voters with hams, bacon, and flour. Another group filled a spring wagon with cases of rotten eggs, and drove up and down the street plastering houses of the opposition. Contempt for civility thrived.

It seemed that Bryan was about to ride to the presidency on the shoulders of labor and agriculture, but by November the price of wheat took a leap because of meager harvests abroad, and Republican farmers were less willing to vote Democratic. On election day, McKinley scored a resounding victory over Bryan. The cry of "Sixteen to one!" died in the miners' throats. The defeat brought rumblings of discontent to the Coeur d'Alenes, and soon the drums were on the roll. Hub Malone, county commissioner, as well as local prod for the Western Federation of Miners, took up the beat.

The mine owners were too busy suing one another for economic advantage to notice the militant union creeping in from Montana, but Dan saw trouble ahead. To rid himself of complete dependence on his job at the Poorman Mine, he accompanied Lennie to work the Seattle docks during the winter lock-down of the mines and returned in March with a pocketful of cash to invest in the Titan. He returned to his job as accountant at the Poorman, and Lennie continued to work at the Titan in exchange for room and board. I put part of my meager salary into the mine.

By early summer of '97 trouble threatened to spoil the comfortable arrangement. It happened one evening after I'd cleared the kitchen table of the supper dishes and was trimming the wick of a hurricane lamp. Dan and Lennie sat at the table with coffee and toothpicks, their chairs tipped back on the hind legs, dusk muting their features. Jeff was stuffing himself with a second bowl of bread pudding.

Lennie brushed a dark forelock from his forehead as if the process cleared a pathway for his thoughts, a habit that heightened his likeness to the serious Abe Lincoln. "We've got that second adit cut in about three hundred fifty feet now," he said in his drawling way. "Isn't it time we started a third, lower down? The vein's giving sign of spreading the deeper it goes."

Dan lowered the legs of his chair and leaned forward, elbows propped on the table. "Guess it'd pay right enough," he said in his clipped manner of speaking. "The report on that carbonate is encouraging."

I took my attention from the lampwick and turned it on Dan. "You stopped by the assay office today?"

"During the dinner break. One batch of samples assayed at fifty percent lead and sixty ounces of silver. In the others, the lead went as high as sixty percent to seventy ounces of silver. Trouble is we don't have the money to prove it out."

Never one to offer an opinion in haste, Lennie lowered his chair so he could prop his elbows on the table, then arranged his fingers like a tent and pressed them against his lips in thought. Several seconds slogged by before he cleared his throat to make a passage for words. "I don't know why you won't sell shares."

Dan shot Lennie an impatient look that said they'd had this argument before so why ask. "We've worked too hard to let a bunch of damned parasites share in something they didn't lift a hand to produce. We'll get our money some other way."

Lennie worked the toothpick around in his mouth, a frown speaking of a struggle waging within him. "I've been thinking that it doesn't make sense for me to keep working the Titan. I could take a job at the Apex for three-fifty and we could hire a short-staker for a dollar less. Put the extra dollar into the mine. That'd be near thirty dollars a month."

Dan brought up a cynical snort. "You wouldn't have a chance. The Apex isn't hiring union men."

"I don't have a union history here on the creek."

Dan's eyes turned glacial. "You'd be considered a scab."

"There isn't a strike going on. And if the company isn't hiring union men, I wouldn't be taking somebody else's job."

"Maybe not, but there's still union men working some of the stopes. They don't take kindly to non-union men." Dan scratched his head in irritation. "I can't figure it—you growing up in a union family."

"You want your mine to go don't you?"

"Sure, but not by hurting the union. Not by paying some bloke a miserly wage to take your place at the Titan."

Lennie shot Dan an accusing glance. "I hear you weren't any too loyal to the union in '92."

"I sure as hell didn't work as a scab. It was just a difference of opinion between me and some of the union bosses. I still believe in their cause."

Lennie turned his scowl on the table and tapped the blue-checkered oilcloth with growing impatience while Dan rubbed his stomach as if anger had caused it to gnarl. The argument was beginning to eat at the lining of my stomach, too. I set the lamp on the table ready for nightfall and sat with my hands clenched around a cup of tea. "You have a right to do what you want, Lennie," I said evenly. "But there is a danger from union men. They've been beating scabs and sending them out of the district."

Lennie sucked a tooth, then with a cynical curl of his lip, he grumbled, "I could go to the Klondike. They say a person can strike it rich overnight. Then I could really invest in the mine."

"I say you're just getting restless," Dan grumbled.

At mention of the Klondike, Jeff's head snapped up. "Boy! Would I like to go to the Klondike. Would you take me with you, Lennie?"

Having fumed at Lennie, Dan now blazed at Jeff. "Look who else is being ridiculous."

"Then what would you suggest we do to make money?" Lennie asked the question in a sullen manner that rejected reply.

Resentful glares met across the table. The tendons tightened in Dan's neck and his jaw stiffened. I was about to suggest we change the subject, thought better of it, and shut my mouth.

Dan wasn't through arguing. "You're a grown man. I won't presume to tell you what to do." Repressed anger put a damper on his voice. "If you work as a scab it'll be on your conscience not mine. And I'll not have you blame me or the Titan for your decision."

Lennie's face darkened and he burst out with an edge of anger in his words. "We're setting blame, are we? After I've grubbed up there all this time. I ought to quit you high and dry. Find a shack of my own to live in. There's only one way you'll accept things. That's on your own terms." He slammed his jaw shut, as if taking the last bite of a tough steak, and strode from the room.

A painful hush followed. No sound but that of steam rising from the teakettle and a faint crackle of wood in the cookstove. Dan glared at the tablecloth. I sat next to him quietly, afraid to breathe for fear he'd snap at me. I'd like to go to Lennie, but didn't dare. I'd learned during my three years of marriage that there were times I must show mute support for my husband. In reality, there was no way I could take one side against the other. Both men were right in their own way. Both had reason to be irritable. They'd been investing too much of themselves at the Titan. Many evenings they'd come home at dark and go to bed right after a late supper, sometimes falling asleep in their clothes, Dan after putting in a full day at the Poorman and three or four hours at the mine on top of that. I was amazed trouble hadn't erupted before this.

Jeff lacked my insight as well as my reluctance to put a red rag to the bull. Without testing the safety of the pasture, he said in his soft, now masculine voice, "I'd like to quit school and work the Titan. I'm fed up with studying."

Dan laughed sarcastically, anger still on the surface. "What would you do? Serve lunch?"

I threw caution down the drain. "Dan, that's cruel! You can see how Jeff's muscled out. I'm sure he could be of help. But I'd rather he didn't. He needs to finish his education. I want that, and I'm sure his mother does." I didn't say that Nelly had written me secretly a while back and was adamant that Jeff finish school. She'd said her husband had been killed in a fight over a gold claim and she was back doing favors for men. 'Don't tell Jeff,' she'd said. 'I'd like him to think I have a better life now.'

"A lot my mother cares," Jeff grumbled. "If she gave a hoot about me or what I do, she'd come home and tell me to my face."

"You shouldn't talk that way. Your mother loves you." I watched Jeff, his face tormented with feelings of rejection, and Dan, his eyebrows drawn tight across the bridge of his nose in a morose way. What those two needed was something to take their minds off their wounded pride. "I think you're nothing but a couple of grumps. It makes me wonder if I want to bring a baby into the house."

Two heads spun toward me. Dan's anger-hardened mouth softened a bit. "Did you say baby?"

I nodded. "You're going to be a father in January."

The announcement sucked the starch from Dan's sullen mood. He stared at me in bewilderment and concern. "But how can we you . . ."

I knew what he was thinking—that I'd lose the baby and suffer another bout of depression. But in the process of dragging myself out of the doldrums I'd learned that no matter how dismal life seemed, if I had one positive thought each day those thoughts would extend until I was able to accept what had happened and could climb out of the emotional grave I'd dug for myself.

I set my cup down and lay my hand on his. "Don't worry. Nothing will happen this time. I feel just fine. There are queens who'd surrender part of their treasure to be in my condition."

Dan continued to study me with an expression of anxiety and foreboding until, finally, he sighed and planted a kiss on my cheek. "I'd say this calls for a celebration." He took three glasses and a bottle of peach brandy from the cupboard and set them on the table. "I'm warning you, when I'm through with my share of this I may revert to song." He poured an inch of the costly brandy in each glass, then raised his in toast. "Here's to my darling wife and to our child to be."

Jeff said, "I'll second that."

I sipped the brandy, savoring its flavor and smoothness, then raised my glass. "And I'd like to propose a toast to family harmony."

CHAPTER 27

After the fierce argument between Dan and Lennie over selling shares in the mine, harmony gradually crept back to our household though it was left for me to set a place for it at the table. I convinced Lennie to stay on at the Black Titan and Jeff to remain at school. They seemed reasonably content for the moment, but that could change as quickly as the direction of the wind. It helped that Dan snapped at them less often. Plans for the baby had softened the rough edges on his nerves, and my healthy pregnancy helped to sustain the calm.

In late January, I gave joyous birth to Todd Adam Rigby, the longed-for child that had Dan's and my blood flowing through his veins. A survivor. As much a part of me as my heartbeat and the air I breathed.

Likely fearing another stillbirth, Della had said nothing during the delivery. Not until the doctor slapped the baby's rump and she heard a healthy squall, did she clap her hands and say as loudly as if she'd put a trumpet to her mouth, "Maggie, you done yourself proud. He's a fine-looking boy."

Her braying had brought Dan into the room, and while she cleaned the baby and swathed it in blankets, he sat on the bed beside me, holding my hand with a grip that spoke of his relief and love.

"You're a papa now," Della said as she lowered the baby into Dan's arms. "Think you can handle it?"

Dan held the child stiffly, as if the babe was a basket of eggs. "He's kinda funny looking." Then, chuckling with delight, "He'll grow out of that, being he has such a handsome dad." He took the baby's tiny hand into his own huge callused one and stared into the blinky eyes. "Not much to you right now, is there, you little urchin. But you'll let the world know you're around and make your dad proud." Then, as though he'd realized he was renewing the cycle of fatherly expectations, he'd added, "Wonder if your grandpa Rigby will think you're fit to keep."

Grandpa Rigby saw his grandchild just four times before a heart attack took his life in mid-summer. After a suitable time for mourning, there was a settling of accounts that stunned everyone. A grudging parent, Adam Rigby had kept his worth a secret and had insisted the amount on the books at the furniture store in Spokane was his sole wealth. As a result, the boys nearly fell off their chairs when the executor of the estate told them they'd inherited thirty thousand dollars each and a shared ownership in the store. That brought whoops of "Hot damn!" and "I'll be a monkey's uncle!" from Dan and Aaron.

Since the Black Titan had begun to show promise, cautious Aaron was now ready to plunge head-first into the murky waters of the mining game. He and Dan agreed to invest their entire inheritance in the mine and to keep their jobs to insure groceries on the table—Aaron as manager of the store in Spokane, Dan at the Poorman accounting office, stuffing his head with figures. I could do as I wished, teach or stay home with Todd in the three-bedroom home we'd purchased. I chose to indulge in the joys of motherhood. It was time to nurture my *own* child and give him a head start on life.

Before the settlement of the estate, Lennie had itched to join the army fighting the Spanish in the Philippines. Now Dan had something to bargain with. "You'd be stupid to leave!" he told Lennie in his blunt way. "There's going to be big bucks in your future. You need to stay on as foreman. I've just hired ten powder and drill men, two muckers, and two timbermen. That's just starters. We're going to grow fast." Lennie seemed to see dollar signs ahead and agreed to stay. That settled, Dan hurried out to buy the necessary equipment, powder, and timbers to bore a new tunnel, hoping to cut the vein of ore by winter.

Blind with optimism, I was slow to recognize events that would alter my life as surely as a flood diverts the channel of a stream. It began when Jeff, now graduated from high school, ignored my fervent appeals to find work in an office, mercantile, or bank and instead hired on as relief mucker and chore boy at the Titan. Always fascinated by stories of treasures waiting to be found, he dreamed that he would share in the Titan's promised wealth. That would have to wait. In his present job, he acted on orders to "Fetch this," and "Fetch that," sharpened tools, used a pick and pry rod to loosen rock, then shoveled tons of rock into a car, wheeled it on tracks to the portal, and dumped it down the face of the hill. He didn't mind hard work, but he confessed that he could hardly wait for Dan to open a business office so he could wrestle with flexible figures rather than unyielding rock. I, too, wished it was possible. As it turned out, I would soon blame myself for not fighting harder to keep Jeff out of the tunnels.

His wish for office work must have traveled on the invisible waves of will and desire, because in September, Harley Hanson offered him a position in the Apex office with the explanation that he'd heard Jeff was good with figures. Because of the prejudice Harley and Clara had shown in the past, Jeff and I couldn't believe Harley would offer him work. For two days, he sat at a desk in the Apex office, bewildered, but with a new suit on his back and joy in his heart. At the end of the second day, he arrived home early from work and stormed into the kitchen, where I was stirring up a batch of cookie dough. He slammed his dinner pail onto the table. "That sonofabitch was bribing me!"

"Jeff! Your language." I looked up from the mixing bowl and saw the square planes of Jeff's maturing face flushed with outrage. "Who was bribing you?"

"Harley Hanson, that's who. He told me if I wanted to keep my job, I'd have to stop seeing Luci."

Evidently Harley had discovered that Jeff and Lucinda had been meeting secretly during the summer. For some reason, for which I was grateful, he'd kept me abreast of the meetings. Sometimes, Lucinda would slip away from home and meet him on a flat above the schoolhouse. At other times, they followed Jeff's secret trails up the hillside through a new growth of pine and fir and looked down on Bixbee unseen. Often, they had only a moment to plan their next meeting. I'd thought nothing permanent would evolve from the relationship, that it would end in a year when Lucinda graduated from high school and entered college. I told Jeff the meetings might lead to frustration and heartbreak, but he was so deeply in love he was willing to take the chance. Now this strange turn of events . . .

"Why that—that—" I could think of no name for Harley that a civilized woman could use to express her anger and contempt, so I merely said, "What did you tell him?"

"That he could take his damned job and stuff it."

"Good for you." I turned my attention back to the cookie dough and beat it with a vengeance, as if it were Harley. "I'm not surprised he'd try something like that. He's used to getting his way by hook or crook. It's hard to believe Luci's his child."

"I guess he thought she'd dump me when the boys at Wallace High started showing an interest in her, but she didn't. He said I distracted her from her studies. He wants me out of her life so she'll get good grades for college." Jeff scooped cookie dough from the bowl and sat in a chair licking it angrily from his finger. "Wait until she hears what he's done. She'll be distracted all right." He cut a piece of baking chocolate from what remained of a wedge I'd set on the table, chomped down on it, and made a face at the bitter taste. "I was crazy to think he'd let me court Luci. He said I was a cripple. That I had 'no future.' That's what he said. I'm every bit as good as a man with his foot on straight and I'll prove it."

• • •

Next day, Jeff was back wrestling rock at the Black Titan, working long hours, burying his heartache in the mountain. He'd decided to disappear from Lucinda's life and made no attempt to contact her.

Her first weekend at home from the fall term at Wallace High, Lucinda sent Jeff a note asking to see him. Thus began another period of secret trysts. Then one day Jeff turned sullen and would hardly speak. I suspected a problem had arisen with Lucinda, but he refused to speak of it.

Two months passed before I learned the reason for his foul mood. It happened on a Sunday in mid-December, when Dan and I attended an ice-skating party Nora and her husband, Josh Hennings, held on the Coeur d'Alene River near Wallace. Clyde Hanson wasn't there, though he'd built a home in Wallace for his baby son and wife of two years, a woman active in Spokane's music circles, and maintained a small office near the railway depot in Wallace where he could supervise shipments of Apex ore. The rift between Clyde and Dan had never healed, and it didn't help matters that the Black Titan was vying with the Apex and other mines for railway cars to haul ore to the smelters. Likely Clyde stayed away from the party because he knew Dan would be there. Just as well, the hostility between them was fiery enough to melt ice.

I was surprised to see Lucinda Hanson at the party, as she was the only person there of her age. I tried to speak to her while the men built a fire with logs and brush on the riverbank, but she avoided me. Giving up on that, I helped the other women start small cook fires and fashion willow tripods for hanging coffee pots over the flames. Soon the aroma of Chase and Sandborn rode the air.

When a haven of warmth was assured, Nora and I took to the ice, our husbands beside us, pushing Todd and Nora's two toddlers in long-handled sleds, the youngsters peeking out from beneath mounds of bedding. The day was as bitter cold as the ice, the sky a fuzzy gray blanket. Ice crystals frosted my eyebrows, scarf, and hood. My nose dripped. But I thrilled to the rhythmic sway and to the swish of blades on the ice. Recently, a hoary draft of arctic air had frozen pools into rinks of transparent ice, and as we rounded each bend in the river, speckled trout darted from beneath our skates—pretty things unused to winter intrusion.

Snow from fall storms bowed the branches of evergreens and covered the riverbank, revealing animal tracks large and small. Those of a coyote and rabbit merged in a blur of red-stained snow tufted with downy white fur. The saucer-shaped tracks of a cougar led from a clump of willows onto the frozen river, the cat's paws leaving circles of snow on the ice.

When we tired, we sat on logs circling the fire to devour a picnic lunch, then Dan lined the men up on the ice to race. Nora and the other wives left the fire to cheer for their husbands, but I stayed to watch over the children napping in their sleds. Because she'd avoided me all afternoon, I was surprised that Lucinda remained hunched on a log across the fire from me, her curly, fly-away black hair poking from beneath the hood of her cloak. She was seventeen, slender, had a face like an apple blossom, and sapphire blue eyes that usually snapped with intelligence and humor. Today, they stared dismally into the fire, as if the hypnotic flames had reduced to ashes any chance she had for happiness.

She didn't leave when I moved to sit beside her, just shot me a glance that said she'd rather I didn't stay. The sun had broken through the clouds and lit her face, emphasizing deep hollows around her eyes.

I put my gloved hand on her arm and tiptoed into conversation. "I'm glad to have a chance to talk to you, Luci . . . I've been so worried. Has something happened between you and Jeff?"

Lucinda was slow to answer, her stare fixed on the fire. When she did speak, her lower lip trembled. "I've been afraid to talk to you. Afraid Josh and Nora might hear." She said no more, simply gazed into the crackling logs.

"Why are you afraid?" More silence. "Whatever happened has changed Jeff. He spends nearly every waking hour at the mine, and when he comes home he hardly speaks to us. Sometimes he just goes to bed without eating. You look like you're skin and bones yourself. Please tell me about it."

"My . . . my father's threatened to run Jeff out of the district if I try to get word to him." The thought seemed to add another log to the charring of her happiness. She drew her quivering lips into a pout. "Nora has orders to watch me like a hawk. And Father hired Mrs. Deek to keep an eye on me when I'm in Bixbee and he mother are out of town." Lucinda looked up then and turned her haunted eyes toward me. "Sometimes I feel like killing myself."

Lucinda's expression said it all, yet the remark, spoken in such a matter-of-fact way, shook me even more than the look in her eyes. "You mustn't say that," I said hurriedly. "Things can't be that hopeless. What brought this on? Did your father find out you and Jeff were meeting secretly?"

Lucinda nodded. "But not until we . . ." She cast her eyes downward, seeming to find as much emotional as physical comfort in the smoldering fire.

I waited for her to say more, wondering how the truth had stolen across Harley's threshold. I'd told no one, not even Dan. Tired of waiting for Lucinda to continue, I said, "Until you did what? What happened?"

She turned toward me and gave a doleful sigh. "Jeff and I . . . we told my parents we wanted to get married. We told them if they said no, we'd run away."

I thought I'd been struck with a sledge hammer. My mouth dropped open as I considered the impact an immediate marriage would have on Jeff's and Lucinda's lives. I could imagine how the Hansons had reacted to the news—Harley like a rabid dog, Clara in shock, looking like she'd smelled something foul. It took a while to collect my wits. "What did your parents say?" I asked at last.

"It was terrible. I was so ashamed." Lucinda squeezed her eyes shut as a tear trickled a path down her cheek. Its twin rolled down the other cheek. Soon a veritable watershed leaked from her eyes and dripped from her chin.

I pulled a kerchief from the pocket of my cloak and dabbed at her wet face. "You shouldn't feel ashamed. It was . . . it was natural for you and Jeff to want to marry."

"I wasn't ashamed of *us* . . . of my father and mother." Haltingly, Lucinda went on to tell of that evening, pausing now and then to dart a wary glance toward the ice, where the shrieking women were welcoming the first men across the imaginary finish line. She first told of meeting Jeff behind the schoolhouse and of their decision to confront her parents, then of the verbal battle that ensued at her home. "It didn't take my father long to figure out we'd been meeting on the sly. He went wild . . . I thought he'd choke Jeff. He said 'Marry that bit of waste paper! As much chance of that as hell freezing over.' He took Jeff's elbow and started to drag him toward the door, said he was going to have Jeff arrested for shaming me. I told him we hadn't done anything wrong—and—and you know what he said?"

"I couldn't possibly guess."

"He said, 'If I had the cheek to meet that brat on the sly, I'd likely be—be slut enough to—" She broke off, quaking, fighting back a new deluge of tears.

I slipped my arm around her and let her cry, then when her sobbing quieted and she was blotting her face with the handkerchief, I asked, "What did your mother say about this?"

Lucinda wiped her eyes and blew her nose. "She-she was terribly upset at first, said we were too young to know what we wanted. Then when she saw how much Jeff meant to me, she tried to make Father hear us out . . . talk us into waiting to marry. But he turned his anger on her. He said, 'How can you take their side? You told me you couldn't stand that cripple. Called him a fatherless brat.'" Lucinda paused, trembling, and went on, "I knew my mother didn't like Jeff, but to say such a horrid thing . . ."

"It must have wounded Jeff to the core," I said bitterly. "It certainly has done that to me."

Lucinda thought about that, pain behind her eyes, as if she was reliving the scorpion's sting. "Jeff . . . he just seemed to cave. He said that my father had made his point. That even if he was good enough for me, my father would find some excuse to keep us from getting married. He told me, 'Your father wants to keep you his little girl. Keep you under his thumb for the rest of your life.' Then he just walked from the house. I wanted to go after him, but my father held my arm so tight I couldn't budge."

My heart sank deeper and deeper within my chest as I pondered the situation, reviewing all that had been said. "No wonder Jeff's behaved so badly. He's decided he's unworthy." I paused, searching for the right words to ease into my next question. "Have you thought past the altar? Have you thought what life would be like as Jeff's wife?"

Lucinda shrugged and said gloomily, "I think about it all the time. Maybe not the way you mean."

"I'm talking about the kind of provider he'd be. Jeff's smart. Capable of earning a good living, but cripples are seldom offered good jobs. He wouldn't be able to provide the things you've had in the past. Not unless Dan's mine proves to be as rich as he claims."

Lucinda glared at me. "I don't give a jot about that. I know the kind of person Jeff is. He could have two heads and I'd still love him."

My heart rose slightly. I smiled. "I thought you'd say something like that. But I wanted you to see the practical side. You don't want it to take you by surprise." I paused, considering the unexpected path my life had taken and related it to Lucinda. "What about college? You'll be missing out on the opportunity to make something of yourself. I wasn't able to finish, and I regret it."

"There are things I can do that are more important than college. Like helping people in need."

"Dear girl, that's what I like about you—always the protector of the lame and rejected. But what if you are the one in need?"

"That won't happen. I could get a job as a secretary to make ends meet."

I hesitated, weighing words that could bend the dialogue in a different direction. After a bit, I said quietly, "You're bound to have children. What if they're born . . ."

Though I didn't finish, Lucinda knew the gist of the question and seemed surprised that I'd asked. "Born like Jeff? Than I'll love them all the more for it."

I smiled sadly and gave her a squeeze. "I can see that you're determined. Is there anything I can do to help? Perhaps if I talked to your parents . . ."

"My father's too hateful. Mother would give in if he would. You know how mothers are. She's afraid I'll run away and stop loving her." Lucinda studied her gloved hands and rubbed her fingers together. Her face saddened to the point of devastation. "Mother would like to pretend nothing has happened. But sometimes I look at my parents and wonder if I can ever love them again. They have no right—"

Blades had cut the ice. Turning, we saw women skate toward us, Nora among them. I rose abruptly. "I wish I could spend more time with you, but I wouldn't want Nora to think I've been trying to influence you. Can I give Jeff a message?"

"Tell him that I love him. That I'll always love him. And I still want to marry him."

"Well, dear girl, I'll see what I can do about that."

CHAPTER 28

The high school had closed for the holidays, and Nora had asked Lucinda to spend a few days in Wallace entertaining the toddlers while she shopped for gifts. Della's gossip ears had funneled in the news that Harley Hanson was out of town as well, and I thought it a good time to brave Clara's wrath. She and I had often traded verbal barbs on matters of school and community, but the Christmas season might have softened her quills.

Wearing my mental and emotional armor, I trudged through the snow to Hanson's house on shifter's row, dragging heavily bundled, eleven-month-old Todd behind me in a wooden coffee crate Jeff had fastened to runners. It was bitterly cold, and I felt the chill eating at my insides as well as numbing my face, hands, and feet. A brisk wind brought tears to my eyes.

Clara came to the door as slender and erect as the day she'd stopped at the school with Hester Reap and Maude Tatro to complain about Jeff's enrollment. She'd aged in other ways during those nine years—the fine lines that netted her eyes and mouth had grown deeper, the driven look in her eyes more compelling, her nostrils more pinched. Apparently I'd interrupted her while she was dressing a Christmas tree, because she held an angel aloft as if she'd caught it in mid-flight.

Surprise registered on her face. "Why, Maggie . . . what . . ." Her gaze crawled over Todd and me as if we were a couple of stray dogs in need of shelter

I said, "I'm sorry to disturb you, but I'd like to talk about Lucinda and Jeff."

"I have nothing to say." Her tone spoke of distaste for the subject.

"I know you're busy, but we really must talk."

"You mean you must. I have no wish—" She broke off as a gust of wind scooped snow from the roof above us and swirled it through the open doorway. "Oh, come on in," she said grudgingly. "You shouldn't have your child out in this icy blast." She motioned me into the drawing room and indicated a sofa made of green silk brocade. "Sit down. I'll be with you as soon as I put this ornament on the tree."

I settled on the sofa, gave Todd orders to sit beside me like a gentleman, and looked around the room. I'd been in Clara's home only once, but I'd heard that the two-story house had never met her criteria for quarters befitting a mine operator. Lacking space in the canyon for building, it was rumored she and Harley would soon move to Wallace to join Nora and Clyde as citizens of that center of commerce.

To me, the house and its fashionable clutter of deep-toned furnishings seemed splendid. Velvet brocades in rich sepias, greens, and golds that matched the Brussels carpet hung from windows and interior doorways. Figurines, lamps, books, and ferns adorned every flat surface. Tapestries and immense paintings transformed the walls into a beckoning forest. Today, the spacious drawing room seemed especially festive. Gifts in luxuriant wrappings lay beneath a fir tree that sparkled with tinsel and gossamer, and the scent of a fire crackling on the hearth of a marble fireplace mixed with the tantalizing fragrance of apples, spice, and rum wafting in from the kitchen. On a tea table in front of the sofa, bowls of ornate cut glass held green and red candies. Despite the room's Christmas mood, it struck me that it would be difficult for Clara to wear a face of good cheer when Lucinda was so miserable.

After she'd hung the angel from a fir bough, Clara selected a straight-backed chair across from me and sat on the edge of the seat as if ready to show me to the door. Her back was rigid, her lips set in a tight, thin line. A piece of tinsel had caught on the pompadour that crowned her head like an inverted mahogany bowl. She hadn't asked if I wanted to remove my coat, and the warm room was sucking a mist onto my forehead. Her cold, unwavering stare countered the warmth somewhat and prodded me to state my case and be done with it.

I said, "I don't want to interrupt your Christmas preparations, so I'll get right to the point. Lucinda and Jeff are in a miserable state of mind. I'm afraid they might do something desperate. I saw Luci at Nora's skating party and she was very depressed. She'd like to see Jeff, but said Harley won't allow it."

Clara's sharp nose wrinkled with a sniff of scorn. "How we deal with our daughter's childish fantasy is none of your business."

"It is my business. Jeff is my ward. I'm responsible for his well-being. How can I ignore it when he's so discouraged with life. It troubles me to see him—" I broke off as Todd slid from the sofa and headed for the Christmas tree as fast as his toddler's legs could carry him. I jumped to my feet to prevent disaster.

When I'd retrieved the child and set him on my lap, Clara unsheathed an accusing finger and pointed it at me like a sword. "Jeff brought his problems on himself by pursuing my daughter. And I'm sure you encouraged him."

I'd kept Jeff's meetings with Lucinda secret. Perhaps in Clara's biased view of things, that could be construed as aiding the lovers. So I lied by omission. "Luci and Jeff fell in love. I did nothing to foster that, though I admit to having great affection for both of them." I paused, stroking Todd's blond hair, wondering how I could prolong the discussion before Clara told me to leave. "I didn't come here to anger you, Clara. I came to share my concern about the youngsters. We're both mothers and I know we must have the same feelings."

Clara pondered that briefly. Very briefly, her eyes diffused, her gaze bent on hands beginning to gnarl at the joints. "It's not easy to be a mother," she said glumly. "If you keep a child from making a mistake, they hate you for it. If you let them have their way and they end up feeling wretched, they hate you for that."

"Children hate us when they're distraught and confused. We need to help them find solutions and make their own decisions."

Clara gave another of her scornful sniffs and glared at me as though I'd said something stupid. "What if they're wrong?"

"They grow through making mistakes."

"Marriage to Jeff would be the greatest mistake Luci could make. Now or at any time," Clara retorted. A flush of anger blotched her cheek. "It would cause my daughter nothing but misery."

Resentment crawled up my neck and heated my face, making it difficult to keep my calm, but I tried. "Jeff is a kind, loving person. He'd do everything in his power to make Luci happy. Even if the marriage has problems, and what marriage doesn't, when Luci comes to terms with that, she'll thank you for giving her a choice. If you don't let her test her judgement, she might hate you forever."

A long moment passed, while Clara thought about that, her eyes murky. I'd hoped something positive would result from her musings. Instead, she rose abruptly, wagging her head as though shaking dust from a mop, and motioned toward the door. "This discussion is useless. I have work to do."

Disappointment and anger mixed as I pulled Todd's woolen cap down over his ears, but in those few seconds I resolved to make one last plea. "Clara, if you value Luci's love, let her meet with Jeff now and then. Here at your house, if you must. And don't put it off, or it might be too late."

CHAPTER 29

A few days later, I could hardly believe my ears when Jeff told me he'd received a note from Lucinda saying her mother would arrange for her to meet Jeff at the Hanson's house whenever Harley was out of town. I was pleased that the lovers would be reunited, but acutely aware that in the end there'd be hell to pay with Harley.

Jeff and Lucinda met at her house three times in as many months. Each time, Jeff returned home like a beaten puppy and said that visiting Lucinda with her mother on the prowl, ready to pounce if they so much as touched each other, was almost worse than not seeing his sweetheart at all. I counseled him to give Lucinda the chance to finish high school before they eloped—if that was what they intended—but they were so desperately in love, I had no faith he'd take my advice. All I could do was to hope for a postponement of the inevitable.

I'd often wished since then that I'd helped them escape Bixbee to find the happiness they craved, as it wasn't long before Fate solved the problem in a tragic way. It began with tremors of union violence, as it had in the spring of '92. Threats of bombings and the like didn't affect the Black Titan. It had gone into full production in March, using both union and non-union workers. Dan made working conditions as safe as possible, paid his miners a dollar more than mines with union contracts, and operated on an eight-hour-day. The generous wage scale and shorter day caused the union to look on the Black Titan with favor, but the Bunker Hill and Sullivan Mining and Concentrating company at Wardner and the Apex Mining and Milling at Bixbee were thorns in the union's side. These mines paid rock-bottom wages and made a habit of striking union men from their payrolls as soon as company spotters discovered them.

The Western Federation of Miners had become the strongest union force in the West, with hundreds of local unions and thousands of members. Mines with union contracts challenged the Federation to do something—either force the Bunker Hill and the Apex to raise wages to the union scale, and thus even the profit advantage, or union mines would lower their wages to Bunker Hill and Apex levels. The latter was unthinkable for union minds.

By April, grumblings against the Apex and the Bunker Hill had grown to a roar. Miners could hardly wait to fuel the fire that had been smoldering all winter. One murder had been committed in the name of unionism. Further trouble seemed assured. I wouldn't allow myself to believe the recurrence of "Shit Creek Fever," as Dan called it, would take the ailing miners beyond the point of recovery. Surely the union bosses would apply salve to the rash of discontent before it festered into outright war.

I was wrong. Rather than soothe the irritation, union officials chose to pour on turpentine, especially those who'd started the itch. Newspapers predicted the violence of '99 would equal that of '92. Headlines pointed in that direction. *WARDNER AND BIXBEE ARMED CAMPS—UNION HEAD DEMANDS NON-UNION WORKERS IN WARDNER JOIN UNION AT ONCE— MANAGER OF BUNKER HILL SAYS COMPANY WILL SHUT DOWN FOR TWENTY YEARS BEFORE IT WILL RECOGNIZE UNION.* It seemed the news of '92 had been dug from the files and blazoned across the pages. I waited with dread for the shot or blast that would signal open warfare.

I'd heard that Federation members from Butte were arriving in the district to help local unions force a showdown, and wondered if the Tatros would be among them. If there was to be a repeat of '92 they'd want to be there. I watched constantly from my windows, recalling Maude's warning that someday Jim would take revenge for what he considered Dan's treason.

Then one morning in late April, as I stood at the ironing board I'd set near the window, I glimpsed Jim, now wearing a straw-colored handlebar mustache, among the throng of armed men who'd gathered in front of the union hall one hundred yards from the house. The sight of his repulsive face made me wonder if the malicious brier had grown longer thorns since his release from jail. Like many of the men, he wore a bandana handkerchief around his neck, I assumed to hide his identity during the violence they planned. My instant reaction was concern for Jeff. He'd left with Lennie early that morning to mingle with the miners in the street and pick their brains for details about the march on the Bunker Hill, and he might encounter Jim. Likely hatred for Jeff lurked in a dark niche at the back of Jim's mind.

No sooner had the thought provided grist for my worry mill, than Jeff hurried into the house, slamming the door behind him. Eyes wild with excitement, he reported that the officers of the Executive Miners Union had held a meeting in Gem the night before and had decided to blow up the concentrator at the Bunker Hill in Wardner. The men swarming along the tracks had come from a meeting held at Burke that morning to vote on the plan, had returned home for handguns and rifles, and were waiting for union officials to commandeer a train to take them to Wardner.

The union men at the Titan planned to take part in the stand against the Bunker Hill. Though Dan disapproved of the union's tactics, rather than work with half-a-crew, he'd closed the mine and was enjoying a day of rest. He'd been lounging on the sofa in the sitting room, rolling a red ball across the floor into Todd's eager hands, when Jeff brought the news about the bombing. He shot Jeff a look of disbelief. "They're not going to do anything to the Apex?"

"Harley agreed to their demands last night," Jeff said as he headed for his bedroom. "He's gone to Wardner to try to talk the Bunker Hill into doing the same thing."

Dan caught the ball Todd threw at his feet and gave it a bounce that nearly touched the ceiling. "Hallelujah! I thought the canyon might be in for it."

I set the heel of the flatiron on the board and looked up from the shirt I'd been ironing. "What about the people in Wardner? They've lost everything to fire twice. Now this. Don't they count?"

Dan raised his arms in a half-hearted gesture of apology. "Of course they do. I didn't mean it that way. It's just that The Creek took the brunt of the trouble in '92. If it has to happen again, let it happen somewhere else."

"Will the union ever learn it can't use brutal force to gain its ends," I said with disgust. "President McKinley will send troops, and the men who dynamite the mill will land in jail. The union won't win a thing for all the trouble it's caused, and the operators will get even by lowering wages and keeping the union out of the mines."

"Yeah, but they'll have to use dumb, green labor to get out the rock." Dan rolled the ball one more time and waved his hands at Todd to signal the end of the game. "However it turns out, it won't hurt me any," he went on. "If I need more men to work the stopes, I can take my pick of the union men out of work."

I slid the shirt onto a hanger, hung it on a rack I used for drying clothes in wet weather, and was pulling a housedress from the basket of clothes when Jeff rushed from his room tying a bandana around his neck. He'd made friends with Milt, one of the younger union men at the mine, and I guessed what he had in mind. "Where are you going?" I said in an ominous tone.

He shrugged. "Milt's going to Wardner and I'm going with him." He spoke as if blasting a mill to smithereens was an everyday occurrence.

I could feel Dan's scowl from across the room. "You stay clear of all that trouble, you hear. It's nothing for a young kid to get mixed up in. Just land you in jail."

Jeff yanked on the doorknob. "I'm not a young kid! I'm perfectly able to take care of myself."

"Jeff! If you don't follow orders, you might as well find another job."

Jeff turned slowly, deliberately, and sent Dan a look of utter resentment. "Why didn't you tell that to the rest of the crew?"

"Because they're not family."

I held my breath while the two glared at each other like stallions about to do mortal battle. I hated conflict, especially between those I loved, and felt torn in two directions. Several seconds sneaked precariously by before either spoke. Then, "I want you to go up and guard the mine," Dan said in a tone that demanded compliance. "A big fracas like this brings a lot of bindlestiffs into town. While everybody's caught up in the hullabaloo, they'll steal everything they can get their hands on. While you're up there, you might as well clean out some of yesterday's workings."

Jeff threw the weight of his disappointment against the coercion in Dan's voice. "Why me? Everybody else has the day off. Nobody's going to bother anything way up there. You just want to keep me from the action." He pulled the door open. "Get somebody else to stand guard."

"Jeff!" Dan blared. "Maggie and I have been good to you. You owe us some consideration. Maggie will worry herself sick if you land in jail."

Jeff swung his head part way around and settled a questioning gaze on me. I tried to speak, but tension clogged my throat. I merely nodded.

Jeff took his time to ponder Dan's words, his expression sliding from anger, to frustration, to resentful submission. At last, he heaved a disgruntled sigh. "I have to tell Milt I'm not going. I'll come back for my boots."

I managed to make my vocal chords work as he went through the door. "I'll fix you some sandwiches and a thermos of coffee. Then Todd and I will walk with you a little ways."

"You're not going out among all those rebels," Dan bellowed.

I shot him a look that matched Jeff's for resentment. "Yes, I am. I need to talk to Jeff. To make him understand we're thinking of his welfare."

Twenty minutes later, I was pushing Todd's baby carriage into the broil of male humanity that clogged the street. The day was typical for that time of year, the sun warm enough I had no use for a winter overcoat, yet not too warm for a jacket. The flag at the union hall fluttered in a light breeze. The same breeze tore a few wispy clouds to tatters, plucked paper scraps from trashcans and set them spinning across the tracks.

Jeff seemed in no hurry to reach the mine and dawdled as we wormed our way through the noisy crowd. Every few yards he'd stop to eavesdrop on men with eye masks who were circulating among the miners, warning against any kind of demonstration. There were no women in the street, and I felt like a dove in a flock of ravens. Even more so, when I spied Jim Tatro in a knot of men huddled in front of the union hall. When I brought him to Jeff's attention, Jeff eyes startled as if I'd said there was a rattlesnake at his feet, but he feigned indifference. "I don't give a straw if he's here or not."

Despite his claim, I noticed that he glanced over his shoulder now and then as we walked the two miles to Burke. When he spelled me with the baby carriage, I assumed the rear vigil and caught a glimpse of Jim's brazen face amidst the comings and goings of armed miners and urged Jeff to speed his pace.

We'd reached Burke and were pressing our way through a crowd gathered at the depot when someone came up from behind and took my arm. I shied, thinking it was Jim, then sagged with relief as I turned to find Lennie standing there glum-faced, his black hair riffling in the breeze.

"You'd better go home, Maggie," he warned. "This is no place for a woman." He took note of Jeff's lunch pail. "Where are you going? We gave you the day off."

Jeff snorted with disgust. "I was going to Wardner with Milt, but Dan wants me to stand guard up at the mine. Likely I'll never get a chance for that much excitement again."

"Dan thought he'd end up in trouble that was none of his making," I put in hurriedly.

"He was right," Lennie aimed the reply at Jeff and added. "You'd stand a good chance of getting hurt if you tagged along on this pooferah. And you'd better be ready for trouble at the mine. I've seen some tough looking drifters in town. Do you know where we keep the rifles?"

"In that metal box just inside the portal."

"Right. Here's the key." Lennie unhooked a key ring from his belt, removed one of the smaller keys, and handed it to Jeff with an admonition. "Don't lose it. And don't use up all the shells on target practice."

Rather than walk the muddy wagon road Dan had built to connect the Black Titan with the railroad terminal at Burke, I parked the baby carriage on the edge of town and took Jeff's pail so he could carry Todd along a trail soggy from receding snows. A forest of small second-growth timber and a groundcover of beargrass, chinquapin, and elkberry closed around us, muting the sound and feel of insurrection we'd left behind. Jeff usually tuned his senses to nature, but he was so filled with anger over his exile to the mine, I had to bring his attention to a pine tree oozing sap from a scar made by a black bear.

Now and then we heard blasts and wondered how that was possible when the mines were closed. Eventually, we decided the explosions were coming from Harry Day's new mine up one of the gulches. Harry was at the same point in his exploratory work that Dan had been before he'd invested his inheritance in the Titan, and Harry and his brother did much of their own blasting.

A melting snowdrift blocked the trail beyond the ball diamond where Dan and I had married, so I left Jeff with several words of commiseration and started back down the path at the snail's pace that suited Todd's short, wobbly legs. On the way, I heard the snap of brush and something squish mud in a wallow off the trail. I took it to be a deer on its way to the creek for water, but the flash of movement I saw when I peered into the forest shadows was that of a man, not a deer. Recalling Lennie's warning to be on the watch for drifters, I pulled

Todd into my arms and fled through the woods as fast as the extra weight would allow.

●●●

Neither Jeff nor Lennie returned home that night, and I lay on my bed with eyes closed, stumbling about in a world of dire imaginings, some of them conjured from the flash of movement in the woods, others rising from the rebellious nature of the union brotherhood. Dan said not to worry, but I noticed puckers on his forehead as he sat down to breakfast the next morning.

I fed Todd his oatmeal and sent him into the sitting room to play with his clutter of toys, then I poured the coffee and set a tower of pancakes on the table. I was about to sit in the chair across from Dan when someone hammered on the front door.

Dan said, "Better get that, Maggie. Somebody sounds real anxious."

"It's Link," I said from the doorway. "He says he has to talk to you."

Link was a non-union foreman from the Titan, a slim ropy man, with graying hair and the cough of a constant smoker. His stony, dry-eyed countenance marked him as a seasoned hard-rock miner. Dan called him into the kitchen and invited him to share breakfast, but he declined, saying, "I ate early. Went up to the mine to check on things. I'll take a cup of coffee, though." He ground the stub of a cigarette onto a saucer I set out for his cup and sat next to Dan.

"What were you doing at the mine?" Dan said around a bite of pancake. "I told you we wouldn't work until the union men were back on the job."

"Lennie said Jeff was keeping watch, and he wanted me to spell him."

I poured Link a cup of coffee, sat down at the table to drink from my own cup, and sent Link a sharp look over the rim. "Where is Lennie? I haven't seen him since yesterday morning."

"He went down to Wallace to see if his crew made it back from Wardner. Wants to know when they'll be back on the job. Rumor has it that Hub Malone wants the brotherhood to go back to work as if nothing had happened." Link gave a snort of a laugh. "From the amount of drink they took along, they'll be hung-over for a day or two."

"That figures," Dan said with a snort of his own. He stuck his fork into the last of a pancake, and held it speculatively in the air. "So, why are you here?"

Link drew in a breath, as if preparing for a major pronouncement. "Like I say, I went up to spell Jeff." He dragged out the words. "Couldn't find him anywhere, but there's a cave-in."

Dan clanged his fork onto the plate. "Christ! How can that be? Our timbering's good and strong."

Link gave a vague shrug. "I know. It don't make sense. And the cave-in ain't where we been working. It's only about a hundred and fifty yards from the portal . . . you know, that drift we give up on a while back . . . where we been storing dynamite."

Dan thought about that, frowning at the wall as if it held the answer. "Must've been a shift in the mountain, but I haven't felt a quake." He turned his worried gaze on Link. "Have you?"

Link shook his head. "One thing, though, I heard blasts up that way yesterday. Thought they was coming from Day's mine. Except one sounded like it come from a different direction. Maybe the Titan."

"That's crazy . . . unless . . ." Dan let the germ-of-a-thought hang in the air for a long moment before he breathed life into it. "You don't suppose Jeff . . ." He let the idea fade to an early death as if it was absurd.

"Jeff's been wanting to try his hand at blasting," Link said haltingly, guilt in his voice. "I'd showed him a little about it. But not enough for him to set a charge on his own."

Dan gave a burst of air and shoved his weight against the back of his chair. "Why in the hell would he do that?" He seemed to aim the question at himself more than at Link. "Maybe to get even with me for sending him up there."

"He wouldn't," I blurted in anger. Then to Link, "Why don't you find him and ask him?"

Link shifted in the chair and coughed in a defensive way. "Well, ma'am . . . that's why I come. He ain't in the cabin . . . ain't nowhere around . . . I think he might be buried under the rock." His voice was brittle with the same hint of fear in it that I saw on his face.

At first I was too stunned for speech. Then as reality set in, "No! He couldn't be. Maybe he went for a walk and—and fell and hurt himself." I felt as if I was drowning, reaching for a twig to keep me afloat. "Have you looked for him on the hillside?"

"Enough to know there ain't tracks going anywhere except to the portal, the cabin, and down the trail."

I didn't know which was greater—my shock or outrage. It was outrage that pointed an accusing finger at Dan. "You were the one who insisted he watch the mine. Likely he thought he didn't dare come home."

Dan seemed not to have heard me, just leaned forward, ready to spring into action. "What makes you think he's underneath?"

"I found his dinner pail just inside the portal, nothing eat from it. And a candlestick was in the loose rock at the edge of the cave-in."

Dan's face turned livid. "Your men could've left a sleeper, and Jeff swung a pick into it."

"No way! I told you, the rock ain't anywhere near where we left off working. Besides, I noticed a length of wire gone that we had ready for the next round o' blasts. If Jeff was standing guard, he had no reason to be in that old drift. He musta been experimenting with the powder."

Dan shoved off from his chair and started to pace, as if too shocked to know what to do. "The wire could've been stolen. Used for the blast at Wardner."

"No, sir. They got that wire from the Frisco Mine. And stealing don't explain the candlestick."

Something closed inside Dan's mind. I could see the change quite clearly, as if anxiety and anger had translated to a deep sadness. "I guess we have to face it," he said morosely. "Jeff set off a blast and got himself killed."

My head wheeled picturing the chain of events—Jeff wanting to go with his friend to Wardner, the disappointment of having to bend his will to obey Dan, the possibility he'd tried to put a thrill into his day by setting a charge. The thought affected me like a chilling wind from the north that turned my blood to ice and froze other worries into silence. "I don't believe it," I said numbly. "I need some proof."

"All right, I'll look for some." Dan gave a heavy sigh and headed for the boot bench near the door. "I'll put on my boots, Link, and we'll see what we can find."

"I'm going with you," I cried.

Dan sent me a look that mixed anguish with concern. "You stay with the baby. Wait for Lennie."

"I'll go crazy waiting here. I'm coming."

Dan swore under his breath, sucked in air, and said grudgingly, "All right, but hurry it up." I was used to his tone of voice. I'd heard it often when worry ate at his insides.

I readied myself as if the furies were at my heels, my heart sick, my mind a jumble of rage, fear, and dreadful regrets. I changed into heavier shoes, threw on my coat, and took Todd's little overcoat and cap from a peg on the wall. "Come, Todd," I said more sharply than I'd intended. "You can go to Della's and play with her pots and pans."

Todd had backed himself into a corner, his face white from the tension in the house, his blue, child's eyes wide and quizzical. "Jeff bye bye?"

The words tore at my heart. I wished I could cry, wished I could rid my throat of the claws that gripped it. This little child, though just beginning to utter a few words, had always understood more than was right for one so young. And now he'd picked up on the tragedy. Thank heavens Della understood little children. She'd set his mind on something else.

While Dan paced the floor and Link slouched against the door smoking a cigarette, I put Todd's coat on him and tucked a few of his toys in a diaper bag. We were about to leave when someone drummed lightly on the door. The door opened a crack, and a girl's voice called in, "Anybody home?"

I turned to Dan in alarm. "It's Luci," I hissed softly. "What will we tell her?"

Dan put a finger at his lips, "Nothing 'till we know for sure." He went to the door and motioned Lucinda inside. "This is a surprise." He forced a smile. "How did you manage to escape your house?"

"Father's in Wardner and Mother's in bed with a lame back. She's taking medication that makes her sleep."

Dan offered a stiff smile. "And you took advantage. Can't blame you for that."

"I-I wish I could ask you to stay," I said hurriedly, "but we're on the way out." I felt horrid, denying Lucinda, when she'd obviously taken a risk to come.

"Then Jeff isn't here? I thought he might be at home because the mines are shut down. I baked him some cookies." She held up a paper bag that smelled of cinnamon

"He-he's out . . ." I paused, searching for a lie and looked to Dan for help.

"I-I had him run an errand for me," Dan said feebly. "I'm sure he'll be disappointed that he missed you. Would you like to leave the cookies?"

The sober-faced Todd had returned to his corner, and in a voice of innocence uttered words that fell like the notes of a dirge. "Jeff bye-bye."

Lucinda looked at the child, at me, Dan, and took note of Link standing near the door, shifting his weight from foot to foot. Evidently our distraught expressions hadn't escaped her. "Is something wrong? Has the union caused you trouble?"

"No, nothing like that," Dan hastened to say. "There's just a problem at the mine."

Lucinda stood there a moment letting her bewildered gaze wander among the rest of us, then said in a worried, tentative way, "I-I hate to leave without seeing Jeff. There-there's something I have to tell him. Would you mind if I waited? I don't know when I can see him again."

My heart had crawled into my toes. How should I answer? When I did, I dragged the words out, sensing I was perpetrating a lie. "I'm not sure when he'll be back, but if you'd like to wait for a while, feel welcome."

CHAPTER 30

On the way to Burke we met six members of Dan's crew. He enlisted five to help search the cave-in for signs of Jeff and sent another to find Lennie. To spare me the possibility of seeing Jeff's body mutilated by explosives, he insisted I wait at the Titan's portal until he and the crew had cleared the drift of fallen rock.

I hadn't waited long before Lennie arrived, Lucinda at his heels, her face taut with alarm. Evidently Lennie had found her at the house when he went to fetch his boots and thoughtlessly had told her where he was going and why.

I was already drowning in gloom. Now I had to keep from pulling Lucinda in with me. I put a comforting arm around her trembling shoulders and said, "Luci, you shouldn't have come. Dan won't let you go inside. There's nothing to do but wait."

She pulled free of my arm and scowled at me as if I'd caused the problem. "Then I'll wait. I have to know what's happened to Jeff."

"Your mother might need you. We'll send word when we know something."

"Jeff is the one who needs me! I'm not leaving until I know if he's hurt or not." Having rejected my appeal, she stood to one side, shivering with dread in the crisp morning air, watching Lennie's dark figure fade into the blackness of the tunnel.

And so we began our long vigil at the portal, the sound of compressors coming from within. Most of the time we paced back and forth in front of the portal. Now and then we slumped wearily on benches just inside the entry. Unable to put our anxiety into speech, we said little. The wait seemed unbearable, a nightmare without end. I spent the time imagining the horror of the blast, grasping at straws to find an explanation other than the obvious. I recalled the flash of movement I'd seen in the woods and thought Jim Tatro might have followed Jeff to the mine. He was capable of murder and had always hated Jeff. But how would we ever know?

Too distraught to set blame, especially for something so elusive, I let my thoughts wander sadly back over the years. I recalled the day Nelly had brought Jeff to school, a shy nine-year-old, dragging his deformed foot along like a prisoner drags a ball and chain. Likely to him it had been such a punishment. I recalled the bullying he'd suffered and the way Lucinda had protected him at every hand. She'd pecked away at his shell of insecurity until he'd emerged a confident young man ready to prove his mettle to anyone who tested him. My heart ached when I thought of Nelly's failure to return. I'd made my own mistakes in raising Jeff, but if I lived to be a hundred, I'd never understand her frailty.

So I passed the time in worry and reflection, feeling guilt at the thousand and one things I would have done differently if I'd had them to do over. More than once, I found myself creeping farther into the entry, listening, anticipating the worst. Just as often, I caught Lucinda's arm as the distraught girl tried to slip past. I questioned the crew each time one of them trudged from the shadows, grunting a carload of rock along the tracks to dump down the hillside, but received no satisfaction.

Shadows of sundown fell across the canyon, chilling the snow-drifted mountain-tops, and still Lucinda and I waited. A cold draft funneled up from the creek bottom, causing night birds to fluff their feathers and voice their mournful calls. To escape the chill, I stepped farther into the cavernous portal, taking Lucinda with me.

The seconds, the minutes, the quarter-hours slothed by without the sound of another ore car on the rails. Lucinda and I were about to defy orders and enter the tunnel that held the compressors, when footsteps echoed in the dark void ahead of us, but without the accompanying rumble of wheels. The steps lost their hollow sound and became the crunch of boots on fractured rock as Dan came near. His shoulders were stooped, as if they bore the weight of the mountain.

I lurched toward him and forced the question past my fear-dry lips. "Is Jeff . . . "

I needn't have asked. Dan's expression said it all. The ripple of horror that washed over me matched the portal's icy draft.

Lucinda gave a heart-rending wail and began to sob. I folded her in my arms, my own nameless horror as deep and black as the tunnel. I'd invested so much of myself in Jeff, had loved him so dearly, only to have him snatched away as quickly as a thieving wind plucks dust from a summer street. I wondered if I could endure.

On the brink of hysteria, Lucinda tore free of my arms and started to run down the tunnel.

Dan caught up to her in a few steps and seized her wrist. "No! It's not for your eyes. You need to remember Jeff the way he was. Not the way he is now."

"I have a right to see him!" she cried. "To touch him one last time."

"It won't help," Dan said more gently. "It'll make the pain worse, believe me. I've seen enough of this sort of thing to know." He held her until she quit struggling and crumpled into his arms, tears running down her face, the breath dragging in her throat.

She stayed there for several seconds, gasping tears that flowed from the fragile lining of her soul. Then with a last despairing glance my way, she ran out the portal and down the hill, stumbling, sliding, sending her cries back on the wind.

CHAPTER 31

Jeff's funeral was held at the cemetery near the Bixbee school, a small fenced plot guarded by two cottonwoods that had escaped the woodcutter's axe. The loss of life in Bixbee should have warranted more graves, but only a dozen headstones dotted the flat. At death, most miners were sent home to families in the East and in Europe. Just the bones of those without ties, like Jeff, lay in the stony ground.

I thought the wretched little plot too lowly for Jeff, but during that period of mourning, I would have considered the most elaborate mausoleum unworthy. I consoled myself with the thought he'd be near and I could tend his grave.

Only a handful of friends braved the steady mist that seeped from the sky and dripped from trees and brush. Dan, Lennie, and I huddled together, the damp like a sodden cloak around our shoulders. I'd left Todd at a neighbor's house, and the Tuttles were there for the brief ceremony, as well as Dan's brother Aaron and Nora and her husband. Milt and another young fellow from town who'd been Jeff's buddies stared glumly at the dank pit as if it foretold their own youthful demise. A few of the soldiers sent to occupy the district after the bombing strolled by on patrol. Likely, the stability they brought to the canyon would last only as long as they remained. Then the usual rumblings of discontent would return. Governor Steunenberg had said the state couldn't afford to suppress a revolution every three or four years and he believed the Western Federation of Miners should be wiped from the face of the earth.

Such matters had the importance of a grain of sand on that day of the funeral—the overwhelming sense of loss had swamped my mind and heart until I feared I'd burst from so much feeling. I wondered why Lucinda wasn't there dressed in mourning clothes like the rest of us, though I guessed she was the one who'd left a bouquet of buttercups and wild violets at the open grave. I half-way expected her to materialize from the mists while our heads were bowed for Dan's and Hank's eulogies, but no one came. Surely Harley wouldn't deprive her of that last goodbye. I could imagine how she must be suffering.

When Jeff lay cradled in the earth, I blanketed the grave with branches of serviceberry, the white blossoms splotched yellow by the rain. I placed Lucinda's soggy bouquet at the head of the mound near Jeff's heart. Then the two young men played a shaky rendition of Jeff's favorite tune, *Clementine,* on their mouth organs.

Back at the house, the mourners sat with me for a while and ate a simple dinner Della had prepared. The women attempted a light conversation, while the men dwelled on the recent union uprising. When they left, Dan went for a walk—likely to have the good cry he'd denied himself—and Della lured Todd to the boarding house with a promise of tarts. She had the best of intentions, wishing to give me time to myself, but I would have preferred Todd's distraction. His absence left me to face the empty silence of the walls.

I closed the blinds to shut out the gloomy day and sat in my rocker with a shawl around my shoulders, somber portraits of family scowling down upon me. From beyond my thoughts, I heard the clock counting away at life, and the hiss of water from an open pan splattering the hot stove lid. I stared into nothingness, seeing phantoms of the recent past, reliving the sights and sounds of Jeff's comings and goings, hearing the gentle fall of his voice upon my ears.

When the men had retrieved his body from the rock-fall, they'd discovered that someone had shattered his crippled foot with a bullet, his body then hidden by the blast. They'd found that he'd fired the rifle that lay at his side, one that belonged to the Titan. They had several theories about what had happened—that Jeff had shot himself in the foot that had caused so much misery and then set the blast, but suicide was a possibility I refused to believe. Another theory was that Jeff had confronted a thief stealing dynamite in the storage area and gunfire had ensued, or that the thief had heard Jeff coming, hidden behind the stacks of dynamite in ambush. It was possible that gunfire had struck the dynamite and caused the blast.

It was too soon to know if someone had killed him or why, though I had my suspicions. The fact of his death was enough to bear. Anger and vengeance couldn't bring him back. But it was of some satisfaction to know he hadn't carelessly caused his death by experimenting with dynamite. I thought of the courage he'd likely shown in the face of the enemy and of the loss of so much goodness. Never would I forget the pain of grief as it drew threads of longing from my heart.

● ● ●

Evening shadows had crept into the canyon before Dan returned. I was in the bedroom packing a suitcase, the mirror on the wall reflecting the image of a woman whose hair seemed a Bastille torch above the intense black of her dress. I'd take clothing from by bureau, give it a quick appraisal, and either stuff it into a brown leather suitcase that lay open on the bed or return it to the drawer. I'd already sorted Todd's clothes. A carpetbag held his dresses, long stockings, and undergarments.

I didn't turn when Dan's familiar footsteps crossed the parlor and entered the bedroom, but I could tell he'd stopped just inside the doorway and sensed his eyes drilling a hole in my back. I feared those eyes. Facing them would shake my resolve. As it was, I'd forced myself to pack. My heart wasn't in the leave-taking, just my frantic mind.

Though I knew Dan was there, I still jumped when he asked, "What in the hell are you doing?"

I didn't turn. Instead, I took a chemise from the bureau and laid it on top of the other clothes in the suitcase. "Nora invited me to spend some time with her in Spokane and I've decided to accept. Little Chris has developed asthma and she's taking him there for treatments. She's rented a flat."

Dan's footsteps closed in, hard on the bare floor, soft on a rug. In my nervousness, I spilled face powder from a box I was tucking into the suitcase and splotched the patchwork quilt that served as a bedspread.

Dan turned me by the shoulders. His squint lines had deepened, making it seem he was smiling. He wasn't. Rather, he seemed shaken. "Maggie, are you mad at me because of what happened to Jeff?"

I shrank from the direct encounter of our eyes, but managed to stammer, "Yes . . . yes, I'm mad . . . a little . . . no, not really . . . except he was killed because he wanted to work in your mine. I'd like to blame everybody. You, Lennie, Harley, Nelly for leaving him. But I know that isn't fair. It's just that . . . just that it's all so senseless. So unreal. Nothing seems real." I paused to gather the weight of my resolve, then went on in words that tumbled from my lips. "That's not why I'm going. I'm going because I'm so afraid of what this place will do to Todd. I don't want him struck down in the prime of his youth like Jeff. Where each time he leaves the house I'll wonder if it's for the last time. In Bixbee, death is always chasing at one's heels, always filling people's lives with torment. I just have to get away from here for a while."

Dan firmed his hold on my shoulders. "Bixbee isn't to blame. Life is hard everywhere. You think you can find a place where sorrow and pain don't exist. Well, there is no such place. There's misery wherever you—"

"Bixbee *is* to blame! It and the stupid mines. You left in '92 because of what happened here. So did Nelly. Jeff was killed because of what's happening now. The district is always to blame. But I'm not going to let it take Todd from me." I twisted free of Dan's grip and turned back to the bureau, where I fumbled among handkerchiefs, ribbons, and bows in the top drawer until I found a neatly folded linen scarf.

When I turned to put the scarf in the suitcase, Dan blocked my way, meeting my defiant gaze with an expression that blended disappointment and reproach. "Be honest with yourself, Maggie. You're not doing this for Todd. You're doing it for yourself. You think you can run away from your grief. But face it, you have to expect sadness in your life."

"Expect it, yes. But I think I've already had more than my share. If I stay on I'll be asking for added heartbreak." The thought brought a sudden weariness. The bones seemed to leave my flesh. I dropped to the bed, saw Dan blur through my tears, and covered my face with the scarf. I swallowed to stifle sobs that were clawing their way up my throat. "I just can't bear the thought of Jeff being shot . . . the blast . . . meeting death in the mountain. I feel like I want to die, myself."

Gently, Dan eased down beside me on the bed and dabbed at my face with the scarf. "I understand how you feel. Jeff lived under my roof, too. I may not always have showed I cared, but I did. I'll never stop blaming myself for his death. But that doesn't mean the end of life for us." He lifted my chin and peered beneath my wet lashes. "We can work things out so you'll be happy. You have a duty to try."

I gave a little sigh and replied, "I read a poem the other day. I can't remember the exact words, but it went something like this, *If you're false to duty, you break a thread in the loom, and you'll see the results when your lifetime unravels.* But what is my first duty? To my son—to you—to our marriage—to the success of your mine?"

"All of those. And I'm beholden to the same."

"But how long must I live two lives—one within myself tortured by grief, the other meeting duties and obligations?"

Dan thought about that, exhaling a long breath of conciliation. "Maybe it was a mistake for you to quit teaching. We'll have to find things for you to do so there's less time to grieve." He paused to wipe away tears that welled over my eyelids and spilled down my cheeks. "I've been thinking . . . maybe . . . as soon as the mine comes in strong, we can build a house in Wallace."

When the mine comes in strong? It was always 'when the mine comes in strong.' The Titan held a record for existing on nothing but promise, though I had to admit, prospects had improved three-fold. And Wallace? No different than Bixbee, just larger. I couldn't believe that not long ago I'd considered such a move an improvement.

Dan seemed to have read my thoughts. "I admit Wallace isn't far enough to suit you . . . full of miners and mining talk. But the town has a lot more to offer than Bixbee. There'd be a chance for you to meet people with broader backgrounds. You already have a few friends there. And . . ." A smile, exceedingly tender and sad, spread across his face. "you'll have Todd and me." He kissed my cheeks and lips in a soft, tentative way. "Promise me you won't stay in Spokane for long. It'll purely kill me if you aren't around to love. I'll turn into dust and blow away."

Something about the sorrow in his voice, the feel of him, and the smell of him, brought a gradual rippling away of my resolve. I kissed the damp creases in his neck, ear, and cheek, ran my fingers through the ringlets of wheaten hair at the nape of his neck, and hugged him. "I promise I'll not stay long. I'm not sure I can live without you for even a few weeks."

A rapping at the front door interrupted the tender moment. Grumbling about the timing, Dan went to see who was there. "It's Clara Hanson," he said when he returned. "Do you feel up to seeing her?"

A groan shuddered in my chest. "Tell her I'll be there in a minute."

"Then I'll go to Della's and pick up Todd."

When I entered the parlor, Clara was pacing back and forth in front of the window, her brown silk skirts rustling over petticoats. I was surprised she'd come. I hadn't expected her to offer sympathy. To her, Jeff's death meant Lucinda's deliverance.

She turned toward me, her face pale, drawn into a mask of calamity. "I'm sorry to bother you at a time like this," she said. She seemed short of breath, as if she'd walked the road too fast.

I tried to smile and failed. "Please sit down." I motioned toward an armchair with a tapestry seat, then settled in the rocker whose curves had the familiarity of an old shoe.

"I really can't stay," Clara said from the armchair. " I know you must be devastated over—over the death." Her words sounded tinny and false. She couldn't even bring herself to speak Jeff's name. She looked out the dusky window behind me, blinking her way into a thought, then focused her distracted gaze on me. "I'm worried sick about Lucinda. She's disappeared. I thought you might know where she is."

The news jolted my numbed senses back to life. "She's gone?" I said with a start. "The last I saw of her was at the mine, just after they'd found Jeff. Didn't she come home?"

"Yes, but she was terribly upset. She wouldn't talk to me . . . said I wouldn't understand . . . went into her room and locked her door. I begged her to let me in, but she wouldn't." Clara paused, blinking as she had before. Her expression said she found this humbling confession hard on her pride. Several seconds crept past before she continued to drag out the details word by grudging word. "I went to her room at daybreak hoping she'd talk to me . . . the door was open . . . so I went in. Her purse, brush and comb were missing from her dressing table . . . when I checked the closet, I found she'd taken some of her clothes and the suitcase she used when she stayed at Nora's on school nights." Another pause, likely to consider how much more she was willing to reveal, then a large, gasping sigh. "I called Nora, thinking she might have gone there, but she didn't. I know she's run off for good!"

I recalled the evening at the mine, picturing Lucinda's shock and grief, as deeply troubling as the anguish that made me want to run away. It could have driven her to do most anything. Clara knew that. No sense adding to her fears nor confronting her with the fact she and Harley were responsible. Trying to suppress blame, I said, "I know from experience that grief can make a person act in a senseless way. Jeff's death tore Luci apart. But she's a sensible girl. She'll come home when she's feeling better."

Clara shook her head in doubt. "I wish I could believe that, but she was so unreasonable when it came to Jeff. I should never have let her go on meeting him. I should never have listened to you." Clara's voice had grown loud, angry. "Heaven knows what she's done!"

"How would you feel if they'd never had a chance to be together?" I could no longer keep reproach from my voice.

Clara pushed off from the chair in anger. "I'd still have my Lucinda, that's what. If anything happens to her, I'll hold you and that-that cripple to blame. May you both rot in hell!" With a resentful jerk of her head, she marched from the room and slammed the door behind her.

CHAPTER 32

I fretted over Lucinda the whole two weeks I stayed with Nora. Wherever I went—the park, the mercantile, the theater—I watched for her brunette head bobbing in and out of the crowds. The worry continued when I returned home. Even worse than Clara's accusation was the blame I showered on myself for being the indirect cause of Lucinda's heartbreak. No matter what I might be doing at the time, remorse staked claim to my thoughts, linking itself to grief for Jeff.

One evening, I stood at the kitchen's sink-stand washing dishes greased from a supper of ham and beans. A breeze drifted through the window, fluttering the curtains and drying steam from my face. The wisp of air carried the lemony fragrance of buckthorn blooming along the hillside at the back of the house. Beyond the window, ruffles of bright rose drifted across the turquoise sky and snared the mountaintops in their glow. I breathed in the beauty in an attempt to lift my spirits.

Dan had gone to spend another evening at the mine. His union crew was jailed and he'd been forced to hire Missouri farm boys who didn't know the difference between their thumb and a stick of dynamite. They were turning him gray. Todd would have to be the one to listen to my worried chatter. He might not make conversation like his daddy, but he was looking more like him every day—the same broad, shining face, same springy curls, though flax-colored, the same blue eyes, sparkling like crystals. He liked to be near me when I worked. The minute I started to clear dishes from the table or work the pump handle to cool the dishwater, he'd toddle into the kitchen, pull pots and pans from the cupboard onto the linoleum and clang the lids together. He was doing just that when the back door opened and Della shuffled into the kitchen, puffing after descending the several flights of stairs from the boarding house.

She waved a couple of envelopes. "Hank was at the post office and picked up your mail. He forgot to leave it off. Thought I'd take a break from scrubbing pots and pans and bring it to you." She turned up the wick on the table lamp. "Don't know why you're working in the dark."

"Just enjoying the sunset." I left my hands in the sudsy water. "Who are they for? Me or Dan?"

Della sank into a chair, wiped sweat from her face with a corner of her apron, and studied one of the envelopes. "This one's from your mother. The other's from . . ." She searched both sides of the envelope for a name and return address. "No name. No return address. Just a Yukon Territory postmark."

"It must be from Nelly. I haven't heard from her since last summer. Maybe someone told her about Jeff." I raised my hands, letting suds drip into the sink. "My hands are all soapy. Open it and read it to me."

Della ripped open the flap with a ragged fingernail, removed a sheet of white note paper, and began to read in her throaty voice:

Dear Maggie,

A friend of mine who still works the cribs in Bixbee wrote me the news about Jeff. I feel awful that I never came back to see him, and I thought it was time I told you that Harley Hanson is Jeff's father.

Della gasped and stared at me in a disbelief that matched my own. "Why, that son of a bitch! All the time pretending to be so high and mighty. You oughta—"

I was so stunned I could hardly speak, but managed to say, "Go on, read the rest."

Della ran her finger down the page to where she'd stopped and went on:

I was Harley's mistress in California. He knew Jeff was his son and helped pay for his care. When he movedto Bixbee, he stopped paying, so I moved there and told him if he didn't go on paying, I'd tell Clara. He set me up in business and paid me a little. Not as much as before. It was hard to keep our relationship a secret and he stopped coming to my bed. He'd give me a few dollars now and then, not much. Enough to feed Jeff and buy his clothes. Things like that. I think he was glad when I left town.

"Lord, how I'd like to ring that rooster's neck!" Della said through clamped teeth.

I was still too paralyzed with shock to say anything, just stood there with my hands in the water, my mouth agape, and listened to Della's furious voice as she read on.

Anyways, I wanted Jeff to have a good job when he left high school, so I wrote Harley and told him if he didn't give Jeff a job in his office, I'd write Clara and tell her everything. My girlfriend said Harley gave Jeff a job, but Jeff quit. She didn't know why. She also told me Jeff wanted to marry Lucinda Hanson. That would make Lucinda his sister once removed. It wouldn't be right for them to marry. Maybe Harley told Jeff, and that was why he quit.

I figured it was time you knew the truth. I'm sorry I waited so long to tell you, but I thought it best that nobody knew. Especially Jeff. Bless his heart. Thank you for taking care of him all this time.

Air burst from Della's lungs. "Kinda hits you between the eyes, don't it? Life ain't simple. It just ain't never simple."

Struck dumb with disbelief, I dried my hands on a towel and snatched the letter from Della's hands in a most ungracious way, almost ripping the paper. As I read the letter silently, doubt translated to an unforgiving reality that flushed my cheeks and strangled me with repressed rage.

In the world beyond my shattered senses, Della was saying, "It makes sense of some o' the things that's happened. First, Harley hates Jeff worse'n a case o' hives. Then he gives him a job. Then he says Jeff can't see Lucinda. Gawd-a-mighty. Why didn't he tell those kids the truth?"

I stared out the window, blind to everything but my rage. "He's not going to get away with it. I'm going to see him first thing in the morning. It's time that man came tumbling off his throne. I'm going to make him crawl—no, grovel on his hands and knees for forgiveness. I want to humiliate him the way he humiliated Jeff."

"I'm going with you," Della declared stoutly. "I've been wanting to give that Limburger cheese a piece o' my mind for years."

"No! I want Harley all to myself."

"All right, but don't go easy on him." Della heaved herself from her chair and fixed her angry eyes on me. "Give him hell for me and Hank."

●●●

I let Dan read the letter, and despite his advice to let the matter drop, I left Todd in Della's care early the next morning and tramped off to the Apex, following the railroad tracks that separated the sooty shops in town. I was in a lynching mood. Wearing the black of mourning, all I lacked was a broom to ride and a Halloween sky to release the witch in me. I took little note of the absence of miners on the street or of the black soldiers patrolling the outgoing train. Governor Steunenberg had called for more troops, and they'd filed into the district like ants. Each day, I'd seen a contingent of blue coats head up the canyon, looking for miners who'd sneaked back to the Creek from hideouts on the ridge. They'd taken every miner prisoner except those who could prove they were employed as non-union miners at the time of the Bunker Hill blast.

Just as the presence of troops made little impression on me, I only vaguely noticed a small-scale drama taking place between a pair of scavenging cats and a half-dozen ravens who claimed the same garbage heap. My black bonnet allowed nothing but the darkest ruminations beneath its round dome.

When I walked into the outer office of Apex Mining and Milling, the heads of the accountant and his clerks were bent over ledgers and file folders that cluttered the four desks. Little in the room had changed in the eight years since I'd forced my way into Harley's office to challenge his stand on the unions—same bench near the entry, flanked by spittoons, same Regulator clock clacking away the seconds, same two-gallon coffee pot squatting atop a boiler-tank stove.

I told the man at the head desk, a wizened blond, but not the blond I'd seen before, that I wanted to talk to Harley. He stuck his head into the open doorway to Harley's office and stated my request. I heard, among other things, a muffled oath rise from the interior. The blond returned, saying, "Mr. Hanson would like to know the nature of your visit."

My black mood broke its flimsy dam and gushed from my lips. "He would, would he? Well, I'm happy to oblige."

Anger propelled me toward Harley's doorway, the accountant close behind, sputtering, "I didn't mean you could go in. I merely intended to relay a message."

It was too late for relaying messages. I already stood in front of Harley's county-sized desk, inhaling smoke from the cigar clenched between his teeth. I glared at him, despising every inch of his six-feet-two, especially the callous look in his storm-gray eyes. I despised the fact that he looked ten years younger than his sixty years. He had no right to look so young. I could hardly wait to give him a piece of my mind.

I didn't. As soon as the accountant closed the door, I pulled Nelly's letter from my purse and thrust it in front of Harley's face. "This is from Nelly Mearns. She says Jeff is your son. Is that true?"

Harley didn't reply, merely jerked the letter from my hand and skimmed it, stiff-faced.

"Answer my question, damn you!" I slammed my fist on the desk. "I want to watch your face when you deny it."

He glared up at me. "What makes you think you're privy to that information?"

"Jeff was my ward. I have a right to know."

Harley's face flushed. The corner of his mouth twitched. He shifted in his chair and laid the cigar in an ashtray. "He's dead. What difference does it make?"

Outrage rasped from my throat. "What difference does it make? The difference between life and death, that's what."

Harley lowered the letter and scowled at me from under his hedge of silver brows. "What's done is done."

I leaned forward over the desk, shoulders rigid as planks, my voice screaming accusation. "I take that to mean you *are* Jeff's father. Why didn't you tell him? Why didn't you tell Lucinda? If they'd known, they would have understood why you didn't want them to marry. Was it because you didn't want Clara to know? Or was it because Jeff was a cripple—not good enough to be your son?"

"Both." Harley's lips curled into a sneer. "Now, does that make you feel better?"

I wagged my head in disgust. "No, but it confirms my low opinion of you. Whatever the reason, you drove Jeff to his death and Lucinda from her home."

The charge had struck deep. Harley shot to his feet, throwing his weight on the desk, his defiant chin almost touching mine. "I may have been a cad about many things. But I had nothing to do with Jeff's death. That was his own stupid doing. As for Lucinda . . ." He paused, working for breath. The twist in his lips slackened a bit. "I . . . I regret treating her so shabbily. I had no idea it would come to this."

He slumped back into his chair, his gaze fastened on a picture of Lucinda that stood in a gilt frame at the edge of his desk. For a long, suspended moment, the room was without sound, without movement, except for the irrepressible motion of the pendulum clock.

Slowly, the anger drained from Harley's face. His eyes lost their glare and began to water. The deep sadness that fell across his face transformed the creases at the corners of his mouth into aisles of shame. With an almost imperceptible nod, he took the picture from its place of prominence and held it before him. He started to speak, but his voice choked. He began again in a ponderous way, with great feeling. "I swear by all that is good and loving between a father and daughter, that I would have told everything if I had it to do over."

Anger had leached the starch from my spine. I dropped into a chair and pondered Harley's admission, letting my bitterness fall away, replaced by an uncertain scorn. When I spoke next, my voice was small and distant, seeming to issue from a throat other than my own. "I believe you, Harley. But I'll never forgive you for the misery you've caused."

He looked up then, his eyes reflecting a deep remorse. "I've already suffered more from my poor judgement than you can imagine. All of your scorn . . . all of Clara's contempt . . . could never cause as much pain. I hate myself for what I've done. I've lost Lucinda. I'm afraid she'll never come back. I've destroyed everything that had meaning for her. If I tell Clara, she'll leave me, too."

I let silence take possession of the room while Harley's words echoed in my mind, over and over until they'd etched an indelible pathway through my thoughts. Eventually they led to a heavy sigh of resignation. "I wish I could say I'm sorry for you, Harley, but I can't. You brought Jeff to his death as certainly as if you'd shot him and lit the fuse yourself. If you'd told him the truth, had admitted your responsibility to him, he'd still be working in your office, instead of going to his death at the mine." I rose unsteadily, leaning on the desk for support, and went on, "I'll always loathe your cowardice. But you needn't worry, I'll not cause a scandal by revealing what you've told me today."

I picked up my skirts and started for the door, then felt a need to leave Harley with one last discomfiting comment. "Rest well tonight, Harley. If your dreams will allow it."

Part III

THE BATTLE
IS
JOINED

CHAPTER 33

Not long after I visited Harley's office, he announced plans to retire to Portland and to turn over the business end of Apex Mining and Milling to Clyde, the operation of the mine to Ted Busby, long-time mine superintendent. I wondered if his feelings of guilt had factored into the decision. I hoped that was the case, because I found it nearly impossible to keep mute about his bad judgement, even more difficult to keep Della from spreading the scandal.

As time passed, conversation in the Rigby household centered less on speculation about the reason for Harley's move and more on events at the Black Titan. Such was the case one Saturday morning, the hot breath of July flowing through the kitchen's back doorway. Dan had announced he had exciting news to share and had asked Aaron to come from Spokane. He wanted the Tuttles and Lennie to gather at the house as well.

Thus, we sat at the kitchen table, coffee and scones at each place, making idle conversation, trying to control our curiosity. When Dan clacked a spoon against his cup for attention, the casual chit-chat stopped and all heads turned his way. Slowly, a secretive gleam in his eyes, he pulled back the tablecloth and poured what appeared to be black ash from a leather pouch onto the oilcloth.

"Looks like stove-ash," Della said with snort of a laugh. "You brought us here to show us that?"

Dan grinned. "Likely the richest stove-cleanings ever found in the district. Here, I'll show you." He worked the blade of his pocketknife through the *ash* and held the knife up to the sunlight lancing through the windows. "See those little crystals reflecting the sunlight. Like tiny wires. Pure silver."

"By God!" Hank and Aaron said in unison.

Lennie didn't seem surprised. He just sucked a tooth and said after a resulting smack of his lips, "My greenhorns broke into a pocket of this stuff at four-hundred-fifty feet into the mountain. The rock around it's rich, too. Full of galena. Never seen the likes."

In the past, Dan had showed me samples of ore that was supposed to make us rich and hadn't. This ore was different, but I kept a leash on my hopes. On the other hand, I didn't want to douse water on his enthusiasm, so I said, "How wonderful."

Dan's eyes rivaled the gleam of the crystals. "Maggie, you oughta see this stuff in place. A miner's lamp makes it look like a million stars blinking on a dark night. It's going to make the Black Titan the most famous mine in the whole goddamned district. Mum's the word, though," he added hurriedly. "We don't want to start a stampede before we can file claims on the land around us."

Aaron had experienced Dan's groundless exuberance in the past and didn't seem convinced. "What if the mineral pinches out?"

Dan wasn't deterred. He fairly bounced in his chair as he explained, "The rock around this mineral it is at least sixty-five per cent lead and about three hundred sixty ounces of silver. Worth two hundred and sixty-nine a ton. Even if there isn't much of this black stuff, we have a paying mine."

Hank had focused his doubts in another direction. "Bet you wish you didn't have to mess with the lead and zinc."

Dan thumped a forefinger on the table in disagreement. "Don't sneer at lead. It's our bread and butter. The days of getting rich on high-grade silver are past."

Della had been unusually quiet for her, possibly weighing the likelihood of the Rigby fortune while she maintained an air of attention and interest. Now she raised her ample bosom with an intake of air and said in her horn of a voice, "At least you'll be making money after all the dry years."

"Not just me. I want everybody at this table to share in the profits." Assuming a certain magisterial attitude, he motioned toward the end of the table. "Take Lennie for instance. Besides his salary as superintendent, I want him to have a sixth of the shares."

Lennie grunted and picked at his fingernails. "I don't want any favors."

"Christ, Lennie, you've already worn your ass off at the mine. You know it inside out. Not afraid to keep the men in line. You're going to get a sixth of the shares, like it or not. So is Maggie for putting in part of her wages, helping with the books, and putting up with my long hours away from home."

I gave a modest, though honest laugh. "What else was I supposed to do? Rebel like the union?" I laughed again and was joined by the others around the table. All except Aaron.

Dan took note of that. "Of course, Aaron might not approve."

Aaron didn't reply at once, simply squirmed in his chair and avoided the probing stares of those around the table, his face as unreadable as a salamander's. "I guess it's all right," he said after a bit. "You folks have been doing all the work. That should count for something." He tried to sound agreeable, but I noted Grandpa Rigby's parsimony in his tone.

Dan flicked a wary smile. "Then you won't object to giving Della and Hank a sixth of the shares."

Aaron's mouth dropped open as if someone had opened a trap door. "Well, now," he sputtered, "I don't think you should get carried away. After all, they're not—"

"They might as well have been working the tunnels," Dan prodded. "They've always lent Maggie and me a helping hand, stood up for us against the opposition, were there for Maggie during those years I was away. We're more beholden to them than anybody else I know."

Hank waved a hand in protest. "Don't feel obligated. We helped because that's what we wanted to do."

"You're like family," Della added with motherly warmth. "We love you as if you were our own."

"Dan, give them my sixth of the shares," I suggested whole-heartedly. "It's only fair. That way you and I won't own the bulk of the shares."

"Sounds reasonable," Aaron agreed above a torrent of opposition from the Tuttles.

And so, before the morning was over, it was decided that Lennie and the Tuttles would each have a sixth of the shares, Dan and Aaron to divide the remaining shares between them.

●●●

Not long after the meeting in the kitchen, Aaron sold the furniture store in Spokane and walked onto the mining scene full-time. For the time being, he made his home at our house, and Lennie spruced-up the mine cabin to make living quarters for himself. Dan quit his job at the Poorman office and became general manager of the Titan. Aaron became the business manager.

Building the Black Titan into a strong competitor in the silver-lead market demanded that Dan, Aaron, and Lennie give of themselves to the point of exhaustion. They had much to learn. Other mine owners

were market and management wise. Pioneers in the district had looked
to both coasts for financial backing and had found wily, well-heeled
investors who bet their spare cash on the future of the Coeur d'Alene
mining district—men such as Darius Mills, a poker-faced philanthropist
of California and New York, Cyrus McCormick the havester king,
William Crocker of the Woolworth-Crocker Bank, and John Jays
Hammond, an engineer and world traveler.

Now the upstart Black Titan was born, promising a giant's
adulthood even in infancy. The mine expected its share of the district's
dollar, if, in the daily arm wrestling for the ore market, it could hold its
own with the Coeur d'Alene Goliath's. Dan's main task was to find a
smelter for Titan ore. To succeed, he'd have to lock horns with men
such as J.P. Morgan and John D. Rockefeller Jr. These, and other
heavy-pursed interests in the East had tied-up the smelting industry by
merging eighteen of the leading smelters in the country into a trust, the
American Smelting and Refining Company. A.S.&R.'s stranglehold on
the district lay in the fact that it already had contracts with district
mines and refused to contract with new mines. In that way, A.S.&R.
could regulate the amount of tonnage each mine could sell in a month.
By limiting production, it raised the price of ore, increased the demand,
and swelled the profits of the trust while it hog-tied the mines. The
trust's influence with the railroads, monster trusts in their own right,
made it possible to raise the rates for ore shipments and add more coins
to its pockets. To cap that, no independent smelter had the capacity to
treat the district's output.

Since A.S.&R. wouldn't contract with new mines, Dan took some
of the precious money from the sale of the Spokane store and hounded
the offices of independent smelters on both coasts. He traveled for
weeks before he was able to persuade a smelter in the East to let him
ship ten carloads of ore samples. Soon, the firm sent an agent who saw
a shoot of ore that would keep the Titan in business a long time, and
within days, a contract came in the mail for two hundred cars of ore per
month. On the heels of that agreement came word from a smelter at
Everett, Washington that it would accept two hundred fifty tons of ore
per month. At last, the Black Titan could haul the ore it had been
stockpiling.

Dan immediately hired men to improve the trails for the go-
devils—ore carrying platforms pulled by eight-horse teams. With a

huge log tied to the rear of the platform for a brake, the go-devils carved deep troughs down the hillside. The troughs had to be kept smooth for the safety of the horses. He also hired four top-flight teamsters and a relief driver from the Palouse farming country, two teamsters for handling the go-devils, two to drive ore wagons from the foot of the hill to the railroad terminal at Burke.

Meanwhile, Aaron had rented a small brick building at the upper end of Burke and furnished it with desks, chairs, and filing cabinets. He'd hired a bookkeeper but hadn't yet found a clerk who suited him, and boxes of office supplies needed to be unpacked and shelved in the office's storeroom. I offered to tackle the job. On the day I chose for the task, Dan and Lennie had spent most of the night at the mine helping the engineer deal with a leak in the ventilating system. Lennie's clothes were wrinkled from falling asleep in them at the mine cabin. Dan's heavy tweeds were in the same condition. Bone-weary, they lounged in swivel chairs, their feet on Dan's cluttered desk.

Aaron sat at his tidy roll-top desk, near at hand a cup of coffee and a roll he'd bought at the local bakery. He was working on a production report for the smelter at Everett. Dan had shifted a candlestick phone and a new Underwood typewriter to one side of the desk he shared with Lennie to make room for coffee and the bag of rolls. Their cups held black, syrupy coffee, brewed cowboy style on the room's pot-bellied stove.

The office furnishings were simple—four desks with swivel chairs, a huge double desk for Dan and Lennie, a roll-top for Aaron, a smaller desk for the bookkeeper, who was busy making entries in a ledger, as well as an extra wooden chair at each desk for visitors who had business with the company. Another desk had no occupant, but a geological map of the interior of the mine hung on the wall behind the desk, suggesting it belonged to the new geologist. An incandescent light with reflector shade hung over each desk and at the entry, a luxury paid for dearly with the purchase of power from the Poorman's hydroplant a short distance up the creek, power too expensive for use in the Titan. A Regulator wall clock hung to the left of the door, and in the center of the room a pot-bellied stove strained against the chill of a blustering November wind.

Stacks of manila folders waiting to be filed sat atop three wooden filing cabinets. Rather than face the tedium of setting up files for the folders, I began the morning by opening boxes in the combined storeroom-washroom a few feet from Dan's desk. From my vantage-point I could listen to the conversation and see most of the office.

I heard Dan rattle his throat and say wearily, "Now that we're pretty well set, I think it's time to pass on a few of the bucks to the men who've been busting their guts to bring in the mine."

I looked up from cutting twine from a cardboard box, saw Aaron take the green visor from his sandy-blond head, and rub the indentation the visor had left on his forehead. "We might be able to tack an extra quarter onto their $3.50 a day."

Dan puffed his lips, now free of mustache, and shook his head. "I want them to have four dollars a day," he said on a loud stream of air. "There isn't a mine in the country where wages are any higher than they were in '90. The Titan's going to be an example for the rest."

Dan's plan was news to me. My instant reaction was that he might have a fight on his hands. Aaron was always ready to do battle when someone tampered with his money belt. Hostility was already evident in ice-blue eyes that bulged in apparent shock. "Your wheel's slipped a belt!" he yammered. "We've got Leyner drills ordered for the third level. A compressor plant—power station—sawmill—mess hall—and bunkhouse underway. Two high-powered mining engineers added to the payroll. More levels in the works. If we raise wages to four dollars a day, we'll be so tight in the crotch we can't move."

Dan flexed his jaw and made a defiant gesture. "Then take the raise out of my dividends."

It was my turn to register shock. I'd counted on the dividends to build a house in Wallace. I walked to the doorway and started to say as much, but Aaron's tirade offered no opportunity.

"Martyrdom isn't your bag, little brother," he said with the scorn of a teenager refusing to share a box of candy with a younger sibling.

"Generosity sure as hell isn't yours!"

The sudden heat of the argument caused Lennie to lift a heavy eyelid and look out from beneath it in question. "I'm all for the miners," he said with a yawn, "but I'm not sure the ones we have now deserve higher wages. Damned Missourians drag their asses around like they were filled with lead."

I hadn't expected reluctance from a union man like Lennie, but it provided Dan with a new direction in the war of wills. "If they didn't get so dragged-out, they'd do a hell-of-a-lot better job. And if they had money in their pockets for something beside a bed at the beanery and a few beers, they'd end up with more self-respect."

Aaron's face had turned pink. He stabbed the air with his pen. "Damned if you don't sound like one of those John Dewey pragmatists. The eight-hour day gives the men too much time for boozing and raising hell. They come back to work more shiftless than ever." Likely Aaron had read about John Dewey's recent influence on social philosophy, and his reactionary stand wasn't surprising. His ethics had always focused on the ledger side of the business world.

"I'm not sure I'm a pragmatist," Dan said sourly. "I just want to play fair with the men." He went to the stove and poured himself some coffee from the one-gallon enamelware pot. I decided not to insert my woman's voice into the skirmish and went back to work, stacking invoice pads on a shelf. "There's another reason we have the eight-hour shift," I heard Dan say. "The ore's so rich the men are getting leaded. If making money for us sends them to their beds, we oughta raise their accident and health benefits."

That bit of philanthropy made me straighten from my work abruptly and look Dan's way in pride. He'd returned to his desk. "I think our payments ought to equal those we deduct from the men's salaries," he said through a mouthful of breakfast roll.

Aaron slapped both hands on his desk, startling Dan into a choke. "Why don't you just give them the mine!"

It took Dan a minute to stop choking and swill the crumbs down with coffee. Then he cleared his throat and grinned slyly, "I've considered letting the men operate the mine under a cooperative plan. Some of the smaller mines in Colorado are trying it."

It was Lennie's turn to choke. Sputtering, unable to speak, he slid his legs from the desktop.

Aaron hauled himself from his chair and began to pace back and forth, rubbing his forehead. "What in the hell is it with you?" he said after the third pass up and down the office. "Now that you have a little extra change in your pocket you feel like John D. Rockefeller. Well, let me tell you, we're a long way from that. We have to keep the purse strings tight if we want to stay on top. We need to use common sense."

I held my breath, wondering how Dan would reply. He began with another sly grin. "I'm willing to forget the cooperative thing. I don't think Lennie would stand for seventy-five men telling him what do—be two hundred before long." It seemed Dan had purposely tested the waters, knowing he'd have to retreat from a wave of opposition. The tactic had provided more room for compromise. "I won't give an inch on wages or the eight-hour day," he said adamantly. "Soon as you can, write up a contract to take effect the first of the month. I'm going to—"

A clap of thunder from Aaron drowned out the rest. "You're railroading us! So damned stubborn you shut off any reasoning you don't want to hear." He thumped back into his chair, took up a pen, and set it scratching savagely across a sheet of paper.

"No more stubborn than you, big brother." Dan checked the clock on the wall and ran a hand over his face. "Gotta shave my mug and get down to Wallace with that report."

Lennie was on his feet, scowling. "I'm not ready to go along with that contract. Not with the men we have now." He took a long stride to a coat tree that stood by the door and shrugged his arms into a black woolen overcoat that seemed an extension of his shaggy black hair. "You're not giving me and Aaron enough say in the matter."

"Better get used to it. It won't be the last time. Not as long as I'm general manager." Dan took off his jacket and tossed it over his chair. "The Titan's going to be the biggest mine in the district, but not at the expense of the men in the stopes."

Lennie sent Dan a look that could curdle vinegar, said, "Don't forget—it's *our* mine," then went through the door and slammed it shut before Dan could reply.

Dan's reaction was a peevish look he darted Aaron's way. "Better hurry up with that report. I'll need it in fifteen minutes."

My own reaction was a gnarl in my stomach. It seemed to me that no success was worth destroying family unity.

CHAPTER 34

I was pondering the argument between Dan, Aaron, and Lennie when Dan walked into the storeroom carrying a teakettle that'd been heating on the stove. He poured hot water into the washstand at the rear of the room, set the kettle on the floor, and tempered the hot water with cold from a tap fed by a year-round spring that bubbled out of the mountain two hundred yards above the building. "I suppose you heard all that?" He said as he draped his suspenders over his hips. I mumbled 'uh-huh' and opened a box of ledgers, hoping to avoid discussion of the matter, but Dan was bent on it. "So what do you think?"

I straightened, thought a moment choosing my words carefully, and eased into a reply. "I agree with your idea of what's best for the miners. I just wish the others would go along without a fight. I hate to see trouble between you."

"Don't worry your pretty orange head. They'll see the light when my policies bear fruit."

"I hope so. But it might take a while." I started to shelve ledgers on the shelf while Dan peeled off his shirt and hooked it over a peg near the washstand. "You shouldn't get too impatient with your partners. They've done their share to make the Titan a success."

"Maggie, I've waited ten years for this. I'm tired of being patient." Dan took a shaving brush and thundermug from a shelf above the washstand, dipped the brush into the water, and was about to swirl it in the mug when someone burst into the office.

I turned and saw Clyde looking like a poster for *Macbeth*. His darting glance missed Dan and me standing partly hidden behind the door of the dimly lit storeroom, so he sicked his temper on Aaron. "What are you trying to do with your dastardly wage scale? Send the rest of us on the road to ruin?"

Aaron looked as if he'd been accused wrongly of robbing a bank. "How did you know about the wage scale? I just found out about it myself."

Dan walked past me swirling the brush in the mug. "That's what I'd like to know. Who told you?"

Clyde spun toward Dan with a startled look, saw me staring at him from the storeroom, and stammered, "Maggie, it-it's good to see you." The lie showed in his tone and in the set of his full lips. "It's been—"

Dan gave him no chance for further comment. "I asked how you knew?" His menacing tone matched the fury with which he swirled the brush in the mug.

Clyde backed up a step and squared his shoulders and his brunette head. "I have ways of finding out."

"How in the hell could you? The only person I told was Sorenson, one of the shift bosses. I wanted to get his opinion of—" Dan stopped his suds-making abruptly. "Don't tell me he's a plant. You dirty bastard!"

Clyde raised his arms with a show of indifference. "Just improving the odds. A man has to keep his eye on the competition. You'll be hiring spies before long."

"I'll shut down first."

"You say that now, but a man will pay dearly to keep his whistle."

Grumbling to himself about crooked sneaks, Dan stomped back into the washroom. I opened a box, trying to pretend I was invisible.

Clyde followed as far as the doorway and said across my bent back. "I'll wager that's what you're doing with your new pay scale. Purposely ruining the rest of us so you can stay alive."

"I'd say he's trying to ruin *us*," Aaron muttered from the other room.

Dan shot Clyde a look of disgust from a mirror that hung above the washstand. "You can tell my brother and I don't see a cow in the same light. I'd feed her grain so she'd produce lots of milk. He'd feed her corn husks so he could make more money per gallon."

Clyde pulled a muffler from around his throat, then dragged a chair to a spot just outside the storeroom door and sat with his arms folded across his chest in a belligerent manner. "You're mad as a Chinaman on the seed. My miners will strike for better wages as soon as the news is out. With the military about to leave, I'll have a devil of a time keeping them under control."

So that's what this is all about, I thought to myself. Clyde was shivering in his boots because the troops were leaving.

"How can your men strike?" Dan said through a froth of shaving soap. "You bilkers in the MOA have killed the unions. That employment agency you run is nothing more than a damned permit system."

"Humbug! The union sneaks memberships wherever it can. Every mine has a few miners waiting to stir up a revolt. I can't believe you're still shouting *Hosanna* for the union."

I turned from my shelving in time to see Dan's eyes flash at Clyde's image in the mirror. "With operators like you around, the men need a union. With the right leaders a union could work."

Clyde gave a snort. "The kind of leaders who come in here are all the same. Strong but stupid."

Dan took a blunt-faced, nickel-plated razor from the back of the washstand and wagged it in the air in a taunting way. "I got me one of those new-fangled Gillette safety razors with disposable blades. Have you tried one?" Clyde looked skeptical. "What's wrong? No spies to keep you abreast of tonsorial progress?" Grinning like a cat who'd cornered a mouse, Dan tilted his cheek toward the glass and made a careful pass through the beard of soap.

"Don't try to derail me with your glib humor," Clyde countered. "I came here as a favor to you. The Association wants to destroy you."

The naked remark caused Dan to nick the skin beneath his ear. He swore, dabbed at the cut with a towel, and applied alum he kept in a jar on the shelf. "The MOA didn't have to send their little errand boy here to tell me that," he said spitefully. "I know they're putting on the screws, especially Sweeney. He's buying up claims around the Titan as fast as he can—taking up land that keeps us from railroad access— refusing us right-of-ways to move our ore." Dan referred to Charles Sweeney, a mine owner and ruthless businessman who'd steam-rollered his way to riches in Idaho and other parts of the West. Dan pulled his long upper lip tight for the razor, made several strokes, then turned toward Clyde, waving the Gillette. "How would you like to have to haul your ore by wagon to the terminal here in Burke and hand-load it instead of chuting it right into cars? Sweeney's trying to kill us off so he can buy the Titan dirt cheap."

A sneer deepened the cleft in Clyde's handsome chin. "You can't blame him for that. Mining is no business for the faint of heart."

No longer could I pretend I wasn't there. "Then why are you in it?" I said with a cynical smile. "You're not known for courage."

Dan chortled, but Clyde glared at me. Thinking it best to make myself scarce, I took a box of desk supplies into the main room, brushing past Clyde's knees.

From the washroom came the sound of Dan splashing water on his face, silence, likely while he dried on a towel, followed by his growling voice, saying, "I suppose Sweeney'll find some way of keeping us from the independent smelters. There are times I'd like to bloody his face." The smell of bay rum drifted in from the washroom as Dan slapped some on his cheeks. Soon he walked into the office, stuffing the tail of his shirt into his trousers. "I suppose you're in favor of the smelting contract."

Clyde's long fingers trailed down his vest to his stomach and pushed on it as if suppressing pain. "I'm going to New York with Sweeney and a couple of the other operators to talk to American Smelting and Refining. It's a matter of survival."

"And ethics? What happened to that old-fashioned idea?"

A small, cold smile hardened on Clyde's lips. "You can hardly speak of ethics. You're stabbing me in the back with your new wage scale. We're a new generation, Dan. We have to be practical. The only ethics a business man can afford are those that bring greater profit."

Dan pulled on his vest, and in his fury, sent his fingers flying down the row of buttons. "That's the difference between us, Clyde. My wage scale benefits the miners. Your contract benefits your stockholders. Which is the higher purpose?"

Clyde's smile slid into one of condescension. "Come now, Sir Fretful, your stubbornness is showing. You know eight-hour shifts slow production. They'll turn into seven-hour shifts by the time we let smoke clear the tunnels. And we'll still be paying for eight. Every time we shut down between shifts it means less money coming in. Less money coming in means fewer jobs. It's as simple as that."

Aaron looked up from stuffing the Everett report into a manila envelope. "I agree with you there, Clyde. But my little brother always has to wave a banner."

Dan stood at the coat tree, slinging his overcoat across his shoulders. Twin pockmarks pulsed in his shiny, clean-shaven jaw. "It doesn't save money when a tunnel's blown because some stiff was too wrung out to be careful. It doesn't save money when the man at the hoist dozes off and sends a cage full of men into the sheaves." He jabbed an arm into a sleeve. "I'm leaving. This room's beginning to smell. Clyde, you can tell your tight-fisted friends in the MOA there's no way I'll back down. If they had any brains they'd see the wisdom in what I'm doing."

Clyde shot to his feet and gave a satirical bow. "Oh, Mighty Rigby! Wizard of the Rock! I humble myself before your oracular wit." Then, with a sudden fierceness, "Most operators have been in business longer than you can ever hope to be with your ideals. If you haven't already, you'll soon learn it's dog eat dog."

CHAPTER 35

The next time I was privy to the conflict in Dan's business life was during an encounter he had with Charles Sweeney of New York and Wardner, the mining town twenty-five miles west of Bixbee. Sweeney was one of the hungriest of the *dogs* Clyde had mentioned during his visit to Dan's office, Sweeney dealt in real estate in several states, dabbled in politics, speculated in mines, and was becoming the catalyst in the transformation of the district from small-owner mines to giant corporations. Under his leadership, the mine owners retaliated against American Smelting and Refining's production quotas by shutting down their mines. The tactic worked and A.S.&R. increased quotas and offered a better price per ton, but it retaliated by wrangling long-term contracts with pig lead buyers, keeping new smelters from the market, and bringing more of the existing smelters into A.S.&R.'s fold.

Amid the industrial brawling, Sweeney pursued his private game for profit and power. Ruthless, indomitable, predatory, imaginative, daring, he was determined to merge the district's mines under his direction, even if he had to play into the devil's hand to do it. Backed by Rockefeller money, he sent his agent to each of the large mines in the district to wheedle an anonymous purchase.

In December, Sweeney approached Dan in person. As often happened between men of strong wills, the battle between the two had been joined before they met, and I was there to witness it. By coincidence, I was on my way to deliver fresh-baked cookies to the men at the Titan's office when I met Dan at the railroad terminal in Burke. He'd been at the mine, had caught a ride to town on one of the Titan's ore wagons, and was watching over the horses while the driver rounded up a crew to transfer the ore to a freight car. He introduced a man standing on the far side of the pair of lead horses as Charles Sweeney—a tall, graying Irishman with a great paunch, fierce, large-balled eyes, and a jaw like a rock. He had extremely heavy brows, a full, mobile mouth, and a smug self-satisfied expression. The collar of his coat was turned up against the cold, giving the impression of a neck like a stump.

"He wants to buy the Titan," Dan told me by way of explanation. "I'd rather sell to a rattlesnake."

Sweeney drew on a cigar and sent a puff of smoke across the horses' backs into Dan's face. "I'll ignore the insult this time, me boy. I don't think you realize what this sale would mean." He had a loud, domineering voice and spoke as if he enjoyed the sound of it. He walked around the heads of the horses and stood facing Dan with an air of unshakable confidence. "You might as well face it, me boy, sooner or later, every mine in the district will belong to one giant company with meself at the helm. We'll be able to wallop the tar out o' the trusts, maybe build our own smelter. Mind you, each owner will be given a mighty fine price for his mine and—"

"You call two million a mighty fine price?" Dan hissed on a steaming breath. The Titan's worth ten or eleven million, at least."

Sweeney glanced down the loading platform to where another team of special-bred American whites were waiting for a crew of men to relieve their eight-ton wagon of Titan ore. "Keep your voice down. I don't want all o' Burke to know me business."

Dan sneered. "Everybody's onto your secret dealings," he said without lowering his voice.

I felt like a fly in the middle of a hornet's nest. "I-I really must be going," I said in an attempt to escape the hostile exchange.

Dan put a restraining hand on my arm. "Stay. I want you to know what I'm up against."

"Up against?" Sweeney forced a smile. "You'll own stock in the new company—a seat on the board of directors. Just think, money in your pocket." He thumped a finger on Dan's chest. "And none o' the worries."

"You may slick-talk the other operators into selling. Some of them are going out of business anyway. But I know three of them, including Hank Day who'll never sell to you. So where does that leave your giant company."

To a man with few scruples, Dan's moral opposition must have seemed a temporary obstinacy, not an immovable barrier. His tone suggested that when he said, "Maybe they're not as smart as you, Dan."

Dan's teeth clenched. "Don't patronize me. I'd rather go belly-up than be part of your mining trust. You've done everything you could to keep me from getting a start. So go join the rest of the leeches in hell." Dan took my arm. "Come on, Maggie. I've heard enough."

Before we could start across the railroad tracks, Sweeney caught Dan by the shoulder and spun him around, his eyes flashing a warning. "Listen to me, you stubborn whelp! Federal Mining and Smelting will be a reality in a few months. And I'll be its head. You won't stand a chance o' getting railroad access. Nor the cheap Washington Power I'm bringing in. What's more, I'm dealing to buy the Everett smelter. Your ore will rot in the bins."

Dan's expression said he'd like to pound Sweeney's nose. He didn't. Nor did he shout. He seemed too choked with rage. "You goddamn conniving sonofabitch. Why don't you break into my office—steal my safe—steal my horses off the wagons." He shook a finger in front of Sweeney's nose. "I'll find me another smelter. Maybe build my own. What's more I'm going to get me a damned good lawyer. You try one more trick, and I'll take you to court."

● ● ●

Three years passed before Dan carried out the threat to sue. In the meantime, Sweeney merged two large mines in Burke Canyon with his own mines to form Federal Mining and Smelting. He purchased mines in eastern Washington, as well as the smelter at Everett, Dan's major purchaser of ore, and canceled Dan's contract with that smelter.

"That bastard!" Dan exclaimed at dinner one night when Aaron told him the news. "That shoots our plans for expansion of the mill all to hell. We'll have to shut down everything until I find a new smelter."

He found the smelter, but not until he'd spent several weeks haunting the offices of smelting companies in New York and San Francisco. This time, the reputation of the Black Titan preceded him, and the Selby Smelter in San Francisco agreed to take his ore. Selby would use the contract as a mutual stand against the Rockefeller mining trust headed by Sweeney, and the Guggenheim trust known as American Smelting and Refining. Harry Day's Hercules Mine, another developing giant near Burke, also signed with Selby, giving both trusts a case of financial indigestion.

The trusts' cure for a bellyful of profit projections gone sour was to eliminate the cause—put the squeeze on the Selby, Titan, and Hercules until they had to sell-out cheap. A.S.&R. pressured the Southern Pacific Railroad to raise rates from the Coeur d'Alenes to California. Sweeney, who held properties that blocked Dan's direct access to the railroad tracks, convinced the Northern Pacific to cut the supply of cars reserved at the Burke terminal for the Titan and Hercules.

The outlook was grim. The time for ethical conduct had passed. "I don't care how you get the cars we need," Dan told Aaron. "Bribe the agent. If that doesn't work, steal the cars."

Bribery didn't work. Stealing was next. Men from the Black Titan began nightly raids on cars parked along a siding at the Tiger mine. They weren't alone. Harry Day's men were there as well. Each night the shadows rippled with crews of hooded men rushing to be first at the cars, often using fists to eliminate the competition. The victors pried loose the cars with pinch-bars, hitched teams of horses to the couplings, and hauled the cars to the terminal in Burke, where they loaded them with ore.

While Dan put his energies into the battles of the marketplace, I tried to find peace in the new home we'd built in Wallace, a two-and-a-half story house built on a raised foundation, around it a small yard enclosed with a fancy ironwork fence. It had a veranda, colonnades, dormers, bay windows with arches of stained glass, and an octagonal tower that jutted into the sky. The walls of the upper story were decorated with bands of square and diamond-shaped shingles, shape competing against shape, color against color, texture against texture.

Dan had spared no expense on the interior—marble fireplaces, decorative scrollwork, walls wainscoted with black and white walnut, the upper half papered with gold silk damask embossed with satiny *fleur de lis*. Elaborate stairways were polished to a golden patina. I thought it too pretentious, but Dan had worked hard for his wealth and wanted to spend it. I tried to combat the feeling of ostentation by keeping the Queen Anne furnishings to a simple luxury.

Disgusted to overflowing with the tactics he must use to keep his wealth, much less survive in the mining game, Dan had engaged a lawyer, Henry Penoir. I was with him when he picked Penoir up at the railroad depot in Wallace and gave him a tour of the town in his pride and joy, a new 1904 Peugot. Dan and I sat in front. Penoir settled his dapper Frenchman's frame on a bucket seat in the back.

Dan brought the Peugeot to a wheezing stop on the outskirts of town so that we could watch a crew of men raising poles for a transmission line. Along the canyon's midriff, a playful wind whipped a trail of mist into a pattern of breaking surf. In the bottoms, leaves on the cottonwoods made splashes of pumpkin and yellow against the somber hills.

Dan let the car idle, and it kept up a soft jounce and putter while we relaxed against the sun-warmed leather upholstery. Penoir peered at Dan over his spectacles, horn-rimmed with heavy bows that disappeared into his coarse black hair. "This is quite an auto," he said. "I'm told baby Peugots like this cost around six hundred and fifty dollars."

"That's right," Dan said over his shoulder. "It's the best one-cylinder on the market. I ordered yellow and black so I could look like a damned sunflower running around town."

"My, how wealth does addle a man's brains."

We all laughed, then I added, gesturing humorously, "It took a long time to get it here from France, though. Can't you just see it riding the waves of the Atlantic with a Frenchman at the wheel singing the Marseilles."

We laughed again. Penoir was still chortling as he reached for something at his feet. There was the sound of his valise being opened, then he held over the back of our seats a five-by-seven-inch box with a pebbled black finish and a turnkey on one side. "While we're stopped I'll take a picture of you and your wife in the auto. Have you seen one of these before?" We shook our heads. "This camera uses that new transparent film of Kodak's. It comes with the film rolled inside. When I'm through snapping my pictures, I send the camera back to Rochester, New York. Kodak develops the film, prints the pictures, and sends it all back to me with a new roll of film in the camera. I used it a lot in Boston a while back. Got to watch Cy Young pitch Boston to a victory over Pittsburgh in that new World Series."

"That musta been some game," Dan said enviously.

"The whole series was a whale of a success. Guess they'll be holding it each year from now on. Do you like baseball?"

"Sure. I used to play on the teams in the canyon. The Titan has its own now. But I don't get much time to play. Only played twice last summer."

Penoir stepped from the auto, snapped several shots from different angles, them climbed back in. By then, the transmission crew had dug a hole using a ten-foot shovel made for that purpose, and a team of horses had dragged a thirty-five-foot cedar pole to the lip of the hole. Grunting and shouting, several men lifted the pole onto a tripod of two-by-six beams. While the rest of the crew kept the pole from toppling, two muscular workers used pikes to raise the pole upright, then heaved it into its socket in the ground with an earth-shaking thud.

"That's quite a process," I said from my seat beside Dan. "To think it wasn't long ago we used kerosene lanterns."

Dan should have been impressed by the team effort. He wasn't. He had other things on his mind. "Makes me maddern' hell to think the Titan's cut off from cheap power," he said over his shoulder to Penoir.

"Why is that?" Penoir said. He'd been sent by the Selby Smelting Company, and being from San Francisco, didn't know all the details of Dan's problems.

Dan's shrubby brows met in a scowl. "Sweeney is using his voting stock in Washington Power to block our appeal for an electric line to the mine. We'll have to limp along with our one-horse generating plant. But, by God, by the time they have the main system complete I'll see to it that we get a line. That's one of the reasons I've called on you."

"How long will it take them to complete the system?" I asked.

"About three years, they say." Dan revved the auto's soft jounce to a massaging vibration, let out the brake, and drove the Peugeot alongside the railroad tracks while the spicy air of fall streamed over the yellow hood into our lungs.

"In a way it's safer to be without the high voltage. It's bad enough with generators." Penoir punctuated the remark with grunts that matched the jogging of the car and the depth of the potholes in the wagon road. "As soon as you get wires and transformers coming in from everywhere, you're going to have accidents. Miners are pretty dumb when it comes to volts, ohms, and amps."

"I am, too," I replied with a self-effacing shake of the head. "I can't understand why it happened, but just last week a man working a mine in the southern part of the state was killed when he touched a transformer that'd been disconnected for twelve hours."

"That's what I mean," Penoir said. "Operators will have to educate the men about residual energy, and have the shift bosses watch them like hawks."

Dan slowed to ease over a pothole that seemed bottomless, then sped up, saying, "We won't have to worry about that for a while thanks to Sweeney. It took me a while to come to it—I hate dealing with the courts—but I'm glad I've decided to sue him and Federal for blocking access to the railroad."

"Do you know what you're getting into?" Penoir's tone had the reflective note of past experience.

"Damned right I know, but it's time Sweeney got his due."

"It'll cost your company a fortune in fees, not just mine but for my assistants, court fees, et cetera. It's going to be hard to prove Sweeney bought the property with the intent to hurt the competition. It could take years in the courts, especially with Republicans on all the benches in the district and in power in the county. They'll make it hard on you, maybe impossible."

"I expect hard, but I won't accept impossible. I want you to file the suit right away. And—" The auto jumped out of the wagon ruts as Dan swerved to avoid a cat that streaked across the road chasing one of its kind. "I have another assignment for you," he told Penoir after he'd turned the wheels back into the ruts. "I understand the Guggenheims have sent Baruch out to the coast to round up smelters for A.S.&R. Seems they're afraid the Rockefeller interests will end up being a big competitor. Your boss tells me his small stockholders want to sell out to A.S.&R. We've got to keep that from happening. When you go back to 'Frisco, I want you to buy up their stock."

"I don't think Rockefeller is interested in anything but playing a chess game for quick bucks," Penoir said from behind me. "What he really wants is to control the railroad mileage of the country through his ties with Harriman. That way he'd have the mines and smelters in his pocket regardless."

"Any way you look at it, all the wrangling for power means trouble for Dan," I said, hoping to show an understanding of the quicksands of the marketplace.

Dan pulled the shift lever, touched the brake, and brought the car to a sputtering stop in front of the brick office building he'd recently built in Wallace to conduct Titan business. He looked over his shoulder at Penoir. "You go on in. Aaron can give you all the paperwork you need. I'll drop Maggie off at the house and come back here for a while, then we'll go to the house for lunch."

Before Penoir could climb from the auto, a man bore down on us and asked Dan about the car. "Yeh, Bob, Peugot's a great car," Dan said in answer. "Look it over if you'd like."

Automobiles, fancy houses. I wondered, as I often had if they were worth all the sleepless nights. Dan was turning into an ogre. He needed a respite. So did I. Somehow I'd find a way for us to escape, if only for a while.

CHAPTER 36

T he opportunity to suggest an escape from the stress presented itself a few nights later when Dan and I returned home from a dinner party the Mayor of Wallace had given for all the mine operators in the district. Dan sat on the canopied bed in our first-floor bedroom, his white vest loose at his sides, his black dress jacket, celluloid collar, and tie beside him on the green velvet bedspread. Dressed in blue nightgown and wrapper, I came from the adjoining bath, pulling a styling rat from my hair and paused in the doorway to study him. One minute he'd cradle his head, next minute he'd rake his fingers through his thick wheaten hair in what seemed a purposeless, unsatisfied gesture.

Too often of late I'd found him sitting in the grips of depression. His dark mood was hurting our marriage. He seemed to have lost interest in my efforts to please him and no longer took me into his arms to sniff the fragrance of Cashmere soap. He was always too tired, too preoccupied. I was painfully aware that the little affection he showed and the endearing terms he used had become habitual, mechanical. The spontaneity had left.

I took the remaining pins from my hair, put them in a pink luster-ware box that sat on my dresser, and opened the French windows a crack, letting the sharp fragrance of chrysanthemums drift into the room. Some people thought the night air deadly, but I found it refreshing, especially when it reminded of the autumn flowers growing along the foundation of the house. The quiet on that night was vast, only the ta-hoo of a great horned owl and the whisper of a breeze in the solitary pine at the front of the house.

I slipped onto the bed beside Dan and kissed the strong curve of his cheek. "Want to tell me what's bothering you?"

He grunted and shook his head.

"It might help if you talked about it."

He ran his fingers over his mouth and rubbed his chin. A full minute passed before he replied in a tentative way, "I was just . . . just thinking about those operators at the dinner tonight . . . thinking what the mining game can do to a man . . . to the things he used to believe important."

"Such as?"

Dan's lips tightened. His eyes blinked out from beneath their protective hedge as though they saw beyond the morning glories twining on the wallpaper. "For one thing . . . me and Aaron. We used to be friends as well as brothers. Now we're always at each other's throats."

"You had another fight?"

"You know how it is. One continuous haggle."

"What's the problem this time?" I asked the question to give Dan the chance to release his tension rather than from the need for information. I was more aware than I liked of the disagreements between him and Aaron over the management of the mine. They happened at the dinner table as often as not. Though Aaron had bought a home of his own, he liked to come to our house for a home-cooked meal.

Dan covered my hand with his thick palm, its touch smoother since he'd quit working the stopes, and let his gaze probe mine long and hard. I thought I saw remorse there, as well as a reluctance to confess it. "Aaron and I have different ideas about how the money should be spent. I guess it's because of his years at the store . . . always looking for a profit . . . keeping costs down. Dad always said Aaron could squeeze a penny until the Indian got a nosebleed. Can you imagine that coming from somebody who gave meaning to the word 'tight-fisted?'"

Dan tended to think in terms of black and white and I wondered if I dared comment. In the past, he'd been upset when I'd pointed out the value of another's opinion. I spoke anyway. "You can't blame Aaron for everything. You benefited from his thrift. He kept the mine from going under when the trusts wouldn't let you contract with a smelter."

Dan's scowl told me what he thought of that remark. He kicked off his shoes and peeled the socks from his feet, grumbling, "I can't live with Aaron's business ethics. If I see something that needs fixing, I want to fix it. If I see a machine that can up our production and make it easier on the men, I want to buy it. But he always puts up a fuss."

"You knew how stingy he was before you went into business together. You must have expected it."

"I didn't know it would be this bad. I get tired of the wrangling. It uses up energy I need to fight off the mining vultures. Their black carcasses are always up there, circling, waiting for me to give up the fight and die. I'm scared to death they're going to out-wait me."

I sensed in Dan's words not fear as much as resignation to the inevitable, to the insurmountable. I thought of the nightmares he'd been having the past few months, recalled the oaths, the grinding of teeth. Perhaps the night vultures had been plucking the flesh from his bones. How should I approach this man who directed his every corpuscle into the battle to save his real-life dream?

Stroking his shoulder, I waded into the murky stream of his thoughts. "Have you considered selling the Titan . . . getting into a business less cutthroat . . . less demanding."

Dan spun his head around with an expression of utter disbelief. "You'd like that wouldn't you! You've always been jealous of the mine. Oh, don't look so hurt. You know it's true."

I averted my eyes and stared resentfully at the carpet. How could he say such a thing? I'd never been jealous of the mine. Just angry at it, sometimes bitter for what it had done to our lives. It had made us rich but had caused misery in the doing.

"Christ!" Dan muttered. He hauled himself to his feet, took his clothes from the bed and threw them onto the back of an armchair. "Look . . . I'm sorry. I had no call to say you're jealous. But the idea of selling the Titan tears me up. I'm the one who breathed life into her and nursed her along. I couldn't sell. It'd kill me." He removed his vest and struggled to work the buttons through the tight holes in his dress shirt. "It's probably damned mean of me, but I feel my purpose in life is to wallop the tar out of the greedy bastards who are making it hard for me to stay afloat. Likely you'd be happier if I didn't feel that way."

Eyes still fixed on the carpet, I answered hoarsely, in a voice slightly above a whisper. "You do what you feel you must. I wouldn't want to change that."

Dan didn't reply immediately, just sent his shirt sailing onto the mound of clothes. Then he said in a tentative way, "I've considered shutting down for a while. Aaron's made enough investments to keep us going as a company. We own smaller properties we can mine that wouldn't deplete our funds as much." His words were directed at me, but he seemed to be trying to convince himself.

I looked up and said hopefully, "We could manage on much less."

The comment resulted in a loud, "Damn it, Maggie, I want like hell to prove a man can make it big in this business and stay honest."

The hope I'd held for a brief moment dissolved, leaving a hollow for disappointment. "Then you should try," I said through dashed

expectations. "Otherwise you could never live at peace with yourself."
I may have failed to convince him to sell the Titan, but I could still
suggest a temporary respite from the broil of the marketplace. "You
need a rest before you end up in the hospital. Why don't you take a
month's vacation and we'll go on a trip?"

Dan had sat on the bed to remove his pants. His head shot up. "I
can't leave here for a month! Lennie and Aaron would have things in a
helluva mess."

I'd been prepared for an explosion of temper, but not the acid in the
eye. I tried to ignore it. "You don't give them enough credit. They're
perfectly capable of keeping things running for a short while. Just tell them
they can't take up any new business or change policy while you're gone."

"Now you're telling me how to run my business."

"Not at all. I just . . ." I took a firm grip on my courage. "We
haven't had a vacation since our three-day honeymoon."

A snort. "We've gone to both coasts."

I felt at once indignant and regretful. I felt partly to blame for Dan's
success, definitely cheated by it. "Business trips don't count. You're
always caught up in meetings and I never do anything but sit in a hotel
room. And when I suggest a pleasure trip you always have an excuse—
some important person to contact—some crisis that only you can
handle. It's time, Dan," I said adamantly. "We need a real vacation—no
business, just relaxation. And we could . . ." I knew I'd gone too far
and let the rest fade.

Dan threw his pants on the chair and lay down on the bed with a
thump. I retreated to the adjoining bathroom and came face to face with
my reflection in the mirror. I noted the lines that anger and frustration
had brought to my face, noted the yellow sparks in my eyes, and the
tightness of my jaw. I saw myself as Dan had seen me a moment ago, a
shrewish, meddling wife. If I was to have any hope for a peaceful night,
I'd have to make amends.

Reluctant to crawl into bed with Dan in our present mind-sets, I
dawdled as I washed my face and brushed my hair. When I returned to
the bedroom, my frustration had subsided a bit, but my sense of futility
over the vacation remained. I expected to find Dan with the scowl on
his face. Instead, a sheepish smile played across his lips. "Tell you
what," he said. "I'll settle for two weeks. Let Lennie and Aaron face
the vultures for a while. Where would you like to go?"

My frustration leaped into utter surprise. I couldn't believe Dan's change of mind had happened so suddenly. But he could be that way, prone to decisions that thumbed a nose at the expected. It seemed his obligations had thrashed it out with his leanings of the heart and he'd warmed to the idea of a vacation. Perhaps he'd hungered for escape all along.

"Where would you like to go?" he repeated as I lay my wrapper on the bench in front of the dressing table. "How about the city? New York and Chicago aren't bad in late September."

I slipped between the cool linen sheets and touched his warm body. "I'd rather not go east. Maybe San Francisco. You could take me to that wonderful seafood restaurant you discovered when you were there looking for a smelter. And we could go to the seashore. Todd would like that."

Dan's smile broadened to include the creases in his cheeks. "I know just the place. The president of the Selby offered to let me use his cabin on the coast south of 'Frisco. He calls it a cabin, but it's as big as this house. I was there for a meeting with his board. We'd have a quarter-of-a-mile of beach to ourselves, no neighbors to bother us." He put a leg over mine and grinned slyly. "We could go swimming in our birthday suits and make love on the beach. Enjoy ourselves outlandishly."

"You're a rogue," I said with a laugh. Though I protested, I was aware of a tingling inner delight at the return of Dan's interest to something besides mining. "I'd love it. And it would be good for Todd." Good for Dan, and me too. After so many busy years we'd have time to enjoy one another.

I relaxed in his arms with his breath on my cheek, the scratch of his coarse hair on my forehead, and felt my heart stir with love.

●●●

Pullman berths, plush chairs, gourmet food, sparkling linens—so different from my trip west in '89. Unlike the squalling babes on that trip, Todd enjoyed his first train ride with the glee and curiosity of an eight-year-old.

The two weeks on the coast were delightful, the weather unusually dry for mid-autumn. Each day began with fog that cleared by ten, revealing the flash of white wings against the intense blue of sea and sky, and ended with the great ball of the sun plunging into a sea of copper sunpennies.

The beach-house south of San Francisco was an ideal hideaway. A private place hidden deep in a remote section of coastline, accessible by a narrow wagon track that wound through fir, cedars, azaleas and rhododendrons. A series of terraced lawns sloped down to a beach flanked at each end by jumbles of rock and steep cliffs. The rumble of surf and the piercing cry of gulls and terns drifted upward to a house that stood beneath a spiderweb of mosses and creepers. Apples hung from trees in the garden, and wasps tried to find warm cracks in the eaves. It was as comfortable as our home in Wallace, with a housekeeper and cook to keep us happy and well-fed. Stocked with cords of stovewood, shelf after shelf of books and magazines, and a children's playroom, it was an ideal retreat for foggy mornings and late evenings.

Seduced into drowsiness by the sea air, Dan and I spent much of the time relaxing on the beach, the stress of the mining business distant, almost non-existent. We saw no newspapers, heard nothing of events beyond the retreat, and made no attempt to follow a schedule. We slept when we wished, ate when our stomachs demanded it, and explored the beach at leisure. It was too cold to go bathing in the nude or to make love on the beach, but we did many times in the comfort of our bedroom and bath.

●●●

I returned home refreshed, happy for the keening of mind and spirit, and with the seed of a new child planted firmly in my womb. Dan returned to face the challenges of the marketplace with renewed vigor.

Lennie met him at the station with the news, "The boys have drilled into a shoot of ore that promises to be the richest yet!"

The Tuttles greeted us with a different sort of news but just as exciting. "Teddy Roosevelt's coming to Wallace," Hank crowed.

"Clyde Hanson and the Republican crowd's gonna put on a big shindig," Della said in a mocking way. "I figure us Democrats need to outdo them. Maggie, you and me gotta make plans."

CHAPTER 37

"We'll put on a breakfast for the President," Della said as she huffed and puffed across the bedroom, helping me unpack one of the several heavy suitcases Dan and I had taken on our trip. Dan had stayed at the office in town, and Hank had gone to check on the kitchen help at the Silver Spoon, a restaurant he and Della had opened with dividends from the Titan. They'd built a house in Wallace as well, and we saw them almost as often as we had in Bixbee. "We'll call it Democrats for Roosevelt," Della went on. "And we'll put on a feed that'll put them local Republicans to shame. We can hold it at the Silver Spoon."

I considered that, thinking of alternatives. "That would be nice, but we could have it here. It would be more intimate, and I have that huge dining room I seldom use."

It was Della's turn to ponder the choices, her expression changing from one of disappointment to a conspiratorial gleam. "In a private home. Just like we was Teddy's good friends. By Gawd, that'd best Clyde Hanson's dinner at the Elk's Lodge."

●●●

I admired Teddy Roosevelt, and was familiar with many of his writings. Most presidents had seemed American, but Theodore Roosevelt *was* America, the America of the West as well as the East—he considered himself a westerner because of the ranch he owned in the Dakotas. The purpose of his trip was to bring his fellow westerners a message about labor, trusts, national finances, and tariffs, as well as to sow the seeds for future conservation policies. The stop in Wallace was convenient, since the town was the Republican stronghold in Shoshone County and on the railroad between important speaking engagements in Helena, Montana and Spokane.

He charged into Wallace on an iron horse rather than on his favorite steed, Manitou, and stepped from the special Pullman car into a drizzly rain that trickled down the steep roof of the new depot and over the fifteen thousand Chinese bricks that formed the walls. Wallace looked prosperous now. In twenty years it had grown from a single cabin to a bustling county seat of five thousand, with railroads connecting it to east and west, and spur lines running up Canyon Creek and Nine-Mile Creek. The town had lured a population of restless, driven entrepreneurs who built their stores on the flat above the Coeur d'Alene River and built their homes on the fringe of town or high on the crowding hills.

A traveling journalist had described the town as a "veritable little jewel of a city, set snugly in its beautiful velvet case of green-clad hills . . . clean, bright, wide-awake . . . only about a dozen blocks long and half as wide . . . streets paved with rolled tailings from the mills that would run something like four or five dollars per ton in lead and silver if carefully treated." The description was overstated but often quoted by the local officials. On this day, they whisked Teddy Roosevelt away in an open carriage and paraded him through streets lined with ten thousand cheering citizens of the district, the storefronts and lamp posts behind them draped with rain-soaked flags and tri-colored bunting,

At the park, Teddy spoke to an umbrella-carrying audience that looked like a sea of black mushrooms sprouting in the rain. The weather might have been dreary, but with Teddy Roosevelt as guest of the town, the occasion couldn't possibly be dreary. The steel of his clipped voice cut the soggy air, infecting those sympathetic to his cause with the same rage and desire for reform that motivated him, and incensing those whose stature was threatened. The applause proved that the forty-five-year-old Republican was popular with most of the audience. Perhaps his popularity derived from the philosophy he expounded in his speech that day: "The worst foe to American citizenship, to American life, is the man who seeks to cause hatred and distrust between one body of Americans and another, and no matter to whom the appeal is made, whether to inflame section against section, creed against creed, or class against class."

I couldn't help wondering how Clyde Hanson had reacted to those words. Needless to say, Dan and I didn't attend the dinner party Clyde hosted for the President, despite the fact that Clyde had no great love for the President's plans for reform. While Dan shut himself in his study to read some of Roosevelt's works, Della and I supervised the preparations for the breakfast to be held the following morning. We opened the pocket doors between the formal dining room and parlor and set tables in the shape of a T. Rather than continue the theme of American flags that had followed Teddy around Wallace, we decorated the tables with bouquets of rust-colored dahlias and yellow asters. Earlier that day I'd hired extra help, and they'd scrubbed the house from top to bottom, waxed the furniture until the patina of polish shone like a glaze of honey, and beat the carpets on the line until not a fleck of dust rose from the nap.

I was quaking like an aspen leaf when Teddy arrived next morning with his bodyguard and cortege of officials, but he soon put me at ease. I'd intended for Todd to eat his breakfast in the kitchen after he'd met the President. Instead, Teddy asked him to sit at the head table in a chair beside his own and insisted Todd's grinning spaniel be allowed to lie at their feet. I thought I'd burst my seams at the sight of Todd, dressed in his best knickers and bow tie, carrying on like a grownup, telling the President how he'd come by a bandaged finger. Dan's grin said he was just as proud.

Aaron, Lennie, and the Tuttles beamed from across the table. Like the other thirty Democrats in attendance, they'd never dressed in such finery, nor been so anxious to make an impression. Hank had even decorated his lapels with pins and badges of the several fraternal orders to which he belonged. I was just as guilty as the rest and had bought myself a morning dress of bottle-green taffeta for the occasion. Dan liked me in green because it made me look like a marigold. Since red hair had become popular, I no longer thought it a curse, and had piled it into a fashionable pompadour.

The room held a tantalizing aroma of entrees that included baked ham, bacon, grapefruit, applesauce with lemon and raisins, three kinds of eggs—Benedict, scrambled, and shirred with sausage—biscuits, caramel rolls, and sourdough pancakes dripping with butter and chokecherry syrup.

I needn't have worried about Teddy fitting in. His verbal gymnastics and his vitality stirred those around him into a light-hearted banter. "By Godfrey," he said after he'd stuffed himself, "you Democrats have outdone the Republicans in your culinary offerings."

I smiled across the plundered serving dishes at Della. "Della Tuttle is responsible. She supervised all the cooking."

Della made no attempt to soften her habitually loud voice as she said, "All of us Democrats are good cooks. If a woman can't put a tasty meal on the table, how's she expect to keep her man voting right." She dug an elbow into Hank's ribs.

He gave the President a knowing wink. "There's no living with these Idaho gals now that they have the vote."

"They're fortunate," the President said. "I'm afraid their sisters in other states still have a fight ahead of them. It's a bully shame some women make bad publicity for themselves. They push too hard for the vote. As for myself, I think there are two times when a woman's name should appear in public, when she marries and when she dies."

Della and I exchanged glances of disbelief. I strangled the impulse to speak, but Della pounced. "I can think of another time, Mr. President—when she gives the leader of our nation the raspberry for saying such a thing."

This bold piece of wit drew a spasm of coughing from those at the table, an outburst hastily smothered with hands, but deceiving no one.

Teddy gave a hearty laugh and slapped the table. "A ripping good barb like that would certainly make the news. The papers are always ready to poke fun at the President, but I like to think I can laugh right along with them." His chuckle reduced to a grin. "A man has to laugh, you know. Detractors, like politicians, don't wear silence very well."

Della opened her mouth to speak, but the President was still wound up in his own thoughts. "My dear artist of the cook range," he said to her, "so you don't think me a complete cad, let me say I believe zealousness possesses some virtue. How utterly dull the world would be if every man was completely prudent."

Dan grunted in agreement. He sat next to the President looking a bit stiff in a new suit of brown Irish wool. The suit's heavily padded shoulders made him as broad as an anvil. He raised his voice above the clatter of china and silver as the servers removed the breakfast dishes and refilled cups with coffee. "That's what life is all about, wouldn't you say, Mr. President? A man needs to let the world know what he stands for. He needs to fight for what he thinks is right."

"Life wouldn't be worth living otherwise," the President agreed with a nod. "I'd rather dare and succeed or fail rather than find safety in cowardice. If I didn't use the presidency as a bully pulpit, I'd feel I'd neglected the people's trust. But I admit, sometimes it seems there's no end to the obstacles." He dropped his gaze to the damask tablecloth, his jaw firm, as if he were remembering something unpleasant. His eyeglasses reflected the dancing flame of a candle that stood beside the floral centerpiece. It gave him a savage look. He took a sip of coffee and brushed a drop of it from his thick mustache. "My advisors tell me you've been having a time of it with the trusts."

Dan shrugged. "It's hard to buck them. Some of the local competition is no better. Here in Wallace, the only ethic is no ethic. An honest man is considered a fool."

Dan's comment sparked Aaron to speech. "I'm afraid my brother considers certain business tactics unethical when they're strictly good economics."

Roosevelt's eyes showed empathy for both men. "Likely Dan's frustration has colored his opinion somewhat. But there is truth in what he says. Chief Plenty Coup once said that the white man keeps his religion and laws behind him to take out and use when it's convenient. As far as I'm concerned, every town has its men of honesty as well as those of corruption. The dangerous crook is the smart one, the one who succeeds. I make no distinction. If he's a poor man, I'll cinch him. If he's a rich man, I'll cinch him a little quicker if I can."

Side conversations had ceased, the only sounds the clack of cups on saucers, a cough or two. All eyes were directed toward the President. He cupped his hands around his coffee mug and spent a brief moment staring at it in thought. "I was born rich, as you likely know, but I had battles of my own to fight. I vowed long ago that I'd rule life, not be its slave. I vowed no enemy of any kind, no complaint of my own, no external criticism, could take command of me." He spoke in a crisp, emphatic way, his jaw rigid.

"All rulers in this world must leaven confidence with humility," he went on. "Dan, now that you're in a position of command, don't forget how you felt after a day of breaking your back. I do the ranch chores at my spread in Dakota whenever I can—which isn't as often as I'd like—so I can remember what it's like to work hard. Sweating does something for a man's soul."

"You don't have to worry about Dan," Della said with a prideful swelling of her chest. "He's always looking out for his men. Pays the best wages for the shortest hours in the whole district—likely the whole state—the whole country."

Roosevelt put a hand on Dan's shoulder and looked at him with obvious pleasure. "Bully for you. Then you and I won't be at odds. For I intend to see that rich men are held as accountable as the poor man. This country wasn't founded to create more of the traditional elite, the kind of hypocritical robber barons that would turn us back to feudal times. I've promised to expand the elite to include opportunity for all men."

I'd been listening to Roosevelt's percussive speech with half an ear, my thoughts latched onto his statement about women's place in the public eye. When I caught the words, "opportunity for all men," I longed to ask if he believed opportunity should extend to women as well, but Roosevelt's determined chatter was difficult to interrupt. And Todd's face was lifted toward him in adoration. I held my tongue.

" . . . your eyes on the stars and your feet on the ground and you'll do all right," Roosevelt was telling Dan in a badgering staccato. "But I can't resist mentioning that glittering stuff you take out of the mountain." He motioned toward the fireplace mantle, where a huge spiraled candle cast its light on bits of galena and other samples of sparkling ore. "Have you ever wondered at your right to take silver out of these hills without a thought to setting some aside for the future. It's finite, you know. It's not like trees. It can't reproduce. We aren't building this country for a day. It must last through the ages. What does a nation do when it depletes the source?" He awaited Dan's answer with intense eyes.

"Actually, that question has bothered me a lot. But owning a mine is a man's dream . . . his child . . . his life's career. It drives him to the point that nothing else matters. Sort of like a disease he can't control."

My lips parted in surprise. This was the first time Dan had admitted the extent of the mine's hold on him. I chanced to reinforce the assessment. "I'll vouch for that. The Titan is a demanding mistress. She keeps Dan away from home much more than I'd like."

"I wish he'd stay home some, myself," Lennie said a bit sarcastically. "Maybe then I could ease up a bit."

"You and your sister see he tempers that drive of his, Mr. O'Shea. Especially you, Maggie. See he give you and your son more of his time. Before any man tells another how his business should be run, let him show he can run his own house. Home should be his first duty. A man needs a woman. He needs children." He patted Todd on the head. "He discovers how great that need is when his wife passes from this earth." Slowly his eyes lost their focus as if he were remembering a great personal loss. A minute dragged by before his paunch raised with a sigh. "Dan, there are ways to channel that drive of yours and fulfill your duty to mankind at the same time. You might consider politics. The nation needs men with enough sand to carry the big stick against corruption."

Dan gave a snort. "Politics turn my stomach. Besides that, I don't have time."

"Then take up the cause of conservation. Help the people of Idaho see that greedy consumption will be the downfall of this nation." Roosevelt put a hand on Todd's reddish-blond curls. "You could be a fine example for this boy of yours. As Oliver Wendell Holmes would say, 'Every boy needs to know his daddy left some of his fleece on the hedges as he passed by.'"

CHAPTER 38

Idaho had its men of courage and intelligence, men politically and financially astute who lived according to their own high standards of behavior, but none were more devoted to the cause of honesty and fair play than Theodore Roosevelt. His sincerity, his passion for truth and duty made no slight impression on those captive to his charm, whether those impressions brought a smile or a frown.

Some of Teddy's remarks had caused me chagrin, but others had dug a trench of inspiration in my mind, as they had in Dan's. The depth of that imprint revealed itself several nights after Teddy's visit when I joined Dan for a light supper in his study. Whereas my small study was finished in light woods and wallpaper, Dan's large, squarish study had the somber appearance of leather and mahogany that carried the scent of tobacco, wood smoke, and cowhide. A log smoldered on the hearth of a stone fireplace set between tiers of bookshelves. Across from the fireplace hung a tapestry that depicted deer drinking from a pool in a forest glen. The housekeeper had pulled a small table set with sparkling white linens and gleaming silverware into the space between two Queen Anne chairs upholstered in green plush that matched the forest scene. In Bixbee I'd dressed in gingham and calico, but here I wore a dress of yellow house satin with skirts that whispered when I moved. When I sat in one of the green chairs, Dan said I reminded him of a buttercup in a mountain meadow.

Todd was always hungry and had eaten an early supper in the kitchen, leaving him free to play. No sooner had I seated myself than he ran into the room and sidled up to Dan, followed by his bouncy black and white spaniel and tortoise-shell cat. Dan gave his blond son a hug, the dog's ears a roughing, the cat's whiskers a tease, and sent the three off to the playroom in time to avoid a collision with the housekeeper. Dressed in blue percale, white apron, and cap, she carried a tray with a silver tureen that wafted the steaming aroma of chicken soup and a covered basket that had the fragrance of browned rolls.

With the food before us, and the housekeeper gone about her business, Dan and I settled down to savor the meal. I was the first to rest a soupspoon long enough to speak. "I've been mulling over Teddy

Roosevelt's comments about fighting corruption. I'm sure he was speaking of male responsibility, but women are just as able to lash out against foul deeds . . . perhaps more willing. I think I've found a way to do it."

"Oh . . . how's that?" The question seemed to come from the surface of Dan's mind, as if he considered my statement of little importance or was preoccupied with his own thoughts.

I was having enough trouble forcing myself to broach the subject without contending with apathy. I hadn't wanted to speak of my plans that evening, but my thoughts had been so locked on the idea that they'd carved a groove that was hard to avoid. Steeling myself for Dan's disapproval, I blurted, "*The Wallace Weekly* is up for sale, and I'd like to buy it."

That seized Dan's attention. "You what!"

"I have plenty set aside from my share of the dividends to cover the purchase and to buy new presses. Bud Lamont, the present owner says—"

"You mean you've already looked into this?"

From Dan's tone, I knew I'd erred. When I took important steps without his knowledge and approval he made me feel as guilty as a thief caught breaking into a house, even though I made such decisions when he was out-of-state and it was necessary. He wanted me to show independence, but not if it overshadowed his role as king-of-the-roost.

I said, "Yes, I talked to Bud. I wanted to know the details of the sale before I discussed it with you."

Dan's face had turned livid. "A woman can't run a newspaper. You'd have the whole damned town snickering at you."

The insult struck me like a lance. I'd never been able to take one of Dan's barbs without it hurting, likely because his approval meant so much to me. But this time he'd gone too far. I felt betrayed. Stripped of worth. Digging my fingernails into the arms of the chair, I leaned forward, chin jutting in defiance. "What makes you think I can't? I studied journalism at college. I worked as a reporter for Aulbach and spoke to him many times about the mechanics of running a newspaper. And since when have you given a jot about what the town thinks."

"Aww, c'mon. Don't look at me as though I was the Devil. It isn't that I doubt your ability. You've been a damned good teacher . . . always done well at anything you set your mind to. But a newspaperwoman? Open to gossip—insults—dealing with rough men."

"I'm able to deal with rough men. I lived in Bixbee, didn't I? The worst place I can imagine for a woman to keep her self-respect. I can handle the men here in Wallace every bit as well—better, because I'm older."

Dan thought about that, eyeing me with doubt, then finally said on a puff of air, "I still don't see why it has to be a newspaper. Why not a book store?"

"It's important for women to be part of the press. They need to state their opinions about something beside the latest fashions. Other newspapers show such a flagrant bias. I want to publish a paper based on fact, not fiction and omission."

"They'll crucify you."

"You told Roosevelt that what mattered in life was fighting for what was right."

"I'm a man. A man is expected—"

"To think? To show his superiority? While his wife stays home and beats the wash against the rocks?" I left the chair and sought the window, my mind latched onto the insult I'd been dealt, my armpits damp with the sweat of my fury.

At that moment the housekeeper brought in dishes of gingerbread topped with whipped cream. Seeming to feel the electric charge in the air, she hurriedly took the soup bowls and left the room.

It took a while for my thoughts to run through the litany of Dan's transgressions, but by the time I sat back at the table my anger had begun to drain into the sinking feeling of regret. Dan still glared at the wall. "I don't understand you," he mumbled. "You have all the money you need and yet—"

"Having a bank account does little for me. I was happier living in a three-room shack and teaching. I want my life to amount to something."

Dan curled his upper lip. "Seems to me you've been doing that. Sure been into enough projects around town. Promoting the arts. Soliciting funds for a library."

"Any woman can do that. I involve myself for the sake of the cause and to stay busy . . . to keep from thinking about things that bother me."

"Then go back to teaching."

"People would say I'd taken the job from someone who needed it."

Dan pulled on his ear lobe several seconds in thought, looking as if he'd sucked a lemon. At last, he said sourly, "I don't like the idea of you working . . . as if I can't support you."

"People will know I'm not in the business to make money. Every newspaper in this town has gone broke at one time or another. I want to do this to keep from turning into a cabbage."

"Why can't you be happy making a home like other women? And what about Todd?"

I hadn't told Dan I suspected I was pregnant. I wasn't sure myself and didn't want to complicate matters with that uncertain news. I merely said, "I can find a nanny to watch him after school and any other time I'm not here. I'll hire a managing editor for the paper so I can spend time at home."

Dan was mute a long while, picking at the gingerbread with his fork, his face bruised looking. He still wore the grumpy expression when he looked up. "If that's what you want, I won't stand in your way. But you'll have to agree to one thing before you sign any papers."

I put my hand on my heart to keep it from beating too wildly. "Agree to what?"

"I'll take out a first option to buy the newspaper. It'll be in my name. That way the gossips won't get started. Then you sleep on it for a month. If you still want the paper after that time, you can go ahead and buy it."

● ● ●

I knew without sleeping on it that I'd soon own *The Wallace Weekly*. I brought out textbooks from my journalism courses at college and visited newspapers in Spokane. The doctor verified my suspicions that I was carrying a child, but I didn't tell Dan until I was four months pregnant. Only Della, Nora, and the housekeeper knew, the housekeeper because she made soda crackers to ease my morning sickness. By then, the newspaper was mine.

I had no tolerance for the editorial comment prevalent in newspaper reporting—the floridity, the bias, and the play on emotion. The daily grist of the news—reports on the mines, marriages, births, deaths, social events, knifings, arrests, listed the bare facts. Only in my editorials did I let opinion, passion, and drama color the page. In these personal missiles, I attacked local and national corruption, called upon the reader to support Roosevelt in his skirmishes with the *malefactors of great wealth*, as he called them. Because I regarded the written word a stronger tool for progress than unionism, I championed the miner, no better off in 1906 than in the '90s. To balance the scale, I supported the mine operators, deploring the rate of mine taxation, the removal of protective tariffs, and the increase in lead imports.

Using my editorials as a sounding board for political opinion, I backed those candidates for office whom I felt deserving, or moaned the lack of them, and lamented the sleeping citizenry. Opposing papers in Wallace and Spokane often tore my views to shreds and locals confronted me in my office and on the street.

"Whose side are you on?" they'd say, accusingly.

Or, "You don't know what you're talking about."

I wondered if the attacks arose because of my opinions or because I was a woman, likely both. Still, I believed I could placate public opinion by reporting without recourse to gender, by being at once direct and caring, and by being thoughtful in the conduct of my journalistic duties.

Five men worked for me besides the managing editor. But a change to bi-weekly publication and the purchase of equipment for job printing turned the newspaper office into a bustling, often frantic workplace. I left the mechanics of the print shop to the men, but gave a helping hand when needed. There was much else to do to help the editor—line the copy hook with time copy and live copy—check the news exchanges—prowl the local sources for news—prod the advertisers—check the affidavits on legal advertising—read and revise galley proofs—read page proofs—update subscription lists—see that the local merchants received their dodgers on time—see if I couldn't speed along the orders for type—and on and on to the point of physical and mental exhaustion. But how I thrilled each time a new edition hit the street.

Because of the increased business, I left Todd with the nanny more than I liked. I hadn't planned it that way and felt wretched about it at times. I'd return home of an evening bone-weary, wanting to lie back and throw my feet up on a pillow, only to be pounced upon by Todd. He chose that time to tell of the day's disasters and of the injustices suffered at the hands of the nanny. He seemed to delight in the tales, as if the distress it brought me made the telling worthwhile. I felt such guilt, always guilt. But to give up my newspaper work would mean to relinquish my independence and resign myself to a life less than I'd hoped for.

IN THE SHADOW OF REBELLION   263

Finally, the time came when I had to take temporary leave. Cally arrived in June, when Nature, herself, was giving green birth, the days sunny and mild. >From the first, my feelings for the baby were different from those I held for Todd. She was a girl-child with the potential of womanhood running through her tiny veins. Likely the deep affection I felt for her arose in part from the way she'd been conceived—a beach baby with the song of the sea and the wind in her soul.

It didn't take Cally long to live up to the promise of her June birth. She became a sunny- faced cherub with reddish-gold ringlets. Because of her bubbling laughter and disposition of a contented child, she received the small amount of time Dan had to give to the family. He'd look at her with unbelieving eyes, as if she was a dream, a miracle. He marveled at her loveliness, at the roses in her cheeks, and at the long, silken lashes.

Once he remarked, "How can such beauty and innocence be possible in this larcenous world?"

Often, he'd sit with her on his lap and tell funny stories, delighting in the soft trill of her child's-voice. And he'd smile at her toddler's walk, as quick as that of a baby chick after its mother. At times he would get down on his hands and knees, roll a ball across the floor to her dimpled fingers and laugh with her in glee. How good that he had Cally for comfort. How good that, as he grew older, he had more appreciation for the delight-giving nature of early childhood.

As for the grumpy attitude Dan presented to all but the baby, I saw clearly it was not a deliberate act on his part. If there were no ugly battles waging within him he'd be the Dan I'd loved so completely. The best way to help him was to continue to love him. The next best was to use the power of the press against his enemies.

●●●

In 1907, my *Wallace Weekly* carried the following stories:

February: TRUSTS PLAY FINANCE GAME
Guggenheim Sons, owners of American Smelting and Refining, has purchased Charles Sweeney's Federal Mining and Smelting. It is well-known that John D. Rockefeller Sr. loaned the money for the formation of Federal. So it comes as a surprise that the Guggenheim takeover was financed by J.D.'s son.

Charles Sweeney, reported to have made over a million dollars on the sale of his common stock alone, has been reelected as Federal's president . . .

March: GUGGENHEIM TRUST BUYS SELBY

American Smelting and Refining Company has purchased two smelters, one in Tacoma, Washington and the Selby, located near San Francisco. Dan Rigby, owner of the Black Titan was offered a contract with A.S.&R. for the purchase of ore, but refuses to sign unless given access to the railway terminal at Burke. The purchase of the Selby Smelter by A.S.&R. has forced Rigby to contract with an independent smelter in the east.

April: MINE OWNER ESCAPES QUAKE

Dan Rigby, Wallace resident and owner of the Black Titan Mining Company was in San Francisco during the severe earthquake that jolted the area. He escaped unharmed when fires caused by ruptured gas mains ravaged the hotel where he was staying and razed much of the city. Rigby was in the Bay Area to bring suit against American Smelting and Refining for breach of contract.

Written in stark black and white. Cold, unemotional. Objective reporting. Reflecting in no way the insane anger and desperation in Dan's eyes when he learned of the sale of the Selby to Federal Mining and Smelting. Nor did the hieroglyphics that marched across the page speak of the black fury Dan loosed on Sweeney before his suit.

In the meantime, the union had gained strength after suffering setbacks that resulted from the bombing of the Bunker Hill and Sullivan. The Western Federation of Miners still smarted from having its members arrested by government troops, jailed in sweltering boxcars, and later crammed into hastily built barracks. Seeking revenge, it hired hatchet-men to murder men in Colorado and Idaho who had caused trouble for the union. The most prominent on their list was Idaho's Governor Steunenberg. Though sympathetic with the miners, he was an American first, a politician second, and had ordered government troops to invade the district after the rebellion of '99—a day I remembered vividly because it had happened on the day Jeff was killed. Beyond that, the WFM considered Governor Steunenberg responsible for the mine owners' blacklisting of union members who'd taken part in the bombing.

Harry Orchard, one of the union's assassins responsible for a score of murders executed in behalf of the union, had been arrested for setting a fatal bomb in Steunenberg's yard. He'd confessed to the killing and had implicated three top WFM leaders from the headquarters in Butte. They, in turn, had pointed the finger of guilt at Hub Malone, who'd worked closely with Orchard.

The defendants spent fifteen months in Boise awaiting trial, then in May of 1907 the electrifying defense lawyer Clarence Darrow was hired to represent the men. Della and I had watched Darrow's theatrics when he'd defended a union man in Wallace the previous month, and we could hardly wait for the results of the trial in Boise.

"You and me are going to Boise," Della declared one day. "See if Darrow can win this one."

We weren't disappointed in the proceedings. Darrow spoke with such eloquence. Such nuance. Such feel for drama. All of it stowed in a head that could only be called bovine. Unlike Della, who'd always championed the union extremists, I thought it sad that Darrow had chosen to defend the dangerous element in the Western Federation of Miners. But that was to be expected. He'd sung the virtues of radical socialism for years, and was leading the chorus for the new socialist-based trade union, The Industrial Workers of the World, founded that winter with the aid and blessing of the Federation.

Darrow's opponent in the trial, Willam Borah, an attorney of rising fame and political importance in Idaho, presented his closing argument with perhaps less drama than Darrow, but with a poetry of equal effect. "What a scene we have passed through in these sixty days of trial," Borah began. "Twenty-odd murders proven and not a single man punished. Think of it—laboring men trying to earn their daily bread, trying to plant the dimple of joy upon the faces of prattling babes, trying to drive the shadows from the simple hearth—blown to an unrecognizable mass because they were not union men." He went on to outline the conspiracy that had resulted in the murder of ex-Governor Steunenberg at the gate to his home, and finished with, "Right here at home we see anarchy, that pale, restless, hungry demon from the crypts of hell, fighting for a foothold in Idaho. Should we compromise with it? Or should we crush . . ."

Despite Borah's eloquence, the jury issued an acquittal. Conspiracy not proven beyond a doubt. I was stunned, as was most of Boise and the nation. Though Teddy Roosevelt expressed a willingness to work with those "whose socialism is really an advanced form of liberalism," even *he* branded the released union heads as undesirable citizens. Miners everywhere scored Roosevelt by wearing buttons that said, "I am an Undesirable Citizen," and in Chicago a parade of thousands supported the union "martyrs."

I returned home with an amazing story to tell of the release of conspirators and anarchists, but when I asked Max, my editor, to read an opinion piece I'd written that was critical of the jury, he said "Maggie, you may think these men—their acts—their views abhorrent. But if our laws of justice set them free, so be it. If we alter the system to trap those with whom we disagree, then we endanger our own right to dissent."

"But murder? Everyone knows those men ordered it done."

"Only if proven beyond a doubt. It's the doubt that may one day free you, your husband, your son, or some other innocent from injustice."

I'd heard that Hub Malone, while serving two years in jail for his leadership in the bombing of the Bunker Hill, had helped plan the organization of the Industrial Workers of the World, and I wondered if his recent release from the Boise jail boded ill for the district.

It wasn't long before my fears were confirmed. "Hub Malone just arrived from Butte," I told Ken, my reporter, one day in June. "He's called a mass meeting at Burke union hall tonight, and I'd like you to take notes. I'd go, but they wouldn't let me stick my little toe in the place." What I didn't say was that I'd caught a glimpse that morning of Jim Tatro leaving the Wallace depot with Malone. Likely he still harbored a grudge, and I was in no position to test the possibility.

"I heard rumbles about the meeting," Ken said. "Sounds like every union man is going to go."

I nodded my head in worry. "I'd hate to think Malone is here to stir things up."

Ken gave a snort of a laugh. "A man who just missed being sent to the jug for murder isn't going to sing the guys a lullaby. He's here to throw grit into the operators' oil."

CHAPTER 39

My high-ceilinged newspaper office on Bank Street had two rooms. The print shop, domain of the journeyman printer and the typesetter, filled a back room that smelled of ink and damp plaster. Run by waterpower from a creek that plunged down the hillside at the rear of the building, the two Wood presses were capable of ten to fifteen thousand impressions each day. A Linotype machine, folder and perforator, rolls of newsprint, piles of job stock, cans of ink, and barrels stuffed with wadded first-sheets and other scraps of paper crammed the room.

The front office held my desk, a huge roll-top with pigeon holes at the back and room for an Underwood typewriter and phone. Four other desks lined the walls, another roll-top for the managing editor and one for the bookkeeper, smaller desks for the compositor and Ken, the reporter. A long table held galleys and galley proofs, scissors, paste pot, scraps of paper, and at the moment, the compositor's lunch pail. He and the bookkeeper had gone across the street for schooners of beer to wash down their lunch. Ken was away on assignment, the editor home for lunch.

The morning had bred problems and my shoulders drooped beneath a white Gibson-girl blouse. Wisps of hair from my pompadour strayed over the collar. From the back room came the sound of rolling presses—k'thud, k'thud, kthud, slam, k'thud, k'thud, k'thud, slam. The noise drowned the clack of my typewriter as I worked to meet the deadline for an editorial on the speech Hub Malone had delivered to the local unions urging support of the Industrial Workers of the World. Ken had filed his report on the meeting, and the notes he'd taken lay beside my typewriter. The latest issue of *McClures Magazine* lay near the phone, its cover a cartoon sketch of the IWW personified in miner's garb, embracing diversified workers of the world. Inside the cover, the magazine reported on Eugene Debs, DeLeon, and the other Socialists who'd given birth to the new union. They advocated the amalgamation of the working class into one big union that would own and control the world's production and flow of goods.

Ken liked to take copious notes, and his report on the union meeting at Burke was no exception. It included physical descriptions and all the dynamics of the contentious meeting. The report as published would be scaled down to essential facts, but his notes reflected the atmosphere at the meeting, invaluable for my editorial. I'd read the notes in their entirety and was going through them again as I wrote my editorial, keeping in mind Ken's description of Malone—*He looked haggard. The hair at his temples has turned white, and one wide swath frosts the length of his stringy black hair, but he hasn't lost his oratorical powers.* Along that line, I might use a quote or two from Malone but without the dialect Ken had included. Such as, "Me lads, since '99 we've been drifting on the waters o' doubt. But we haven't been waiting for a stiff breeze to come along and fill our sails. We've been working behind the scenes, reorganizing, getting ready for the big push. Miners are no better off today than they were in '90."

Building on that idea, Malone had gone on to say, "We've tried the path o' political action. But they've shot us down time after time. There's only one way we can overcome the warlords of capitalism. We must bare our fists in revolution. We must put the working class in power. We must control the production and flow of goods without regard for the capitalist masters." Ken had noted—*Only slight applause at this.*

"Me boys, the Federation can't do it alone. We have to have help. 'Tis time for the amalgamation of the working class into one big union—The Industrial Workers of the World. 'Tis a grand sounding name. And well it should be. For 'tis this child of revolutionary industrialism that will round our sails with the winds of hope and speed us across the sea of capitalist greed to the promised land of social and economic equality." Ken had noted—*Only mild applause.* I could understand that. Socialism was making strides in the country, but it was by no means popular as yet. Not even in Burke Canyon, where at one time anarchists had found rich bedding for their spores of revolution.

According to Ken's notes, a solitary voice rose above Malone's saying, "I'm no Socialist! You and the WFM can't legislate socialism into me no more than you can legislate religion into a hog." *Coarse laughter.*

From another miner, "You can take Eugene Debs, DeLeon, and the rest of them Socialist windbags that hatched the IWW and feed 'em to the coyotes." *Angry voices in agreement.*

Malone raised his hands for quiet. "All I ask is that you think about it, me lads. There's a class struggle going on in our society. That struggle will go on and on, festering from generation to generation until the worker is master of his product."

From the rear of the hall, "What am I gonna do with ten ton o' rock a day? Take it home for the missus to pay the groceries?" *Gritty laughter.*

"Dump it onto the Super's yard." *More laughter.*

Malone's face lit with a new fire. He leaned over the speaker's table and pointed a finger at the small sea of faces. "A yard? How many o' you have a yard? How many have two and three-story houses? Any o' you ever lived in anything that big except a beanery?" *Miners shake heads.*

"Think o' the injustice, me lads. While the operators take their ease in mansions with running water . . . electricity . . . soft beds . . . and fancy food, those who make them rich have to rest their tired bones on a hard bunk in a drafty beanery, or in a one-room shack with the rats. How much better that those mansions be turned into homes for the workers. Into hospitals for the miner and his family. Into sanitariums for those miners with The Dust. Into orphan homes for those who've lost their daddys to the mines and their moms to hard work."

A voice in the crowd. "I don't want their damned mansions. Just want a decent house of my own."

"Me boy, you don't stand a chance in hell o' getting that house until the working class is emancipated. Until we are no longer wage slaves. Not until then. Not until we are free."

—*Note: Hub's speech not well-accepted. Some miners don't like far-left socialism. Even strong union men have their doubts. The IWW will not last.*

A counter with a hinged flap at one end stretched across the front of the newspaper office to keep the public from the rest of the room. The latest issue of *The Wallace Weekly* lay in a stack at one end of the counter, and beneath the counter lay piles of back issues. The worn pages of large-city editions hung from a rack near the front window. Despite a stop that held the door open to the hot summer air, the room smelled of ink and paper fiber. I was so engrossed in my work, the job press making such a clatter, I hadn't noticed when a man came through the front door and lifted the flap in the counter. Not until I caught the scent of tobacco and whiskey did I turn my head.

Behind me stood a coarse-grained blond, tall, orange-faced, with a raw canker at the corner of his mouth. He wore no coat and his vest was open, revealing a white-shirted belly that lopped over his belt. His features were the same as before, though hardened over the years, the head set on the body of a man in his early thirties instead of on a scrawny youth. He had a new feature—tiny red veins that threaded his nose. Jim Tatro.

My chest rose on a sharp intake of air. Nerves prickled the back of my neck. My hands froze on the typewriter.

Jim laughed in a cruel way. "You remember me, don't you."

The answer caught in my throat.

Jim moved closer, leering through uneven, tobacco-stained teeth. "Glad to know I make a mark on the ladies." He glanced toward the door of the print shop as if someone might be watching, then settled his fierce gaze on me. "How's Dan? I hear he's been bloodying his knuckles on the trust."

While I was deciding whether to answer, Lars, my young Scandinavian typesetter, came from the print shop, letting the full rattle and clank of the presses into the room. He shot Jim a questioning glance, took a galley from the compositor's table, and returned to the back room.

Jim's face turned grim. "We'll catch up on Dan later. Got more important matters." With a scaly hand, he took Ken's notepad from the desk

I tried to grab the pad, yelling, "That's none of your bus—"

"More my business than yours. I sat next to your reporter at the meeting. Saw him writing on this." He held the pad out of reach as he scanned the notes, then tossed it back on the desk. Clearly displeased, he tore the sheet of paper from my typewriter and read it slowly, moving his lips with the words. A hardness came over his face, a twitch of the lips, a sharp concentration of the eyes, like the quick shift in mood of a purring cat when it sees a mouse run across the floor. He gave me a sneer, not for any particular reason but because it was an ingrained mannerism. "I wouldn't print this if I was you." He crumpled the paper and threw it into the wastebasket next to my desk.

"You have no right to do that!" I plucked the paper from the basket and began to smooth the wrinkles.

Jim snatched it, tore it into bits, and threw them on the floor. "You ain't going to spoil things by dirtying Hub's name in your shitty paper. Hub don't like being called a radical and a revolutionary. It puts 'im in a bad light."

"How can he be viewed in any other light? He's stood for strikes and violence since '92. If it was left to him, the mines would go to rack and —"

"You're just afraid the IWW will take your big house. It'd make a mighty nice boarding house for miners or a rest home for men with *The Dust*."

"They're best helped through legislation, not anarchy. Malone's twisting the miners' arms, promising a utopia that can't possibly happen. Most of them don't want to have anything to do with the *Reds*, as they call—"

"Bullshit! Hub knows what's best for 'em. You moneybags'll catch it before long." Slamming his jaw shut on the thought, he stormed over to the door to the print shop and threw it open.

I hurried after him, yelling, "You can't go in there!" heard him grumble something to the Linotype man, and watched angrily as he explored the room, the press men looking on in bewilderment.

He motioned toward the press. "It'd be a shame to ruin a nice press like this," he said in a harsh, insinuating tone.

"You wouldn't dare!"

He locked rigid fingers around the sateen sleevelet that protected my blouse. "You know I would. I told you when you helped Dan run off that I'd make you sorry someday."

"Let go of her!" Lars made a move to hit him.

Jim shoved the smaller Lars aside, walked with a resentful stride into the front office and out into the street. Lars and I followed as far as the doorway and watched him enter a saloon. Still that swagger, I thought bitterly. Still the *I don't give a hoot about anybody* attitude he'd learned from his father. Nothing of his mother in him. I wondered if Maude still lived and if her life was as wretched as ever.

Feeling weak from the encounter, I sent Lars back to work and slumped into my chair. Why must Jim Tatro, that poor excuse for a human being continue to plague my life? About the time he'd passed from my mind, he'd slithered back to the district, baring his fangs like a reptile on the prowl. *Well, Jim, you may have fanaticism running through your veins like a swill of cheap whiskey, but you aren't going to tell me what to do. I'll print what I please.*

CHAPTER 40

When I arrived at work two days later, my distraught editor, Max, met me at the door—a slight man with a pale, melon-shaped face, wearing thick spectacles beneath a green eye-shade. Always nervous in his manner, on that day he was like a child fidgeting his way through a tale of misadventure. "We could have been ruined!" he exclaimed. "Absolutely ruined."

"What happened?" I said, fearing the worst.

"Come, I'll show you." With much wringing of his hands, Max led the way into the print- shop, where four other employees stood around in varying shades of gloom. "See what I mean." Max pointed to fuses, caps, and several sticks of dynamite lying on the floor near the large press. "He was going to blow it up."

"Who was going to blow it up?" I thought I knew the answer.

"Same man was here two days 'go," the typesetter said glumly. "Lars not forget that face."

"Lars scared him off," Max put in with a nod of appreciation.

My hand went to the base of my throat as I considered the scenario—Jim bent on destruction and Lars with the courage to run him off. "I can't believe Jim had the nerve to come here in broad daylight."

Lars shook his head. "Was before sun up. Max say he need dodgers for Golden Rule Store, so I come early. I hear noise in back room. Take pistol Max keep in desk. When man see me, he run out back door. I think I should shoot, but I afraid he shoot back."

I blew an anxious sigh. "You were lucky. I'm surprised he ran."

Max had removed his glasses and was wiping his watery blue eyes with a handkerchief. "Do you think he'll try this again?"

I thought about the possibility, imagining a hateful man determined to ruin the press and succeeding next time—a madman seeking revenge for Dan's desertion of the union in '92— revenge for my daring appraisal of Hub Malone—revenge for whatever reason his demented mind gave substance. "Let's hope he won't try for a while. He and Hub Malone left for Butte on the morning train."

The compositor's dark features were set in a frown. "Shouldn't we report this to the police?"

The journeyman printer and his helper nodded in unison. "You should, Mrs. Rigby."

I shook my head adamantly. "If Dan finds out, he'll make me sell the paper. No, just dispose of the blasting materials in some safe way and go about your business as if nothing has happened."

●●●

Although I kept the Wood press rolling with assaults on the radical union, The Industrial Workers of the World, Jim Tatro didn't return to torment me. He was violent, not careless. And like most bullies, he had a streak of cowardice in him. Besides, his muscle was needed in Butte. To everyone's surprise, the *Wobblies,* as people jokingly called the members of the IWW, were having trouble surviving in that radical copper camp. Most workers would like to rid themselves of the old-line American Federation of Labor with its division of crafts, but this common grudge was not enough to unite workers of diverse skills and needs.

Rather than union matters, it was a natural disaster that brought the *Wallace Weekly* to its knees. Due to the town's location at the meeting of four river canyons, during high waters, Wallace was vulnerable to rubble and silt that spewed from the canyons onto the flat. The worst offender, Canyon Creek, flushed tailings from the ore mills into the Coeur d'Alene River, and these tailings clogged the channel east of town. The city fathers had asked the operators to stop dumping tailings during the rainy season, and most had, but their efforts had fallen short. Sludge had raised the bed of the river to a hazardous level.

November brought a leaden sky that pressed down upon the town like a smothering lid and rain poured for what seemed an eternity. Then the sky opened a few hours to sunshine and closed again, releasing punishing drops that struck the ground like bullets. Dan and the other operators with mines on Canyon Creek ordered their men to the river to build a dike. Too late. Swelled to overflowing, the river escaped its banks and fled down the streets like an incorrigible child. Wallace's youngsters splashed up and down the walks in their rubber boots and sailed tiny shps of bark and sticks.

Storekeepers stood in their doorways and scowled at the rising waters. Saloon keepers with establishments near the river tended bar in waders while they kept an eye on the murky water seeping through the floorboards. Afraid to delay longer, merchants loaded provisions onto wagons hub-deep in water, or heaped their goods onto makeshift rafts to the point of capsizing. Dan and his miners worked to save the section of town that stood on higher ground.

Teams of horses strained at their harness as they tried to clear the railroad right-of-way of mudslides that had carried a jumble of trees, rock slabs, and other debris down the mountain. Frustrated railroad crews fought to repair washed-out track and telegraph lines. Hurricane-force winds sent huge cedars to their death. The river raged several feet deep through every street in town, flooding basements, supplies of food and fuel. People fled their homes or worked in desperation to save their possessions. There were no lines of communication. Train travel was out of the question. Evacuation impossible.

Because of its raised foundation, our home was safer from floodwaters than most, and I opened the house to those who'd been forced into the streets. Anna, the housekeeper, and I kept on the run passing out blankets and dry clothes, offering solace to those whose loss had been great. We made pot upon pot of strong coffee and tea, kettles full of soup and beans. Delicacies from the pantry disappeared within minutes. Case after case of beer and whiskey Dan sent to the house seemed to evaporate before our eyes.

Della's house had flooded and she came to help. Her voice penetrated the walls as she made new arrivals welcome and barked orders. "This ain't a picnic! You young gals get in here and help stack these dishes." Or, "Cally, scoot upstairs and get your brother and the rest o' the boys. Tell them to get their behinds down here and fetch me some dry wood or they'll be going without supper."

Dan brought men into the house, wet, bedraggled, chilled to the bone, and found hot coffee and fresh rolls waiting in the kitchen. They gulped down platefuls of stew and bowls of thick soup, stuffed their mouths with chunks of fresh bread, washed everything down with a bottle of beer, then went out again into the night.

Through it all, Cally tore around the house with the blush of excitement on her cheeks, smiling, making new friends in her effervescent way. Todd took the boys up to his room to tell ghost stories and play dominoes and checkers. For the grownups, nothing but a bone-tired weariness, frustration, and puffed eyelids that drooped from lack of sleep. The women talked of Wallace's floods past and present and spoke of the possessions they would have saved from mud's-way if they'd had time. Silly little things, personal items that had no meaning for anyone but themselves.

●●●

It took a week for the waters to recede. When they did, Dan left the house wearing a pair of waders to round up help for the nasty job of swamping out the Titan's office building. He said he'd take a look at the *Weekly* as well, but I couldn't restrain my curiosity. After putting on several pairs of his socks beneath his gumboots, I went downtown to inspect the damage myself.

Ugh! What a horrid sight!

Silt and rubbish lined the streets and sidewalks—paper, bark, dead leaves, water-logged tree limbs, fence boards, shingles, waste from outhouses, manure from the local liveries, upturned wagons, all capped with a putrid, yellowish-gray froth. The stinking pudding had formed ridges against the curbs and made miniature dunes in the street. Gasses bubbled up through the mush. Next to the newspaper office a barber pole advertised *Baths.* I smiled at the irony and thought of adding the word *Mud* to the sign.

I was lifting my skirts to step around a brown miasma heaped at one side of the *Weekly's* doorway when several mud-spattered men approached. One of them, a tall rod of a man, complained, "Hope you operators are satisfied. Look what your dumping's done."

"Yeah," grumbled another. "Why don't you print that in your paper? You're always spouting for every other cause."

A third said sarcastically, "Now, how would that look? Her a loyal wife. Likely she's too scared to speak out against her husband and the rest of the rich mucky-mucks." He laughed as if he'd made a joke.

I felt the heat rise beneath my wraps. "You know full well my husband has worked to stop silt from entering the streams."

"A lotta good a little blasting and wing-dams'll do," the man countered.

"It's a start. And he'll do more. It's the other operators who've been dragging their feet." "That's what you say," the tall man countered. "Your husband oughta pay to dump the tailings somewhere else, then you wouldn't have so much money to play newspaper gal with. A woman has no business running a newspaper. Pretending she's a man. What she says is really her husband talking, not—"

"Dan has never told me what to print and what not to print. You just—" A heavy hand on my shoulder cut off the rest. When I turned, I saw Della standing there.

"You don't have to make excuses to this bunch o' belly-achers," she said. Then to the men as she propped a hand on her hip, "Ain't you men got enough to do without kicking up a row with this poor girl?"

"Huh, poor girl? I wish I was as poor."

"Aww, go on with you." Then, as she slid the hand from her hip. "We brought some dry coal down from Mullan and the stove's working. The Spoon's offering free coffee. Tell Hank I said to give each o' you an extra cup on me."

Somewhat subdued by Della's offer, the men headed for the restaurant, muttering complaints at me over their shoulders. Della motioned in the direction the men were taking. "Come on, we've got the Spoon's kitchen cleared enough so we can heat up a pot o' tea."

"Later. I want to see what's happened to the presses."

Della waved an arm. "Max and the others have been in there for hours. Give 'em a little more time and maybe you can face it without screaming."

"Putting it off won't make it any easier. I'll come as soon as I can."

Max and the other men had shoveled a path from the door to the print-shop, and I stood there mouth agape, thinking I'd be more able to cope if I was a salamander. I'd expected to find a layer of silt a few inches deep on the floor. Instead, the walls had contained the mud to the depth of a-foot-and-a-half. A coating of scum and grime three feet high ringed the walls. The place held the odor of mildew and rot as well as the sour smell of paper soaked for days in slime. Furniture lay on its side or upside down in the muck along with books, paper, stinkbugs, and a mouse or two. Blue-black streaks showed where inkbottles had wedged in the mud. Newspapers lay in soggy sheaths. I felt numb to the bone.

Max shuffled from the print-shop, scoop shovel in hand. Mud had slopped over the top of his galoshes and plastered his pants to his legs. From the room behind him came the scrape of shovels against sand and wood. "I think it'd be easier to dynamite the building, Maggie. The machinery's clogged with mud and it's rusted."

I raised my arms in a hopeless gesture and said in an attempt at cynical humor, "Right now, dynamite sounds good. I could call Jim Tatro in from Butte and let him do the honors." Then seriously, "Just salvage what you can. I'll have to decide what to do with the rest."

CHAPTER 41

I was about to cry when I walked into the kitchen at the Silver Spoon. The room's appearance did nothing to cheer me—the same filth as at the newspaper office, offensive to the nose and streaked black from coal the waters had sucked from the bin. Della had washed the huge Monarch stove as well as a table and chairs and had put coffee pots and a teakettle on the hot stovelids. She and Nora sat with their elbows propped on the table in a mood of dejection, a pot of tea and cups in front of them. Any other time, Nora's eyes would have twinkled from her round, dimpled face. Today they looked clouded and flat.

"I can tell you've been to the newspaper," she said to me. "I have the advantage of living on the hill—at least my house didn't get flooded." Nora's lawyer husband had bought Clyde Hanson's spacious home on the hillside above Wallace. Clyde had purchased a deluxe apartment building in Spokane and had moved there to please his socially-conscious wife. He spent weeknights in a Wallace hotel, the weekends in Spokane.

I put my hat and coat on the scrubbed counter and sat at the table where an empty cup was waiting. Della pulled a folded sheet of stationery from her apron pocket. "I was about to show this letter to Nora," she said. She pushed a sheet of expensive silk bond in front of us. "It's from Abigail Scott Duniway in Portland. Likely you remember her from our suffrage work in '95. Now she's editor of that reform paper, *The New Northwest*." She said this more for Nora's benefit than mine. I knew Abigail well—a remarkable feminist who'd helped us crusade for suffrage in Idaho. It was after I'd lost my first baby and I'd plunged mind and soul into the movement. Recently, I'd visited her when I was thinking of buying the *Wallace Weekly*.

"Anyway," Della went on, "she says she's going to start a campaign to get women the vote in Oregon and Washington State. She wants us to organize the gals here to help in Eastern Washington."

Nora gave that a few seconds thought while her restless fingers poked absently at a Marcelle-type pompadour intended to keep her curly brown locks repressed. Though she and Della often argued, in the mutual caring for some cause, they'd worked together with a shared understanding. "We have a lot of contacts in Spokane," she said. Why don't we start putting pressure where it'll do some good?"

"The best place to put pressure is at men's necks," Della said with a hearty laugh.

I looked up from the letter and laughed with her. "As much as I'd like to strangle them sometimes, that might not go over too well."

"Show me a better way."

"Will you two stop it. I'm serious." Nora's small frame seemed charged with sudden energy. "We ought to put our heads together and see what we can come up with. We made a good team in '95 and we're a lot smarter now. Maggie has her newspaper. She could print flyers to send out and about."

●●●

Thus, at a time when I could barely face the prospect of salvaging the newspaper from the muck and mire, the idea of using the press to forward the cause of suffrage in the Northwest renewed my sagging spirits. I bought new presses and furnishings and for the next two years did my best to help the crusade.

One of my first efforts was to interview May Arkwright Hutton, Spokane's self-appointed leader for the cause. May was a diamond in the rough, a figure of political importance. Friend of William Jennings Bryan and Clarence Darrow, she possessed a unique quality that attracted people of state and national importance. I'd known May when she lived in Burke and Wallace, knew her as an aggressive sort with an elephantine figure and a voice like a bassoon. I also knew May for her sometimes-crude behavior, her outlandish way of dressing, and her generosity with her fellow man. She'd recently moved to Spokane, after making a fortune as a shareholder in Hank Day's Hercules Mining Company. I sat in May's luxurious apartment for hours listening to her explain why "women shouldn't be relegated to the kitchen and bedroom and be classified with children, convicts, and idiots."

My views on the status of women weren't as radical as May's, but by the end of the interview I'd jumped onto May's bandwagon, pledging the support of my newspaper, time, and energy. Despite my reluctance to face an audience, as I had in '95, May soon had me traveling across Washington giving speeches attended by from twenty-five to five-hundred people.

Dan objected. "I knew buying that goddamned newspaper would lead to no good. You've turned into a male-impersonating feminist who doesn't give a hoot about her husband or kids."

Dan exaggerated. I could never be unfeminine, nor truly neglect those I loved. I tried to include the children when important suffragettes came to visit. Little Cally used her considerable charms to befriend them, but Todd would say a polite "Glad to meet you," and escape to the outdoors. As for Dan, it was a time in his life when little could please him. A depression had gripped the nation and the price of lead and silver had dropped into a bottomless pit. Many of the Coeur d'Alene mine owners had cut production, put a leash on their moneybelts, and told a thousand men to pack their bags. When the Black Titan cut to one shift, Dan spent much of his time placating Aaron's and Lennie's fears, not just of the depression but of the eventual extinction of the mine. The venerable Tiger-Poorman Mine at Burke, one of the original giants, had been closed and allowed to fill with water, its accessible ore exhausted, its further potential unexplored because of the high costs of mining. Now each mine owner and each miner breathed less easily.

The death of a mine? The death of the Titan? Like other mine owners Dan preferred to ignore the possibility. In the day to day struggle to ship silver-lead ore to market there was no time to consider the end of the dream.

Meanwhile, only a few months remained to file petitions to put suffrage on the ballot and sway the Washington State Legislature. Accustomed now to speaking in public, Nora and I let Della drag us onto Spokane's streets with a soapbox. We braved the comments of passing toughs and the scorching looks of Spokane's upper-crust, when those elegant citizens rode by in open carriages and gleaming autos. With other suffragettes, we'd climb into a horse-drawn coach decorated with slogans and parade through town touting the worthiness of our cause. Mainly we stood on street corners urging suffrage literature onto passersby. And when enough people gathered, one or the other of us would mount the soapbox and give our spiel.

We'd isolated ourselves from May Hutton because her brash behavior had caused a breach between suffrage units in the eastern and western sections of Washington State. We believed more could be accomplished in behalf of the movement by distancing ourselves from the feud. To this end, we gathered about us high-spirited intellectuals full of wit and humor, accomplished but not pretentious. We met weekly at a hotel in Spokane to plan the crusade, discussing equal pay for equal work, equal opportunity for education and jobs. We supported legal protection for mothers who'd given birth within and outside of marriage. We argued in behalf of day care centers for working mothers and payment to those who chose to stay at home with their children. We spoke of birth control and the right to have an abortion. We believed that progress in those areas must be part and parcel of equal suffrage.

Due in large part to our efforts, the legislature passed the bill to allow the referendum on the ballot in November of that year of 1910. Now came the big push to get out the vote and be sure it was for equal suffrage. Realizing that all units of the Washington State suffrage organization must pull together, we made several trips to the coast to plead the case for unity. We'd all but get to our knees and beg, "Please, ladies! Let's be intelligent about this. How will men believe us capable of a rational vote, when we can't make peace among ourselves, when our actions are ruled by emotion rather than good sense?"

I'd made just such a plea before the Seattle unit and was leaving the meeting hall, when I was handed a yellow and black envelope. I ripped it open and read the message it contained, *IMPERATIVE YOU RETURN HOME AT ONCE, DAN.* The telegram simple, direct, but enough to weaken my knees.

The Children! Something must have happened to the children. If only I was clairvoyant and could see across the miles. Suddenly the suffrage movement lost all import.

CHAPTER 42

I tried to telephone Dan before I caught the train for Idaho, but a severe windstorm had raged across the flatlands east of the Cascades and downed the lines.

The trip across Washington was always long. This time the miles seemed endless as the train crawled through mountains scorched and thirsting from drought, beside rivers shrunken to sluggish streams, and across sage and wheatlands dancing in the heat waves of July. At each tedious stop to take on passengers the knot in my stomach drew tighter. I thought I'd shrivel to a bag of nerves before the train finally wound up the canyon of the Coeur d'Alene River.

When I descended from the coach onto the station platform at Wallace, I knew the horrors my distraught mind had imagined had fallen short of reality. Gray puffs beneath Dan's eyes said he hadn't slept much in the last few days. Without a kiss or word of greeting, he hustled me through the crowd arriving for the Fourth of July celebration to be held the next day, then over to his shiny black Reo parked at the rear of the station. When we reached the auto, I pulled back on my arm and said breathlessly, "For God's sake, Dan, what's wrong?"

"I can't talk about it here. When we get home." His voice sounded of fatigue and impatience, along with an edge of anger.

"Has something happened to the children?"

"I told you we'd talk later." His tone was harsh.

The sun had heated the Reo's leather upholstery to the point of discomfort, and Dan threw a lap robe on the seat before he helped me into the car. He seemed reluctant to return to the platform for my luggage, just stood there scanning the hillside behind the station, the thin stand of trees paper-dry and quivering in the warm breeze of late afternoon. He seemed to focus his glazed eyes for an instant on two men standing at the base of the hill, then turned toward me. "I'll be back in a minute with your suitcase."

Actually it took ten minutes, because Dan made a detour to speak to the men at the bottom of the hill. When I asked about them, he refused to answer, nor did he speak at all on the way home. Not even during the worst of his troubles at the mine had he been so withdrawn and morose.

A trim, athletic-looking blond in his late thirties greeted us when we entered our house on Bank Street, a Nordic type with fine bone structure and sky-blue eyes. A scar on one temple and a thin nose that appeared to have been broken in the past hinted at combat of some kind. His bald pate extended half-way back the crown of his head to a ridge of short hair that stood on end. My instant impression was of someone with intelligence and self-confidence.

"Any trouble, Mr. Rigby?" he asked.

"None."

"Are the other two still at the station?"

"They were when I left."

"Good. I'll leave them there to check on the crowd."

Who was this stranger who displayed such an air of authority? What business did he have in my house? I thought I'd hit someone if I wasn't told soon.

Dan turned from hanging his hat and coat on the rack beside the door and made a slight gesture toward the man. "Maggie, this is Ed Stapp. He's an agent working out of Spokane for the government's new Bureau of Investigation."

Stapp offered a benign, thin-lipped smile.

I found no reason to return the smile. "Why is he here? What's happened?" Fear and anger pounded at my ribs.

Stapp raised a nearly invisible blond eyebrow at Dan. "You haven't told her?"

"I was waiting until we got home."

"Then I'll let you break the news."

Dan held out his hand. "I want to show her those letters."

"Sure thing." Stapp took three wrinkled sheets of paper from his coat pocket and handed them to Dan. "I'll need them back." Saying no more, he pulled a pipe and leather pouch from a black jacket hanging on the rack and went into the parlor cleaning the pipe bowl with a metal scraper.

Dan motioned me into his study and closed the door behind us, the room's somber furnishing matching his mood. Once inside, he turned his eyes on me with such ferocity and pain I flinched. "Cally's been kidnapped."

"Kidnapped?" I spoke the word as if it were foreign, without meaning, then repeated it as a near-scream. "Kidnapped!" My thoughts floundered, snatching at bits of hope. "How do you know—maybe she's—maybe she's wandered off—maybe she's lost—or playing a trick. You know what a mischief she is."

"For three whole days! Do you take me for an idiot? Don't you think I looked into all those possibilities right off? Besides, these started coming in the mail." He shoved the sheets of paper into my hands. They were Western Federation of Miners leaflets ridiculing the Industrial Workers of the World with insulting red caricatures that linked them to the Socialists, or Reds as some people called them. Someone had scrawled a message on the back of each sheet. I scanned them fearfully, eyes and lips parted in shock, quit breathing for an instant, and dizzied.

Leaning against the stone fireplace, I rasped, "When did you get these?"

"The first one came the day I sent the telegram."

"And you haven't paid them?" I said with a mix of disbelief and outrage. "They said they'd kill her."

"No, I haven't paid them!" The terrible wrath in Dan's voice made me jump. Before, he'd sounded near disintegration, fear trembling in his voice, now it was joined by an anger that shook him. "I haven't known what to do. The full quarter-of-a-million's in the safe, but Stapp says I shouldn't pay the bastards until he finds out where they're holding Cally." Dan dug his fingers into his scalp and scratched in a gesture of frustration and worry. "They called me this morning. The Burke operator handled the call. She said it came from the Short Stake Saloon in Bixbee. The sonofabitches gave me one more day to deliver the money—told me where to leave it. The sheriff's searching for them in Burke Canyon now."

For an excruciating moment utter consternation stopped the breath in my throat. Then I said with growing frustration, "One more day? This is our baby. You should be moving heaven and earth to—"

"You're a fine one to talk!" He grabbed my wrist. A hard, driving anger reddened his face. "You leave your children for days at a time. You don't deserve to be called a mother. If you'd been here watching after them properly instead of frittering around with your damned women friends this wouldn't have happened. You'd rather leave them with a nanny who's more interested in cozying up to her boyfriend than watching out for Cally."

"Boyfriend? Hester's too old to have a boyfriend."

"She was called out of town for a funeral. She sent a girl in her place."

"What about Anna?" I referred to our devoted housekeeper.

Dan averted his eyes, hesitated. "I'd already given her a couple of days off to visit her sister."

"And you didn't tell me!" I jerked my wrist free. "You're just as much at fault as I am. You blame me, yet you showed a complete lack of judgment."

"How was I to know what to do? Taking care of children is a woman's job. And you've just given up your right to that. I'll find someone who'll stay home and be a real mother to them." He spun, tore aside the green velvet curtains that had been drawn against the sun and stared outside in a black rage.

I felt stabbed through the heart. Dan had made some cutting remarks during our sixteen years of marriage, but nothing that sliced through our bonds like this. It was the truth of his words that struck the deepest. If I'd been at home, Cally might still be with us. I hated Dan for slapping me with the truth, hated him for his anger, hated myself. I stood a long while in silence, hearing the echo of his barb, imagining my poor, helpless baby with some vicious brute. My darling Cally. My sunshine. The child of my womb. And it was all my fault. The thought made breathing difficult, as if I was clawing my way out of a bottomless pit. My shoulders slumped, drained of some of their life.

"Do the police have any idea who . . ." My barely audible words trailed off.

Dan's grumbled reply was no louder. "Not yet. At least they're not saying, if they do."

"All we can do is wait?"

"Just wait."

A sense of hopelessness sucked at my insides and took the strength of my legs with it. My head sank to the mantle of the fireplace, the marble surface cold and forbidding. I felt disowned, everything around me hostile. Tears tried to well in my eyes, but the pain I felt was too great for weeping. I was miserable beyond anything I'd ever known.

My eardrums had begun to throb from the silence when I turned my head to watch Dan brood at the window. As much as I despised his treatment of me, I felt his sorrow. Cally meant more to him than anything else on earth. My throat ached with our common anguish as I crept up behind him and encircled his waist. That simple gesture of love, the gentle clasp of my hands that drew him close, seemed to do more to span the crevice between us than a thousand words of apology. He turned toward me, chin quivering, eyes watering, and took me into his arms, holding me as if his life depended on the love he found there. Together we wept, joining one another in that dark terror reserved for parents who fear for a child.

●●●

When I was able to control my tears, I looked for Todd, another casualty of the kidnapping. I found him sprawled on the bed in his second-story room, the aging spaniel curled at his side. He sat up and pushed his back against the mahogany headboard. His features were caught in that wavering period of adolescence when they were neither a child's nor a man's, neither Dan's nor mine. His eyebrows had always been heavy, especially where they met at the bridge of his nose, giving him an expression of perpetual worry. That had intensified since I'd seen him last. His hair, a light brown now, coarse and wavy like his father's, looked like it hadn't seen a comb for days.

The spaniel slid from the bed when he saw me. I scratched him between the ears while I asked Todd, "How are you son?"

"I didn't know you were back." His voice was as unsure of its timbre as his face was of its true mold. Neither held any welcome.

I said, "I've only been home a few minutes. I've been talking to Daddy. I wanted to see if you were all right." I watched his face and saw disquiet lurking in his deep blue eyes. "We have big trouble, don't we."

His fingers traced the figures of huntsmen and hounds on the counterpane while his jaw flexed in the same manner of displeasure I'd often seen in Dan. "I feel like I'm in jail. They won't let me leave the house."

"That won't last long." I tried for a positive tone, but had no faith in my reply. "Can I sit?" Todd made room for me and went back to his tracing. I covered his hand to still the motion. "Look at me son."

He looked up for a second and lowered his eyes. In that glance I saw an indictment almost as great as Dan's. Todd blamed me for being away when I was needed. He blamed me for the danger Cally was in. He blamed me for his upset and the restrictions placed on his life. My throat tightened. I wanted to speak but could only sit, holding his hand, heaping blame on myself.

Slowly, his hand relaxed and he leaned toward me, resting his head on my shoulder. I slipped my arm around his waist and kissed his forehead. "You mustn't fret, Todd. One thing about Daddy, he's never let anyone get the best of him. He'll get Cally back for us and straighten out our lives. Now that I'm home, I'll keep such a close watch over you, you'll wish you could make me disappear."

CHAPTER 43

As it had before during times of great fear or sorrow, it seemed inconsiderate, almost obscene to me that the sun should continue to shine and the flowers should go on blooming when my world was turned upside down, when getting through that night and the next day was all that mattered. But everything remained the same, except in the Rigby household.

The next twenty-four hours were a living hell—unquenchable fear, self-blame, compulsive pacing. I spent anxious hours at windows waiting for some sign of hope to poke its head from the dark shadows. Despite that moment of clinging together, Dan still viewed me with accusation, though his eyes had softened from a hate-filled red to a censuring ice-blue.

The second evening, Ed Stapp left the dinner table to answer an urgent rapping at the door. After a few minutes of hushed talk at the entry, he returned to the dining room with two sheriff's deputies and a man in plain clothes. Stapp introduced me to the men—Dan seemed to know them already—and returned to his chair at the oval table. The arrivals, after declining an invitation to share supper, pulled chairs from the table and sat with their hats perched on their knees.

"Is there any news?" Dan asked anxiously.

"Your daughter's being held in an old mine shack above Bixbee." Stapp speared a slice of ham and put it on his plate as if the news was of little consequence, but Dan's eyes widened with hope.

"Are you sure?" he asked, hope mixed with skepticism.

"A couple of kids were on the hill hunting squirrels and noticed footprints going up to the shack. They thought it suspicious because the shack hasn't been used for years. They knew we'd been asking about strangers and heard about a reward." The man speaking was Cantrell, in plain clothes, a stocky gray-haired man, with a head that sat like a block on his shoulders. "At any rate, they hid behind some brush and watched for signs of life. After a while, a man came out of the shack to cr—" He glanced at me and decided to change his choice of words. "He came out to . . . uhh . . . relieve himself. Two others came out later."

Too fearful to hope, I put in hurriedly, "Maybe the boys are making up the story to get the reward."

"We checked on that as soon as they told us." This from one of the deputies, a burly blond with a voice that sounded like it rose from a barrel. "We found things just like they said."

"Weren't you putting Cally in danger when you went up there?" Dan's tone was both sharp and ragged.

"Relax, Mr. Rigby," said Cantrell. "We weren't that close. But while we were there a man came out of the shack carrying a little girl."

"Was she alive?" Dan and I cried as one.

"No way to tell. But the other two men came after the first guy and shoved him back inside. My point is, it looks like there's trouble among the three. It could work to our advantage."

I thought his tone too matter-of-fact, too businesslike. Cally wasn't his child, but you'd think he'd show some sympathy, some concern. His job appeared to be nothing more than that—a job.

Dan pondered the news, scowling. "Is Cally worse off because of the trouble between the men?"

Cantrell stuck his tongue in a gap between his teeth and made a sucking sound as he met Stapp's gaze over Dan's shoulder. I read the exchange as a reluctance to tell the truth. "It's hard to say, Mr. Rigby. Men like that aren't predictable. If they're having a disagreement, it might help the little girl. On the other hand, it might not."

"Hell! We deserve better than that from you," Dan exploded. "Tell us what we can expect."

Cantrell looked at Stapp in question, received a nod, and went on, "Like I say, you never can tell. One of them is a hard case. We tried to finger him for putting a match to the Hercules Mill last summer . . . you remember . . . when there was some union doings in town?" Dan jerked a nod, impatient for Cantrell to continue. "I knew this guy when I lived up Shit Creek years ago," the agent explained. "Rotten to the core. A real loony. Now the IWW's hired him to do their dirty work. He's smart, though—using those Federation leaflets to write his ransom notes. He figured he'd throw us off his track and onto the trail of somebody in the miners' union."

"Do you think the IWW is back of this?"

"They could be. Your wife has gone after their hide a few times in her paper. But I think this guy knows we're on his trail for the arson thing and needs money to leave the country."

All the information led to one man. My heart thumped. My skin felt clammy. The question came as a hiss. "What's his name?"

"Tatro. Jim Tatro."

Cally with Jim Tatro! Jim Tatro the pervert, the maniac. For all I knew, a killer. Oh, Cally! I suspended my breathing while my mind flashed with all manner of sordid crimes being committed against my darling baby. Only dimly did I hear Dan swearing or the men making plans to rescue Cally without endangering her.

"If they call about the money, put them off until morning," Stapp was telling Dan. "We'll surround the shack tonight and rush it at daybreak."

"What about Cally? They might . . ."

"We have to take the chance. The way we see it she's in danger regardless of what we do. Likely even more if we wait until you give them the money."

"I don't know . . ."

"Look, Mr. Rigby, those men have no scruples. If you give them the money, who knows what'll happen? If they operate like most 'nappers, they'll send two men to pick up the money so they'll have a check on each other. The third will stay with the little girl. When the two get the money, they might leave the guy at the shack in the lurch."

"In that case would he kill her?"

"Likely he'd be too scared. He'd have to face murder charges alone. If the others go back to the shack they'll have a choice. They can leave the girl tied up and alive, or they can kill her. They may not want to take a chance that she could identify them. Or they might keep their part of the bargain and let you know where they're holding her. Whichever way you look at it, we're playing a game of poker with only one high card—that's the fact that we know where they are and they don't know that we know." Stapp's blue-gray eyes held the self-confident, arrogant expression of a professional who was very good at his job and knew it.

Dan pursed his lips as he considered the options, his expression grave, then leveled a warning stare at Stapp. "All right. But I sure as hell am going with you. If you do anything that gets Cally hurt, I'll take it out of your hide."

• • •

I didn't bother to go to bed. I knew I'd be up and down all night if I did. Instead, I spent most of the time huddled at the kitchen table with a cup of tea in hand, trying to prevent an avalanche of thoughts and emotions from burying me. I wished I could speak to Della or Nora, but Stapp had left orders with the deputy on guard that I wasn't to touch the phone—evidently, he was afraid prying ears on the party-line might gather information that would hurt his chances of catching the kidnappers. He'd even banned Lennie and Aaron from the house.

Utterly exhausted, I dozed off in the wee hours, my head resting on the table and didn't awaken until salmon-colored fingers streaked the eastern sky and illuminated the kitchen with an orange glow. Anna McCormick, the housekeeper, had come into the room in robe and slippers, her narrow fox-like face pinched from sleep. A long braid of graying blond hair flowed from beneath her nightcap and over a bony shoulder.

"Och, you look like a ragged marigold, Ma'am. It will do you no good to be up with the robins. Sitting bleary eyed, with your face afrown willnae make things happen sooner."

"I couldn't go to bed for worrying."

"Let me fix you some breakfast. Too much tea willnae set well with nothing in your stomach. Especially with your nerves all ajangle." She slipped a pinafore apron over her wrapper and took an iron skillet from a row of gleaming pots and pans that hung from hooks above the range.

"Don't fix a big breakfast," I said before she could put the skillet on the stove. "Maybe some toast. Then sit down and have a piece with me. I need to talk to someone." Then, after she'd joined me at the table, a pot of tea and a platefull of buttered toast between us, "Why is it that things a woman considers important turn out to be nothing but wisps of her imagining when compared with matters of life and death?"

"Ah well, 'tis the nature of us silly humans, ma'am. We need something to get us out o' bed each morning so we make up fairy tales to feel important. Not that what we do with our time on earth don't matter. The good book gives us plenty o' rules to follow to make our lives count for something. But this big old ball willnae stop spinning when we leave it."

"It's a frightening thought . . . death," I said to myself as much as to Anna. "I don't know which is worse, facing one's own death or the loss of a loved one. I've lost my father, a brother, a still-born child, and someone else I loved dearly. I was close to death myself during childbirth. But the thought of losing Cally . . ." I bit my lip to stifle tears. "I should have been here to prevent it."

"Don't go blaming yourself, ma'am. You couldnae have stopped it from happening any more than Mabel. Them heathens were real slick about it. Claimed the mister had hired them to clip the hedges. They snatched wee Cally from her swing before Mabel knew what was happening."

I frowned. "Why didn't she watch Cally when there were strange men around? I can't imagine it."

"'Tis true, she should have been more careful instead of treating her boyfriend to coffee and pie in the kitchen. But the poor lass hadn't hardly a minute to herself when I left to visit my sister. I think Mr. Rigby was wrong to send her packing. The gossips have been giving her the treatment over this thing."

I fiddled with my toast, thinking about that. Likely Anna was right, but it was difficult for me to forgive Mabel when I might lose my child because of her carelessness.

●●●

Minutes passed . . . a half hour . . . an hour . . . two hours. Anna had gone about her duties, and I sat in the parlor, keeping vigil at a window that looked out over the street. I'd closed my heavy eyelids for a few seconds, but snapped them open when I heard a car door slam. I saw Dan hurry up the walk to the house, Cally's limp figure draped across his arms. Stapp ran ahead, taking the porch steps two at a time.

I reached the entry just as Dan stepped inside, Stapp holding the door open. Cally looked like a dirty rag plucked from the garbage can, gray as death except for two spots burning on her cheeks. The sight of her lacerated my heart. "Is she . . ." I gasped the words.

"Alive, but real sick." Stapp's voice was as bland as his face.

I followed Dan up the stairs to the second floor, noting every aspect of my child's crumpled form. One concern routed all others. Had they touched my darling baby—molested her—contaminated her for life? I slipped my hand beneath a tangle of curls and felt her forehead. "She has a fever," I whispered hoarsely.

She roused at my touch and opened her eyelids a crack. "Mommy," she murmured, then coughed. A gray mucous appeared at the corner of her mouth, foul-smelling and tinged with blood.

"Oh Lord!" I turned to Anna who'd followed us up the stairs mumping Celtic oaths. "Phone Dr. Kendrick. Tell him Cally might have diphtheria."

Dan lowered Cally onto the flowered pink chintz of her child's bed and looked at her for a long second, as though he'd rather be on the brink of death himself than lose her. When I began to remove her filthy dress, he turned to leave, embarrassed at the prospect of seeing his daughter naked. I called him back and groped for words to ask the question that had been driving me wild. "Do you know if they . . . did they . . . did they touch her?"

He gave me a heart-rending look. "No. At least the bastard we caught at the shack says not. She got sick right away, and they were afraid they'd catch whatever she had. The other two made him take care of her."

"That was all that stopped them?" I exclaimed with outrage. "Beasts! I hope they hang."

"There's only one to hang," Dan said morosely. "A man was shot when he tried to escape and Jim Tatro got away."

"Oh God, no! He's still out there? What deviltry will he try next?"

"Hard to tell." Dan's expression darkened, the skin on his face tight from the anger within him. "I should have killed the sonofabitch long ago when I had the chance."

● ● ●

Before Dr. Kendrick arrived, I bathed Cally, inspecting her for signs of molestation as delicately as I could, and dressed her in a cotton nightgown. I'd isolated Todd in his room until a diagnosis was made. I felt sorry for him. He'd been kept in the house for days due to the kidnapping, now he was shunted aside as if no one cared. I vowed to make it up to him later.

At that time, Dr. Kendrick was about fifty years of age, thinner than in later years, a tall, rangy man with prominent cheekbones, craggy brows, and palms like small hams, but he tended Cally with a gentleness that belied his man-of-the-woods appearance. While he conducted his examination, I hovered near, watching Cally's eyes for signs of pain. Her small chest rose and fell in gurgling spasms as her cracked lips siphoned air.

The doctor gave her shoulder an affectionate squeeze, handed me several tongue depressors wrapped in a rag to burn, then beckoned me into the hall. Dan was there, wearing a path in the carpet. "I see no sign of her being molested," the doctor told us, "but she has diphtheria. She's pretty far along. The only chance she has is for me to give her some antitoxin through the veins."

Dan's eyes startled. "Is that necessary? I hear the antitoxin can be worse than the disease."

"It hasn't been perfected yet, if that's what you mean. There's a chance she can have serum shock—go into a coma—maybe end up with partial paralysis. But it's the only hope you have. You'll need to give it to the boy, too. Likely, he's been exposed."

What a choice! Death or paralysis. I gripped the doorframe to steady myself while I considered the alternatives. "Do you have the serum on hand, or must we wait?"

"There are several other cases of diphtheria in town. I sent to Spokane for enough serum to see me through. We'll need to put some tubes down the girl's throat. They might help her breathe. And you'd better get a nurse to help."

I pushed off from the door and squared my shoulders. "That won't be necessary. I've cared for lots of sick children in my time."

The doctor smiled knowingly. "No doubt you have, but you'll need help bringing the little girl through. She'll have to be watched night and day." He sighed and stared at the floor in thought, then looked up with a glimmer of an idea in his eyes. "Tell you what, I'll send Edith Huff over. She quit her job at the hospital to take care of her husband. Now that he's dead, there's nothing to tie her down. She's a good nurse and easy to have around. She'll know exactly what to do to keep the disease from spreading. In the meantime, you might as well take up the rug. You'll need to mop the floor and put the little girl's furniture out in the sun." That said, he picked up his satchel of instruments and medications and started downstairs. He'd gone but a few steps when he turned back and muttered across his shoulder. "I forgot to mention, you'll all have to be quarantined in the house for a couple of weeks. Maybe long—"

Dan broke in, roaring, "How can I carry on my business? In a few days I have to be in Spokane to testify in a suit."

"That'll have to wait. Consider yourself lucky. I've sent some cases to the pest house up Nine Mile Creek to control the disease. Several others are quarantined. Kids are moping because they missed the fireworks." Again, he turned to leave. "Let me know if Cally takes a turn for the worse. I'll be back later with the tubes for her throat."

CHAPTER 44

The next four weeks heaped misery without end. Afraid to leave Cally's bedside except when the chores demanded it, Nurse Huff and I hung on the child's every breath and moan and constantly checked a pulse that barely whispered of life. Todd's legs were temporarily paralyzed from the serum, which complicated the nursing and heightened the worry. Dan felt as if he was in prison and grew grumpier by the day.

Besides the perpetual cycle of mopping, scrubbing, and washing, Nurse Huff and I had to clear the tubes of mucous on the half-hour and give Cally a small piece of ice before reinserting the tubes. A solution of sulpho-carbolate of soda had to be given every hour, permanganate of potassium swabbed on the throat every three hours. And always, that loathsome odor permeated her room, despite a fan kept in operation to drive off the heat. I worked until I felt squeezed dry of energy. While I worked, I thought of Jim Tatro, hating him for what he'd done, wishing fervently he was dead, wishing I'd never moved to a place that spawned men like him.

The days were exceptionally hot and dry, the sun a huge leering disc that burned through an acrid blue haze. The newspapers reported that fires had sprung to life all over the Northwest and flames a hundred feet high had licked charred paths through the forests. Ash coated Wallace's streets, roofs, lawns, and sifted indoors to lay a film on furniture and floors.

The town suffered from conditions other than the effects of fire— soon after Cally's arrival home, Dr. Kendrick had placed the entire population under quarantine. Anticipating the quarantine, Aaron had chosen to move into the mine cabin with Lennie. Stapp had arranged to be confined to a hotel room to conclude his investigation, rather than in our home, for which I was glad. Of course Della and Nora weren't allowed to visit. I left the *Wallace Weekly* in Max's capable hands, though the quarantine limited distribution.

The epidemic lasted a month, leaving several deaths in its wake. But thank God, Cally lived. The doctor said that in time she'd be her adorable self and said that I should fumigate the house. Despite the smoke in the air, Dan carried Todd and Cally into the yard, then headed for the office to catch up on a month's work. Anna, Nurse Huff, and I hung books on the clotheslines to air and set other household items on the lawn. When we'd removed everything light enough to carry, we stuffed rags in the keyholes and around the windows, lit sulfur candles, and went into the yard to rest beneath the cedars.

Anna must have recognized the thin line I walked between usefulness and nervous collapse. When an agent came to town representing Pennsylvania Mining and Smelting, a company Dan hoped would process his ore, Anna suggested Dan entertain the guest at Della's Silver Spoon and take me with him so I'd have a change of scene.

"After all," she said, "wee Cally is much better. And Todd can thump about on his crutches. I'll have no trouble seeing to their needs."

Dan alerted Della and dressed for the evening, at least as much as he allowed himself—he'd always said that when a man worked his tail off all day, he shouldn't have to tear around and get into his dress-ups for the sake of company. That night was no different. He merely changed his shirt and tie and disappeared into the library to read the evening newspaper. I was still in the bedroom. I'd had to keep the doors and windows open to allow the sulfur smell to dissipate, and the faint perfume of roses and honeysuckle wafted through the French windows beneath the overlying smell of sulfur and forest fires.

I'd bathed, and sat at the dressing table wearing a blue silk kimono over a corset and chemise, the kimono thrown back from my shoulders because of the heat. I was running a brush through my hair, watching in the mirror as the orange waves crackled and stood on end in the dry air.I was forty-one, and it showed. Many years like this one and I'd turn into a granny. Wrinkles had already formed at my mouth and eyes, and a permanent worry frown creased my forehead. My skin was white as a ghost's and dry as parchment from lack of care.

I combed my hair over the frizzy rats that provided a foundation for my pompadour, pulled a few strands down over my forehead, then moistened a finger to test the temperature of a curling iron. Using the hot iron, I curled the strands I'd pulled over my forehead.

As I attacked the last stubborn wisp I caught the odor of tobacco and whiskey. Next instant, a man's form slipped up behind me and filled the mirror. The glass slanted in such a way I was unable to see his face, but I knew it wasn't Dan, and no other man who frequented our house would have invaded my privacy. My first terrified impulse was to scream, but I could will no sound from my throat.

A sweaty hand clamped over my mouth, and something metallic jabbed me in the back. A fierce voice said, "Don't move. Don't yell. Or I'll shoot."

The voice tore a path through my memory, causing my heart to pump terror, hate, and fury. I pulled the hand from my mouth long enough to yell, "How dare you come here, Jim Tatro! After what you've—"

Jim's hand stifled the rest. I heard him cock the gun at my back. "Shut up, or I'll shoot. Put your hands on the dresser." A moment passed before his hand relaxed and he said in a lewd way, "Didn't 'spect to find you half-dressed. A bit o' luck." He took his callused fingers from my mouth and ran them along my neck and shoulders. I flinched and started to squeal, but he dug his fingers into my shoulder. "I wouldn't do that if I was you. Just stay calm and I won't hurt you." Again he ran his fingers along my skin in a lustful way.

My nerves screamed at his touch. I tried to shove his hand away and failed.

"Don't like me messing with you, do you?" His voice was crooning, laced with mockery. He continued to run his rapacious fingers along my shoulder. "You didn't know I fancied you, did you?"

I shackled an inner violent tremble of anger and gave him a frigid answer. "You have a strange way of showing it. You've done nothing but bring misery into my life."

"Just getting even for the way you treated me at school. Always making me out to be the bad kid and praising the goody-goodies in the room. Your eyes sparked like fire when you scolded me. I like that in a woman. Makes my blood heat up. It made me want to take you into the woodshed and pull off your clothes." He gave a coarse laugh.

My sweaty palms trembled against the cherrywood as I said, "You filthy scum! I've been praying you'd had diphtheria and lay dead on some mountaintop with the buzzards picking at your bones." My voice sounded thick and each word came out separately with unrepressed rage.

Jim gave a sarcastic laugh. "That ain't a nice thing to say. I thought you was a lady. But I bet you'll like this." His fingers crawled down to my cleavage.

I started to turn, crying for Dan, but Jim grabbed the base of my neck, squelching the cry as it came from my throat.

"Shut up!" he said viciously. I heard him take a couple of breaths, and in the mirror, saw him turn slightly toward the door and turn back. "I got business to attend to. I come for my ransom money and you're gonna help me get it."

"There's no money here. Dan keeps it at the bank."

Jim clamped his hand on my shoulder. "Don't lie to me! I don't like being lied to. I know there's a safe in the library. I sneaked in the day we snatched the girl. It's behind a picture on the wall."

He was right. He'd planned thoroughly. As a bluff, I said, "It's where Dan keeps important papers." Not the complete truth.

"I told you not to lie. I'm betting he's got money there. And he'll hand it over if I put a gun to your head." I noted a change in Jim's voice from the aroused pervert to the tone of a psychopath. He was breathing heavily, the wheezing breath of a heavy smoker.He'd bent down far enough that I could see his cheese-skinned face. Abruptly, his yellow eyes focused on a picture of Jeff I kept on the dressing table. He took the picture and studied it, the mirror revealing his savage grin. "You cause me any trouble, and I'll kill you and Dan like I did this dumb brat."

"Kill—it *was* you! You despicable fiend." A black fury radiated outward from my stomach, turning sweat to steaming hot rivulets. "Why? Jeff never did you any harm."

The answer growled through thick lips. "To get even. I hated the stupid crip. Shot his ugly foot before I killed him." Jim tossed the picture onto the table and jabbed the gun into the back of my head. "We're wasting time. Get up."

My fingers itched to grab the revolver and use it on Jim. But he was careful, very careful. I scanned the dressing table for a weapon— anything that could do harm. The curling iron offered a possibility.

I said to get up!" Jim repeated furiously.

Pretending to do as he asked, I grabbed the curling iron and whirled, striking out with savage fury, letting the pent-up hatred of year's flow through the metal. The iron ripped across Jim's face—once, twice, three times—and down onto his gun hand. There was the smell of seared flesh.

Jim yawped in pain and dropped the revolver to the floor. I reached for it and closed my fingers around metal wet from his clammy hand.

Before I could aim the gun, Jim lunged, pushing me off balance. As I fell, the gun veered in his direction, and my fingers jerked the trigger. The recoil jarred my spine. The explosion deafened me momentarily. Acrid smoke bit into my nostrils.

Jim had lurched backward and was bent double, gripping his stomach and groaning. Through my partial deafness I heard Dan run down the hall, yelling, "What in the hell's going on?" Anna and nurse Huff's heels clicked on the stairway. Todd's crutches thumped on the landing.

I tried to get to my feet, but was tangled in my kimono. Jim straightened from his crouch and leaped. I had no time to aim, simply raised the revolver's muzzle toward the bloody mass that hurtled down upon me.

It took all of Dan's strength to drag Jim's dead weight from my chest. Took all of my strength to keep from fainting when I stood up, weaving. I was only slightly aware that Anna and the nurse had entered the room, shrieking, and that Todd was crying. A thousand eerie sensations took possession of my mind. I thought I was living a terrible dream.

Jim sprawled grotesquely on the floor, pools of blood flowing onto the carpet. His eyes stared hideously in my direction, and one hand stretched toward me, seeming to point a finger in accusation. A grievous doubt crawled from the tip of that finger. Was I wrong to have killed? Or would Dan and I lie dead if I hadn't?

In the blue severity of Dan's eyes, I saw bewilderment mixed with shock and grim approval. The silence that hung between us was so prolonged I wondered if he'd failed to comprehend my act of murder, had failed to comprehend that I, Maggie, who'd never killed a living thing in my life, who couldn't bear the squeal of a mouse in a trap, had killed a man.

At last he spoke, his voice carrying a vast numbness, but more kind than it had been in months. "I don't know how this happened, or much care, but you did the right thing. I'm proud of you." Murmuring that he loved me, he put his arms around me and pressed my head against his shoulder. I let the gun slip to the floor and crumpled into his embrace crying tears of hysterical release.

CHAPTER 45

D r. Kendrick kept me sedated for two days and allowed me to see no one but family. The sheriff said he understood and would question me about the shooting when convenient. He didn't intend to file charges. After all, I'd done him a favor by disposing of a public menace without his having to invest further time and effort.

The few times I woke, I was too dazed to tell reality from dreams, nor would I accept the bits of real life I perceived, merely lay in numb silence. While I lay, waiting for the heavy load of sleep to lift, the ghost of Jim Tatro would rise to haunt me, reminding me of a time when he ranged free, leaving death and destruction in his wake. The sight of Jim in death had scarred my memory with the permanence of a branding iron. I saw the hideous paths the curling iron had seared across his face, saw his corpse bleeding itself dry. The horror of that moment continued to shake my courage, but I felt no remorse. My resentment toward Jim had been gathering force with every instance of torment he'd brought into my life. Still, if it hadn't been for the kidnapping and the fact he'd killed Jeff I doubted I could have murdered. Those malicious acts had primed me for a deadly rage and had fired me like a match set to a charge of dynamite. The only regret I had was for Maude. She would grieve because of that indefinable bond that connected every mother with her offspring whether loved or not.

On the morning of the third day, I awoke with a renewed sense of time, self, and place, determined to do without the hated laudanum and its feeling of torpor, determined to escape the nightmares that led me along tortured pathways. When nurse Huff brought tea and toast to my bed and offered me the drug, I made an excuse to wait until I'd eaten, and when she'd left I poured the liquid down the toilet.

Toward the middle of the morning, I threw my legs over the side of the bed, slipped on a wrapper, and went to the window to see if the world had changed since Jim's horrible exit. A look outside assured me that Wallace was still Wallace, ash-ridden and hot, and that bees still plied the honeysuckle vines clinging to the shutters. I washed the sleep from my face, brushed two-days-worth of tangles from my hair, and went to check on Cally.

Wrapped in a white mother-hubbard, Mrs. Huff's broad-boned hips were bent over the child's bed as she smoothed the sheet. She straightened, her plain features registering surprise. "Why Mrs. Rigby. I'm glad to see you up." She whispered so as not to waken the sleeping child. "Are you feeling better?"

"A bit weak . . . fuzzy in the head." I sat in a rocker at bedside, the one I'd used to comfort the children when they were babies.

The nurse studied me in a professional way. "Laudanum tends to make one's head fuzzy. I'm surprised you're not dozing."

Pretending I hadn't heard, I bent over Cally and stroked the reddish-gold curls, affection flowing from the well in my heart. She moaned faintly with each breath she took. "How is she?"

"Still weak, but improving," the nurse said in a guarded, sympathetic tone. "She sleeps a lot . . . been sleeping for an hour now."

"I'd like to stay with her while you rest."

Mrs. Huff waved a hand reddened from too much immersion in carbolic solution. "I don't need to rest. The day's just getting started."

"Please, I'd like to be alone with her. I'm sure there's hot water for you to make a cup of tea."

"That does sound good, now you mention it." She took an empty water pitcher from the nightstand and started for the door. "I'll fill this before I come back up."

I went to the window and threw up the sash, letting warm, dry air burst into the room. If nature could sterilize linens hung out to dry, it should help an invalid as well. Today the sunshine was dim, the air filled with the smell of distant fires.

"Mommy." Cally had wakened and made a move to rise.

"Careful, Sweety. You mustn't try to get up." I returned to her bedside and took her cold hand. "I didn't mean to wake you."

"I've missed you, Mommy."

"I'm sorry. I-I've been sick."

Cally studied my face, her eyes full of questions. "Did you really kill a man?"

I stiffened. My smile dissolved. "Who told you that?"

"Todd did. Daddy told me *he* made the big bang when he was cleaning a gun . . . Todd said it was you." She paused to suck in breath, and went on to murmur, "He said you shot a man."

I shuddered. Oh, that Todd! He always liked to sensationalize. Knowing him, he'd have described all the gory details. He should have used better judgement, but good judgement didn't come easy to a fourteen-year-old. I'd give him a good scolding later, but first I must deal with the truth. If I was good at deception, I'd tell Cally I felt remorse, but she was too perceptive, she'd see the lie on my face.

I leaned forward and looked deep into her sky-blue eyes. "I had to do it, Sweety. The man was going to hurt me . . . maybe Daddy."

"Todd says it was the man that kidnapped me. I'm glad you killed him . . . he was mean." The little voice had begun to weaken and shake.

I stroked her head and said soothingly, "Don't let it worry you. It's all over now." I paused to consider my next words carefully, trying to strike the right balance between justification and morality. "It's not right to kill anyone, Cally," I said measuredly. "But sometimes . . . sometimes things happen so fast there's no other . . ." My voice choked.

"Don't be upset, Mommy. I don't blame you . . . I'm glad you . . ." Abruptly her expression changed into one of wide-eyed alarm. She put a hand on her chest. "Will you stay with me?"

I squeezed her hand and said, "Like I was glued to the spot." I wiped a sudden mist from the child's face with my handkerchief and kissed her cheek. "Mrs. Huff tells me you're doing much better." I said this to calm rather than to convince.

"I . . . I don't feel good right now. Please don't leave me."

"Of course not." I studied the wan face, especially the pleading eyes, and tears welled over my eyelids. I trembled inwardly. "Would you like me to read you a story?" The question was an attempt to distract both of us from our anxiety.

"Please. Mrs. Huff reads too fast . . . like she can hardly wait to finish."

"What would you like to hear?"

Cally shut her eyes and thought about that, then opened them and murmured, "The Shoemaker and the Elves."

I took a copy of *Grimm's Fairy Tales* from a shelf above the bed, thumbed through the worn pages until I found the story, and began, "There was once a shoemaker, who through no fault of his own . . ."

I'd read for about twenty minutes when I noticed Cally's eyes had closed. "Are you awake, Dear?"

A mumbled, "Sort of," a gurgle in the throat, then, "Mommy, I need a drink." The words were barely audible, spoken in fright.

I shot a worried glance at the door. "I'll tell Mrs. Huff to bring the pitcher."I called for water from the top of the stairs and hurried back to the sickroom. "Are you all right, Cally?"

No reply came from her cracked lips. I felt her cheeks and put my fingers on her pulse, noting the trickle of life was fading, fading. My own pulse raced beyond control.

Mrs. Huff's quick footsteps clacked on the stairs and across the soap-bleached floor of the bedroom. She poured a glass of water from the pitcher and handed me the glass.

"Here's your drink, Cally," I said softly.

No response.

"Cally?" Then to the nurse, "I guess she's gone back to sleep." I spoke out of hope rather than belief.

Peering anxiously over her spectacles, Mrs. Huff took Cally's wrist and searched for a pulse, set the tiny arm on the bedclothes, and put her ear on Cally's chest.

"Can you hear . . ." The rest faded into despair.

"I think she's . . ." The nurse shut Cally's eyelids. "She's gone."

I turned cold. My quaking became irrepressible. "How can that be?" I said from the hollow in my chest. "She's been getting better."

Mrs. Huff squeezed her lips tight, fighting tears that leaked down her cheeks, and gave her gray head a doleful shake. "Likely it was her heart," she said hoarsely. "Diphtheria can do terrible damage to the heart. The doctor's been worried about her pulse being so weak."

I felt nothing but disbelief—Cally was just sleeping, her pulse too faint to detect. Anxiously, I took her wrist, explored it for signs of life, and found none. *She was dead.* An uncontrollable anguish swept over me and contorted my face. Hot fingers of pain traveled along my spine, into my neck, and latched onto my skull with an intensity that made me want to cry out. I pressed the back of my head, willing the pain to stop. In some other world I heard Mrs. Huff offering solace and felt her fingers trying to soothe me.

Long moments passed before the pain subsided, before I could speak. Then the words rose from my aching throat in huge visceral sobs. "It's not so—I won't let it be so—call the doctor—I want him to see her." I waved a trembling hand toward the door. "And tell Anna—tell her to call Dan and have him come right away."

Not until Dr. Kendrick pulled a sheet over my tallow-skinned child did I accept the fact she was dead—accepted it rationally, not really, not emotionally, not in the depths of my being. Dan stood at my side, stony-faced, as if he hadn't heard the confirmation of death, his silence a deep, deep trench between us. Without so much as a word to those gathered at bedside, he left the room and locked himself in the library. Soon, from behind the closed door, came the sound of a man convulsing from sorrow.

In the midst of my own agony, I grieved for Dan. Cally had been as close to him as his own heartbeat, his love for her generated from some inner spark, not just from the fact she was of his blood and seed. I knew the feeling. Cally had filled my days with a special joy and had sewn a bed of affection deep in my heart. I'd thought of her young life as being a long bright pathway into the future. Now there was only a dark wilderness, a chopping end to all she could have been and done, an end to all the enchantment she'd scattered around her. I wished I had died instead, if only to escape the tear in my heart and the deep guilt that would haunt me the rest of my life.

"Oh, Cally . . ." I called hopelessly in body-shaking grief. "Cally . . . forgive me."

● ● ●

No forewarning, no preparation could have steeled me for Cally's death. I refused to allow her to be taken to the undertaker and asked that he come to the house to ready her for burial. Afterward, I brushed cornmeal through her hair and dressed her in her frilliest white dimity. First, I held the frock to my breast and breathed in the sprinkles of lavender, recalling the bright Easter day when she'd danced up and down the hall giggling, twirling the lacy ruffles in a blithe conspiracy with life. I had images of a sunny-faced toddler running to give her brother a hug—an image of a five-year-old with a gaping hole in her smile, carrying an armful of stray kittens into the house for adoption. Finally, an impression of the six-year-old, who'd shed tears when her Mommy left for Seattle. With the memory came the knife in the heart, the unrelenting flow of tears, the choking from bitterness and regret. If only I could have relived that last month. How different things would have been.

The heat forced me to release Cally to a padded coffin lined with silk and lace. All that night and the following morning I sat like a sentinel beside the casket, my vigil broken only by gusts of sorrow that shook my frame like a violent wind. I took little note of the hushed footsteps, of the whispered words of sympathy, or of the shadowy forms that prowled the hall.

Dan refused to unlock the door to the library until the afternoon we went to watch our beloved child lowered into her grave. As he stood beside me in mute sorrow, I heard the words, "Ashes to ashes and dust to dust." Then vaguely, and unwillingly, I tossed a handful of earth onto the coffin in a gesture of farewell.

Still in silence, Dan followed me to our bedroom that night after friends and neighbors had left the house. Dressed in black swathings and numb from grief and exhaustion, I thought I, too, had perished. I fumbled with the hooks and eyes at the back of my dress, while Dan stood looking out the window, a study in granite. Beyond him, the evening shadows laced black and thick. It seemed that a million miles separated us, miles of unspoken reproach.

"I'll never forgive you," he said at last. His words sounded as if they rose from a tomb, more bitter than the tears he could not shed. Certainly in spirit he shared Cally's grave.

I stopped my fumblings and stared at his unmoving silhouette. "How can you say that at a time like this? Don't you think I've been crucifying myself every minute of the day?"

"I didn't want there to be any question about how I feel."

"For God's sake, Dan. I know how you feel. I hurt terribly because of it. I feel like dying because of it."

"Then why don't you?" Each word fell with the weight of lead. Saying no more, he took a bathrobe and pajamas from a hook in the bathroom and vanished into the hush beyond the bedroom doorway.

I felt as if a lead weight had struck me, as if buzzards had clawed my insides. Dan had always lashed out when he was hurting. He'd done it again, pouring onto me all the festering anger he'd smothered that day in a civilized front. The hope that he still held a glimmer of love for me was left in ruins. The raw revenge in his voice had made a desert of our home. I was past blaming him. My own failures, stupidity, and ambition were the cause.

With a trembling hand, I lowered myself onto the bed, staring into a past moment I would have given the world to change. Slowly, the floodgates of all that misery opened and I wept with a fearful intensity of grief, self-doubt, and blame. *How could I ever heal the wounds?*

CHAPTER 46

I slept heavily in the night and when I awoke next morning I could hardly raise myself off the bed. I was aware of a strange numbness and of a tightness that circled my head like an iron band.

In the days that followed, I had lapses of memory that made me forget what I'd set out to do. I'd find myself in tears without knowing the cause. Sometimes I imagined that I floated outside myself, a stranger to my body. One moment it seemed centuries since Cally had died, and next moment it seemed she'd left my arms less than a minute before. Little by little came the tricks of the mind—the sound of Cally's laughter bubbling from her empty room, her footsteps skipping through the hall, her sunny face staring at me from a patch of wallpaper daisies. I made trips to her room to see if she needed care, only to find the room empty of life.

Visions of Jim Tatro leered at me from every nook and cranny, sparking conflicted feelings of rage and guilt. I imagined I heard his savage voice, imagined his scabby fingers on my bare skin, and I shrieked words of loathing at the walls. Next instant, I'd shrink at the thought that I'd caused his death. I found it hard to believe he no longer skulked through our lives like a predatory beast.

Reality seemed just as cruel. Dr. Kendrick said Todd's paralysis wouldn't last, but how could he know? Todd had been shoved aside in all the turmoil, but as I watched him hobble around with a glum face, the spaniel at his heels, I had little capacity to comfort him. My nature had stability of a willow in a windstorm. Only the vein of iron I'd inherited from my mother prevented total collapse.

Dan spent long hours at the mine, wrapping himself in projects rather than face his sorrow, remembering the pain the minute he paused to rest. When we were younger he'd helped me laugh at my worries and forget my sadness. Now in our mid-life, he'd cast me aside. He slept alone and ate his meals alone. He spoke to me only from necessity, and then with icicles in his voice, as if I was an unwelcome stranger. I wondered how two people who'd once loved with such warmth could skirt their relationship, as though to trespass was unthinkable.

At first, the tears were fairly easy to control, but the periods of grief lengthened until there came a day two weeks after the funeral when I wandered upstairs and down weeping constantly as I watched clouds of smoke billow beyond the steep ridges to the south. Poplars and cedars bowed before a gale force wind. Ash and cinders whirled crazily in the air. I'd read that fires in Idaho had joined into one huge holocaust and were gobbling everything in their path.

An hour earlier I'd called Dan at the mine to tell him what was happening. "It's just as bad here," he'd said. "The fire's jumped the ridge and burned part of the tramway. It's bearing down on the cabin at Level One. Lennie just came from Burke and says the fire is about to cross the creek. We'll have to stay in the mine or crawl down the creek on our bellies if we want to get out of here alive."

Dan had said to call Aaron and have him help me find a way to get Todd out of town, but when I phoned the office there was no answer. Dan and I had survived a kidnapping—a shooting—the death of a child. Now it seemed we were about to lose everything to fire.

Things beyond the window began to spin before my eyes—a horse-drawn wagon cutting a path through the ash, a dog yipping in the smoky yard across the street. I don't know how long I lay in a swoon. Long enough for Anna to find me and call the doctor. "Dr. Kendrick, you've got to come right away," I heard her say. "'Tis Mrs. Rigby. She's terribly ill." A pause while she listened, then, "Very well, I'll do my best."

When she returned to my side, she wore the face of calamity. "Are you feeling better, ma'am?" she asked worriedly. I nodded. "I tried to get the doctor to come, but he's at the hospital treating fire fighters who've gotten burned. He said I'll have to take you to the hospital, but it might be better to get you out of town before it's too late."

● ● ●

Like the rest of Wallace, Anna, Todd, and I spent the next few hours fearing death. Not that any of us had been taken by surprise. For weeks we'd been sweltering beneath a shroud of ash and smoke that smelled and tasted of incinerated trees. Newspapers had kept us posted on the course of fires in north-central Idaho and Western Montana that had blackened thousands upon thousands of acres of forest land. They'd killed eighty-five persons to date and sent ash flying as far east as the Great Lakes. Because of the smoke, ships up to five hundred miles at sea were unable to use their instruments to navigate. We'd read that fifteen thousand men were battling flames in the wilds and that President Taft had ordered troops into the area to help.

It wasn't lack of warning, but the rapidity with which the fire swept down from the ridges on that day of August 20th, 1910 that shook the town's faith in its survival. The wind had scythed in from the southwest that afternoon, gusting from forty to sixty miles an hour, and had whipped lurid smoke into towering thunderheads that obliterated the sun.

We'd been too beset with personal problems to bury family treasures in the garden as Anna had suggested, or to haul furniture into the street like our neighbors, hoping to commandeer wagons. Choking on the smoke, our eyes on the glow in the southwestern sky, we left the house carrying only three carpetbags filled with important papers, cash from the safe, a few family keepsakes, and a change of clothes. Anna helped Todd into the street on his stiff legs, Chippy the spaniel on a leash. Then she returned to slip a strong, ropy arm under my elbow. We feared we might have waited too long. The fire had just crested the ridge south of town and winds were blowing a wall of flames down the slopes toward the business district at the east end of town. Balls of fire, tossed from one treetop to another, broke into showers of sparks that spread the blaze to houses perched on the hillside. Some had already crackled into flame. Nora's was among them, and I wondered if she and her family had left in time. Nature played no favorites, treating the wealthy and the indigent alike.

We started down the walk, the evacuation bell ringing in our ears. A few homeowners were hosing down roofs, but most had given up on saving possessions. I gave Anna a twenty-dollar bill to bribe a burly teamster—one of several with wagons who were earning money by hauling goods to the railroad station. He stopped long enough to lift Todd and the wild-eyed spaniel onto boxes that crowded the seat and to help Anna and me climb atop a load of furniture. Then laying his whip across the steaming backs of his team, he barked them into a headlong rush toward the railroad station located across the river.

When we reached the Silver Spoon, an employee was loading a wagon with silverware. I told the driver to stop so I could inquire about Della and Hank and was told that Della had suffered a life-threatening asthma attack from breathing in smoke. Evidently Hank had taken her to Spokane on the first evacuation train. That unsettling fact gnawing through my other worries, I held tight to the precarious load of furniture while the wagon rattled into the east end of town. Fiery missiles crashed to right and left and a pandemonium of fright assaulted us on all sides. The flames had eaten their way the base of the slope and flapped wildly above a burning office building like sheets on a wind-stretched line. Heat blasted my cheeks as a blizzard of hot ash swirled around my face. The horses screamed and fought the reins.

Most of the town's male citizens had been ordered to stay in town to fight the fire, but at the railway station across the river, women and children were stampeding onto a passenger train that had postponed its departure to help in the emergency. They scrambled onto coaches, baggage cars, and a boxcar, shattering windows and doors in their concern for selves. A few disoriented souls wandered about in a daze, not knowing what to do.

The wagon driver helped us from the wagon just as the doors to the coaches and baggage cars slammed shut. The locomotive's bell clanged. "There's no room. Too many on board as it is," said a harried looking man in charge of the evacuation. He indicated the load of furniture. "There's no room for that, either. The boxcar's filled with townsfolk."

Thwarted on that score, the teamster accepted another twenty-dollar bill to take us to Providence Hospital located a short distance up the Coeur d'Alene River at the mouth of Canyon Creek. The miners' union had built the brick facility—a two story building with colonnades and mansard roof—but had turned it over to the Sisters of Charity to administer. When we arrived, miners who'd escaped the fires up Canyon Creek were hosing down shrubs and trees near the building. I asked them if they'd seen Dan, but none had, nor did they know if it was possible for him to make his way down-canyon. As it was, they'd had to crawl down the creek to keep from being burned alive.

Dr. Kendrick noted my state of nervous exhaustion and had the nuns who ran the hospital put me to bed in a room that smelled of carbolic acid and caustic soap and had them bring in chairs for Todd and Anna. Through the mush and roar in my head, I heard the doctor on the other side of a bamboo privacy screen answering Anna's string of frantic questions.

"There's some doubt that we can evacuate the patients by train," he said dismally. "The wind has driven all the smaller fires north of the

Salmon River into one big front. It's gaining speed so fast it could go on up into Canada. I heard a rumor that the railroad tracks west of here are already burned. I don't know if the train taking the women and children to Spokane will make it through or not."

"Horrid fires," Anna wailed. "What are we to do?"

"There's just one hope. I know the route east is open. I received some medical supplies this morning. We might be able to get you and the patients as far as Missoula, Montana. You can stay at the hospital there or in a private home. I understand the people of Missoula have opened their doors to refugees from the fires." There was a pause along with the sound of movement. "I'm going into town to see if I can help. If I don't make it back, the nuns have orders to evacuate you and Maggie along with the rest of the patients."

CHAPTER 47

I must have fallen asleep from exhaustion, because I awoke to a dark room, to the cloying stench of smoke, and to voices drifting in from the hallway. Part-dream, part-reality. I focused on the loud chatter that stirred me from my drowsy awakening and recognized a woman's tense, high-pitched voice as that of the stern-faced nun who'd helped me into bed.

"We can't just keep them here, Lou," she complained. "We'll be burned out."

"'Tain't nothing left in town but old ninety-seven and a caboose," a man answered in an ominous drawl. "We've used all the big engines, coaches, and freight cars to send the women and children to Spokane. We can't go west now, if we wanted. Fire's burned the tracks."

Another male voice boomed with no apparent thought paid to who might be listening. "We might not even have ninety-seven if the flames have crossed the river to the station." A pause, some mumbling, then, "How many patients did you say you have, Sister?"

"Twenty-five, plus five staff. And there's Mrs. Rigby, her housekeeper, and her crippled boy. Dr. Kendrick made me promise to send them out with the rest of the patients. It seems favoritism to me— the other women and children had to fend for themselves."

"Is Dr. Kendrick evacuating with you?" asked the booming voice.

"He's gone to town with medicine to treat burns."

"He's needed all right," said the man called Lou. "The men are having a time fighting the fire. They've dynamited the part of town that's burned to make a fire break."

The man with the booming voice returned to the previous concern. "You say there's around thirty-three who'll be leaving from here?"

"That's right," said the nun.

"Then we'll try to squeeze 'em into the caboose and hope ninety-seven don't break down before it gets to Missoula." There followed a scuffle of feet, then, "Get 'er ready, Lou. We'll leave in a half-hour."

For several minutes I lay stiff as a board, clutching a sheet while fear streamed through my mind on dark currents of thought. Amid a confusion of voices and movement, someone switched on a light, helped me from the bed, and rushed me into my clothes.

"Where are my son and housekeeper," I cried in a bewildered way. "I can't leave them behind."

"They're waiting out front, dear," said a soft-eyed nun. "Now come along. There's not much time." She spoke in such a condescending tone I felt like a child.

"Where are you taking me?" My voice quavered.

"Where the fire can't get to you."

In the hall—lit by electricity because of the pall of smoke—we joined an outgoing stream of patients, attendants, and Sisters carrying boxes of emergency supplies. Miners carried patients whose faces were like chalk from illness. At the front door, the nun turned my welfare over to a man who guided me down several flights of steps to the railroad tracks in front of the hospital. Lou had gone to Wallace and brought engine ninety-seven and the caboose onto the track. "None too soon," the miner said. "I heard Lou say there's a wall of fire across the canyon between the hospital and town. He got the engine out just in time."

On the hillside west of the hospital, trees crackled into flame and spat embers onto the hospital grounds. Locomotive, caboose, tracks, jumble of faces, everything in that fiery world reflected a red glow that waxed and waned with the dancing of the flames. Waves of heat struck my hands and face.

I turned to the man who held me and said wildly, "Where is my son? Please, will you help me find him."

"My orders are to get you onto the caboose. There's no time to look for anybody."

"But my husband's up at the mine! I'm worried about him, too. He'll worry about me."

Noting the disagreement, an over-wrought nun came up to me and took my arm. "Calm down," she said firmly. "Your son and housekeeper are already on the caboose. Now, come. We can't wait any longer."

The nun linked her arm in mine, and with the miner's help, hauled me onto a caboose crammed beyond capacity with patients sitting on benches in the kitchen area, on bunks in the sleeping area, others standing or sitting on the floor. I thought the nun might stay with me, but she left to quiet a delirious patient. The miner shunted me up a ladder into the crow's nest, where Todd, Anna, and a couple of nuns were seated. Before he left to do what he could to save the hospital, I thanked him and pleaded with him to tell Dan where I'd gone if they happened to cross paths.

I waved Anna aside when she offered her place on the bench and took a firm grip on a rail that circled the roof. Todd slipped one arm from the frightened, sooty spaniel he'd managed to keep in tow during our flight from town and accepted the hand I held out to comfort him. "Mom, I-I'm afraid," he stammered. A revealing confession from a boy trying to become a man. "Do you think we'll make it over the pass?"

"I don't know, Son." I forced a smile. "But at least we're together."

A different worry joined the multitude of anxieties reflected in his eyes. "I wish Dad was here. I'd feel safer. He'd . . ." Todd's chin trembled. Tears squirted from beneath his eyelids. "I'm afraid we'll never see him again."

I stroked his thatch of light-brown hair, taking full note of the panic in his face, wondering if I had the strength to care for him if worst came to worst. After all, he was almost as tall as his father and crippled to boot.

From the crow's nest, I could see into the locomotive, where a fireman was throwing coal into the firebox in a mimic of nature's blast furnace. Steam popped from the safety valve. From trackside came the loud voice I'd heard in the hall. "The road's all yours, Lou!" the man yelled above the hiss of steam. "I've posted men at the switches. Run the wheels off 'er. I'll—" The rest was drowned as the driving wheels took hold.

Soon number ninety-seven was belching up the steep grade to the pass that separated Idaho from Montana, threatening to split its seams when pushed to greater effort. Its oil lamp, a large box headlight at the front of the smokestack, reflected off the dense smoke like an enormous red eye. I looked down at the stunned souls in the main section of the caboose and saw the terrible fear in the eyes of some, saw the expressionless stare of the near-dead, and saw nuns telling their beads. Anna had latched her eyes shut in fervent prayer. From every corner of the caboose came the babble of fear and pain along with the smell of sickness and smoke.

Near the pass, the violent winds had changed direction and cleared away the thick haze. I was able to see the slopes to the southwest where nature was eating itself with greedy orange teeth. At the cleft in the canyon where Wallace should be, I glimpsed nothing but boiling, red-streaked smoke. Up Canyon Creek, flames were crawling down the ridge above Bixbee and Burke. The terror of the moment drove all thoughts of self, of grief, and guilt from my mind. Dan was out there facing nature's fury, and I was being taken farther from him every minute. That terrifying thought brought a reality that had eluded me for weeks. Nothing in the world—not sorrow, not remorse, not concern for my own well-being—were as important as seeing Dan alive and regaining his love. Nothing was as important as holding him in my arms once more.

After the eight-wheeler had mounted the pass, it meteored down the flaming eastern slope with the bridle off, clipping off mile after mile as it careened around curves, crossing smoldering bridges, racing by torches that once had been telegraph poles. In places, fire flowed like a river at track-side and heat-generated winds gusted with a roar that dimmed the noise of the churning wheels. I thought we'd suffocate from the smoke and from the intense heat that penetrated the windowpanes.

Choking on the ash, clutching the rail as if it was an extension of my arm, I struggled to stay on my feet as the caboose rocked from side to side. Tiring from the effort, I squeezed onto the bench beside Todd and Anna, one minute grabbing the edge to keep from sliding off, next minute bracing myself to keep from hitting the window pane.

The village of Taft was a bonfire. People were deserting in wagons, on horseback, and afoot. Some frantic souls had formed a human barricade across the tracks to stop the engine. I wondered how they could bear it when they climbed onto the roof of the caboose and onto the engine's cab—the metal was griddle-hot, and cinders hissed onto the roof.

Farther down the eastern slope we encountered refugees who'd straggled from mountain trails onto the safety of the railroad bed and onto stream-banks that wound beside the tracks. At Saltese, people fought to save homes and sawmills. I glimpsed women and children huddled in a river while deer, bear, elk, and a pair of timber wolves, streaked along the banks to keep ahead of the flames. One crippled elk, its coat aflame, its muzzle raised skyward in squeals of agony, fell to the ground in a writhing death before my horrified eyes.

The fire showed the innocents no mercy that night. Tongues of flame had eaten a path down the slope from the main front and licked at a clutter of animal pens and corrals belonging to a homestead at the base of a hill. Silhouetted against the flaming pens, a man and six children rushed about like tightly wound mechanical dolls slinging buckets and pans of water on pockets of flame while a woman worked a pump to fill containers. Two of the larger children held frantically to the halters of a pair of screaming, rearing horses. A sow had crossed the tracks with her litter and was headed for the river. Not as clever as the sow, three bleating sheep milled about on the tracks. The engineer had no time to stop the train. All he could do was to give a blast on the whistle.

I closed my eyes to the slaughter of the helpless beasts and covered my ears to the thud of bodies, to the cries of agony and death. My stomach churned. I thought I would retch.

Todd slipped his arm around my shoulder and said in a distressed voice, "Don't cry, Mom. It's going to be all right. I heard one of the nuns say we've come through the worst. We'll . . . ." He choked on the rest.

Sensing eyes upon me, I noted two patients were looking up at me, watching me cry, their jaundiced eyes without expression, without comprehension, with less awareness than a babe fresh from the womb. Realizing how close I'd come to their state of mind, I vowed that if I lived through the night, I'd not allow myself to become like them, separated from reality because of illness, dependent on others for care. I'd fight to control my shattered nerves, fight the tendency to cringe at real and imaginary dangers, the tendency to feel guilt and rage. I simply would not tolerate such weakness in myself. To do so would be to give up on life. That was unthinkable. I had a son and husband to care for.

Part IV

IT COMES AROUND
FULL-CIRCLE

CHAPTER 48

The next morning, the Missoulian newspaper reported: " . . . The train from Wallace reached Missoula at 8:30 P.M. after a run through fire and smoke. When the dusty, smoky, tired passengers filed from the caboose under the glare of electric lights on the bridge they were indeed a sorry-looking sight. Everywhere there has been fire . . . Eyes were red and weeping, hands were blistered, and clothing was burned full of holes by flying embers. Great, strong men wearied by a long night of continual mental and physical strain staggered in pitiful weakness. Women, on whom the terror of a fire-filled night rested heavily, fairly crept along the sidewalk, their haggard faces and sunken eyes telling better than their few incoherent words of their fearful experience."

●●●

All that had changed by the time Dan met us at the station two weeks later—the tracks of the northern route to Spokane around Lake Pond Oreille had been repaired and the Wallace railway station, because of its brick structure and location on the far side of the river, was intact. How we clung to each other. It was as though we were afraid to let go, afraid that fate would separate us again. Not until then did I learn of Dan's ordeal in his own words. Not all at once, he didn't want to speak of it, but slowly when things popped to mind, mainly when Todd prodded him with questions.

Evidently, Lennie had remained at the mine with some of the crew, but Dan was beside himself with worry about Todd and me and had headed down the burning canyon. As I pictured it, his escape was a trip through Hades. When he'd arrived in Bixbee, he'd found a firestorm sweeping the canyon, shattering boulders, exploding the resinous hearts from trees. It had already ravaged the town to a mere crash of flaming timbers and the Apex properties were afire.

Dan had always felt invincible. Even in the bleakest of times he'd kept his feet firm while his world crumbled around him. But at that fiery moment he'd had little confidence in his ability to survive. Forty-six years old, he was past his prime, no longer used to intense physical exertion, yet he'd tied a wet handkerchief over his nose and begun the long crawl down the creek-bed. As he told it, progress had been painfully slow. The steep banks had funneled the worst of the heat over his head, but at the same time they'd turned the waterway into a bake-oven that had seared his flesh, sucked the breath from his lungs, and burned his eyeballs. His clothes had steamed to the point of blistering his skin. His brains had felt like they were frying. When he could, he'd closed his eyes against the heat and felt his way along, but there were deep pools to skirt and slippery rocks that defied passage and scorched his hands. At the lower end of the firestorm, he'd staggered out of the creek into semi-darkness, feeling as if he'd been in a kiln, and, from what he could tell from his brick-red skin he looked it.

When he arrived at Providence Hospital he'd found fire raging on three sides. A little French novice, Sister Joseph Antioch, and three miners who'd refused to leave on engine ninety-seven had climbed from a balcony onto the building's mansard roof and were wetting it down with a hose attached to a water closet. Dan had joined them on the roof, and the miner who'd helped me onto the caboose had told him, "Your wife left on the train . . . maybe an hour ago."

Dan recalled that he'd stared up the canyon of the Coeur d'Alene, where the fire was making its reckless advance, and thought for certain I was dead. He'd never been so weary and void of hope.

The Reo had burned, and now that we were reunited, we had to walk through the incinerated east end of town to reach our home on the west side. All that remained standing in the business district were the corners of a few brick buildings, stark monuments to a type of construction intended to prevent damage by fire. Merchants were poking at the ruins of what had been saloons, stores, banks, and cafes, searching the remains with glazed eyes. Everyone looked bone-tired. Tired from fighting the fire and from lack of sleep. Tired at the thought of their loss and at the prospect of rebuilding.

Kicking at the ash, we spent several minutes staring with unbelieving eyes at the ragged shell of bricks that had been Dan's office, then at the charred home of the Wallace Weekly. It seemed as if my own vitals lay in the mix of cinders, mortar grit, and bits of molten glass. I had no desire to rebuild, but Dan had already made plans for his new office.

A change in the wind had spared the western third of town from fire, but houses lay beneath a heavy coating of ash and soot. Trees that once had cooled the walks with solid shade stood shriveled from the heat, but they'd fared better than the fir and pine on the hillsides. We were lucky. Our house had been spared all but the smother of ash and cinders, though the rose garden was dry as paper, and petunias had withered and blown away. Some families had returned to shells of houses. Those whose homes were among the one-hundred-fifty destroyed were staying at the hospital. The floating population driven from hotels and rooming houses had found shelter wherever they could.

Help came to Wallace from everywhere. Tents arrived from Fort Sherman and other points west. Clothes and bedding appeared out of nowhere. Food poured in by the boxcar-load. Thousands of dollars flowed in by wire, mail, and express. Insurance adjusters blew into town as if by magic and set up offices under canvas roofs. In no time, lumber arrived from the coast, and carpenters and brick masons were hired on the strength of their word alone. Above the underlying misery of those who'd lost homes and livelihood, the town soon hummed to the rhythm of hammer on nail, saw on board, and trowel on mortar. Even the Catholics and Protestants of Cedar and Bank Streets set aside their feuds to raise funds for civic buildings.

Lennie and Aaron stayed at our house until Lennie could build a new cabin at the mine and Aaron a new home in Wallace. Nora's husband decided to open a practice in Spokane and moved there. The Tuttles stayed there as well, since they'd remodeled a restaurant in that city. Everyone seemed bent on starting a new life.

I identified with the rebirth among the ruins, because I, too, needed to rise above the ashes. I'd entered my fifth decade filled with vitality and promise, warm of emotion, and tolerant of life's setbacks, but the summer's events had stripped me of those qualities.

Dr. Kendrick said, "You're doing well, Maggie. You survived. Go about your normal life."

I was too proud to tell him of my mental suffering, to tell him that grief for Cally and my growing remorse over the killing had caused a lack of direction and usefulness, like walking in a midnight fog, or trying to carry the perfume of roses in a pan. Bent on curing myself, I devised ways of clearing my mind and calming myself. But how difficult it was to cage the jungle of monkeys in my head without letting the most audacious escape. Each method worked well for a time, then lost its effect. For every two days of success, there followed a day of failure. There was no way I could make the journey to recovery in one leap. Getting through an hour or a day was all that mattered. A step at a time. But little by little I made progress. The monkeys became more docile, or disappeared into that misty world from which irrational thoughts and fears derive.

Noting my need for cheer, Anna tried to help. She'd say, "'Tis a beautiful day, ma'am. Makes one glad to be alive. You should be out and about."

So I dug in the garden preparing the flowerbeds for the winter and took long walks along the river where the cottonwoods hadn't burned. The trees appeared as an island of flame amid the blackened slopes and the faun and dusky green of brush growing along the river. Some tree branches, loathe to relinquish their hold on summer, waved flags of lime-green against the gaudy strip of orange.

"Move slowly, Maggie. Move slowly, in peace," I'd tell myself. "Look around. See what there is to see."

Bit by bit, I learned to escape my nagging thoughts and to focus on the intimate things of nature—on the sun playing its game of shine and shade through the cottonwoods, on the twitterings of pine siskins and other flitty birds, and on the papery tunes the wind played upon nature's witherings. And as fall came to an end, I listened to the soothing drip, drip, drip, of the leaves. Watching nature helped me realize that my concerns were but a straw on the winds of time. Yet in my wanderings, I found a reason to be.

●●●

At first, Dan had pampered me despite the many ugly things he'd said that summer, despite the many hateful looks that had passed between us. Those had been enough to break a marriage that had become a fulfillment of duty, not passion. But the fire had shocked us both into realizing we couldn't bear to lose each other, that there was hope for a future together. Then slowly, Dan slipped back into his preoccupation with the mine, and I noticed he was becoming as abrasive in his dealings with the competition as the men he'd criticized in the past.

Not that times weren't good for mining. They were. The demand for lead was up. Woodrow Wilson, the nation's incoming president had vowed to press for new banking laws that "must not permit the concentration anywhere in a few hands of the monetary resources of the country." The likes of Rockefeller, Guggenheim, and other pillars of the mining and smelting trusts began to squirm. Then in December of 1913, Wilson signed into law the Federal Reserve Act.

Dan, Aaron, and Lennie celebrated with several bottles of beer. "It's about time those bastards got kicked in the ass," Dan chortled.

Wilson had also vowed to press Congress for legislation that would legalize labor strikes and peaceful demonstrations and to press for a bi-partisan commission licensed to investigate anti-trust violations.

The men celebrated again, with Lennie saying, "Things are coming around. Things are finally coming around."

Fearing legislation would strip it of its holdings, Federal Mining and Smelting released some of its mining properties on Canyon Creek to Clyde Hanson. The Foxfire claim was adjacent to the Black Titan, and in no time Clyde's men were caught digging into a tunnel on Titan property. Dan filed suit.

Not long after that, a Spokane newspaper reported:

COEUR D'ALENE MINE OWNER
ARRESTED

Clyde Hanson, prominent miner owner and Spokane resident, was arrested yesterday evening. Details are lacking at this time, but Mr. Hanson's name has been linked to a gambling ring operating in Washington and adjacent states. The ring has been accused of fixing horse races . . .

Mr. Hanson has also been under considerable fire from the Guggenheim Trust. The Guggenheim's Federal Mining and Smelting has brought suit against Mr. Hanson, stating he withheld certain properties illegally in a recent trade of mine holdings with Apex Mining Company. This is in addition to a suit brought by Black Titan Mining Company for infringement on the Titan's property. . .

Clyde's excesses had finally caught up with him. What a waste. With his intellect and talent he could have made much more of his life.

I expected Dan to be pleased that the law had fingered Clyde, but he didn't like to talk about it. When he did, it was without compassion and with an expression of amusement and contempt. Behind the other emotions, I caught a hint of self-blame for Clyde's demise. I understood. Dan and Clyde had grown up together, had been steadfast friends until the stupid mining game had turned them into mongrels fighting over a bone.

Then one hot Sunday Clyde's lawyer showed up at the house and begged Dan to settle out of court—the deed to Clyde's apartment building in Spokane in exchange for dropping the suit. At first Dan rejected the compromise, but the more he thought about it the more it grew in appeal. In the end he accepted, and the current of circumstance steered us toward an uncharted course in our stream of life.

CHAPTER 49

Providence Hospital, 1916

I stood at the window of Dan's hospital room and looked across the canyon, noting remnants of the fire of 1910. Trees that remained standing were blackened spears, but a thick growth of brush greened the slopes, hiding young evergreens that had sprouted from seeds that needed fire to bloom into life. Like the saplings, my family had experienced a rebirth of its own. Acutely aware of our need for each other, we'd been determined to build upon that foundation. We'd succeeded until the cave-in sent Dan to the hospital several days ago. He no longer lay in a coma, but showed little response to people and events around him. His face of humor and dreams had dissolved into a bland, blue-eyed stare, without thought or interest.

Dr. Kendrick had advised me to care for Dan in our Spokane apartment, and I planned to take him there on the morrow. Thinking of the return to Spokane, I turned from the window to look fondly at Dan sitting motionless beside me in a wheelchair, his face bloodlessly white, and recalled how excited he'd been about the move to Spokane in 1914. The time was ripe for the move. Dan's enthusiasm for the mining game was at a low ebb, eroded by the continuous battle with the trusts and suits against other operators for fraudulent practices that cost him part of the market that was rightfully his. Beyond that, the realization had finally hit behind his vast brow that the Black Titan had made him one of the richest men in Idaho, a man who could afford to buy what he pleased. Craving diversion, he dumped part of Titan's problems into Aaron's lap and took on a new challenge.

"When I'm through with Clyde's apartment building it'll be three times the size it is now," he told Lennie one night at the house. "Aaron'll think I've gone loco. He doesn't invest in anything that isn't already making a profit."

"He's a cautious man. Nothing wrong with that," Lennie countered in his easy-going way. "Caution has its place, but what's the use of putting your money into something you can't build and make go yourself."

That in mind, Dan joined a long line of investors in the city of Spokane and businessmen fell all over themselves to help him spend his money. Located ninety miles west of Wallace, the city's spokes of trade radiated in all directions—to the silver mines in the Coeur d'Alenes, to the wheat farms of the Palouse, to the logging camps in the north and east, and to markets for its products all over the west. Its population of around seventy thousand conducted business in a downtown rebuilt after the fire of '89 with classic structures of brick and granite that shouldered six and seven stories high. Merchants, whose purses provided elegant offices in town, owned chalets and mansions in the south hills.

The rest of the city? Modest homes in the creeping suburbs, small homes on the pine-studded flat, a shanty town lying along the river front—the full range of society from the most wealthy philanthropists to beggars and whores, and on the weekends, miners, loggers, and farmhands ready to whoop-it-up in riverfront dives.

We marveled at the conveniences—streetcars, hacks, omnibuses, Gurney and hansom cabs, river water pumped through the veins of the city to home and office, and the most complete electrical system west of Denver. There were many automobiles, including Dan's new Cadillac, and several bridges on which we could whip over to docks on the opposite bank of the Spokane River and take a steamer cruise above the falls.

A steady flow of humanity swept along the sidewalks to shop in the stores, to attend the theater, symphony, opera, or less cultural events—such as The Ziegfeld follies, George White Scandals, Houdini, Al Jolson, Eddie Cantor, and Ed Wynne. Visiting troupes performed in The Auditorium Opera House. Except for San Francisco's opera house, the auditorium was the most complete house on the Pacific slope. There were twenty-one theaters for moving picture and variety shows. Barnstorming troupes put on acts wherever an audience collected. Bawdy shows frequented saloons and upstairs halls. The miners and loggers who visited the riverfront found unrestrained prostitution, fun, frolic, and fights.

To fill other needs, there were twenty churches, four parks, two hospitals, three colleges, a public library, theatrical societies, and halls that rang with voices and instruments raised in symphony and song. Besides the public schools, there was a Sister's school and two select schools.

We plunged into this whir of activity to make the investment of money and selves, removing a half-block of older buildings that had escaped the big fire of '89 to make room for an enlarged apartment complex. By September of 1914, a ten story, million dollar, steel-girded, fire-proof monolith with the largest terra-cotta cornice of any building in the West looked down on its lesser neighbors at the busiest intersection in town. The three-way intersection formed a vee, giving the building the appearance of a wedge, the tip of the wedge blunt enough to hold four swinging doors that opened into a large foyer. From the foyer, doors led into the offices of my recently established newspaper, *The New Century*. Other doors opened into the *Silver Strike,* a large, upper-class restaurant jointly owned by Dan and the Tuttles. The rear of the foyer held elevators and a broad staircase.

Boasting a barbecue pit, a stage for an orchestra, and room for dancing, the restaurant had lured chefs from San Francisco and Seattle who prepared food that pleased the male pallet. Dan and the Tuttles hoped this would attract the mining trade—capitalists, engineers, mine executives, machinery salesmen, and fortune hunters who buttonholed each other in the streets and hotel lobbies to learn of the latest strike or merger before they rushed to the local mining exchange.

As Della said, "We'll serve oysters ala Rockefeller and lamb chops wearing bright drawers. We'll spoil those bigwigs so they won't eat anyplace else."

For this same clientele, the Rigby Building offered spacious offices on the second and third floor. Dan's branch office was among them. The next six floors were devoted to apartments of varying size for permanent or part-time living. The tenth floor held a nine-room suite with a soft elegance, all the modern luxuries, and an unrestricted view of the bustling city and surrounding countryside. This was our private suite. Dan would spend as much time there as possible. When in Wallace overseeing work at the Titan, he'd stay at our house with Lennie and Aaron, who'd settled there with Anna as housekeeper. Todd had enrolled at Whitworth College and divided his time between the apartment and the fledgling campus.

Dan's excitement over the Rigby Building was no greater than mine was over my new publishing child, *The New Century*. The space set aside for the newspaper was more than I'd hoped for—separate offices for myself, for my editor, for the business manager and his staff, as well as a copy room for eight reporters. The composing room and print shop had large staffs. The Wood presses were three times the size of the press in Wallace, and their massive rollers and automatic feeds made a constant rumble and thwack.

Along with my other duties as publisher, I wrote a daily column that focused on important issues of the day. Usually, I left the newsgathering to the editor and his staff of reporters, but now and then an event came along that I preferred to cover myself. The arrival of Elizabeth Gurley Flynn, the cactus flower of female liberation, was such an occasion. Flynn's leadership role in the radical union, The Industrial Workers of the World, and her view on American society had inflamed the nation, and I simply had to see her for myself.

Driven by this curiosity, on a busy afternoon in November, I walked down the noisy aisle that separated the rows of reporters' desks and stopped at one littered with copy. I held a set of keys in front of a chubby-faced blond intent on his work, a young reporter who sometimes drove me around town to gather information for my column. "Would you get my car, Tom? It's parked at the side entrance. And bring your camera."

He looked up in question. "Where are we going this time?"

"To the tenements. The Wobblies are holding a meeting there."

Tom's mouth dropped open a bit. "Are you sure you want to go? There'll be a bunch of tramps. All sorts of rough characters."

I gave a little snort. "I've lived in mining towns. Couldn't be rougher than that. Besides, Elizabeth Gurley Flynn will be there."

"The Flynn! In Spokane again? Do you know what happened the last time she was here."

"I didn't live here then, but I heard she was arrested. Hopefully, this gathering will be more orderly. I'd like to see how she leads a horde of rowdy males unafraid."

I remembered reporting in the *Wallace Press* that Flynn, along with union leaders acquitted of involvement in the Steunenberg murder, had pulled the IWW from the protective folds of the Western Federation of Miners, calling it the "Federation of Fakers." They'd organized converts into rebel units and sped them by boxcar to places where they sensed unrest. Before long, the red card of Wobbly membership had become a necessary ticket for any hobo riding the rails. Most transients accepted their card with a shallow commitment, considering it a ticket to a free meal and a rollicking good time.

Spokane authorities had become notorious for their treatment of the IWW during Flynn's first visit to the city. Prisoners arrested during an outdoor meeting were packed into six by eight cells, given bread and water, sweated with a stoked furnace, then taken to unheated cells in an abandoned school building, this in the middle of winter with near zero readings. The result—three deaths. There were tales that the jailers had run a brothel in the women's section of the jail, acting as procurers or non-paying customers. Despite my feelings about the IWW, if the current street meeting produced similar results, I'd bring them to the attention of the public.

An informant had told me that Flynn had alerted IWW cardholders about today's meeting via an add in the union's newspaper, *The Industrial Worker*. The add said, "Quit your job. Come to Spokane. Fight for free speech alongside the lumberjacks, miners, and pickers. Are you game? Have you been robbed, skinned, grafted on? If so, then come to Spokane and defy the police, the courts, and people who live off the wages of prostitution."

They'd come. Hundreds of them, riding in boxcars, converging on Spokane from all directions like ants on the trail of sweets—the migratory worker, the foot-loose, and the malcontent—then given orders to foment brawls, riots, strikes, and revolution. The main purpose was to fight for the repeal of an ordinance against street meetings, one intended to purge the IWW from the area.

The rally was being held on a street lined with tenement houses scarred by rough use, their lower floors assigned to shabby saloons, small groceries, pool halls, and the like. Basement window wells reeked of urine and garbage, the unpaved street of horse manure the city crews hadn't bothered to collect.

The weather didn't invite an outdoor meeting. The dark cape of a cold front had settled over the land, and chimneys belched great puffs of smoke. I'd swathed myself in woolens and fur, but the cold hadn't deterred the Wobblies, who were there in droves, whisky and Coke bottles in hand. They ignored the sermons and music of a Salvation Army band, a ten-piece band that had the volume of twenty instruments. A few children watched in curiosity. Others played marbles or jumped rope with frayed cords that slapped the sidewalk with a rhythmic thwack, thwack.

Tom parked my blue Thomas flyer along the curb opposite a Chinese market with dried ducks hanging in the window. While he tried to get a close enough to the speakers to take photos, I stood on the fender, notepad in hand, bobbing my head this way and that to peer over the restless mob. There were bristle-faced transients, painted street ladies in gaudy ruffles and plumed hats, young hooligans with cigarettes dangling from their lips, several Chinese, as well as a couple of curious young men of obvious wealth holding bicycles with monstrous front wheels. Especially notable were gypsies in full skirts, fringed pants, and bangled headgear.

A young woman dressed in a man's great coat, slim black skirt, white shirt and red string tie had mounted a soapbox in front of the Chinese market. A broad sombrero covered her long reddish-brown curls. From pictures I'd seen, I knew it was the twenty-four-year-old Elizabeth Gurley Flynn.

Her zealous eyes flashing, Flynn quoted a phrase from Mirabeau, went on to paraphrase Byron, George Eliot, and Maxim Gorky, then addressed the reason for the meeting, petitioning for the right to hold open-air meetings. "This government is not a republic but a hateful oligarchy," she said dramatically. "Do you want the elite to tell you what to do and what not to do?"

"No! No!" The crowd yelled in answer.

"Do you want them to get rich on the backs of the working poor?"

A lusty roar from a crowd that was half-drunk.

"Do you want them to put us in chains when we cry out for justice?" Another roar from the crowd. "Then rise up, rise up against the robber barons. Rise up against . . ."

When Flynn had ended her speech, she held up a long sheet that flapped in a chill breeze. "Each of you take one of these petitions to circulate around town," she said. "We'll show the narrow-minded capitalists in power they can't crush the IWW with empty rulings. Go out and fight! We can't win the battle with lazy minds and feet."

The crowd hailed the challenge with a great waving of arms, shouting IWW slogans, and singing brazen IWW hymns.

Two other speakers followed Flynn, men with a heavy-bearded foreign appearance and accent. Then a vibrant woman, likely in her early thirties, approached the soapbox, her free-roving stride made possible by a mannish suit that had a skirt six inches off the ground. Now and then, the skirt gave a flip, revealing black lisle stockings above blunt-toed boots. A man's felt hat topped curly, fly-away black hair. Unlike Flynn, who was mildly weighted with child, this girl made a quick leap onto the soapbox, waited for order, then began to speak with clear, impassioned words.

The sound of her voice gave me a start. The ringing tone was familiar but unheard for years. The woman's hair curled with the same undisciplined locks I remembered. Her face was too thin, but the lilting voice that said, "Seize the wealth that is rightfully yours," must surely belong to Lucinda Hanson. But how could that be? Why would a child of wealth speak of the common ownership of property and social revolution? If it was Lucinda, where had she been all these years?

CHAPTER 50

I looked more carefully, thinking this woman couldn't possibly be the adult version of Lucinda Hanson. Or could she? The younger Lucinda had always championed the underdog. Why not now?

The woman's gaze roamed the upturned faces in the crowd and met mine with an expression of shock. Seconds passed before shock slipped into a smile that disappeared when the sound of hoofbeats and racing feet came from up the street. From the opposite direction, came the sputter and cough of automobiles and the clang of bells.

The police crashed in, bellowing orders and swinging billyclubs. They tore IWW placards from stubborn hands and stomped the slogans into the ground. The Wobblies sparred with fists, posters, and tongues as if they looked forward to a night in jail.

A second wave of police swooped down onto the crowd, some on handsome mounts, others riding in a horse-drawn patrol wagon and a White patrol car. Heads poked from tenement windows and shouted insults. Fists shook in defiance. Officers in black helmets and slickers pulled a firecart onto the scene and streamed water onto the scattering mob. The initial burst of spray drenched my skirts and spattered them with mud.

Tom ran to the front of my auto and cranked the engine. "Get in, Mrs. Rigby! We're leaving."

I waved a staying hand. "Not yet. But keep the engine running."

Soggy woolens clinging to my legs, I jostled my way through the fracas to where three policemen were herding the leaders of the demonstration into the rear of the horse-drawn wagon. One of the officers was a stocky redhead, the flesh around one eye bleeding. His fist was locked on Lucinda Hanson's shoulder.

"You can't arrest this woman," I said in protest. "She's done nothing wrong."

The redhead glared at me. "She broke the ordinance against street meetings."

I met his glare with one of my own. "That law should never have been put on the books." I put a firm hand on Lucinda's arm and said with more authority than I felt, "I'll take charge of this woman. Also, that one." I indicated Flynn, who was laughing at the police and carrying on a saucy banter. A shaft of light had sheared through the cloud layer striking the lamppost where she'd chained herself, the links accentuating the slight swelling of her abdomen.

The redhead shook his head furiously. "You can't have 'em. 'Specially that tart of a Flynn."

"Rubbish! Just because the politicians don't agree with the Wobblie's views? I disagree with some of their ideas, too, but they have a right to express themselves."

The officer raised his club in threat. "I'm getting tired o' you, lady. Maybe I should take you in for obstructing justice."

The steam of frustration rose beneath my blue cashmere dress and dampened my armpits. I felt like saying something vicious. Instead, I squared my shoulders and said defiantly. "You will not."

"Then let me be getting on with me job." He shoved Lucinda up the wagon steps. "C'mon, trash, you're holding things up. And as for you," he aimed his club at Flynn, "You'd better be putting a key to that lock or I'll saw you outa them chains."

I stepped between the officer and the back of the patrol wagon to prevent him from climbing inside. "If you don't let Miss Hanson go, I'll splash this police action all over the front page of my newspaper."

"Sure you will. Like I'm gonna sprout wings. I don't know who you are lady, but the good citizens of Spokane would be pleased to know the police are doing their job."

Lucinda poked her head from the wagon and said emphatically, "There's no sense getting involved, Maggie. It's not good for the reputation."

"Reputation be hanged!" I spread my arms and legs and dug in my heels to block the entrance to the wagon.

The officer's florid face turned a deeper red. He grabbed my elbow. "I've had it with your brass, lady. You're coming to jail."

An image popped to mind of me, Maggie Rigby, standing in a jail looking sheepishly through the bars at Dan. If I was put in jail, Dan would have to face the scandal. It would be bad enough if he could see me at that moment, soaking wet and badgering the law.

The officer was about to shove me into the wagon when a tall, sallow-skinned, gray-haired man dressed in a well-pressed police lieutenant's uniform stepped from a White patrol car and headed toward us with a purposeful stride. "What's the problem, Red?" he asked the first officer.

"This here lady's trying to keep me from taking in a couple o' these Wobblies. Don't know why in God's name she's siding with tripes like them."

Outrage boiled up in my chest. My jaw stiffened. "Lieutenant, I'm Maggie Rigby, publisher of *The New Century*. I demand you release these two women into my custody."

"Lady, I don't want your protection," Flynn shouted from the lamppost. "I can do more for the cause by going to jail. Besides," she winked at an officer standing beside her, "by the time this bloke gets me there I'll have him converted."

The refusal disarmed me. I could only gesture helplessly in Flynn's direction. "But . . . you're . . . you're . . ."

"Pregnant?" she said boldly. "It doesn't matter. I spend a lot of time in jail. Likely drop my little Red in one of them."

Blushing at her frank words, I said, "Then . . . at least Lucinda."

"Can you get along without me for a couple of days?" Lucinda called to Flynn from the wagon. "I haven't seen Maggie for years."

Flynn shrugged. "Go ahead. You'll have a chance to mix it up with the police before we're through with this town."

My eyes sought the officer in charge. "Lieutenant?"

The lieutenant studied me with an air of indecision and finally said on a burst of air, "All right, Mrs. Rigby. Just this once. But you'll have to pick the wench up at the station after she's booked."

I manufactured a grateful smile and thanked the Lieutenant, then said to Lucinda, "I'll have my reporter pick you up at the station after he's dropped me off at the apartment." I tugged at my wet skirts. "I need to change into something dry before I catch pneumonia. Do you have dry clothes somewhere?"

She pointed up the street. "Some flea-bitten hotel near here."

Tom will take you there. When you've changed he'll bring you to my apartment. You can stay with me." I took more careful note of the changes time had wrought in the girl's face—the cheeks sunken, a depth of experience behind the eyes, though they still held an impetuous glint. "I can't believe it's you," I said in parting. "I'd thought you were lost to us forever."

● ● ●

I'd left the design of the Spokane suite to the French *de'corateur* who'd planned the other apartments in the building. As a result, the suite lacked the homey feel of the house in Wallace, but the abundance of plush, brocade, and French damask wallpaper suited the wealthy mining clientele who visited. My study was the one room I'd decorated myself—a bright, airy room with florals and velvet, chintzes, cream paint, and wallpaper. I planned to receive Lucinda there.

The housekeeper had set a tea table near French doors that opened onto a balcony. On this November day, the storm front had moved to the east like a battalion of gray-sheeted ghosts and the slanted rays of the sun streamed through the panes of glass in the closed doors, making the florals in the carpet so lifelike I imagined I smelled their fragrance. I sat at a small madam's desk with paper and pencil, trying to concentrate on an editorial about the jailing of the Wobblies. But all I could think of was the startling fact that after all these years, Lucinda was coming to visit.

The housekeeper's husky voice came from the doorway. "Miss Hanson to see you, ma'am."

I went to meet Lucinda as she came through the door wearing her bold expression and a dry set of masculine clothes. She had a purse snugged under one arm while the other arm swung in a loose, confident way. A teenage boy followed at her side.

Without preamble, she put a hand on his shoulder and said, "Maggie, this is Scott, Jeff's son."

I stopped in my tracks, staring in disbelief. The boy was Jeff reincarnated, a ghost of the past haunting a new face. It seemed I was seeing a younger Jeff on that afternoon in Bixbee when Nelly first brought him to school—the same chestnut hair, the same wondering expression in the gray eyes. Though this boy, if he was truly Jeff's son, had to be fourteen-years-old. My gaze followed the line of the boy's brown corduroy trousers to the floor. The feet, normal. Thank God.

"I'm pleased to meet you, ma'am," I heard the boy say through my fluster. "Mom's told me a lot about you. She said you adopted my father when his mother ran off. That was good of you." Nothing shy about this boy, though his voice held a tone of respect.

"It-it was nothing," I said weakly. "I did it because he was a dear child." Still recovering from shock, I managed to take the boy's extended hand. "I'm-I'm so happy to meet you, Jeff—I mean, Scott. Forgive me. It's just that you look so much like your father." Unable to say more, I stood holding his hand, marveling at the resemblance between father and son, suffering the ache that always accompanied thoughts of Jeff. Not until the boy squirmed under my scrutiny did I release his hand. "I'm sorry, I didn't mean to stare. It-it's such a surprise. Please won't you sit down." Then, when they'd settled in comfortable overstuffed chairs, "I'm sorry Dan isn't here. He'd be so pleased to see you. But he's in Wallace. The financial panic is causing trouble for the mine."

"Your reporter told me The Titan has become one of the richest mines in the district," Lucinda said with interest. She waved her arm to embrace the room. "This is a far cry from Bixbee."

I combined a nod with a shake of the head. "It is in some ways. Not in others. Wealth doesn't solve all one's problems. In fact, it creates as many as it resolves. Sometimes I wish we were poor again and depended on each other for sustenance."

"There must be a happy medium," Lucinda said with a knowing smile. "I've come to know poverty more than I'd like."

She and I went on to exchange the pleasantries that follow a long separation. Then a few minutes later, with tea and shortbread served on the tea-table and the warmth of the sun making for relaxed conversation, we traded memories of the days on Canyon Creek, Scott asking questions now and then. I had many burning questions of my own to ask Lucinda, but not while Scott was present.

After I'd told of the growth of the mine and of my involvement in the newspaper business, Lucinda said in a matter-of-fact way, "Do you share your wealth with the poor sods in the street?" Her tone suggested she doubted it. I might have thought the question impertinent coming from someone else, but it seemed natural for Lucinda to ask.

She eyed me carefully for a reaction as I said, "Yes, we do. Dan has opened a soup kitchen on the riverfront and has built several tenement houses with flats that rent for a pittance. Just enough to pay for someone to manage the units and cover maintenance. Dan pays for major repairs out of his pocket. Besides that, we donate food and clothing to the needy. And I'm planning to open a children's home where orphans can lead normal lives. You know—separate cottages—a staff for each one so the cottage functions as a family with all the benefits and responsibilities."

"I'd like to work in a place like that."

"Your personality would suit the children. But I'm afraid it will take time." I shrugged and shook my head. "There's a lot of red tape involved, but my lawyer is looking into it."

Anxious for a private moment with Lucinda, and sensing Scott was bored with the conversation, I invited him into Todd's room and showed him a bookcase filled with adventure stories Todd had read when he was fourteen. Then I pointed to a table in a corner of the room. "If you're careful, you can look at Todd's miniature car collection. He took great pains making each piece. I think he'd like to design cars for one of the manufacturers someday. That is, if he isn't killed in the European War."

"Why do you worry about that? The United States isn't involved."

"No, but I fear it will be. Todd wants to quit school and help the French right now. Maybe as an ambulance driver. I don't know if he's motivated by compassion or a sense of adventure. Likely both."

Scott picked up the model of a Reo and fingered it. "I think it's brave of him. I wish I was old enough to do that."

"Let's hope the war is over before you're called. It's a shame that young men are killed before they have a chance to make something of themselves. Or are wounded so badly they can't." I paused thinking what a tragedy it would be for Scott to die as young as Jeff had, without reaching his potential, without enjoying the blessings of life, leaving his mother to grieve. "Promise me you won't give in to the lure of adventure," I said with feeling.

Scott seemed to think about that as he ran his fingers over the model car, then said slowly, "I don't know that I can promise that. A guy never knows what's going to happen, does he?" He held up the car. "But anybody who's clever enough to build these needs to stay alive."

I felt a surge of pride in Jeff's boy. So gentle of manner. Wise in a youthful way. So like Jeff, despite being raised among social rebels. His mother deserved much credit.

Back in my study, I turned a look of deep affection on Lucinda. "Scott's a lovely boy. But what a surprise. I-I just can't believe . . . that you and Jeff . . . that you . . ."

"Had sex?"

"I don't . . . like to put it that way."

"How else can you put it? Unless you believe in immaculate conception." There was a ghost of a cynical smile on her face, one tinged with heartache.

My cheeks warmed. "I apologize for being so inept. I'm too old-fashioned to speak of it comfortably." I paused, reaching for the question that kept returning to mind. "Do you have a husband?"

"I haven't found anyone I could love as much as I loved Jeff." Lucinda offered nothing more, but her eyes told of her longing. Evidently their love had been the kind that touched few lives, one of the heart and mind and soul, and for one fleeting instant of the body as well. As long as I lived I'd never forget the sight of Lucinda tearing down the mountainside, screaming when she'd learned that Jeff no longer lived.

She took a slender cheroot from her purse, lit the squared end with a match struck on the underside of the tea-table, and blew a ring of smoke with an air of release. The process told me more about her worldliness than anything else she could have done. How dramatic the change from bubbling innocent to sophisticated radical. I could tolerate the bold countenance and masculine garb. In fact, the black and white tailored look complemented her vibrance, ebony hair, and the twin circles of red that brightened her cheeks. But a cheroot!

Shoving that thought aside, I bent the subject at hand in a different direction. "What have you told Scott about his father?"

"Only that I grew up with Jeff, that we were high school sweethearts, and that he was killed in a mine accident. Not that he was lame. I'd rather all that stayed buried in the mountain."

I decided not to tell her about the Jim Tatro saga. Not yet. Maybe someday. I wasn't ready to relive that horror. Instead, I asked, "Do your parents know about Scott?"

"I've never written my family. I was too hurt at first, then too ashamed of running away."

I wondered if I should tell Lucinda that Jeff was her half-brother and decided the explanation should come from Clara or Harley. What did it matter now? What did it matter that Scott was born out of wedlock? "You had reason to feel hurt, but your parents thought they were doing the right thing when they prevented the marriage. They wanted the best of everything for you."

Lucinda stared out across the rooftops, her face reflecting a host of emotions. "It wasn't only Jeff's death that made me run, or the fact my parents kept us from marrying. I knew the prattle-tongued biddies in Bixbee would tear me apart if I stayed. And I was afraid Dad would make me give up the baby. So I ran as far and as fast as I could. The Atlantic Ocean finally stopped me—a little cold for swimming." She gave a brittle laugh and drew on the cheroot. I knew the reason for her nervous laughter. In a child, it would conceal feelings of insecurity. Lucinda was no child but she needed to feel accepted by those she'd deserted. She continued the tale through a string of smoke. "I thought about contacting my aunt in Philadelphia. She's a nice soul. But I couldn't face telling her about the baby and I was afraid she'd send me back to my parents."

"I haven't seen them in years," I said hesitantly, recalling the bitter exchange I'd had with Harley over Nelly's letter. "Did you know they'd moved to Portland?"

She didn't, so I explained about Harley's retirement and Clyde's ascension to the Apex throne, without saying anything about the cause. "Nora lives here in Spokane and she mentions her parents from time to time. Your mother is quite ill from lung disease, but your father is doing well. You should visit them. They'd be overjoyed. They'll not blame—"

"Oh yes, they will. Especially when they see Scott. I'm sure mother has consigned my soul to hell without that."

A shadow of remembrance crossed my mind. In it, I saw Clara standing in my parlor in Bixbee as clearly as the day it had happened. "May your precious Jeff rot in hell!" She screamed across the years. "If it weren't for him I'd still have my Lucinda." Clara had never blamed Lucinda, just Jeff. Always Jeff.

I reached across the table and took Lucinda's hand. It was chapped from hard work and from being out in the weather with the Wobblies. "Your mother was terribly upset when you left, but time and distance have a way of healing wounds of the heart. I'm sure she never held it against you. And . . ." I paused on the brink of revealing too much and rearranged my phrasing. "I'm sure she has things to tell you that will help you understand."

Lucinda shook her head. "I'm in no hurry to have her tap me with the finger of shame." She flicked an ash onto her saucer in a resentful way.I went to the bookshelf for an ashtray I kept on hand for Dan, a silver one etched with the picture of a deer. "How is Todd these days?" Lucinda asked as I set the tray on the table. Likely a way to change the subject. "I'll bet he's grown into a handsome young man."

"He looks a lot like Dan. He'll be coming home soon. He's attending college here in town."

"Do you have any other children?"

The question sat heavily on my chest for a long moment before I could answer. When I did, I merely said, "I had a little girl. She died from diphtheria."

Lucinda seemed to sense from my tone that I didn't want to speak of it, and we sat a while thinking our own thoughts, Lucinda looking around the room with mixed emotions behind her eyes. As I refilled our teacups she asked, "Do you ever see Clyde?"

"He owned a lovely estate in the hills south of town . . . got himself into a bit of trouble . . . gambling . . . and lost everything to creditors. Umm . . . he's not here anymore." I thought it best not to explain. "But Nora lives on the edge of town. She was distraught over what happened to you and Jeff. She still agonizes over it and wonders what became of you. I'll take you to see her."

The idea seemed to startle Lucinda at first, then she seemed pleased. "I'd like that. Nora wasn't just a sister. She was my friend and mentor."

"She'll be surprised to know you're with the Wobblies. I guess crusading is in your blood. She and I climbed onto the soapbox for the women's vote." I studied Lucinda for a moment, especially the unconventional clothes and the cheroot lying in the ashtray, sending up a spiral of smoke. "Tell me, how did you ever get involved with the Wobblies?"

Lucinda's smile suggested amusement. "Maggie, you're the first person to call us Wobblies without making it sound obscene. The Flynn would appreciate that. She's a great gal. I met her many years ago when I was doing finishing work in a Philadelphia garment factory. The IWW was campaigning for members among the workers. Lizbeth would catch us outside the factory and preach about Socialism—just a young girl, likely thirteen or fourteen at the time. Her father had been a Socialist for years, so it was natural that she learn about Marx and unionism at an early age. Her father disapproved of her friends and she soon left home. When she came to Philly I was in need of a friend, and she was bright and cheerful. She'd visit my flat of an evening, and after I'd put Scott to bed we'd play cards and talk Socialism." Lucinda's sapphire eyes had grown soft with nostalgia. She drew a long breath and went on, "Not long after that I left the garment district to work in the office of a children's home, and Lizbeth married, but we kept in touch."

"She's such a firebrand."

"She's also kind and loving. She's always traveling around crusading for better conditions for workers of all sorts. It was just a matter of time before she involved me in the socialist movement. She knew I missed the West, so she asked me to come with her on this campaign." Lucinda made a sound that mixed a snort with a laugh. "Riding side-door Pullman isn't the way I'd choose to travel."

"Do you really believe in Socialism?"

"I believe in the basic philosophy. I saw too much cruelty in the factory not to think change was necessary. The bastards who owned the factory built their wealth on the misery of us workers. Women sat at the treadles twelve and fourteen hours a day in rooms with no windows, no fresh air, poor light, hardly time to use the stinking pot." She made a sour face at the dismal memory. "But I'm not sure I agree with the IWW's tactics for correcting the problem. I guess I'm too much a product of frontier capitalism to give it up completely. And I'd like Scott to think in broader terms."

I bent my thoughts toward the boy in Todd's room. He seemed intelligent. Able to converse. Had the potential to make something of himself. "This tramping about with the Wobblies is hard on him isn't it? He's exposed to rough elements."

"This is the first time I've taken him with me. It's the first time I've traveled so far to campaign. I've never left him for more than a couple of nights." Seemingly preoccupied with the thought, she picked up the cheroot, sucked on it, and blew smoke. "I'm glad I came to Spokane. It's made me realize how much I've missed the West. I'm thinking of settling here. In fact, I visited the children's home yesterday morning. I've had five years experience at the one in Philly."

"Did they offer you a job?"

"Yes, but I don't know if I'll accept. The place reminds me of a jail. I'm not sure I could work there."

"I've seen the home. Deplorable. It makes me anxious to build a child-friendly home. Like I said you can have a job there when it's a reality. In the meantime, you could work for me at the newspaper. I have a secretary, but she's completely bogged down. She tells me I take on too many charities."

Lucinda raised an eyebrow in an expression of doubt. "Are you sure I'm qualified."

"Of course. You'd run errands, stuff envelopes, pass out literature, take messages, a thousand and one things. You can learn the newspaper business while you're at it. With your background and personality you'd make a good reporter. Unafraid. Open to the views of others." And, I thought to myself, I'd have you close and could see Scott often.

CHAPTER 51

L ucinda was fortunate to have left the Wobbly crusade. Not until March did Spokane release the prisoners taken in November. Tired of the socialist movement and its cost to the town in wealth and reputation, the city granted the IWW the right of assemblage, the right to print and sell its literature, and the right to rent quarters in town without harassment.

Lucinda and I bade farewell to Elizabeth Gurley Flynn, who returned to the East to bear her child. As for her pilgrims of labor, they'd made their point and were dreaming of a hobo's life in the open or of jobs in forest and field.

Rebel that she was, Lucinda's presence at *The New Century* brought new zest to my job, livened the atmosphere in the copy room, and made me face a shift in the sands of the Rigby fortune. Dan was in Wallace much of the time—not that I wasn't used to it—but something about his absence at this time disturbed me and I'd go to bed without him, drifting on the same ocean of care that was trying to drown him. And I had worries of my own. Todd had completed two years of college and was itching to take a break from his studies before he enrolled in an engineering school. He'd been hinting stronger then ever that he'd like to volunteer as an ambulance driver to help the French in their fight against the Germans. Of course I'd railed against it—Todd was my only child and I'd curl up and die if he was killed. But Nora's boy, Todd's college buddy, was egging him on, saying they could cross the *big pond* together. Nora and I held little hope that we could prevail against their lust for adventure. Dan simply said, "I've tried talking to Todd. God knows I don't want him in the middle of that slaughter. But he's a grown man and can't wait to get out into the world. When I was his age, I drove my mother wild because I was determined to do my own thing my own way, and to try everything. But that independence has helped me survive. Todd's attitude is his way of pulling free, of discovering what he thinks of himself and the world. He needs to stand without the crutches you're always handing him." Dan thought further and added, "Likely he'll change his mind before he actually signs on. Besides that, if the U.S. enters the war, he'll be drafted anyway."

Dan had too many problems to spend much time worrying about Todd. Part of his troubles were the litany of suits the Titan brought against its competitors. The passing of the Apex properties to Federal Mining and Smelting did nothing to ease that. Clyde had been a known enemy. The trust was elusive. A growing financial depression and the war in Europe added to the problems. The price of silver had plunged to forty-eight cents an ounce, lead to four cents a hundred pounds. All of Dan's holdings suffered, but the Black Titan most of all. He gave up operations in low-grade stopes and confined work to ground that would pay at the reduced prices. Mine and mill went to one shift per day. Feeling the pinch, he called for a meeting of the stockholders in his private dining room at the Silver Strike—a room with high, open-beamed ceilings, a barbecue pit, and brick walls splashed with accents of red, green, and gold. Of course I was there, the Tuttles, Aaron, and Lennie. Dan had chosen to limit the shareholders to the initial investors of time and money.

The evening of the meeting was stifling-hot, and Dan delayed the discussion of business until the waitress had cleared away the dishes from a trout dinner and nothing remained to feast on but the hash of aromas coming from the kitchen. Anxious to get to the point of the meeting, the rest of us let the light conversation trail off into silence and turned our eyes to the head of the table.

Dan squirmed in his captain's chair, seeming to feel the weight of our combined gaze. He slipped a finger beneath his tie to loosen it, and began hesitantly, "I . . . I've called you together to discuss the status of The Black Titan . . . and a possible sale of the company." He paused with an expression that said he'd expected an immediate objection to the idea of a sale or at least a show of surprise.

He received neither, just silence that made the humming of an overhead fan more noticeable. Lennie had removed his coat and hung it over the back of his chair, revealing the sweat-stained armpits of his shirt. He hunched over the starched tablecloth smashing breadcrumbs with his thumb. Hank and Aaron had removed their coats as well and tugged on their cigars. Della and I turned to one another and raised our eyebrows in response to Dan's statement, but said nothing. Inwardly, I felt surprise along with a relief I wouldn't express until I'd heard more. It was clear that none of us wanted to be the first to step into troubled waters.

Obviously affected by the silence, Dan went on woodenly, "You all know that the bottom has dropped out of the price of silver and lead. Maggie's heard me grouch about it enough, talking about how we've had to cut our operations in half." He shot me a dismal look, then turned to the others. "The smelting trust has cornered all the cheap Mexican lead and is hoarding it until prices go up."

"The revolution down there might save us," Aaron put in. "The Mexicans are thinking of cutting off exports."

"Won't the war in Europe increase the demand for lead?" Hank asked.

"It could," Aaron replied. "Especially if the U.S. becomes involved in the battle. But wartime is always a boom and bust proposition."

Dan shook his graying head. "Who wants to profit from other men's grief? Not me." He took a few seconds to pull off his tie. He was already coatless. "Even if there was a boom," he went on, "we couldn't meet the demand. We'd have to go to a shaft system."

"Wouldn't that be pretty expensive?" Della asked. "And even more dangerous for the miners?" Dan had discussed the possibility at past meetings of the shareholders and Della was aware of what was involved. Besides that, she'd boarded miners who'd worked in mines with shaft systems.

"It'd cost an arm and a leg, but we haven't room for more surface entries. We'd have to use the fourth level as an entry to the shaft. About a half a mile in, we'd hollow out chambers for hoists and other shaft equipment. Like you say, it'd be an expensive proposition. Especially now, with the price for material and equipment on the rise."

Dan paused while a dumpy brunette in crisp blue uniform filled his cup with coffee and made the rounds of the table, offering coffee and tea. "Another point on the negative side," he added after she'd left the room. "The Titan's been doing a hell-of-a-lot more than our competitors to stop silt from plugging the streams. We've built two dams and hauled out tailings for landfill. Now the city council in Wallace wants more money to cover flood damage. Doesn't seem fair we have to cough up more money when the other operators have been sitting on their duffs doing next to nothing."

There were mutters of agreement around the table and a couple of side-exchanges that deepened Aaron's scowl. "There's that income tax bill to think of. We'll each have to shell out to the government. First the tax on corporations, now the individual. Doesn't pay to be in business anymore."

Dan filled his chest with air and let it string out on a new thought. "There's a positive note. We've just signed a compact with Montana Power. They'll deliver a lot cheaper than Washington. We'll have to put in our own lines from the Montana border, but the cost'll be shared with other companies involved. Aaron can give you the figures on that if you want."

Della made a sound that was half-grunt, half-snort and flicked a hand. "Figures don't mean a thing to me. I just want a general idea of what's going on."

Dan spent several seconds stroking a mustache he'd been nurturing for several weeks, making eye contact with each of us, as if assessing our frame of mind. When he spoke next it was in a labored way, seeming to drag each word from a grudging glue. "I guess that brings me to the point of the meeting. Federal has made some attractive offers. I think they're looking to the possibility of a wartime demand. You all know I'd rather take salts than sell to Federal, but I thought you had a right to state an opinion." A long pause, a painful expression. "How many of you would consider selling?"

The question produced a silence that was more unsettling than words. Hank and Aaron's cigars belched great clouds of acrid smoke. Lennie hung his head, studying the tablecloth. Della played with her thumbs in thought. I watched everyone, trying to imagine what they were thinking, knowing the decision was a struggle for them as well as for Dan. As for myself, though I'd wanted to sell for years, I felt utter sympathy for Dan's feelings along with a sense of disbelief that he was truly willing to sell if the others wanted it. It wasn't easy for him to discuss the sale of his life's work, the child he'd nurtured from infancy to adulthood.

Hank broke the silence by saying around his cigar, "How much are they offering?"

"Fourteen million," Dan said without enthusiasm.

Della grinned. "That's better'n a kick in the rear."

"It's not a bad deal for them, either." Aaron said with an animation that was rare for him. "Last year the six of us drew three million in dividends."

Hank stirred ash in a tray with the tip of his cigar, as if the process helped him to collect his thoughts, then said slowly, "To be perfectly honest, Della's wanted . . . that is, we've wanted permission to sell our shares. You know the trouble she has with asthma. It gets worse each year. Her doctor says she has to move to a warmer climate. We're thinking of Arizona."

Della had mentioned the possibility to me, and it came as no surprise. But I'd hoped it wouldn't happen. Her face had lost its florid appearance and the skin drooped like soft dough. Whereas her dresses used to fit like a well-stuffed gunnysack, now they hung in loose folds on her large-boned frame. The move would be best for her, but I'd miss her terribly. I expressed the feeling by squeezing her hand in a show of affection. "What will I do without you?"

She gave a little snort. "You won't have me putting crazy ideas in your head."

Dan pursed his lips and studied Hank with questioning eyes. "Do you need to sell in order to make the move?"

"Not really. As you know, the restaurant's done well, and we've built our dividends from the mine into quite a savings account. But I'd like to do some investing in Arizona. They say the towns are busting out like mushrooms after a rain."

"Then you definitely want to sell?"

"Umm . . . yes. I'd say definitely, yes."

Dan took a moment to think about that, tapping the table with a fingernail, his eyes cast downward. Finally, he filled his lungs and shot Aaron a wary look. "What about you, Aaron?"

"I'm almost fifty-four. Getting tired."

Dan groaned under his breath and turned to Lennie. "What about you, Superintendent?"

"Oh . . . I'm getting tired, too. I'd like to cut loose and blow my fortune on a few years of fun. But if you decide not to sell, I'll go along with that and stay on as super."

Dan turned a pleading look on me. "What about you, Maggie?"

I felt the force of five pairs of eyes upon me, as if my answer not only determined the fate of the mine but that of each person seated tensely at the table. And it did. A battle raged within me between Dan's wish to keep the mine and my desire to be rid of the troubles it bred. But Dan had supported me when I chose to publish the newspaper. The least I could do was to stand by him now. "I'll go along with you," I said half-heartedly. "Whatever you decide."

Dan let a long moment pass, his brow oozing perspiration, his face reflecting the tug-of-war going on between his conscience and his devotion to the mine,. "I know it's selfish of me," he said at last. "But I have a few years left. I can't see spending them without the mine. Besides, I'll be damned if I'll sell to the trust. I'd rather risk a loss." He glanced at the Tuttles. "I know it's important for you to leave. If you want to sell, I'll buy your shares."

Aaron brought up a cynical laugh. "Does that go for me too?"

"I can't afford it. And you'd better head for the tall timber if I catch you selling your shares to Federal. If I buy Hank's and Della's shares, then they no longer have a vote. So it looks like a tie vote—Aaron and Lennie for the sale, Maggie and I against—in which case the final decision rests with me."

"You sure know how to fence a man in," Aaron thundered. He spent a few seconds obviously fuming inside, then muttered, "All right, I'll give it two more years. Then I'm out."

CHAPTER 52

After the meeting with the stockholders in June, Dan spoke to me often about his long climb out of the stopes to success as mine operator. He'd hated the days when he'd worked in the smell, the damp, and the dark of the Apex stopes and felt sorry for miners who'd never rise from the muck to own a mine of their own. He spoke with a mix of pride and wonder at changes that had come about since he'd swung a hammer with the ring of steel in his ears. Now miners wore hats with lights in them, used a buzzy to drill their holes, and fired shots with an electric blaster. Soon the Black Titan would have an electric hoist that could lift fifteen tons from three thousand feet and run a cage with the use of electric bells.

It was the hoist that plunged Dan into a world as dark as the mine. I was at my publisher's desk when Lennie called on the phone. "Dan was inspecting the room they're digging for the new compressor when a seam ripped open and buried him and two of the men."

"Buried !" I cried. "Can you get them out?"

"We reached them in a few minutes. Wasn't soon enough for one of the men," Lennie said dismally. "He fell on top of Dan and cushioned him from the rock. That man's dead. The other guy's hurt bad, but is alive."

"What about Dan?" My voice cracked from anxiety.

"His head's got a big gash in it. Likely hit it on a chunk of rock when he fell. He's still unconscious. His nose was buried in the other guy's stomach. Must've come close to smothering."

I felt as if was sinking into quicksand. I thought I'd faint. Like other disasters that had haunted my life, this one had hit without warning. A blow to the head. No air. I'd seen such cases in Williamsboro. The men's minds had been affected and they'd lived like vegetables.

●●●

Memories had a habit of meandering their way into the present. The days I'd spent at Dan's bedside at the hospital in Wallace had offered such a journey, beginning with my girlhood in Williamsboro and ending with the move to Spokane and the mine accident that had altered the streambed of our lives. Now it was September 1916.

I'd hoped that the return to our apartment in Spokane might spark Dan's memory, but he showed as much interest in his surroundings as a cadaver dug from its grave. He'd grown thin and his face had lost its lines of character. The flame had left his eyes and they stared absently, their expression shallow as clay marbles. His mouth drooped on one side, and he didn't speak, though at times he made a continuous babble of unintelligible sounds. Once in a while he reacted to noise, but most of the time he gave no indication he heard.

Adding to his helplessness, his right arm was paralyzed and he couldn't be coaxed to use his left hand to feed himself. He controlled his bodily functions and used the toilet if helped there, but walked only when forced to it. Often he'd lie on his bed in a cataleptic state until helped into his wheelchair. He seemed a stranger within a familiar framework of bones and flesh. My spirit sagged with his. How difficult it was to accept Dan in this condition. How difficult to resign myself to the fact that he'd turned into one of my house plants. Except that my flowers rewarded me with beauty and fragrance. Dan gave back nothing.

At first I refused to hire a nurse and cared for Dan with the help of Mary, the housekeeper. Todd had helped for a while, but had left with his friend Kyle to visit the seashore before leaving for the battlefields of France. So I was left to receive the many inquiries about Dan's health and held the phone at my ear for long periods of time or sat at my desk answering letters. For the time being I'd turned the responsibility of the newspaper over to Howard, the managing editor, an intelligent bachelor with years of experience and no obligations except duty to the paper. Now and then he called me for advice.

Lucinda worked part time as my secretary's helper, but often was called upon to write reports on civic affairs. Most days, she'd come to the flat to keep me abreast of happenings ten floors below at the *New Century,* her humor bringing a breath of fresh air and sunlight to the apartment. Sometimes Scott would come with her, giving me that special lift of spirit that happens when youth walks in the door.

That was the case one late afternoon in fall. September had drifted into the past as well as half of October. I'd pulled Dan's wheelchair near the French doors in my library, and I sat in a flowered over-stuffed where I could look down onto the park across the way, its maples shimmering in hues of red and copper. I'd been reading the newspaper to Dan, a daily read-aloud, though I doubted he understood—perhaps he couldn't even hear my voice. He stared straight ahead, his eyes fixed on some bright object or on nothing at all. Still I read, hoping some word or phrase might spark a memory. I wasn't sure how I'd know if it did. I simply watched his every twitch from the corner of my eye and every intake of air for a sign that his mind stirred. Before the accident, he and I knew each other's thoughts so well we had little to say. Now I longed for just one word.

Mary usually announced callers, but Lucinda's visits had become so regular she just knocked and walked into wherever I might be. This time, the knock on the library door was followed by Lucinda saying, "Ma'am, would you be interested in buying the latest encyclopedia? Fifty volumes of copious knowledge."

I turned in my chair with a smile for Lucinda's jest. She never failed to delight me. So fresh, unguarded, confident. She hardly looked to be in her mid-thirties. Scott had come with her, now a good-looking young man of sixteen. "You're getting to be a handsome devil," I said to him with a teasing smile. "How do you keep the girls away?"

He blushed and scuffed the toe of his shoe on the carpet. "I'm too busy for girls." There was truth in that. After classes at the high school, he worked as evening copy boy at the newspaper.

"He won't admit it, but he's become a heck-of-a reporter," Lucinda said with a grin of pride. "Sometimes he tags along when I snoop around town for news. He writes flashier copy than I do." She winked at Scott and added, "Just don't tell Howard that he's taken over my byline."

Scott's blush deepened. "I'm not really that good. Mom just thinks I am. You know how mothers are."

I laughed in an agreeable way, pleased to see that Scott had the same self-effacing manner as his father.

Apparently both visitors had just come from the newspaper office, as neither wore jackets. Lucinda settled in a well-cushioned emerald-green armchair near me and suggested Scott go to the kitchen and rustle up some tea. When he'd left the room, her gaze settled on Dan. "No change?" I shook my head. Her appraising eyes left Dan and fixed on me. "I don't like what I see in your face, Maggie. Defeat, resignation."

"Am I supposed to show joy at what's become of Dan?" I said with mild affront.

Lucinda's eyes flashed. She leaned forward in her chair. "No, I wouldn't expect that of you. But neither do I expect you to curl up your toes and die. Why won't you hire a nurse? I think for some sick reason you feel responsible for Dan's condition. You've turned yourself into a nursemaid for a cabbage that doesn't even know you care."

"Shhh! He'll hear."

"What if he does? Face it. Dan knows nothing. He breathes, his heart beats, his body takes care of its waste. Beyond that, nothing. Why make yourself a slave to that kind of maudlin—"

"He needs me!" I got to my feet and paced back and forth over the floral carpet, twisting my handkerchief as if to wring out support for my argument. "Dan needs someone who cares enough to watch for signs of progress."

Lucinda raised her hands in disagreement. "Any nurse worth her salt can do that."

Pleasure at seeing Lucinda had suddenly turned to dismay. It stung my eyes, stiffened my chin, and pulsed in my neck. I stopped pacing and faced her squarely. "What are you trying to do to me, Luci? What is it you're trying to tell me?"

"I'm telling you not to give up on life." Lucinda left her chair and put a hand on my shoulder. "Don't dig a grave for yourself here," she said more gently. "Come back to the newspaper. Let your mind focus on the outside world. I don't want you to turn into a slug like Dan."

"You know I wouldn't let that happen. The newspaper is always on my mind . . . more or less. But I'm not ready to return. I've saddled myself with such guilt over the years for stealing time from my family I don't know if I could live with more."

Lucinda sighed, took a cigarette from her skirt pocket, found a match on the mantle, and lit the cigarette. "Don't stay away too long," she said after she'd blown smoke. "I'm thinking of myself, too, you know. I need you down there to keep me from going off half-cocked, from sticking my foot in my mouth all the time. I need a nurturing boss with a firm hand and a willingness to forgive."

I lowered myself onto the overstuffed and studied Lucinda with a dawn of understanding. "Is Howard losing tolerance for your point of view?"

Lucinda gave a "huh" of a laugh and said, "You see through me every time." She drew on the cigarette and went on, exhaling smoke, "Howard's raked me over the coals more than once lately. I think he's over the hump as an editor. What we need around the office is a modern thinker like you."

"Don't exaggerate, Luci. At forty-seven it's not easy for me to keep up with the trends."

"At least you understand the human cause. Howard is still back in the dark ages with his chauvinism and his feudal view of society. He's an arrogant prude. Maggie, you've got to go to bat for me. I have as much right as the stupid men on the staff to cover important news."

I thought about that as I brushed a wisp of hair from before my eyes, the rust color reflecting bits of silver in the glow of the chandelier. "I think you've inflated the problem. Howard has his opinions about how things should be done, but he's always been willing to listen to my point of view. Sometimes it takes a firm hand to keep a newspaper headed in the right direction. I admire his courage, his intelligence, his passion for justice, his ability to face almost any kind of truth, and the fact he is never a hypocrite." I paused, decided I'd said enough. "I'll have a talk with him."

Lucinda dropped onto the arm of my chair and took my hand. "What we need is for *you* to be down there watching over things. You have a right to a life of your own. A right to use your mind and talents. You can either stay here and turn into a blithering idiot, or do something worth your time and be glad of it."

●●●

That was a few days ago. Since then I'd begun to take Lucinda's plea seriously. She was right. I should make a fresh start and order my life to suit my needs as well as Dan's. Along that line, I'd redecorate the apartment to my liking. The ornate, executive look had to go. The mahogany, Orientals, and gold wallpaper had been appropriate for gatherings of the mining rich, but I wanted a light, colorful atmosphere. Perhaps light oak or maple, pastels, and light velvets rather than heavy brocades. As I stood in the formal dining room, considering the possibilities, the phone jarred me from my thoughts.

It was Aaron, calling from the Black Titan. He spent no time on pleasantries, simply jumped right into the subject. "Is Todd back from his trip?"

Aaron rarely showed any interest in Todd. Why now? "Yes, he's back," I answered warily. "But he's at the barbershop. Do you want him to call you?"

"That won't be necessary. I just wanted to know if he was in town."
Aaron sounded tense. "I want you and Todd to come to the office at the
mine tomorrow morning."

"Why? Is there trouble?"

"The strikes are keeping me hog-tied, but I'm not calling about that.
I need your signatures on some papers. I've sold the company."

For a moment I could say nothing, simply tried digest the news,
then I exploded with, "You what!"

"I sold the company. Give you the details tomorrow. Be here at
eleven."

CHAPTER 53

T hat evening I was in the drawing room playing music for Dan—
I'd found that when I played music a dreaminess filled his eyes,
and I often played the selections he'd enjoyed before his accident. I
placed a hard rubber disc on the gramophone, rotated the diaphragm,
lowered the needle onto the disc, and soon the strains of Debussy's
Claire de Lune wavered from the machine's large horn.

The descriptive phrases followed me as I walked into the hallway,
where Todd stood before a mirror, slicking his wavy light-brown hair
to each side of a middle part. Brushed with Pomade, the hair seemed
quite dark, but a light over the mirror brought out reddish glints. He
was dressed for the evening in a dusky gray suit and bow tie. A bowler
and fashionable cane lay on a stool nearby. Dan had always been casual
about his appearance, but Todd preferred a look of cool, deliberate
fastidiousness.

I watched him unobserved, his tongue curled over his teeth in
concentration. He was twenty, taller than Dan, his face cast in the same
mold, but softer and without the sunny glow Dan's had when he was
young. Todd's nose flared more at the tip, and his blue eyes had a
darkness about them, as though his mind was full of solemn thoughts.
He couldn't bear to see his father in such a helpless state and had
become irritable and withdrawn since the cave-in. The flame of
communication had never burned brightly between the two of them.
Dan had been so busy before his accident, it seemed that Todd had
looked for something that wasn't there and had given up on it. Now
there was no hope at all. I'd expected him to want his privacy and to
start breaking the filial bonds, but it seemed the accident had sucked
him into a world of his own too soon.

Events abroad hadn't helped. The war had begun officially in 1914
when Germany and Austria-Hungary declared war on France, Britain,
and Russia. Later, Bulgaria and Turkey joined the German alliance,
which came to be known as the Central Powers. President Wilson had
issued declarations of neutrality and had offered to mediate, but the
warring nations would have none of it. By the summer of 1915 the
British navy had stifled nearly all U.S. trade with the Central Powers

and with the neutral states of Europe. To retaliate, German submarines had destroyed ships within the war zone around the British Isles and had sunk the British passenger liner Lusitania with one- hundred-twenty-eight Americans aboard.

With the open seas inviting disaster and German U-53 submarines crowding America's coastline, most Americans had no patience for neutrality. What had begun as a simple matter of choosing sides in the war games had turned into unabashed hatred. People started using terms such as "Huns" and "Bohunks" when referring to members of the Central Powers. Despite a strong compassion for his fellow man—perhaps because of it—Todd had yielded to the same hatred. I couldn't tell if he feared the United States would become involved and he'd have to pick up a rifle to kill the enemy, or if he looked forward to it. I dreaded the day he might have to take up arms.

Now, as I looked at my son, it seemed the shell that had been the boy had cracked and I glimpsed the man inside. "Are you going out with Kyle?" I asked. Since the move to Spokane, Todd and Nora's son, Kyle, had become constant companions, Kyle spending as much time at the apartment as Todd did at Nora's lovely home. Likely they were meeting again.

Todd mumbled a reply I couldn't translate. No further comment, no sound except the whine of the gramophone and the clang of a trolley in the street ten stories below. "Please get home at a decent hour. You always wake your father."

Todd glanced at me with impatience. "What difference does it make. He sleeps most of the day anyway."

"When your father wakes, I have to get out of bed and care for him. Then I can't get back to sleep." I fought a hopeless battle to restrain my tongue and said with a general spleen toward life, "Don't forget we're going to Wallace tomorrow. Aaron said to be there by eleven."

Todd blew disgust. "No, Mother, I haven't forgotten. But I'm not looking forward to a meeting that'll end up in a big argument."

●●●

Early the next morning, Todd and I took the elevator down to the garage in the Rigby Building and rolled out the Pierce-Arrow touring car Dan had bought before the cave-in. Todd made a quick exit from the city, wheeling the auto in and out of traffic, and sped onto the open sagebrush flats to the east. He flew over the road at an alarming thirty-five miles per hour, swallowing the miles in huge gulps, and shattering the nerves of every team of horses we met. Beyond the flats, he tackled the contortions of the road that skirted the north shore of Lake Coeur d'Alene, forcing the Firestone tires to bite into the gravel road.

I panicked the first few miles, but as I gained confidence in Todd's ability to handle the curves, my nervous fuming drained to mild anxiety. Aware of his detached mood, I made few demands on his attention and allowed my thoughts to drift along with scenery that framed the placid lake, its waters reflecting white clouds that strung across the sky like maidens' hair. Clumps of late-blooming purple asters, goldeneye, and crimson currants brightened hillsides that had experienced a rebirth of second-growth trees and brush since the terrible fire of 1910, but cinders from recent lightning strikes blackened patches of bare earth.

On up the road, I glimpsed the abandoned millpond where Dan and I had picnicked with Clyde and Nora my first September in the Coeur d'Alenes. The pond was larger now, its dam built high with tailings to prevent silt from seeping downstream onto farms along the flat. Ice fringed the pond's sluggish green waters this day, and only one young angler fished from the banks. I had trouble remembering what it had been like to be so young, so full of the dreams and emotions of youth, thinking that love was wonderful and life was forever. The mental images were there, but the sensations and emotions were obscure.

"Would you believe that twenty-seven years ago your father brought me boating on this pond. In a way it seems like yesterday. In other ways nothing but a hazy dream I have trouble recalling."

Todd managed a dutiful smile. "Let's see, you would have been twenty. It's hard to imagine either you or Dad that young."

I laughed. "Is it because of how I look, or how I act?"

A tease came to Todd's eyes. "Both." The tease slid into a speculative look. "I'll bet you were a real looker then."

"What do you mean, *then?*" Light laughter. "You know, it's funny how life works. The older we get the more we become like one parent or the other in looks and actions. I look more like my father than my mother. I can even feel Patrick's audacity racing through my veins at times. But before I can do anything rash my mother's prudence rises up and puts a stop to it."

"I hope I'm never exactly like you or Dad."

"Why do you say that?"

"Umm . . . I want just the best qualities of each of you."

I smiled to myself. At least Todd had the sense to take his foot out of his mouth without leaving the shoe.

On up the canyon of the Coeur d'Alene River, the intervening years had wrought startling changes. New towns had sprung up along the river while old ones had grown as large as they dared in the narrow confines of the canyon. Mine portals gaped from the hillsides, one after the other, mile after mile. The floor of the canyon carried a maze of railroad tracks—main lines, spur lines, ore runs. Because of strikes, huge mills were belching half the usual amount of indigestible gray puffs into the air, some of them none at all.

Wallace looked more down than up. Miners leaving the troubled district waited at the Prussian-domed railway station, suitcases and other belongings at their feet. Others slumped against the brick walls or loafed in the shade of the porch waiting for nothing in particular. The gasoline station where Todd stopped for fuel and to have the windshield washed looked starved for business. The district's perennial labor problems made the pyramid of glittering ore samples at the intersection of Bank and Sixth Streets seem inappropriate.

I checked the watch that hung on the lapel of my coat. "We have time to stop at the house," I said to Todd. "I'd like to freshen up and visit with Anna."

We drove by the rebuilt newspaper building, now a shoe-repair shop, drove a few blocks farther west and stopped in front of the house. The curtains of the three-story Queen Anne were drawn, the lawn a yellow-green from autumn frosts, the trees turning into skeletons, the brittle flowerbeds in need of grooming for the winter. The sight of the bleak house and of the gardens I'd once tended with loving care prompted a shower of memories that constricted my heart. A sunny-faced toddler danced into my mind's eyes, giggled and twirled, then dissolved into a ghastly gray death. A husband drained of the juice of ambition crumpled at the child's feet in a half-death of his own. The wide-toothed smile of Teddy Roosevelt sitting at my table dissolved into the leering, cheese-rind face of Jim Tatro. Then the hostile feel of gunmetal—a body sprawled on the floor, the clawed fingers groping, groping, groping.

Unable to stem the torrent from the past, I said hurriedly to Todd, "I-I've changed my mind. I don't think I can bear to go inside."

"I don't much want to go in either."

Relieved by that decision, we left town and started up the narrow mouth of Burke Canyon. Only eight miles to the mine office. Soon I'd have to endure the meeting with Aaron and Lennie.

I studied my son and saw that his face was still clouded and surly. "Why do we have to go to the mine?" he complained. "Wouldn't it have been more convenient to meet in Wallace?"

"Aaron implied that the strikes are tying him to the mining property." I paused, thinking of Dan and the argument that lay ahead. "Your father had hoped you'd take over the mine one day."

Todd showed his agitation by pressing on the throttle. "I'm not Dad. I've never liked mining. I want a career of my own."

Stubborn little jay. He might not share his father's interests, but he'd inherited his stubbornness and drive. I had to admit I'd done everything in my power to keep him from going into mining. "I know how you feel. I've often wondered if *we* possessed the mine or if *it* possessed us. I've also wondered what right we had to take mineral that should belong to everyone for eternity. Sometimes I think I have rock dust in my soul. Nonetheless, your father worked hard for his dream. It will break his heart if we sign papers that turn it over to the trust he despises."

Todd spun his head around. "Break his heart! How can it do that. He has no heart to break. No feelings. He's nothing but a lump of clay."

"A lump of clay?" The question was the gentlest and saddest of reproaches. "That's cruel of you. He does have a heart. My heart throbs for his. If you sell, his heart will break because of the tear in mine."

Todd seemed to ponder this, his dark brows knit into a frown. "You make me feel like the lowest kind of turd. Maybe I deserve it. But you're not thinking of what's best for me. I'm going to need the money to go to engineering school after the war."

"I can pay for that."

"I want to make it on my own just like Dad."

My heart gave an erratic flutter. It seemed that any conflict brought on a similar reaction these days. And this was the conflict I hated most—between mother and son. I'd denied the possibility Todd might want to sell. Now reality shook me by the shoulders.

For a while I sat in unhappy silence, my damp eyes stinging from suppressed emotion while the hillsides swam by. "You're right," I said at last. "I'm sorry I sounded so dogmatic. I want what's best for you."

Todd slowed the throttle and stared murky-eyed at some thought, while the Pierce Arrow rumbled through Gem, past hillsides that had echoed the yammering of a hundred rifles many years ago. Union pickets were marching in front of the various mining properties as they had so often in the past. They were no longer members of the Western Federation of Miners but of the Miners and Smelters Union and the Industrial Workers of the World. No matter, the purpose was the same—a demand for better conditions and wages. I recalled the day I'd arrived in Bixbee riding an ore car and had met Dan after his encounter with Rafe Tatro over union affairs. I remembered the hopelessness on Dan's face when he'd told me he was leaving for Canada. And I felt the grip of his hand on my shoulder during the union troubles that had brought Jim Tatro to the canyon and caused Jeff's death. "You can't run away from life," Dan had said. Here, again, rather than submit to a longing for escape, I must stand my ground.

Children played in the yard at the Bixbee School. It was larger now, with a fresh coat of paint. Little remained of the first tiny shack Dan and I had called home, mainly the slate foundation and a few weathered strips of clapboard. The boarding house that had rung with Della's laughter had been enlarged into a saloon and hotel. How I missed Della's brash, light-hearted conversation.

At the lower end of Burke, a line of women had plumped themselves in the road to keep strike-breakers from entering the mines. From their loud banter, I could tell that most of them were southerners. In my day, I'd have heard the inflection of the Irish and Swedes.

A blond woman with the build of an ox demanded to know who we were and where we were going. When we told her, she made an awkward bow accompanied by a sweep of her arm. "Well now, we wouldn't want to keep your majesties from going about your business," she said in a sarcastic southern drawl. "Give 'em room, girls."

The line of women parted with the reluctance of molasses, allowing the Pierce-Arrow barely enough room to grind into town. With an inane comment about the mining business, Todd continued on through Burke, through the smoke-blackened railroad tunnel that cut beneath the Tiger Hotel, and pulled up in front of the office at the Titan mill. A few minutes later we'd climbed two flights of stairs and settled in straight-backed chairs in Aaron's stark, utilitarian office. He wore his usual down-in-the-mouth expression, and Lennie's eyes gave no clue to the thoughts behind them.

We spent a brief moment answering questions about our trip up the Coeur d'Alene then Aaron went to the window and looked down at pickets blocking access to the mill. "Good thing the strike's come at a time when the market for silver is slow," he said, "or we'd be losing our shirts to the out-of-state competition."

"Why are they striking against us? Dan has always been more than fair in his dealings."

"I lowered wages."

"You know Dan wouldn't have approved," I said with reproach.

Ignoring my protest , Aaron left the window and tapped a cigar over an ash-stand beside his desk. "I tell you, Todd, I'm so anxious to turn the business over to someone else I can taste it. Same old problems over and over—labor, taxes, tariff, pollution suits. I've had enough."

"You've never made a secret of that, have you Aaron?" I regretted the remark the minute it left my lips, but I was primed for trouble. I was likely to say a lot worse before the meeting ended.

Aaron shot me a venomous look and went on speaking to Todd. "It'll be easy for the trust to hang on until the market improves. They have the bank accounts for it. They're chomping at the bit for us to sign the sale agreement."

"Mom said you were asking fourteen million last time you talked about selling." Todd's words were a question as much as a statement. He was part of this meeting because Dan had put the shares he'd bought from the Tuttles into Todd's name. I was there with power of attorney to act for Dan.

"The Titan itself isn't worth much anymore," Aaron said in answer to Todd's question. "Likely, four million. The seams are pinching out. Maybe two years of production left in her. It was stupid to invest in a hoist system. Our other mines and the mill could bring twelve million. We're asking Federal for sixteen million."

I felt like throwing something. I hated the way Aaron inflated like a helium balloon at the mention of large sums of money. I'd always considered the preoccupation with money ignoble when compared to higher dreams. Sadly, Todd seemed to have inherited some of his uncle's avarice. His eyes lit like blue lanterns at the mention of dollar figures. "I'm ready to turn over my shares," he said eagerly. "I'll need the money when I get back from Europe."

"You still thinking of volunteering?" Lennie asked with true concern.

"Seems likely."

Aaron showed no such concern. "I'm glad we caught you before you left," he said coolly. "Federal's lawyers want to finalize the deal tomorrow."

An ugly pride seized me, anger raking my vocal chords as I complained, "I can't believe you drew up papers without my consent. I'll never sell to those cutthroats."

"Better get off your high-horse," Aaron crowed. "Before Dan's accident he signed a paper that gave each shareholder permission to sell if something happened to him."

If something happened to him?

My eyes widened with suspicion. I pointed an accusing finger. "Likely you caused the accident so you could do just that."

Lennie shifted in his chair and said emphatically, "Take it easy, Sis. I was there. It was an accident. Nothing more."

Disarmed by the rebuke, I made no reply, simply sat with rage pulling at my chest and rippling up and down my spine.

"You can keep your shares if you want," Aaron said, smirking, "but when Lennie, Todd, and I sell you'll be part of the trust and all their shenanigans. The measly percentage of Federal's shares you'll get in trade for your Titan shares won't give you any drag with the men who make policy."

I felt like slapping the smug look from Aaron's face. I didn't. Just said between clenched teeth, "It's trickery! Nothing but." Leaving Aaron with his eyes bulging, I stormed from the office and hurried down the steps to the car. At the bottom of the stairs I stopped to lean against the rail, gasping for breath, my heart dancing a jig. I shouldn't have let Aaron upset me. It didn't matter if he sold, I told myself. I owned a newspaper and had invested well. I didn't need the money and wouldn't accept it even if it was offered.

Above me, the door to the office opened and closed and feet tapped down the stairs. I felt an arm at my back. "You all right, Sis?" Lennie asked. I gave a slight nod. "Here, sit down." He helped me onto one of the steps, gathered my skirts around me, and sat down beside me, his arm around my shoulders. "You shouldn't let this make you sick." There was anxiety in his drawling voice. "All things come to an end sooner or later. Sometimes it hurts when they do. The Titan's given us a good life. But it's time to let go."

"I don't care about the Titan," I said, wheezing. "I care about Dan. I feel like a traitor. I'm not going to let him down . . . not at a time when he can't defend himself."

"Face it, Maggie, he's never going to be able to defend himself. We have our own lives to live. We're none of us getting any younger."

"You think I don't know that? I see it every time I look in the mirror. I feel it every time I walk up a flight of stairs." I paused while my lungs pulled at the air, then continued, pausing now and then to wheeze. "Age has taught me that what I've worked for is nothing more than dust in the scale. If I was to kick up my heels and die, how many would grieve, and for how long? I haven't given enough of myself to those who really mattered."

Lennie started to interrupt, but I put a quieting hand on his knee. "Just hear me out. I haven't had a chance to bare my soul to you for a long time." I sighed as if the sigh might be my last. "You see, Lennie, for the first time I'm really feeling my age. Lots of things are bothering me. Some of them are physical, beyond my control, things that happen to a woman my age. But mainly it's Dan's condition. He doesn't even know I'm around. I feel useless. That's why I fought this sale. It was a way I could do something tangible for a relationship that's past. Sort of *in memoriam*."

Lennie made a vague sound and patted my hand. "Stop talking like a mopy old grandma."

I turned pleading eyes on him. "I will if you promise to do something for me."

"What's that?"

"All I care about is keeping the original Titan from the trust. I don't give a whit about the mill or the other mining properties. I want you to let the Titan fill with water. The trust won't want to take on the expense of pumping her and finishing the shaft system just for two years worth of ore."

Lennie looked stunned. He blinked several times and stammered, "See-see here, I've put a lot of myself into that mine. It-it'd be like committing murder."

I shrugged. "Aaron said there's not much left of her anyway."

"But to kill her with my own hands . . . " Lennie shook his head adamantly. "Aaron would never stand for it."

I gripped Lennie's arm in desperation. "He doesn't need to know. Think of it as saving what little mineral there is left."

A minute passed while Lennie hunched over his knees, pursing his lips in thought, rubbing his thumbs together. "I'd have to do it when Aaron is out of town," he said at last. "He's going to take a trip east as soon as the sale is finalized. I could do it then. We're shut down because of the strikes anyway."

"How?" Now that I'd suggested it, the thought frightened. I didn't want harm to come to Lennie. "Can you do it without getting hurt? I couldn't bear that."

"Umm . . . sure . . . just set off some charges . . . seal the tunnels and let them fill with water. The fourth level would be best, because that's where we'd started the shaft system. I know a couple of tight-lipped miners who'd help me and keep it a secret. The law will think the Wobblies did it. They set fire to the Hercules a while back . . . and done other sabotage." Lennie turned silent, running his fingers worriedly through his mop of black hair, darting looks up the hill toward the Titan. Finally, he exploded with, "No, I won't do it."

I gripped his arm more tightly. "You must! There is no other way. For my sake and Dan's. If it weren't for him you'd still be working the stopes."

Lennie sat a long while chewing the guilt I'd laid on his plate, his sallow face ashen. When the door above us opened and voices drifted outside, he turned an unforgiving look on me and said, "All right, I'll do it. But I feel like I'm committing a sin." He rose and helped me to my feet. "I'll let you know when it happens."

CHAPTER 54

A week-and-a-half had passed since the meeting at the mine, and I'd settled into the semblance of a routine, tackling a mound of paper work that had accumulated on my desk at *The New Century*. Howard had admitted he was ready for a vacation and had left to investigate an orange grove in California that he was considering as a place for retirement. It was my duty to see that the paper left the presses in time and my fingertips had turned sore from thumbing through newsprint and reporters' copy, my nerves frazzled from the press of deadlines.

Now, with the fat Sunday edition safely on newspaper stands and porch steps, I put on a flowered smock and disreputable blue quilted slippers I refused to part with because of their comfort and puttered up and down the rows of slatted tables in my garden room. By piping water from the adjacent bath, adding more lights, windows, work tables, shelving, and sinks, I'd converted a sunny, south-facing sewing room into this one spacious area. The room had become a jungle that smelled of wet sphagnum moss and mica flakes, spicy geraniums, and the primeval scent of ferns and hanging vines. With potting soil stuck to my hands, I spoke to my favorites, checked the shine of their leaves, snipped off a wayward stem or yellow leaf, and gave them a drink from a thin-spouted watering can. From time to time I'd sit and rest on a bench below the bay window.

The last month had worn me to a nubbin and I was relieved to slow my pace for the afternoon. Caring for Dan had been exhausting, but hiring a nurse had lightened the load. Then I'd had to endure the painful leave-taking, when Todd and Kyle departed on the train for New York and the trip across the Atlantic to France. The worry he'd be killed hovered over me constantly and often I found myself short of breath.

The awful meeting at the Titan hadn't helped. It had spent more of my energy than a full week at the office. Too bad it had come to that. I'd like to forget the wrangling, but couldn't. With the sale a fact, I could only hope that Lennie would follow through on his promise, feeble as it was. I didn't blame him for not wanting to turn the Titan back to nature—not that it could ever return completely now that the character of the mountain had been changed—but if I was to keep it from the trust, what other option was there?

The wall phone jangled in the hall. A second or two passed before it dawned that it was the housekeeper's day off. I rinsed my hands, dried them on a towel, and made a dash for the phone before the switchboard operator gave up. Luckily, Kristine knew my Sunday habits and let the phone ring several times.

"Maggie Rigby here," I said breathlessly.

"A long distance for you, Mrs. Rigby."

Long distance? A somersault of the heart. Todd said he'd call before he departed for France, but would he be leaving so soon? I heard Kristine saying, "You can go ahead, sir."

A male voice on the other end of the line. "That you, Maggie?"

"Yes." It wasn't Todd, but I'd so expected the voice to be his that I was having trouble accepting the fact it was someone else. The connection was poor and it sounded like Lennie with a frog in his throat. "Is that you, Lennie?"

"Right. I thought I'd let you know that I went through with the plan. It's done."

An erratic fluttering of my heart. "You mean the mine—"

"I don't think we should spell it out on the phone. I just wanted you to know I kept my promise. The sale went through a few days ago and I'm leaving for 'Frisco tomorrow. I'll take a ship from there to Hawaii."

"So soon?"

He gave what sounded like a snort. "I've been waiting to take off for years. You oughta join me when Dan . . . you know what I mean."

"I-I don't want to think about that possibility."

Lennie waited for the phone to clear of static and asked, "Is he doing any better?"

"Not really. Some days I can't get him to eat. Dr. Kendrick said that all of a sudden he might start fading for no obvious reason." A lump came to my throat. I swallowed.

Before I could continue, Lennie said haltingly, "I don't know what to say . . . except you might be better off if he . . ." Silence, as if Lennie might have regretted the statement. Rather than pursue that subject, he reverted to the former. "By the way, you'll read in the paper that there were some blasts at the Titan. The sheriff thinks the Wobblies did it, but the law will have a hard time proving it. Too bad for Federal." He laughed. "Don't think they'll want to go to the expense of clearing out the muck and water. They'll get what they can out of the other mines."

"Then it's worth the chances you took."

"I guess, I almost got caught in a rock sl—" He broke off, paused, then said tersely, "Gotta go. The sheriff just walked into the office."

"The sheriff? Does he suspect . . ."

"He wants to talk to me about the strikes and other union activity. I'll stop by tomorrow before I catch the train."

"Please do. I'll want to hear . . ." My voice trailed off as the receiver on the other end of the line clicked in my ear. I pressed my own receiver to my chest and leaned against the wall. Visions of the mine collapse I'd perpetrated made my ribs resound with the hammering of my heart. My knees buckled, and I slid onto a chair beneath the phone. Would Dan have approved? Or would he condemn it?

The receiver in my lap clicked several times and Kristine's voice said faintly, "Mrs. Rigby, you there? Are you all right?"

I stirred and raised the receiver to my ear. "Yes . . . yes, I'm all right. At least I think I am."

●●●

Lennie stopped by the following morning when I was at my publisher's desk. Worried that he might miss his train, he stood rather than accept my invitation to sit. "You shoulda been there. I never heard the likes of it," he said in telling of the death of the Titan. "My friends and I set charges every hundred yards from the rear of level four on out to the portal . . . took out the pump lines . . . water's likely already building up behind the fall. Besides that, we set fire to the timbering. That'd bring down a lot of rock."

"How on earth did you manage all that?"

"Lots of fuse. Couldn't have done it without the McCarties . . . had to time things just right. We set the blasts and ran like hell."

"Will they be free of suspicion?"

"The old galoots live way back up the South Fork. Hermit like. They stay holed-up back there during the winter. I'm the only one in town who knows where their cabin is."

"Did you caution them to stay there for a while?"

"Didn't need to. They're squatters on Forest Service land and keep out of sight. They'll be gone setting their trap lines for the winter.

Doubt if anybody'd think of suspecting them." Lennie checked the clock on the wall and said, "Gotta go."

I rose to give him a hug. "Thank you, Lennie. It was a brave thing you did. I hope you don't feel as much guilt as I do."

"'Course I do, but where I'm going I'll soon forget all about that. Just lie on a beach with coconuts and sunshine. You oughta come along . . . start a new life."

I gave a wistful smile. "It sounds like heaven. Maybe someday. For a vacation. I don't think I could ever leave Spokane and the newspaper for good. I've invested too much of myself." I kissed him on the cheek. "Have fun for me. And please be careful."

"I will. And if Aaron talks to you about the Titan, pretend you're innocent as an angel."

That was in the morning. It was mid-afternoon when I returned to the apartment. Mary, the housekeeper, followed along as I headed down the hall removing my soft, suede jacket. "Did your brother find you in time?" she asked. "He said he had to catch a train."

Accustomed to Mary's curiosity, I knew she'd asked because she wanted more information. "Yes, he did. He's quitting the mining business and going to Hawaii. How does that sound to you?"

"Like paradise." She took my jacket and hung it on a hook beside the hall mirror.

"How is Dan?" I asked worriedly.

"Kinda peeked," she said with a shake of her head. "He's out on the balcony. The nurse thought the air might do him good. This Indian summer won't last much longer."

"I'm surprised it's lasted this long. Already the third of November."

Kristine, the nurse, caught the drift of the conversation as she came down the hall to meet us. "I've lived here twenty years and never seen it this late." Her voice had a flat, mid-western quality. Her full-cheeked face wore a constant expression of concern.

I repeated the question I'd asked Mary. "How is Dan?"

"Getting as light as a feather. Wish we could get him to eat. You may need to talk to Dr. Lewis about him." She referred to the doctor whose office was in the Rigby Building. He'd taken over the responsibility for Dan's health.

"I'll talk to him tomorrow." Making a mental reminder, I started up the hall, Kristine at my side. "I can watch Dan now. You take the rest of the day off."

"But you must be played-out."

"I'll manage. And Mary will be here until seven."

It didn't take Kirstine long to latch onto that idea. "Then, I'll do just that. My sister's coming in on the evening train and I have to tidy up my flat."

When Kristine had gathered her things and left, I tiptoed up the ramp that led from the drawing room onto the balcony and stood beside the frail figure sitting in the wheelchair. Dan's chin had slumped onto his chest and his arms dangled down over his thighs. Still asleep. I'd not disturb him, just leave the door ajar so I could hear him grunt when he awoke.

I took a moment to look down on the busy street ten stories below and at the park across the way. In the street, horse-drawn wagons crawled among lamp-eyed beetles that went by the name of Ford, Packard, Oldsmobile, and others. An electric streetcar clanged a delivery truck out of its path. On the sidewalks, people-ants met, passed, and trailed in and out. Across the street from the apartment, on marigold-lined greens, bright butterflies with the voices of children climbed, slid, swung, spun, and fluttered from one end of the park to the other. Oldsters sprawled on benches beneath maples that had lost most of their leaves. I thought it rewarding to have donated the land to the city for a park when we built the Rigby Building, nice to have a bit of greenery amid the bricks and buzz of the city.

By the time I'd gone to my bedroom, removed my dress, and thrown on a willow-green velvet robe and slippers, the sunlight caught only the southeast corner of the room. I went into the bath and took a new bar of Woodbury Soap from the drawer of a dressing table cluttered with glass jars and little China bowls that held face powder, creams, pastes, and strips of cotton—all a woman in her late forties needed to look younger. I felt unusually tired. Just removing the wrapper from the soap took special effort and concentration. "For the skin you love to touch," the wrapper claimed. I smiled ruefully. I'd learned not to expect anything from a bar of soap except a good cleansing.

Next, the garden room to check on a fern that had been ailing, a stop that extended into several minutes. Finally, a collapse onto a floral sofa near the French doors in the drawing room. At its afternoon angle, the sunlight reached the cushions, soothing as a warm blanket. I let the numbing weariness melt from my bones and allowed my mind a moment of blankness before it reminded me of letters I must write telling my relatives in Norway about Dan's condition. My mother had died in 1902. Ned from black lung contracted in the Roros mines. The older boys were still in America, scattered to north and south. Carl had returned to the states and worked as a detective for the Pinkerton Agency. He stopped by whenever his assignments brought him west.

My eyelids shut on a vision of six-year-old Carl lying hidden in a root-hollow, except for his orange top-knot, which rose like a furry mushroom above a bed of leaves and sticks. I was a phantom in pursuit of freshly-baked cookies that had disappeared from the kitchen table. The boy leaped from his nest and flew down the wooded paths, always faster than me, always beyond reach.

I awoke, breathing rapidly, heart thumping, still feeling the frustration, the ghosts of the dream drifting in and out of my vision. Snatches of absurd conversation faded into reality. The landscape of my fantasy dissolved into the pastoral countryside depicted in the wallpaper above the maple wainscoting. The evasive youth was transformed into a stoic face looking down from a shelf of portraits on the wall.

I became aware of the loss of the sun's warmth on my legs and of a cool breeze playing with strands of hair. I sat up with a start. I hadn't meant to sleep. What time was it? The grandfather clock next to the shelf of portraits warned of the approach of six o'clock. Good heavens. Dan. I jerked to my feet, trotted up the ramp and into the murky gray of evening.

Dan's chin still dug into his chest. Something wrong. I shook his shoulder. "Dan? Dan!" No movement, except a wobbling of his head from my attempt to waken him. I slipped my hand under his shag of sand-gray hair and felt his forehead. Cold. But not without reason. The air was chill. But why didn't he stir?"

"Oh Lord, please don't let it be that!"

I felt his wrist. No pulse. No pulse in his neck cavity. I put my hand on his chest and detected no rise and fall. My own gasping breath clawed at the lining of my throat.

I went to the doorway and screamed for Mary, hoping my voice would carry through the drawing room, down the long hallway, and into the kitchen where she'd be preparing supper. Hearing no response, I started the wheelchair down the ramp, leaning backward, digging in my heels to control the descent of the chair. Dan's body slumped forward, almost doubling over. The chair lurched. It took all of my strength to keep the chair upright, and suddenly I had so little. My heart was thudding, skipping beats.

"Mary! Mary!"

An answering cry from the far pantry, then Mary's footsteps racing to the kitchen door and up the hall. Next instant she was at my side, keeping the chair from falling.

"Good Lord, Mrs. Rigby, what happened?"

I explained as Mary wheeled the chair down the hall to the master bedroom. "Help me get Dan onto the bed. Then call Dr. Lewis just in case."

When Dan lay on the bed and light from the chandelier made it possible to see him clearly for the first time, I knew there'd be no "just in case." His face was ashen, the broad lips stiff as parchment. There was no hope. My beloved was dead. *Dead.* The word had the thud of a door slammed shut. If only I was mistaken. But no, it was true. I'd lost him. I felt deserted, adrift in a world without Dan. How dare he leave me alone, after I'd tried so hard to keep him alive.

Breathing heavily from the struggle to get him onto the bed, I reached out slowly and touched his cheek. Even that small effort was too much. The chalky face began to swim before my eyes. The bed became a misty pool that had no substance. I felt light-headed and disoriented. It occurred to me I was about to faint. Mary was saying things that blurred when they reached my ears. I tried to concentrate on the words, but a searing pain ran down my neck and circled my chest, tighter, tighter, like the jaws of a giant vise. The pain stabbed through my breast, demanding what remained of my fading senses. Muscles stiffened, contracted. With a cry, I folded my arms over my chest, squeezing, then crumpled to the floor, strangling from the pain. I'd never known such agony. I seemed to be floating in a sea of black, my current of life ebbing, flowing, ebbing, flowing. A voice warned from deep inside—I was going to die, just like Dan.

I felt Mary's arms slip around me and try to drag me onto a chair. I managed to wheeze, "Please . . . the bed."

"Oh no, ma'am I can't do that. Not with a dead man."

"Please, the bed . . ." With what remained of my waning strength, I leaned over the bed, Mary's strong hands at my back to help. A last hazy glimpse of Dan's face. Then a final sensation of my cheek touching his.

CHAPTER 55

The apartment had taken on the quiet of a morgue. Mary and Kristine tiptoed up and down the hall with long faces, trying not to disturb me while they went about their chores. The doctor hadn't sent me to the hospital after the heart attack, but had left orders that I was to stay in bed, Kristine to watch over me, a tank of oxygen and medications at bedside in the event of another attack. During the brief periods when I lay awake, I thought of Dan. Of all the times to lie abed. I should be up attending to a proper burial. When I asked Mary about the funeral, she told me not to fret, that Mister Rigby's brother was attending to everything. Lennie was on his way to Hawaii. They hadn't been able to reach Todd before he'd left on a freighter bound for France. That saddened me, not only because he was headed for battle, but I wanted him near.

The day of the funeral I woke to the sound of voices in the hall. I'd asked Mary to pull the drapes so the sun would rouse me, and I'd expected to see daylight when I opened my eyes. Instead, the sky was a dismal gray and raindrops struck the windowpanes. Fighting a sedative stupor, I felt awash in unfamiliar waters, the raindrops strange to my ears. When I switched on the bedside lamp to ring the handbell, my heart raced from the effort.

Mary appeared sleep-drunk in a maroon bathrobe. Usually, she wore her long brown hair in a tight bun at the back of her head. Now it fell over one shoulder in a braid. "You feeling all right, Mrs. Rigby," she said with a yawn. "Sorry I look like this, but it was my turn to watch over you in the night. I went to bed when Kristine came, but she had to go to the drugstore for medicine. I didn't mean to sleep while she was gone."

"No harm done. I heard voices. Is someone here?" I felt my lips move, but the words seemed to come from behind my ears.

"It's Miss Lucinda. I was going to ask her to come back later, but since you're awake . . . would you mind?"

"Please, send her in."

Mary shook a finger at me. "You must lie quiet and try not to get too excited."

I raised a hand in acquiescence.

A moment later, Lucinda came through the doorway and up to the bed. She was dressed in black, uncertainty and grief written on a face that was normally wreathed in smiles. I took her hand as she stood at my bedside, the skin warm to my cold touch. "It's good of you to come."

"I wanted to come sooner, but the doctor said 'No.'"

She stood watching me, her dark brows knit, as if I was someone she didn't know very well. For the first time since my illness, I was conscious of how I must look—my hair an orange tangle on the pillow, my face without powder and likely showing the effects of the heart attack. I could tell that my eyes were puffed from illness and tears of mourning. No doubt they had dark circles under them. I brushed unruly strands of hair from my cheeks. "I hope I don't look as bad as your face says I do."

Lucinda stammered, "Oh, no-no. I was just thinking of all that's happened to you lately. Enough to give anybody's heart the willies."

"Please, sit down. I'm uncomfortable with you standing there." I waited until she pulled a chair to bedside and asked, "When is the funeral to be held? Aaron seems to be avoiding me, and Mary pretends ignorance . . . likely so I won't worry. Do you suppose I could sneak out and . . ."

Lucinda raised a protesting hand. "Mary has strict orders to keep you in bed."

"Oh, bosh! Then tell me about the plans. I get agitated not knowing. With Aaron making the arrangements the funeral's not likely to be what I want. And now this rain. Why did it have to rain today?"

"Don't get upset. It's supposed to clear by afternoon. The funeral is scheduled for three o'clock."

"Will there be music?"

"The usual funeral selections—a guest organist, harpist, and small choir. We left it up to the funeral director."

"You say, 'we.' Who's we?"

"Aaron, Nora, and I. We've tried to arrange a nice funeral, no expense spared. We're expecting a large crowd."

"No expense spared?" I gave a feeble laugh. "Likely Aaron is glad he's not paying the bill."

Lucinda smiled knowingly. "You might say we've done what we could in spite of him." She reached into a pocket of her skirt, as if for a pack of cigarettes, caught herself, and shrugged sheepishly. "Force of habit. Don't want you breathing smoke."

My mind was still hungry for details. "Tell me more."

"We're having a reception catered at the funeral home. Nora wanted to have it at her house, but Aaron didn't like that idea."

As I considered the arrangements, I found it hard to show approval. I'd much rather the burial was a small affair, friends of the family saying a few words about Dan, perhaps Lucinda singing *Rock of Ages*. She could sound deceptively like an angel. Dan would have preferred that. He'd never been comfortable with public demonstrations of grief.

Lucinda sensed my doubts. "I . . . I thought you'd be pleased."

"Oh, I-I am," I lied. "Funerals always distress me." I paused, chin quivering. "I thought I wanted to talk about it, but I was wrong."

As if my discomfort with the conversation had produced some obscure connection with Mary, she entered the room carrying a vase of hot-house roses Lucinda had brought, providing the needed change of subject. We spoke of the exquisite hues of the salmon-colored roses and smelled them. Then Mary placed them on the dresser.

When she'd left the room, I asked Lucinda, "Did Nora hear from Kyle before he and Todd boarded the ship? Mary said Todd called here, but of course she didn't tell me until later."

"Kyle said that New York was fabulous and he could hardly wait to see France."

"The devastation there might come as a shock. Perhaps they can visit parts that haven't been ruined by German artillery." Tears came all too readily, and again, I felt a need to change the subject. "How are the twins? They'll graduate this spring won't they?" I referred to Kyle's younger sisters.

Lucinda nodded, adding, "Nora's busy looking into colleges. The girls like the idea of Mills College. That's a women's college in California. Nora's asked me to go with them during the spring break to see what it's like." She paused, a light coming to her eyes. "Say, why don't you come with us. You'll be on your feet by then. A change will do you good."

"Right now it sounds like more effort than I could summon. But, who knows? By then, I might be ready to escape for a while. First, I'll have to make sure the newspaper's on track."

"I've been watching things for you on that score. Howard has actually delegated some of the responsibility to me." She seemed to note a troubled look on my face and made a gesture of apology. "I shouldn't talk shop. I'm tiring you. I need to go."

"I do feel like I've been tied in a few dozen knots and given a good booting."

She rose and kissed my forehead. "I'm sorry about all this . . . so many terrible things happening at once. It doesn't seem fair."

"Dan told me once . . . at a time much like this . . . after Jeff's death, in fact . . . that life wasn't meant to be fair. Sometimes we have to drink from a bitter cup. But later, when the acid has left our lips, we begin to smile again and think how wonderful it is to be alive."

My mother's philosophy, I recalled as Lucinda slipped from the room and I closed my eyes in weariness. Its message had helped me through those violent mining wars in the Coeur d'Alenes. Through the tragedy of Jeff's death. Only after Cally's death and my shooting of Jim Tatro had its wisdom eluded me. And now? Events seemed nearly as dire. Even the sealing of the Black Titan loomed as a tragic mistake. The one redeeming thought was the knowledge that the trust wouldn't want to work the abandoned tunnels. That was as it should be. The mine had been the tinder that fired Dan's ambition. And now it was dead. As dead as the man who'd given it birth.

As I lay, drudging up the past, thoughts crowded one upon the other, pushing, shoving, vying for supremacy, driving off the lethargic need for rest. Giving up on that, I propped my back with pillows, and from a shelf in the nightstand took a notepad and pencil I kept on hand to record editorial ideas that often encroached upon my sleep. Using my knees as a desk, I began in a shaking hand:

OBITUARY OF A TITAN

Today my heart is heavy, for I grieve the loss of my husband and I grieve the loss of his dream. Indeed, in my mind I cannot separate the man from his dream, their identities are entwined. Dan Rigby—the Black Titan. When we speak of the man, we inevitably speak of the mine. When we speak of the mine, we cannot help but speak of the man.

The passing of the man and his dream marks the end of an era, of a time when a man could make it on his own by hard work and vision. A time when a man could gain respect through a compassionate stewardship of his mine, his mills, and his land. Through personal heroism he could endure. Now, only the large corporations endure. Not through heroism, instead through financial wizardry and political shenanigans. Few of the managers of these corporations have known humble beginnings. None have known the sweat, the fear, and the blackness of the tunnels. These industrial barons send others against the rock to tear their hands and souls, while they, themselves, reap the wealth.

Dizzying from the intensity of thought, I took pencil from paper and let the pillow feel the weight of my head. I breathed slowly, shed a few tears, and dozed for a while. When I awoke, I continued to write, hoping to finish before Kristine returned and took away my tools for thought.

I grieve not only for a remarkable man and a remarkable mine, but for the Coeur d'Alene's and the mining district that has supplied such wealth. The district's honeycombed slopes have a rendezvous with death. It won't happen in my generation, perhaps not in the next, but sooner or later the large corporations and trusts that rob the district of its treasure will leave it destitute of mineral, will leave its rugged mountains a catacomb of exhausted dreams.

To borrow somewhat from the poets, I say, "Farewell, my husband. Farewell Black Titan. I hear your death chant murmuring from the mine-scarred hillsides, from the mountain's empty bowels, from the tired lips of men who tread the black tunnels. You chant not of the past, but of the future. May we learn from your death song. May we learn to restrain our greed before our fate is sealed.

I lay back, my shallow breath passing over opened lips, and wondered what Dan would have said to such candor. In a way, he was as guilty as the rest of the industry of gouging the heart from the mountain. Because his fortune was forged in silver, it suffered the tarnish of over-ambition and lack of foresight. I felt the guilt as well. What right had any of us to claim and squander treasures that should belong to posterity, we who pass but a wink of time on this ageless earth?

Hearing footsteps head for my room, I slid the notepad under the covers, put the pillows back in place, and pretended to be asleep.

• • •

It was evening before I had the energy to edit the piece I'd written. Kristine had left for home and Mary was reading in the study. I was free to pull my notepad from beneath the covers without fear of discovery. Pencil ready to change a word here and there, I read the pages over with a critical eye, cringing a bit at my accusations of the mining industry. I'd have to send the piece to the copy room before I lost my courage.

I turned to a clean sheet in the pad and wrote a note of explanation to Howard, the script marred here and there by a trembling hand. Note and obituary tucked in a manila envelope that had contained materials Howard had sent me, I picked up the phone. The clock on the stand showed quarter after seven. Scott should be at work, putting in some of the extra hours he was accumulating to fatten his savings for college.

The phone at the other end of the line rang several times before Scott said in his jaunty voice, "Copy room. Scott Mearns here."

"Scott, I'm glad you're there. Would you mind coming up? I have some copy for Howard."

"I thought you weren't up to that sort of thing."

"Let's just say it's something I had to get off my mind."

I was sitting up with a pink shawl around my shoulders when Scott arrived a few minutes later, trailing into the room behind the hulking Mary. Bright red suspenders ran down his striped shirt and rubber sleeve protectors covered the elbows. Mary issued the usual warning for him not to stay long and went back to her reading.

"You look pale," Scott said when she'd left. "The doctor'll be mad at you for sitting up and writing."

"I am a mite tired, but I had to do this." I handed him the envelope addressed to Howard. "Did you go to the funeral?"

His expression sagged. "Everybody missed you. But it's a good thing you weren't there. It lasted a long time."

Tears welled in my eyes. I felt cheated to have lost my husband and to have missed the funeral. "How was the music?"

"Beautiful. You would have liked it."

I swallowed at a thickening in my throat and forced the words that awaited speech. "I'd rather talk about you. I've been wanting to speak to you about the way you push yourself. You don't have to be a straight A student to succeed in life. Make time for fun. I didn't. Now I realize what a mistake that was. Though I'll admit that circumstances didn't allow time for much frivolity."

"Was school harder then?"

I laughed. "I'm not ancient. It wasn't that long ago. I'm sure it's just as hard now. I only wish I hadn't taken life so seriously. And you mustn't. I don't mean that you shouldn't care about something more than yourself. You should. If you care about something deeply enough, just wanting to do your best moves you along toward success. As for the money you'll need for college, you'll be able to get a scholarship, and I'll pay for whatever that doesn't cover."

Scott blinked and stammered, "You-you don't need to—"

"I don't need to. I *want* to. You say you've decided to major in journalism?"

Still stunned by my offer, Scott began in a fractured way, "Umm . . . yes . . . that's right. Working for you has given me the bug . . . and Mom helps that along. When I graduate, I'd like to work for you."

"I insist. You can work your way up through the various editorial positions and learn along the way. Who knows? Maybe you'll be managing editor some day."

Mary entered with a sponge in one hand, a bottle of rubbing alcohol in the other and said firmly, "You'll have to leave, Scott. I need to get Mrs. Rigby ready for the night."

"Remember, Scott," I said in parting. "Make time for fun."

I felt a surge of affection as I watched Scott disappear into the hallway. I'd never have guessed that by helping Jeff so many years ago fate would have blessed me with the devotion of his son.

CHAPTER 56

I spent the next month regaining my strength, grieving for Dan, and worrying about Todd. The body rallied and healed, but the mind wandered and sometimes became snared in remembrance. I hated to inflict my gloom upon others and received few visitors. Instead, I passed the hours sorting photographs and going through Dan's papers. To add to the mountain of personal effects, Aaron brought two cardboard cartons of correspondence from the office of the Black Titan, letters he thought would someday have significance for Todd.

At times I feared I'd lapse into the same despair that followed Cally's death, so I reminded myself that grief had a way of coming to a head after a time, of finding an inner resolution that would give me reason to think of tomorrow. Yet, winter had stolen across the countryside on a trail of fallen leaves before I was able to control the flow of grief.

Early in December, I woke from a dream I couldn't remember in detail, except that Dan, Jeff, and Scott had played important roles. The dream left me with a happy fluttering of the heart and a strange stirring of spirit. For the first time in a month I breathed without effort. I felt at peace with the world, anything and everything a possibility.

I put on my dressing gown and went to the window to look out on a world dusted with snow. The sun had risen above the jumbled horizon of brick and stone and glittered from snowflakes on the balcony. Far below, children raced each other across the park on their way to school, leaving erratic trails in the white. Oh to be a child again, filled with the joy of living.

Well, Maggie, happiness doesn't come automatically. You have to work at it. And it's time you did.

I found Mary standing in her blue housedress and apron, washing up the dishes from her own small breakfast of tea and toast. The doctor had pulled Kristine from her duties at the apartment for a more critical nursing chore, and Mary had been waiting for me to rise before fixing my breakfast. The small round kitchen table was set with cloth, silverware, and napkin.

"Good morning," I said with the first true smile I'd presented in weeks. "I'm so hungry I could eat the silver."

Mary's broad face wrinkled with a smile. She dried her hands on a towel snugged in the band of her apron and headed for the stove with cup and saucer. "It does my heart good to see you looking so chipper. I knew you'd come to it in time."

"Well, as they say, life must go on. It's just taken me a while to accept the fact." I drew a deep breath and sat at the table.

Mary put a steaming cup of coffee in front of me and asked, "What do you intend to do today with all that energy kindling your spirit?"

"I thought I'd go to the cemetery."

Mary's pleased expression changed to one of disapproval. "Now, ma'am, must you do that? You'll get to feeling down again."

"It's time I went. I need to get it over with so I can think of other things."

I wolfed down breakfast, gave my ferns and ivy a drink, then dressed in a green knit suit topped with a mourning cloak, the skirts a modern eight inches below the knee. I'd make the offices of *The New Century* my first stop. I'd neglected my duties. Time to make amends.

I saw the astonishment on Lucinda's face the minute I walked into the noisy, smoke-filled copy room. She left a desk glutted with newsprint and copy paper and ran down the aisle, her arms spread wide.

"Knock me over with a feather!" she cried over the erratic clack of typewriters and one-sided phone conversations. "Look who's returned to the world of nincompoops. Are you here to make order out of our scrambled brains?" She threw her arms around me and hugged. "Now we can get back to our normal amount of confusion." Then in a serious tone, while she held me at arm's length and looked me over. "Are you feeling better? You look swell in that suit."

"No false flattery, please. My mirror won't allow it. But I am feeling better, thank you."

"Are you going to spend some time with us today?" Her tone was hopeful.

"I thought I'd just stir around a bit . . . get used to being in the whirl again. I've almost forgotten how to carry on a conversation about something other than household affairs and—"

A hand took hold of my elbow. I turned and saw that it was Howard, a man of medium build. His finely-chiseled features were obdurate, the unyielding chin and black spade beard a measure of the man. His eyes were old and tired, mirroring a journalist who'd seen three lifetimes' worth of human drama. He nodded me toward his office. I told Lucinda I'd see her later and followed Howard's lead, leaving behind the haze of smoke and the strong smell of coffee brewing on an electric plate.

Once inside his stronghold, Howard released my arm. "I'd begun to think we'd fallen from your graces completely." He stood looking me over, his dark blue-gray eyes filled with concern. "How is it going?"

"It? You mean this miserable thing called grief? Oh, it's still there, but I've gotten the best of it. I'm ready to take on the world again."

"Good. Sit down. There's something I want to talk to you about." He took a manila folder from an overstuffed chair he sat in when his desk chair brought an ache to his back.

I dropped into the overstuffed and asked. "So what do you want to talk about?"

He sat behind a desk littered with newspaper clips, notepads, and galleys, started to say something and hesitated, fiddling with a pencil on his desk. "I hope it's not too soon to ask. I wouldn't want to overtax you."

I gave a little laugh. "How will I know unless you ask."

Again he hesitated, then went on measuredly, "It's just that I've been invited to attend a conference at the University of Washington in February. They want me to be on a panel to discuss the problems of newspaper publishing in the Northwest . . . possibly speak to some of the journalism classes. They want you to serve with me . . . sort of as a team. It seems they want the perspective of editors and their publishers. I'm sure you'll find a letter on your desk with all the information."

I sat quietly, avoiding his eyes, fiddling with the straps of my purse. This was a little more than I'd expected my first day back on the job, but Howard didn't make a habit of asking favors.

"I hope I'm not rushing this," he said with apology. "I have to give them an answer in two days."

I shrugged along with a dubious wag of my head. "It is kind of sudden. But I'd like to help. I'd especially enjoy speaking to the students." I paused to think further. "Tell you what, I'll give it some thought and let you know tomorrow."

Howard broke into the semblance of a smile. "Well, that's much better than a flat rejection."

"Don't get your hopes too high. I wouldn't want to disappoint you."

"Needn't worry. I learned long ago that if I held my breath too long, I might strangle." He rose as I got to my feet. "Where are you off to? You're not dressed for the office."

"I'm going to the cemetery. I haven't been there yet, you know. I'll be back in a little while."

"Let me drive you. I need to get out of this squirrel cage for a while." He reached for an overcoat hanging on a hook by the door. "I'll stay in the car so you can be alone."

"I'd like that. It's been a while since I've driven in traffic."

●●●

Howard stayed in the car reading the competitions' morning editions while I mounted a sparsely wooded knoll on the edge of town, leaving prints in the trace of melting snow. I climbed slowly, not so much because of the ascent, but because of a reluctance to face the ultimate truth—the history of a man translated into a few etchings on granite. I carried two bouquets I'd bought at the florist on our way out of town—one of red roses, the other of violets. The blush of autumn had faded from the cemetery grounds, baring the ghostly limbs of trees and browning the lawn. A wrought-iron fence enclosed a plot of frost-bitten lawn, the name Rigby on the gate. I hesitated briefly, then worked the latch and closed the gate behind me as if its open tracery could offer privacy.

I passed father Rigby's massive monument, six feet tall if an inch, and that of mother Rigby, a woman I'd never known. Cally's modest, little girl's grave was next in line, moved from its original plot in Wallace. *So few years to show for a life.* I stood a long while before the headstone, suppressing tears, letting my thoughts steal into the past, avoiding the fresh diggings a few feet to the right.

With reluctance, I turned to face the new grave—a granite base and marble pedestal topped with a silver miniature of a mine's headworks. Aaron's idea, no doubt. The grave seemed that of a stranger, the name foreign in that setting, the span of life stated as March 20, 1864-November 3,1916, a mere nothing in the eons of time. How miserly the habit of computing a man's impact on people's lives with a few meaningless numbers.

I stared at the inscription with an eye as cold as the granite base that barred me from my love forever. It seemed to say, "Go peddle your sentimentality elsewhere, let this man rest in peace." If I'd had my way, I would have left Dan's remains in some rocky crevice high on a ridge-top above the Black Titan, the bluebirds and mountain zephyrs to sing a requiem, the gnarled roots of a pine to serve as a grave-marker. Dan would have liked that.

I thought I'd grieved myself out. But now that I faced the grave, the awful finality of death struck home. *Dan was gone. Truly gone.* I placed the flowers on the grave, one bouquet at a time—the velvety purple of the violets as a symbol of the depth of my love, the flagrant crimson of the roses as a symbol of its ability to endure. Then I sank to my knees and crouched like a lost child, tearful, my chest heaving.

Several minutes passed before I wiped the tears from my face with the corner of my cloak and spoke as if Dan could hear. "I'm sorry, my darling, I didn't mean to burden you with my grief. I just wanted to visit and talk of old times. I've dwelled on the old days these past few weeks. How can I measure my loss except in memories? Some days my recollections are like a book I want to read over and over. Other days, they seem a long, dark, lonely winding. The high moments go round and round in my head. The low moments make me shrivel and want to cry. But I count them all—pearls of remembrance right along with those made of acid and clay.

"I remember you most often as you were years ago . . . young . . . sunny of face . . . strong. I remember the day we met, your curls blowing carelessly in the hot wind. And the day you appeared as if by magic in my schoolroom. I remember the way you walked and talked, the way you held your head, the way your whole face crinkled when you smiled. I recall the warmth of your flesh and the feel of your lips. I wake in the night and see your face lurking in the dark, or see you standing before me whispering of your love. I see myself as a phantom drifting into your arms. I feel once more the tenderness of your kiss.

"I've loved you through the years for what you've meant to me and for what you've meant to others. I've loved you for things only I could know. I've loved you dearly, though the cost of that love has run high. Now, my darling, I must say goodbye, but my soul will drift with yours forever, while I, the woman, go on longing for you, living the best I can."

With a sigh in my chest, I planted a kiss on the headstone and started down the knoll. I'd met the challenge of the graveyard and said my good-byes. Now, on to the morrow.

A breeze had risen and was blowing fallen leaves across the light snow. Squirrels streaked from tree to tree, cache to cache, storing seeds and nuts for the winter. Dan's death and my own encounter with mortality had left me with the squirrels' sense of urgency. I'd led a full life, but one was always greedy for more.

With each step I moved more easily, feeling the faint warmth of the December sun. It was a relief to look forward rather than back at what might have been. I'd make sure the newspaper was on track, then I'd help Howard at the conference in Seattle. After that, I might travel to California with Lucinda and Nora. Next summer, provided Todd had returned from France, I might take him with me to visit Lennie in Hawaii. Later on, Lucinda and I could breathe life into the plans for a children's home.

I'd always embraced beginnings and hated endings. What lay ahead was a beginning. An adventure. A challenge. With luck it would be a joy. A sudden longing to get at the changes in my life propelled me down the hill and into the lure of what lay beyond.

Printed in the United States
127312LV00005B/62/P

9 781605 940700